THE
GUINEVERES

Center Point
Large Print

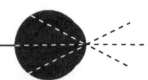

**This Large Print Book carries the
Seal of Approval of N.A.V.H.**

THE
GUINEVERES

SARAH DOMET

CENTER POINT LARGE PRINT
THORNDIKE, MAINE

This Center Point Large Print edition
is published in the year 2017 by arrangement with
Flatiron Books.

The text of this Large Print edition is unabridged.
In other aspects, this book may vary
from the original edition.
Printed in the United States of America
on permanent paper.
Set in 16-point Times New Roman type.

ISBN: 978-1-68324-333-5

Library of Congress Cataloging-in-Publication Data

Names: Domet, Sarah, author.
Title: The Guineveres / Sarah Domet.
Description: Center Point Large Print edition. | Thorndike, Maine :
Center Point Large Print, 2017.
Identifiers: LCCN 2016058851 | ISBN 9781683243335
      (hardcover : alk. paper)
Subjects: LCSH: Female friendship—Fiction. | Teenage girls—Fiction. |
Convents—Fiction. | Orphans—Fiction. | Large type books. | GSAFD:
Bildungsromans.
Classification: LCC PS3604.O456 G85 2017 | DDC 813/.6—dc23
LC record available at https://lccn.loc.gov/2016058851

For Robbie

THE
GUINEVERES

The Assumption

We were known as The Guineveres to the other girls at the Sisters of the Supreme Adoration because our parents all named us Guinevere at birth, a coincidence that bound us together from the moment we met. We arrived over the course of two years, one by one, delivered unto the cool foyer of the convent and into the care of Sister Fran. Each of us had our own story. Usually, our parents whispered that they loved us; they told us to behave. Our mothers gave us lipstick kisses on our cheeks, or our fathers said they hoped someday we'd understand. Then they drove away for good, up the one-lane drive and into a world that was easier without children. They all had their reasons.

But The Guineveres had our reasons for wanting to run away, which is how we found ourselves stowed inside the cramped quarters of a parade float, wheels whirring beneath us, gravel bumping us like unpredictable hiccups so that we had to brace ourselves against the chicken-wire frame that cut into our skin. Inside the float, the air was suffocating, a thick blanket thrown over us. Through tiny gaps in the tissue paper, we could see Sister Monica, the handle of our float thrown over her shoulder as though she were heaving a giant cross up that graveled hill. Half-circle sweat marks appeared at her armpits; she grunted as she struggled with the weight of us.

Soon we heard Sister Fran's voice snap from behind, "Keep with the pace. This is a parade, not a pilgrimage." She appeared in our line of vision, her whistle swinging around her neck in place of the cross pendant that the other sisters wore. Sister Fran looked almost translucent in the sunlight, her arms and legs exposed and her veins appearing like little road maps beneath her pale skin.

"It's quite heavy," Sister Monica said between short breaths.

"*Sin* is heavy," Sister Fran said. She trilled the whistle three quick times into a wincing Sister Monica's ear, then marched ahead toward the front of the parade.

Our float was the largest entry in the parade, and for good reason. We'd designed it to hide us. Eight feet at its tallest point, it was shaped like a hand of benediction—two perpendicular fingers set closer than a victory sign, resembling a double-barreled, gun-shaped hand pointed toward the air. Win and I stood crouched in the upright fingers, Ginny had curled her tiny body into the thumb, and Gwen pancaked herself inside the narrow hollow of the plywood base. Outside we could hear the cheering of onlookers, some squealing and hooting. The band boomed in the distance, not the slow, haunting organ music we normally heard in the chapel during mass, but something infinitely more upbeat, with horns and guitars.

The parade itself capped off the Sisters' annual August festival celebrating the Assumption of Mary, her earthly departure. At the end of her life, Mary was carried up to heaven on the wings of angels, her body too sacred to remain on earth, succumbing to dust like the rest of us. To be certain, The Guineveres didn't believe we were perfect, not like Mary. How could we, with Sister Fran's constant reminders of our waywardness or the sins of our bodies that shamed us for the simple fact that they *were* bodies and thus subject to the laws of biology? "The Flesh, girls, the Flesh," Sister Fran warned, her habit swaddled tightly against her face so she appeared to have no ears, though she always seemed to hear us, to overhear us, and so we often found ourselves whispering, even when we were alone. For The Guineveres, the festival marked not Mary's departure but *our* departure, *our* freedom. We refused to wait until we were eighteen; we were leaving the convent for good.

Of course, this was nearly two decades ago, and some of the details I've since forgotten. Call it willful amnesia or an act of forgiveness. I'm not sure which. I gave up writing in my notebook a long time ago—life got in the way, and I grew out of the habit. Besides, after everything that happened that year, there were some things I didn't wish to remember, some questions I couldn't bring myself ask. Back then, I hadn't yet realized that time had a way of providing the answers. Back then, I believed The Guineveres were all I had.

I was the first Guinevere to arrive at the convent, the only Guinevere that summer when my mother left me there. Almost thirteen then, I shared my name with Saint Guinevere, who, at my very age, was martyred for her faith. Beheaded by a vengeful suitor after resisting his advances, she miraculously rose from the dead. She lived on as a nun for many years after, her head apparently functioning just fine. I could understand how she must have suffered—to have her head severed from her body, but then be forced to go on living. That's how I felt when my mother left me. But I wasn't as wise as Saint Guinevere, and I wasn't a saint. They called me Vere. I was a sensitive young girl, a girl who still had faith. I prayed often, as I'd been taught to do. I prayed for someone to come rescue me.

And eight months later, during Morning Roll, my prayers were answered. Sister Fran stood at the head of the Bunk Room, yelling out names like insults, and when she hollered "Guinevere," her voice rising as she spoke that last syllable, another voice joined mine in response. "Here," we both said in harmonious unison, like the opening chord of a song. Our eyes locked. There stood

12

Ginny, arms akimbo, her skirt twisted on her skinny waist, pleats askew.

Ginny resembled a bird only in that she was a delicate creature, as prone to unpredictability as the spring that ushered her in. "Blessed are those servants whom the master finds tidy," Sister Fran would say, motioning for Ginny to tuck in her shirt or tame the wild red hair that framed her face like a lion's mane. After learning about stigmata wounds during Morning Instruction, she'd sit mesmerized by her palms, tracing her thin fingers along invisible sores. Ginny liked to think of herself as an artist—not so much a person who created art as a person who was misunderstood. When she felt things, she felt them deeply.

Winnie—we called her Win—arrived another eight months later, near Christmastime, when the hallways were strung with pine rope and holly. When Sister Fran called out roll and hollered "Guinevere," sternly this time, as though we were in trouble, three clear voices answered back. "Here," we said, a triumvirate chorus. We scanned the room and located the owner of the smoky alto that had joined us. We found olive-skinned Win, her arms folded in front of her, her skirt low on her hips, her bold, broad smile revealing a slight gap between her front teeth. At breakfast, we motioned her toward our table, and she skeptically slurped her Cream of Wheat as we explained the extraordinary coincidence of our trinity.

To pass the hours during Rec Time that winter, Win practiced braiding our hair, which we grew down past our shoulders. We were allowed to wash our hair only once a week, so braiding helped it appear less greasy. Despite her dexterity, Win had knotty knuckles, big hands that when balled into fists made an impression on the other girls who, if they were afraid of us, were afraid of her the most. Sometimes the younger girls pressed their backs against the wall as we passed them in the hallway, so The Guineveres could walk side by side.

Gwen was the last of us to arrive, late one fall, after the Sisters brought out our sweaters that smelled of must and mothballs. The night before, we had witnessed the new girl changing into her nightgown without even pretending to turn her back to the Bunk Room. Her eyes were glassy, a startling blue, and as she undressed, neatly folding her uniform, we noticed a heart-shaped birthmark right above the bone of her hip. In the morning, she leaned despondently against her bunk, her long blond hair appearing smooth, even after a night of sleep. Sister Fran rattled off the roll, pausing as she neared our name, her beady eyes scrutinizing her clipboard. "Guinevere," she finally said. We rose to our tiptoes as though lifted by the spirit. "Here," we sang in our most gleeful voices, and when we recognized Gwen had joined our song, we tried to contain our excitement but could not. "Here," we answered as dozens of other girls swiveled in their skirts, looking on in disbelief. "Here! Here!"

"An abundance of Guineveres," Sister Fran said, clicking her tongue, which we took as acknowledgment that Gwen's arrival was no coincidence but a miracle indeed. That morning at breakfast, over stewed prunes and dry toast, we sat together, the four of us, now with Gwen, complete.

Of The Guineveres, Gwen was the prettiest, and she understood this as fact, not opinion. Someday she hoped to become an actress. She clipped out photos of beautiful people from the only magazines she could find in the library, and she tacked them to her bunk, staring at the images while she sat up in bed brushing her hair—exactly one hundred strokes every night before Lights Out.

It was Gwen, herself longing to wear lipstick, who taught us to stain our lips with the beets we were served for dinner or the berries we picked out of the fruit salad. It was Gwen who instructed us to stuff our bras with tissues, not by wadding but by folding so as not to create lumps. It was Gwen who demonstrated how to do toe touches to slenderize our middles or how to perform the pencil test that we all passed, except Win, or how to roll up the tops of our gray uniform skirts so we didn't look old-fashioned. It was Gwen who showed us how to steal butter from the dinner table—"It's borrowing," she explained, as she

15

tucked a pat into the cuff of her sleeve—so that we could later massage it into our hair and skin made brittle by the dry air of the convent. She dedicated herself devoutly to grooming.

And it was Gwen who, after living at the convent for less than a year, devised our hollow-floated plan to leave it.

"We're running away," she had said. She was reclining on one of the plaid couches in the Rec Room, propped up on pillows like Cleopatra awaiting hand-fed grapes. "And I know just how to do it." She smiled with one corner of her mouth, for dramatic effect, the way she sometimes did. The rest of us sat on the hard ground beside her and leaned in to listen.

She had gotten the idea from a movie she'd once seen back home, in her Unholy Life. In it, a giant cake was wheeled into a party at a mansion—an executive's house—and a chorus girl popped out of it, her arms raised in a V. Gwen soon demonstrated the scene for us, jumping up from behind one of the couches and putting her arms toward the ceiling as Father James some-times did during mass. In the movie, everyone gazed upon the beautiful woman as she burst through the cardboard cake, including the man who would eventually fall in love with her. This was Gwen's favorite part, the marveled, amorous expression on the man's face.

We worked on our float for weeks, every

evening in the courtyard, right after dinner until Lights Out. Win, whose grandfather had taught her to use tools, built the frame for us, a wooden base supporting chicken wire that we all helped bend into shape: a giant hand offering the victory sign. It was a universal symbol, The Guineveres agreed, and only one finger away from the other universal symbol we wished to offer the convent upon our departure. We painstakingly covered the frame with yellow tissue paper, twisting each piece around the wire and flaying it out at the ends until the frame was completely covered and our fingers numbed. The end product looked primitive, at best; the oversized fingers were set too vertically together to look much like a victory sign.

"Victory?" Sister Fran had questioned when she came to assess our creation. "A rather secular theme, don't you think?"

"The victory of our souls," one of us said. After all, she reminded us daily about the battle between good and evil that raged inside our young bodies.

"This won't do." As parade master, Sister Fran made it her earnest duty to ensure every float met a particular standard. The prior year, some girls weren't allowed to enter their Holy Chalice because she said it looked too similar to a martini glass. "Quality, like cleanliness, is a sign of godliness, girls," Sister Fran muttered as she circled our float. Her nose was an equilateral triangle, and she tapped

17

the tip of it while thinking. A few tedious moments of contemplation passed, and then she spoke again. "Ah, a hand of benediction. Yes, yes. A hand of benediction."

"Whose hand?" Ginny had said. Win elbowed her.

"Yes, Sister," Gwen said. "A hand of benediction."

"It's settled," Sister Fran said. She turned toward Ginny. "It's a hand of blessing. That's what this"—and here she paused to wave in the general direction of our float—"will be announced as in the parade." She made some markings on a clipboard. "You'll need to add the papal ring," she'd said without looking up. "You can't very well have a hand of benediction without the papal ring."

To complete our Hand of Benediction, we cut out an oval from poster board and painted it. We didn't have any gold paint, so we mixed brown and white together to form a color closer to beige, but it looked okay. Finally, we glued the oblong ring to the float, somewhere near where the knuckle would be. It wasn't perfect, but Sister Fran agreed to let it march in the parade. She *did* like to reward hard work, she had said.

Of course, The Guineveres would not pop out of our Hand of Benediction. No party awaited; no dazzled lover's eyes would gaze upon us. We knew that once the floats were paraded up the long driveway of the convent and, farther, into the courtyard of the church, they'd be left there until Sunday mass to help commemorate the Assumption. They'd be left alone. Overnight. Unguarded.

In the empty quiet of the church courtyard, once the sun had sunk and the sky turned to shadow, we planned to unfurl ourselves from our hiding spots. We'd stand on firm ground again and stretch our limbs, free to set about our lives that didn't involve the Sisters or their rules. Lives that didn't involve rising early every morning to Sister Fran's whistle and dressing in our monochrome uniforms—gray skirt, white blouse, white knee socks, black loafers. Lives that didn't involve single-filing to the kitchen, where we were served oatmeal and a piece of peaked fruit for breakfast. "We must be modest in our wants," Sister Fran would say when we asked for something more substantive, like eggs or waffles or a cream cheese Danish, the things we'd been accustomed to at home. We had little awe for the routine of convent life. After breakfast, we endured an hour of silent prayer, three hours of Morning Instruction, a break for lunch, chapel, more Instruction, and then Rec Time after dinner.

We simply wanted to be ordinary girls.

During the two blissfully unstructured festival days, under a canopy of tents, we could at least *pretend* we were ordinary girls, like before our parents left us here. When we weren't working the booths or cleaning the trash from the courtyard, where the garbage cans overflowed with grilled corn husks and sticky paper cups, we ate sugary foods, played tear-offs with names like Bars and Bells, and watched as the local parishioners aimed for the target on the dunking booth where Father James sat beneath a handmade sign that read DUNK-A-PRIEST. We placed bets at Turtle Downs, a booth run by Sister Tabitha, Sister Fran's second in command. She gripped a microphone and held it close to her reedy lips as the creatures ambled across the track in a leisurely race to the finish. Sister Tabitha had a stutter that she bore proudly, perhaps to demonstrate how God loves us despite our flaws.

"Sc-c-c-scales of Justice takes the lead," she called out, rattling off the names of the creatures as she called the race. "The Holy Sn-n-n-snail is close on his tail. Though Sh-sh-sh-sh-Shell Fire is making a si-si-significant comeback from behind."

For these two short days, the Sisters possessed a sense of, if not lightness, then at least not their usual costume of pressed lips and tight faces. They dressed in pink skirts and white cotton shirts, a drastic departure from their usual black habits, but they still covered their heads with veils. Without their tunics, they looked gaunt; their thin frames resembled a prairie animal we'd seen in a *National Geographic* in the library. It was our favorite magazine, and we turned those pages especially slowly when they featured photos of naked men and women.

"It's like they're not embarrassed or anything," Ginny said.

"It's like Eden before the Fall," I noted.

"I'd hate to live in a world without makeup," Gwen added.

Win said nothing, just sat there and stared at the picture as if it were the most perplexing thing she'd ever seen.

We used to joke that we lived at the Sisters of the Supreme Constipation School for Girls. Behind the Sisters' backs, we'd contort our mouths in imitation, in what Win dubbed our Holy Constipation Faces. During Morning Instruction, while we sat in varnished desks reading about the lives of the saints, Ginny doodled pictures of the Sisters, their cheeks sunken and their expressions strained, cradling their torsos and sitting on a toilet as a heavenly light shined down upon them. *This too shall pass,* the caption read. We laughed, but not Gwen. She told us we were too old for such antics, and in some ways she was right. Had we lived "outside," we'd be in high school, learning to drive cars, getting part-time jobs at Woolworth's, and smoking cigarettes on our breaks in order to appear older and occupied and, thus, more attractive to boys. But the convent stalled the progression of time, stunted our growth. We lived cloistered lives, and in that way we *were* like all those saints.

"And look at how they turned out," Win reminded us. We had spread ourselves out on the lawn near the bandstand, watching the trumpet player's face redden and the saxophone player's cheeks blow in and out like a fish's.

"Yes. They died! It was horrible! I don't want to die," Ginny said, clasping her forehead, then pulling back her palm to examine it for stigmata wounds.

"And most of them never even got laid," Gwen said.

"There are more important things than that," I added.

"Like what?" Gwen asked, but it came out like a yawn. She constantly preened herself, and at that moment she picked dirt from beneath her nails, grimacing as she flicked each speck to the grass.

"Like faith." I was the only true believer among us.

At the far end of the lawn, we saw Lottie Barzetti, the sun reflecting off her glasses. She was handing out tufts of cotton candy to her friends like manna, bending at the waist to administer each piece. Her curly hair had frizzed out in the heat, and she had her socks pulled up to her knees, even though the Sisters said we could go without socks for the day. Lottie was never one to break the rules. Her devoutness bordered on ascetic. The Guineveres once found her in the Bunk Room hitting herself over the head with her Bible. "Stupid girl, stupid girl," she kept repeating with each thwack.

From behind her we could hear the crowd cheer, and we watched as Father James emerged from the dunking booth. His now transparent undershirt revealed his wide chest, patched with dark hairs. His shorts clung to his body in a way that showed a lump of manhood. We looked on in horror, not like we did with those *National Geographics*; something seemed irreverent about it.

During the festival, even the old folks from the convalescence wing seemed livelier. During the day, they'd usually sit stone-faced at the tables in their lobby. Some would stare out the window toward the parking lot as though waiting for someone, but they seldom received visitors. These decrepit old men and women were left behind, forgotten, like us, and so we felt sorry for them. But still, we didn't ever want to be put on Sick Ward duty. We called it the Sick Ward, even though most of them weren't visibly sick—like Mr. Macker or Miss Oatley—just old and dying slowly of age.

The Sick Ward comprised the entire east wing of the convent, a different world altogether. Old men and women would moan from their beds, call out the names of people they'd once known in voices that sounded ghostly, like the slow hand-spinning of a record. It frightened us. The Guineveres agreed that this must be a kind of purgatory, where souls of old people went when nobody else would claim them. And purgatory, we repugnantly observed, smelled like rubbing alcohol, bleach, and urine. From a distance, the old folks looked like a militia's front line. Their wheelchairs pointed toward the church, and the balloons tied to their armrests shifted in the breeze like colorful flags. Mr. Macker had fallen asleep in his chair, his head leaned back at a forty-five-degree angle, his mouth parted as if he were waiting to take communion. His crooked toes poked out of his slippers like an atrophied hand.

For more than a month The Guineveres had planned our escape; we'd held meetings in the Bunk Room while the other girls played Ping-Pong; we'd even followed every rule, down to ensuring our uniform skirts hit the proper length, draping the floor when kneeling, as we did every morning before prayer under threat of a JUG. A JUG was similar to a detention, only worse. It stood for Justice Under God, and it usually involved extra Bible study and some undesirable chore detail, like scrubbing the old folks' lobby or changing one of the convalescents' bedclothes or washing down the blackboard in the Instruction room, then clapping out the erasers that coated the insides of our noses with a fine layer of chalk.

Each of us had our role in the grand escape plot. Gwen was charged with securing extra blankets that she'd pilfered on the most recent Wash Day when Sister Claire wasn't looking, then tucked beneath her mattress. Win, who had recently been assigned to kitchen duty, was tasked with appropriating food, no easy feat since our uniforms had no pockets. She managed to stow away a few bags of dry oatmeal, some raisins, and a jar of peanut butter, placing them in the sanitary closet, where nobody would think to look. Every girl felt shame when she opened the sanitary closet each month, as though her body had betrayed her, and so our food supply remained in there for two weeks, untouched. For my part, I gathered grooming sundries, items Gwen said were essential: toothpaste, tissues, a bar of soap, a hairbrush. Poor Ginny wasn't given a task at all. We found her unreliable but well-intentioned—a weakened constitution, she claimed, from her asthma—so we asked her to carry the burden of worry for the rest of us. She did that with ease.

We planned to find our way to the city. The Guineveres had pulled together what we knew of the surrounding terrain from our memories of being brought to the convent. Ginny had the most specialized knowledge, having been taken to the hospital last year for yet another bout of asthma that the rest of us knew was really just hyperventilating brought on by excessive concern.

"We're practically in the middle of a desolate forest," Ginny had reported. And when we pressed her further she conceded that she did remember passing houses along the way to the hospital, and a general store, and a bank, now that she thought of it. "It had a clock so bright that from a distance I thought it was the moon," she said.

The Guineveres would hike through the woods to town; it couldn't be more than fifteen miles, we figured. We'd avoid the main roads. We'd stop to rest if we had to. "But we won't get dirty," Gwen had said, reminding us of our need to keep our dignity. Then we'd take a bus to the city, where we'd get jobs as secretaries at first, and we'd rent an apartment, the four of us. Ginny wanted to go to art school, eventually. Gwen wanted to work as a sales clerk at Tiffany's while auditioning for theater productions.

"Of course," Gwen had said, "later we'll all get married. To executives."

"Yes, to executives," we all repeated.

Win thought she would become a hairdresser at first, maybe eventually earn a beautician's license. Braiding our hair felt like a logic puzzle to her, she said, and she had great spatial awareness. Plus, she preferred manual labor to paperwork. Win was big-boned and strong, a fact that led the Sisters to recruit her help carrying the large sacks of flour and potatoes that were delivered to the convent each month. As for myself, I hadn't developed many specialized interests or skills, except a keen memory for church history. At night, while the other girls slept, I'd write in my notebook all the saints I could remember. My mother and I used to do that, memorize parts of the Bible together: Adam begat Seth who begat Enos who begat sons and daughters and so on. I'd jot down as many of their names as I could, pretend I was listing the branches of my own family tree. Because that's what I wanted to do when I got out—to belong somewhere, to someone, to a big family. When I told The Guineveres this, they scoffed, said I needed grander dreams than that. I never mentioned it again, and if prodded, I explained to them that I wanted to become a schoolteacher. This answer pleased The Guineveres just fine.

When it was time, we walked through the festival, now buzzing with people, with women in sundresses and strappy sandals, with small kids who held balloons that floated like the Holy Ghost above their heads. At the high striker, Regina, one of the newest girls, swung the rubber mallet. She went by Reggie, and despite her thick frame and legs set a shoulder's width apart, the puck didn't rise even halfway to the bell. After each attempt, she'd tuck the mallet between her legs, and she'd wipe her sausage hands on her uniform skirt. Next to Reggie, cheering with strained facial expressions, stood her sidekick, Noreen, mute as always. She had a green apron tied around her waist, and she was supposed to be selling raffle tickets, but considering The Guineveres had never heard her speak, we didn't know how this would be possible. Some of the older girls—the ones who were almost eighteen—had spread out in front of the bandstand, kicking off their shoes and leaning back on their elbows. A few of them had only a matter of weeks before their birthdays, and then they'd be sent away, off into the world, forever free. We envied them their ages.

"Any cute boys?" Gwen asked as she scanned the crowd. Her lips were still stained pink from the cotton candy we'd eaten earlier when we worked the concessions booth. She had pressed strands of fluff to her mouth and let it melt there.

"None that I see," Win said.

"Maybe they're turning them away at the gate," Ginny said.

"Lead us not into temptation," I added.

Oblivious to all but our own purpose, The Guineveres walked through the crowd transfixed, like Moses must have felt when he parted the Red Sea, leading his people to the Promised Land.

The convent itself towered behind the festival tents. Its gray stone had grown lightly mossed, and to see to the topmost cross affixed to the highest spire, we had to crane our necks back, giving us the feeling of staring straight up into the heavens. And as we stood there, doing just that, our necks exposed, the backs of our heads resting on our shoulders, we felt the weight of the convent, the sheer enormity of it. Its windows were eyes staring down on us, unblinking. Unsympathetic, too.

We climbed the steps to the main archway, and from there we saw that the Sisters were beginning to corral the old folks toward the parade's staging area. We made our way inside, down the long corridor that, though it had plenty of windows, was shrouded in shade. Regardless of the time of year, the hallway felt chilled, the way dirt does if you dig down far enough. The size of the convent taught us how space related to time. It took us several long minutes to cross through to the Sick Ward. Nobody was in the main room, except Mrs. Martin, who sat at one of the front tables, a deck of cards stacked in front of her, two hands neatly dealt. She didn't look up as we walked past.

We arrived at the back door to the courtyard just in time to catch a glimpse of Sister Fran holding her clipboard. She walked on the tips of her toes, bouncing as she exited through the open gate in the direction of the festival crowd. We could hear the squeal of her whistle, short staccato beats, and though she was yelling something, it sounded to us like the garbled warble of a bird. Gwen shoved my back, and I stumbled forward a bit.

"Go," she said. "Move."

I sensed the urgency, and I can say that up until

that point, I hadn't been scared. But now, faced with the reality of the situation, my limbs felt mired in quicksand. It'd been three long years since I'd stepped foot off the convent's grounds. What did I know about the world?

"Vere," Win said. "Go!" Her voice was not unkind, and so I stumbled forward, and, despite my fear, my legs carried me the rest of the way.

A tall stone wall stretched the perimeter of the courtyard, enclosing it. We could see above the wall to the striped tops of the festival tents that billowed in and out in the breeze like they were breathing. Because the Sisters believed that functionality preceded beauty in all areas of their lives, and because they did not tolerate waste of any sort, they had filled their old black shoes with soil and lined them along the base of the wall in tiers, using them as planters. From these rows of leather lace-ups sprang purple geraniums that were pretty enough, except for how creepy it looked. The toes were scuffed, angled out from one another in pairs. Moss had grown in the shoes' worn crevices or along their busted seams, and every so often the head of a geranium popped through a weak spot in the leather, eaten by decay. These shoes gave us the distinct impression that the previous owners, whoever they were, wherever they were—alive or dead— were guarding the courtyard like invisible sentinels. Even out of doors, these shoes reminded us, we could not escape the omnipresence of the Sisters in our lives.

We tried to put this out of our minds as we made our way to the concrete patio in the center of the courtyard where the floats were parked, lined in rows. Our Hand of Benediction wasn't so shoddy compared to some of the others: an enormous fish with streamers for a tail; some lumpy nondescript saints; a dove with an elongated neck; a lamb that looked more like a dog; a tree of life that resembled pom-pom fronds; and a float that simply spelled out L-O-V-E, each letter in a different color. We hurried in silence toward our Hand of Benediction. Sister Fran had made a sign that read A BLESSING FOR YOU and affixed it to the front of the float; the smell of fresh glue stung our noses.

Getting into the float was like getting into a canoe—it wasn't easy. Though the float didn't tip and turn, the angle was tight as we climbed through the hollow plywood base and into our hiding spots. We hadn't accounted for the space taken up by our stash of blankets and supplies, so I scraped my back as I slid up into position, and I grabbed hold of the chicken wire to get my balance.

"I can see your fingers poking out, idiot," Gwen snipped, so I loosened my grip a bit and allowed the frame to hold my weight. Waiting for everyone to take their places, I felt like a caged animal ready for transport.

"Okay, ready," Win said.

"Hurry," I heard Ginny say.

Gwen grunted somewhere beneath me. The float rocked and knocked as she slid inside the platform below.

"Okay," Gwen said.

"All aboard," Win said.

"God save us," Ginny said.

"Amen," I said.

We didn't have to wait very long. Only a few minutes later the short punctuation of Sister Fran's whistle grew louder. Through small gaps we could make out the outline of some Sisters approaching. We closed our eyes, hoping if we couldn't see them, we'd be invisible. Our hearts were beating quickly; we swallowed pitifully. We could hear our stomachs grumbling from too much funnel cake we'd eaten earlier in the day. We didn't know when we'd be able to eat again. Soon we could hear footsteps surrounding us, and then Sister Fran began coaching the others.

"Parade route is same as last year. Be sure to keep moving at all times—and stay a good ten feet back from one another. No accidents this time, please, Lucrecia." Sister Fran then began calling out the assignments. Sister Margaret would march with the L-O-V-E float; Sister Magda would be pulling the lamb; Sister Claire would walk with the Saint Theobald.

"Which one is Theobald?" we heard Sister Claire ask.

A pause. Claire was not known for her brains. "The monk," replied Sister Fran with a tone of disappointment. She sighed audibly, then continued her list of assignments.

Sister Fran answered our prayers and assigned Sister Monica to pull our float. She was the largest sister in the order, so presumably the strongest. Her hips were wide, her back end was huge, and she sort of hunched and waddled when she walked, swinging her legs out and around her body, earning her the nickname Sister Hippomonica.

Now Sister Monica's enormous derriere faced us. It looked like two oblong melons beneath her skirt, and I thought I heard Win restraining a laugh. Sister Monica picked up the long handle attached to our float and jerked it lightly to test its weight. "Jesus help me," she muttered, then turned to face front.

We heard Sister Fran's whistle again—a long, low sound followed by an up-pitched zip. Soon we were moving—not quickly, but moving. Inside the float, our muscles already began to ache from the odd angles at which we held our bodies. We couldn't think of where we'd sleep or how the woods at night would be crawling with spiders and snakes. We couldn't project our thoughts very far into our futures. We could only recall our pasts in silence. We considered our present, too, and we marveled at what had become natural in our lives: the stone structure itself, now looming behind us;

the Sisters who normally resembled black-cloaked matryoshka dolls; the alabaster statues of saints that lined the corridors of the convent, staring down at us like disapproving parents. But not our parents. Our parents were far away. What would they think of us now, we wondered, as Sister Monica unknowingly pulled us up the hill, our bodies twisted and contorted inside our Hand of Benediction. Together we took a deep breath of stale air and exhaled. All these years later, and I can attest: This may have been my only out-of-body experience. I felt like I was watching the scene from a distance, from the crowd of onlookers in the parade. In fact, I'm certain I can see it in my memory, that jalopy of a float, our Hand of Benediction, slowly wobbling its way up the hill, the four of us hidden inside.

Once we got to pavement, the ride felt smoother; the wheels purred beneath us. The crowd now clapped in rhythm with the band. Sister Fran clapped along with them, her broad smile revealing her teeth that were small and pointy like a cat's.

The float in front of us had no wheels, and so it was carried by handlebars at both ends. From behind, it looked like a giant misshapen mushroom, but it was supposed to be a saint. The float kept tilting from side to side, swaying so it seemed as though Saint Whoever was dancing, but once Sister Fran marched up beside the Sisters carrying it, the dancing stopped and the float straightened.

Tucked inside our Hand of Benediction, we felt dizzy with excitement. The world looked overmagnified somehow. Though we'd often fantasized about leaving the convent, conjuring up great scenes of escape—with tied bedsheets thrown out the Bunk Room window and Sister Fran in hot pursuit, her whistle bouncing up and down on her chest as she ran after us—in the end, we simply believed our parents would come back for us. That they'd show up one day, wet-faced, frantic with apology. We even figured we'd forgive them. They were our parents, after all, and though they let us down, we wanted to love them. That's how love works. It conquers all. Back then, the solution seemed pretty simple.

Sister Monica's breath grew labored as she strained to pull us up the incline of the long drive. Her face glistened. She kept stopping to wipe her palms on her skirt and to get a better grip. Just as we began to crest the top of the drive, Sister Fran walked toward us again with a look of stern indignation on her face. Holy Constipation.

"Here," Sister Fran said, grabbing the handle; then her voice changed. "Dear heavens," she said. "It's like hauling the Rock of Gibraltar."

We all froze, our muscles stiffening. Anxiety overcame our cramped hiding space in the form of warmth, as though blood simultaneously rushed to our faces, which kicked on like little space heaters.

But the float kept moving forward, upward, toward the top of the hill, to where, just a little beyond, sat the church and our salvation. Our Mount Sinai. Our Promised Land. Sister Fran and Sister Monica each gripped the float's handle with one hand, waving to the crowd with the other. Sweat soaked the backs of their thin white blouses. Their smiles looked more like winces.

Onlookers lined the parade route, their gazes aimed toward the top of the hill, where Sister Tabitha now stood announcing the floats in the same scratchy voice that had called out the names of the turtles at Turtle Downs. She held the megaphone to her lips and lifted her head to the sky, so she resembled a bugle player in a marching band made of one.

"The S-s-sacred Heart," she said, "by Lottie Barzetti, Sh-Sh-Shirley Mitchell, and Nan Waggler." We could hear the crowd clapping slowly, either tired or unenthused. We couldn't blame them. Who, after all, really enjoys parades after the first ten minutes, The Guineveres had wondered while building our float in the courtyard, twisting paper around wire. Certainly not us. We found it all so embarrassing somehow.

"S-s-s-saint Philomena, patron s-s-saint of youth," Sister Tabitha said through her megaphone another minute later, as the brown hump of a float in front of us cleared the top of the hill. The crowd's clapping grew louder, and we knew we were almost there. Our breathing became shallow; our heads buzzed; our fingers were wet with sweat and anticipation. We'd never felt closer to freedom.

"A Hand of Benediction: A Blessing to You," Sister Tabitha hollered, and she read our names off, one by one. We winced when we heard them, spoken so publicly. We could tell by the volume of the clapping and the angle of the float that we'd reached the top of the drive. If we could have seen behind us, we'd have waved good-bye to the old gray building shrinking in the distance. We'd have waved good-bye to years of loneliness, of guilt because we never felt we could live up to the expectations of perfection demanded of us by the Sisters. They say good-byes are always hard, but not for us. Not on that day.

We eased up as we rolled farther away from the convent and toward the churchyard. Sister Fran surrendered the handle to Sister Monica, and we were gliding along the smooth pavement, which bumped every once in a while when we hit a crack or a rock. The hypnotic sound of the wheels on concrete nearly lulled us to sleep.

Soon the sounds from the crowd quieted, and we could feel the coolness of the shadows in the courtyard. Some Sisters giggled in hushed tones; wheels scraped and grated. We knew we'd almost made it, and tension rose up from our bodies like souls from the departed.

"Right over there," we heard Father James say. He'd changed out of his indecent swim trunks and wore his usual black outfit, slacks and a shirt. The Hand of Benediction turned one hundred and eighty degrees before coming to a quick stop. And just like that, we arrived.

We began to feel edgy with excitement, but we knew we couldn't risk moving. We'd wait until we heard no more voices, until long after we heard no more voices. We weren't allowed watches—we lived on God's Time at the convent—so we'd decided to say the rosary three times in our heads, since praying it three times, from start to finish, all fifty-nine beads, lasted about an hour.

We waited. We recited the Our Father. We'd learned patience while sitting through long sermons or tedious lectures given to us by Sister Fran during Morning Instruction. We waited. We recited the Hail Mary. We'd learned to be still while kneeling in rows during prayer time, our knees growing numb from the wood. We waited. We recited the Glory Be. We'd learned to be silent while single-filing through the convent, treading as gently as possible through the stone foyers that felt chilly even in the summer.

We heard some murmuring and muttering, idle chatter among the Sisters. We heard Sister Lucrecia's laugh, five high notes descending the scales. Sister Fran asked Sister Tabitha for the bullhorn back; Sister Tabitha hesitated to relinquish it. She sang into it—"La, la, laaaaaaaa!"—until she lost her breath and gasped for air. This aural display was followed by subdued snickers, a sound that unsettled us, for we'd never known the Sisters to be jovial. The Guineveres wondered what else we didn't know about them.

The band's happy cadence faded. We heard a running faucet in the distance. We heard some birds chirping somewhere beyond. Then we felt the lightest sprinkling of water—was it raining? It hadn't looked threatening. We hadn't noticed any clouds. The cool droplets would have been a welcome respite from the heat, if not for our next realization: Tissue paper dissolves in water.

It was like coming to from a dream, or maybe like Jonah when he first emerged from the belly of the whale. We were disoriented; we couldn't see clearly at first. The spray of water revealed the blue sky above us, bit by bit. Then the water came on heavier, the full force of it stinging our skin till we were crying out in pain. "Stop!" we screamed in unison, breaking our vow of silence. We couldn't open our eyes, only stand and wait for it to end.

And when it did, we opened our eyes slowly, one at a time. There stood Sister Fran, holding a hose like the staff of Joseph. "Where are the others?" she asked, then hunched down to peer inside the base of the float. She stood again, slowly, brushing her skirt with one hand to smooth out wrinkles. She was quiet for a moment, and the quiet was excruciating, so we just stood there, blinking slowly and waiting for the end.

"Get. Out," she said in two sentences.

Win looked like a wet, rabid rodent. Her hair clung to her forehead and cheeks, and her dark eyes were glossy, stunned. Beneath me I could hear Gwen and Ginny untangling their bodies from their hiding spots.

Sister Fran squeezed the nozzle again, and water pelted our skin. Then she dropped the hose, and it became a serpent in the grass. Water dripped down our faces. Or were they tears? I can't remember. The Guineveres stood paralyzed with fear, with disappointment.

"Out," she said again. This time she said it softly, but not without anger.

One by one—much more slowly than we had gotten in—we climbed out.

Saint Rose of Lima

FEAST DAY: AUGUST 23

As Saint Rose grew into womanhood, her body became her burden: hands white and tidy as church gloves, a slender nose, dark almond eyes, round hips, and an ample bosom. Everywhere she went, people stopped to appreciate her beauty; they stared at the lovely sight of her clear, porcelain complexion, so out of place on the dirty streets of Lima. Rose, afraid that such admirations would lead to temptation, cut off her long raven hair. She was saving herself for one man and one man alone.

Her parents encouraged her to marry, but she refused. Instead, she'd rub her face with pepper, splotch her skin with welts and berry-shaped blisters. Once, an admirer swore hers were the most delicate hands he'd ever looked upon. Disgusted, Rose went home and rubbed them with lime, burning them so badly she couldn't move them for a month, not even to button her nightshirt.

Her body troubled her. It was her home, her prison—this thing that stirred her at night sometimes; she could not escape it. During the day, she'd wear a wreath of thorns concealed with roses, pressed into her scalp so firmly it pierced her skin. Light drops of blood crowned her head like morning dew. In this manner, she'd toil in the garden, and at night she'd labor by candlelight on her needlework. *Increase my suffering,* she'd pray.

And her suffering increased. She was lonely. Her friends and family ridiculed her, yet she remained obedient, steadfast in her devotion. To help her family, she sold her flowers and her fine, hand-tatted laces at the market. With her leftover profits, she fostered the sick and the poor. Rose fasted weekly, then started abstaining from meat altogether, until eventually she ate only the paltry amount of food required to survive. She grew thin, but this thinness only highlighted her perfect bone structure, her fine jawline, her high cheekbones. She didn't often leave her little room, a grotto she'd built in the garden. *Increase my suffering,* she'd pray, and she'd go to sleep on her bed made of broken glass and stone.

Her suffering increased. She toiled in the garden, numbed her scarred fingers with her lacework and embroidery, carried her goods to the market, fed the poor, tended to the sick, all while press-pressing that thorny wreath into her scalp. She grew tired, but the dark circles under her eyes lent her an exotic look. People praised her beauty, even then. Rose smeared lye on her face and retreated to her grotto, where, hidden away, she awaited even the smallest of signs from above. She felt such distance between herself and the sky, such distance in the world, such sadness.

Then one morning, in the quiet of the dawn, when the light cast gray, grainy shadows on the wall of her grotto—so early yet, the birds had not begun their warbling—she saw Him, standing above her. He wore a simple robe, His hair moving as though stirred by wind. His eyes were gentle. He smiled as He touched her, and when His hand grazed her skin her face cinched in ecstasy, and her body: It unfolded; it tensed; it bloomed.

Rose was thirty-one when illness took her. As the first saint of the New World, she's remembered for her devotion, for her pious suffering, and, above all, for her beauty. She died a virgin; yet, she never regretted a day of her suffering—not a single day. For in the end, she knew He'd come again. And He did.

Penance

The Guineveres resolved to face adversity with grace, as the greatest of the saints had done. We'd recently learned during Morning Instruction that Saint Marguerite had survived Iroquois attacks, fires, and plagues, and that Saint Barbara's own father had locked her in a tower for years. Still, we couldn't help feeling more than a little defeated. We sat on the cool tile floor of the Bunk Room, which felt like a prison with its slate-colored walls, with the meager amount of light let in from the single window. Bare rafter beams ran the length of the ceiling, forming bars above us. At that very moment, we should have been bounding through the woods or boarding a bus to the city. Instead, Ginny kept rubbing her palms together, crying that she was afraid she might never see her father again. Win reassured us that we'd find another way out.

"Did you see the look on Sister Fran's face?" Win said, trying to lift our spirits. She had positioned herself behind Gwen and began finger-combing her hair, parting it in pieces. "Pure constipation!" We all laughed, even Ginny. We spent the rest of the afternoon in silence, watching the room turn gray, prohibited from joining the other girls for the picnic supper. When we stood by the window, we could hear squeals of laughter and the murmuring of the festival crowd that, when we closed our eyes and pretended, sounded like the ocean. Ginny wept quietly; Gwen slept with a pillow covering her face; Win braided tiny sections of her own dark hair until she looked like Medusa. As for me, I prayed my usual prayers; I prayed for my mother to return for me.

The next day, Sister Fran brought Father James in to take our confessions, though he must have known what we'd confess: We didn't want to live here anymore. We didn't want to wear our scratchy uniforms, so out of fashion, according to Gwen; or fast on Fridays when we were already hungry; or single-file from place to place like a row of ducks, minus the quacking. Only silence. We'd grown tired of staring out the window during Morning Instruction, and up the hill toward the church, wondering what our families were doing now. Did they think of us? Did they regret leaving us here? Maybe things could be different, if they'd only take us back. The Bible contains all sorts of stories about second chances. Look at Noah, or Samson, or Abraham's son Isaac, who was nearly slaughtered by his father. Even Isaac forgave Abraham in the end.

One by one, Father James called us into the chapel confessional, a small room with an opaque penitential grille to obscure him. Father James was a young priest then; he'd taken over as pastor only shortly before I arrived at the convent. However, to us he seemed old. He even *smelled* old, like aftershave and something sweeter, but sour, too, something Win told us smelled like the way her mother often did after her father had left. Since Father James was tall—or the grille was short—we could still see his smooth forehead, his dark, bushy brows, his hair, prematurely gray, combed flat to the side.

"Bless me, Father, for I have sinned," we had each said during our separate visits to the confessional.

"I wanted to run away," Ginny confessed, "to visit my father. He can't visit me, you know. He would if he could." She curled herself into a ball on the confessional bench, tucked her head between her knees.

"I designed the float to hide us," Win confessed. "It was originally supposed to be a victory sign." She crossed her arms in front of her chest, self-conscious of her well-developed breasts. Of all The Guineveres, she wore the largest-sized bra, a fact that Gwen resented.

"It was my idea," Gwen confessed, peeking above the grille and smiling with one corner of her mouth. "I'm full of ideas." Father James nodded sanctimoniously.

"I wanted to go," I said, and as soon as the words flew from my lips, I recognized my utterance as sin. I felt disloyal in admitting my relief that we'd been caught. It's not that I didn't want to be out in the world—I did. When I couldn't sleep, I'd reach for my notebook hidden beneath my bunk, and I'd remember myself on a bus, circling a city. My mom and I used to do that, sit for hours in the back to observe other riders because Mom believed that's where one got the truest glimpse of humanity. She was giving me a lesson, one I couldn't get from school. Who stood to offer up his seat to someone else? Who tugged impatiently at the cord that ran above the windows like a clothesline? Who refused to move over, or fell asleep against the window, pocking it with grease marks that looked like tic-tac-toe boards? Who smiled at us, even though we looked like Gypsies, our hair unwashed for days? The bus would stop and start, stop and start. From my window, I'd watch the cityscape, tall, angular buildings passing above me like geometric clouds, and I'd wonder who was inside. This is what I dreamed of at night: the fullness of a world.

However, the thought of leaving the convent scared me, too. I was only fifteen. How would my mother find me again? How would I find her? "I don't like it here," I confessed to Father James, and that part was true. I could see his half-moon eyes above the divider. They were the eyes of God Himself.

After confession, The Guineveres sat squished together in the first pew, so close we could still smell grilled meats and grass in one another's hair. Father James stood before us, listing forward against the front of the pew so that his arm muscles bulged. It was hard not to notice. He had a small scar above his mouth that cut into his upper lip, and his nose and cheeks were rosy in a way I'd later learn was an alcoholic's rouge. Sister Fran perched herself just far enough behind Father James so she appeared like a menacing bird on his shoulder.

"Your sins may be absolved, girls," Father James said, "but your work has just begun." We sank deeper into the pew as if our spines had dissolved, our bodies now putty. He continued, "After all, young girls need guidance. I don't think a singular JUG will suffice this time. Three months of service in the Convalescence Ward will hopefully reawaken your sense of gratitude. For when you wish to see yourself as fortunate, you should spend time with those who have less. Happiness, girls, is a matter of where you place your attention."

Father James examined us closely, focusing on us one at a time, trying to determine the fates of our souls. He could have been handsome if he weren't a priest, but he was a priest, which made him seem almost otherworldly to us. At that moment, he was running his hands down his sides as though counting his ribs. Gwen later claimed he was trying to imagine us without clothes on, sizing us up, as men are wont to do, which is why Sister Fran intervened.

"Thank you, Father," Sister Fran said. "I think you've shown more leniency and graciousness than the case warrants. Don't you agree, girls?" she asked.

"Yes, Sister," The Guineveres said, even though we didn't.

Father James nodded and began to walk away. But then he stopped midstride, turned around, and smiled a sad kind of smile, no teeth, just the bending of his lips. "Life is not always better on the outside, girls," he said gently. "Remember that."

The Guineveres knew exactly what Father James was referring to, and in some ways he was right. As we brooded churlishly in the chapel, as we repented and bewailed our fates, outside the convent the War had already been declared. There were soldiers in the War, boys who would fight, boys who would become injured, grievously so. Some would die. But we could think only of ourselves in this moment. We didn't care to know how a war a continent away could impact our lives or that it would. It did. But that day, while we sat in the first pew of the small chapel at the Sisters of the Supreme Adoration Convent—and despite the War—we were sure Father James was wrong.

To The Guineveres the outside meant leaving behind our histories as throwaways. We'd heard what the other girls said behind our backs in the cafeteria. They would cluster together at their tables, paying no attention to the way sound carried through the arched ceilings and into our ears. *Their parents just gave them away,* they whispered. Outside we wouldn't have to worry why our parents didn't write, even though we begged them in our letters, or why they didn't come back for us. Sure, they had problems, but why? Why us? We were tired of asking why, of throwing up our prayers to some higher being that ignored our pleas. Outside we could reinvent ourselves, create our own lives, become The Guineveres, the ones with an apartment and jobs, with boyfriends who worked in the city. We'd wear high heels and lace bras and lipstick, and we'd laugh, and men would clamor to light our cigarettes. We wouldn't have time to feel sorry for ourselves. Outside we could make something of our lives, something out of nothing, like the fishes and the loaves. And maybe then we'd find our families and ask them that burning question in person: *Why?*

Because what we wouldn't have given to be *normal* girls; that's all we really wanted. We wished we could tell Father James that we knew the outside was far from perfect—we all remembered our homes—but it was better than convent life. That's what we thought we knew back then. But what we didn't know, what we couldn't yet because the spirit works in mysterious ways, was that the universe had a larger plan for us, one that was taking shape, even as Father James left the chapel, even as Sister Fran laid her now sorry eyes upon us and said in a perky tone, "God loves a gracious giver." The Guineveres collected ourselves from the pew, straightened our skirts, and walked slowly to the cafeteria for lunch.

Although girls were assigned to beds in the Bunk Room, we could freely pick our seats in the cafeteria. As a result, the cafeteria became a microcosm of the convent's social order, designated by the very girls who resisted such order in the first place. We hated that Sister Fran assigned us to desks during Instruction or, with the zip of her whistle, commanded us to line up alphabetically by first name when we filed as a group from one room of the convent to another. And yet, meal after meal, you could find each girl in exactly the same chair at one of the cafeteria's long wooden tables that the Sisters waxed so often it felt sticky beneath our arms.

We divided ourselves by story. The Guineveres called them our Revival Stories, our reasons for coming to the convent. During Morning Instruction, Sister Fran had taught us that a revival was a moment of spiritual reawakening. She said we'd been given a second chance at an obedient life, a clean slate. "It's hard to stumble, girls, when you're on your knees," she said, taking long strides in front of the chalkboard. We held our pencil tips to our notebooks. "I think this is an important point, and you should write it down." We did as she instructed. For us, however, our Revival Stories were those moments when our eyes *really* opened to the truth. At the table closest to the serving buffet sat Lottie, Shirley, Nan, Dorrie Sue, and the other girls who still had contact with their parents, who received letters and birthday cards and postcards and—the lucky ones anyway—occasional phone calls that had to be taken in Sister Fran's office since that was the only phone at the convent. Ginny nicknamed these girls The Specials, because that's how they acted, even though they weren't special, not in our book. Their parents had good reason for leaving them, and these girls knew as much. They sat with stiff postures of superiority. Their noses tilted ever so slightly upward as though attached to the ceiling by an invisible string.

Barbara and Irene and Judy and those girls—they were stationed at the table nearest the Sisters, who arranged themselves at the far end of the room, closest to the kitchen. Win pointed out that these girls never appeared to be speaking to one another, and rightly so. They were the ones we called The Sads, the girls with the most depressing Revival Stories, the ones whose parents had died suddenly and sometimes violently: in fires, in automobile accidents, in suicides. The Sads hunched over their trays, even the weight of gravity making them despondent.

The next table over, the one right beneath the only large rectangular window in the room, sat The Poor Girls. These girls, Jeanette and Polly and their friends, we'd heard, had been taken away from their parents. Most of these girls came from destitute families, poorer than ours, even. The kind of poor that meant their ribs were showing like little accordions on their torsos when they first arrived. We'd heard the rumor that in Jeanette's Unholy Life, she used to eat only grease sandwiches made of bread and lard. She, unlike the rest of us, actually thought the convent's food tasted good. The Poor Girls were usually the first to return their trays to the bins; their plates never needed scraping.

Next to The Poor Girls sat Reggie and silent Noreen, just the two of them, all by themselves. They'd been at the convent for only a few months, and since they weren't much of a group, we didn't have a nickname for them yet. If we had, however, it might have been The Delusionals, because Reggie claimed that their parents were coming back for them any day now, just you wait and see. She swore to God—even though we were forbidden by Sister Fran from swearing to anything holy— that they weren't staying at the convent for long, just temporarily, not like the rest of us. Nobody believed her.

Reggie was broad-nosed and pear-shaped. She had short arms and big, fleshy wrists, and sometimes when she'd walk through the vaulted hallways, she'd stop midstride and say to whoever would listen, "When I'm out, I'll write you letters just so you don't feel so sad." Reggie meant well, though she annoyed us, and we never knew when she was telling the truth. Her feathery eyebrows arched dramatically, giving her the constant looked of feigned surprise. When she first arrived at the convent, before she found Noreen, she had asked to sit with us.

"Is your name Guinevere?" Win had asked. Reggie shook her head.

"My dad almost named me Guinevere," she said. "I swear."

"This table's reserved only for *actual* Guineveres," Gwen said, rubbing her lips with the guts of her grapes.

"You can call me Guinevere," Reggie said, biting her lip and swiveling her wide body to scan the cafeteria. Her water glass sloshed as she steadied her tray. "It's my middle name," she added, then scratched the inside of her ankle with the tip of her shoe.

"We're sorry," Ginny said sincerely. "Rules are rules."

"It's God's plan," I added. Gwen smiled at me in approval, and Reggie found somewhere else to sit.

At the table next to Reggie and Noreen sat

The Delinquents, a dead-eyed, slack-jawed lot. These girls could only blame themselves for their current predicament. In their Unholy Lives, The Delinquents had been a source of trouble, truants or users—the kind of girls you'd find in the backseats of cars smoking cigarettes that didn't smell like cigarettes. A table over from them sat the girls who were almost eighteen, the ones whose friends had already left and who'd be leaving the convent themselves as soon as their birthdays arrived. And next to them sat us, The Guineveres, who, as we rested our trays on the table, heard the other girls snicker in our direction.

"Guess you thought you'd *float* away," Shirley hollered, cupping her hands like a bullhorn around her already large mouth, and at that the cafeteria roared with laughter so boisterous Sister Fran had to zip her whistle several times to call for order. The Guineveres poked our forks at the hard crust of the potato pie. We swallowed away the lumps in our throats. Despite the fact that we hadn't eaten since the funnel cake, we weren't hungry. None of us took a bite.

Our punishment required that immediately following Afternoon Instruction, during Rec Time, while the other girls visited the library or congregated in the basement for Ping-Pong tournaments, The Guineveres report to the Sick Ward on the east wing of the convent. Sisters

Connie and Magda, who supervised the ward, dressed in all white when they were on duty, from their frocks to their stockings and shoes, and each wore a white paper hat pinned primly to her head. They were an odd-looking duo: Sister Connie was almost unnaturally tall, willowy and fair. Sister Magda, on the other hand, was short-legged and swarthy. They both had formal training as nurses and, we later learned, had even worked in a hospital overseas. It was hard for us to imagine a time when they were not nuns, a time when they were single young women on a boat to a foreign land. We pictured them standing on the bow of a ship, their long, silky hair blowing in the ocean breeze, their young faces tilted toward the open sky. We wondered what would make them want to return here to the convent when they could have traveled the world instead, the way The Guineveres had planned to do someday when we were older. We never did, of course—not together. But we couldn't imagine a future where we weren't together, where we didn't live the same days or dream the same dreams.

Ebbie Beaumont had also recently been assigned to Sick Ward duty. Tall and pretty, with dishwater hair she wore in a low ponytail that draped over her shoulder, Ebbie was almost eighteen, and we admired her for that fact alone. Her pin-straight bangs fell just above her dark brows, and sometimes when she was wringing out washcloths or scrubbing the floor, she'd blow them out of her face with a slow puff of air, as if she were exhaling cigarette smoke. Of all the girls who were almost eighteen, Ebbie, The Guineveres believed, was the most sophisticated, despite her Revival Story. Her mom, we'd heard whispered through the darkened Bunk Room, was a prostitute, like Mary Magdalene only less pious. Nobody knew what had happened to her dad. Ebbie had been placed on Sick Ward duty because Sister Fran discovered she'd been scratching tick marks on the wall beside her bunk with the point of her compass. When confronted, Ebbie explained in a calm voice, but one that contained a recognizable resentment, that she was tracking the number of days until she could leave the convent. "Then we shall make good use of your time here with us," Sister Fran had scolded. "Every one of those tick marks will count." "Yes, Sister," Ebbie had replied politely, but we knew from her glazed look that she didn't care. In her mind, she was already gone.

Ebbie was quiet, but never rude to us. It was a generally accepted rule of the convent that the girls who were almost eighteen rarely spoke to the younger ones, so we didn't take offense at first when, on our breaks, Ebbie chose to sit in the corner of the courtyard alone, her back to the stone wall. Her knees were bruised purple from kneeling to scrub the floor, and she'd lean back her head and look up at the sky with a half-crooked smile, as if it were the most beautiful thing she'd ever seen. The Guineveres looked up at the sky, too, to see what she was seeing. Above the trees, small planes sometimes left billowy white streaks, the sight of which reassured us that a different world existed out there and someday we would join it.

At that point, the Sick Ward was still just a repository of old men and women; rows of beds lined the white walls, parted by a wide aisle between them. This made the place feel like a church, especially when Sister Fran ceremoniously walked up and down the aisle when she visited, the hard bottoms of her shoes clunking on the linoleum, rhythmic like the ticking of a clock. "Christian charity, girls. That which you do to the least of my people . . . ," she would say. Most of the patients were like us—left behind, clinging to hope—and so we couldn't say we *hated* them, even though we pretended to. We were only girls, after all, hadn't yet learned to be kind, hadn't yet realized that we're all fighting a great battle. That's something Win says to me now; she regrets her behavior in her younger years, though I tell her not to. We all did the best we could.

The Guineveres usually kept to the Front Room of the Sick Ward, away from Ebbie and her domain, not because we were afraid of her but because we found her intimidating. It wasn't just that she was older, though that was certainly a part of it. There was an easy unflappability about her that we couldn't quite pinpoint. We tried to mimic the way she wore her uniform, which seemed utterly cosmopolitan: the waistline mid-hip, her socks just barely slouched, her shirt softened, on the verge of wrinkled, so that she always looked relaxed. In the Wash Room, we'd witnessed Ebbie and her friends dampen their shirts to remove the stiffness of the starch. They swung them over their heads to dry, like white flags of surrender. Of course, when nobody was looking, The Guineveres tried this, too, but the result was never quite the same.

The Front Room of the Sick Ward was reserved for the most lucid patients, the ones who occasionally got out of bed, the ones who didn't have regular coughing fits that left them breathless. It's not that we weren't allowed in the Back Room—we'd later spend a great deal of time there—but from the Front Room we at least had a good view out the windows, beyond the wall that lined the property and above, to the trees just starting to turn, their leaves tipped red like little tongues.

To begin our duties, we selected a Bible stacked in a black cabinet—the Holy Cabinet, we called it, though it was also full of board games and decks of cards and puzzles—and we stood by the bedside of an old man or woman, wrapped up in blankets like a mummy. "How are you doing today?" we asked, but we didn't often listen to the replies. We took the temperatures and pulses of our patients and recorded the vitals on the clipboard fastened to the bed. Sister Magda taught us to count the beats in the neck, since some of the patients had circulation problems.

"Our country has a great need for nurses," Sister Magda told us. Her face grew serious, and when it did, her wrinkles relaxed. She lowered her voice reverently, her eyes, too. "Especially now." We watched as she demonstrated on the half-dead Mr. Worlizter how to properly adjust a bedpan beneath a patient. "I was a war nurse once, you know," she added. "It's a noble profession and not a bad choice for girls like yourselves." Forget the fact that The Guineveres felt odd about placing our fingers against the clammy skin of an old person's neck. Forget the fact that the warmth of a full bedpan made our stomachs lurch. Forget the fact that we had no desire to be nurses, believing secretary to be a much preferable occupation since secretaries had access to executives.

Next, we took a seat, flattened our skirts on our laps, crossed our ankles, sat up straight, and read the selected biblical passage for the day, bookmarked as such by the Sisters. Sometimes the stories inspired hope in us, like how a prostitute on the brink of death was spared from stoning, or how Lazarus awoke from the dead, or how a puny little David killed Goliath. Stories of triumph were well and good, but we enjoyed the stories of hardship the best, of punishment, of anguish. Sure, our lives were tough, but the people in the Bible had it worse, The Guineveres concluded, and it lightened our moods to read about others who suffered more than we did. Commiseration was comfort. Sick Ward duty was nothing compared to being banished from paradise, or to a great flood that wipes out most of humanity except one lucky guy, his family, and their pets.

"That means we're all related," Ginny explained as we walked back to the cafeteria, the anesthetic smell of the Sick Ward still penetrating our noses. We slowed our pace and let Ebbie walk ahead of us, watched her long, smooth gait, and even that seemed admirable. "We're practically sisters."

"Noah was a creep," Win said.

"He's the father of mankind," I protested.

"I thought that was Adam," Gwen said. She was quick, good with her facts, receiving high marks on our church history tests.

"We have two fathers of mankind," I said. I was good with my facts, too.

"Noah had to have sex with some of his relatives, right?" Ginny said. She swung her body out to face us and walked backward down the hallway. When we passed the door to Sister Fran's office, we lowered our voices. "How could all humans descend from him otherwise?" Ginny questioned.

"He had three sons," Win explained. "And their sons had wives."

"I bet the old guy knocked up his son's wives," Gwen said. She stopped walking, placed her hands on her hips, and began gyrating her torso.

"Like father, like son," Win said. "It's practically the same genes."

"Those poor women. Can you imagine having to repopulate the world?" Gwen shook her head. "Sounds exhausting. And they probably never regained their figures."

"Basically we're all inbred," Ginny said.

"That's not it," I said.

"Then explain it," said Gwen as she began walking again. One of us swung open the door to the cafeteria, and the smell of cooked milk hit us, so we knew we were having porridge for supper.

"Not everything can be easily explained," I said. Everyone agreed with that. We found our table, and we waited for Sister Fran to call us to the serving buffet

Luckily, the old folks in the Sick Ward rarely asked questions, and if they did, we rarely replied. We simply read. The sounds of four girls reading at once, along with the whirring and beeping of the various machines, filled the room with a noise so textured it had a musical quality. Our patients rested listlessly in their beds, their eyes closed to the sound, or asleep altogether. Their mouths hung open, even when they swallowed, and they smelled the way old people sometimes do, like a noxious mix of baby powder and natural gas. We never felt much for these sick and dying, except guilt for our discomfort, guilt for the way we pulled our heads back when they took toothless sips of water, guilt for the way we held our breath when we took their pulse.

We told the priests about it at our monthly confession. During Wednesday chapel service, Father James brought with him a small group of other priests from nearby parishes to accommodate all the girls at the convent. Since there was only the one confessional, the other priests would station themselves around the perimeter of the chapel, their backs to the stained-glass windows so their heads glowed with a halo of light. The Sisters—due to either graciousness or to church canon, I'm still not sure—allowed us to select the priest to whom we would confess, and we cherished this, one of our few freedoms.

Choosing a priest required some strategy. You had to size up the length of the line, the speed of the priest, and the temperament of the person immediately in front of you. Some girls, like Irene and Judy and the rest of The Sads, waited until toward the end of the service, when the lines were only two or three girls deep. That way, they wouldn't have to wait as long, and if they were the last in line, nobody could hear what they had confessed, which was depressing, no doubt.

Others like Reggie and Noreen and the girls who were almost eighteen raced toward a priest once Sister Lucrecia hit the first somber note of the organ. They wanted to be first—get in and get out—so they could sit back in the pew, close their eyes, and pretend to pray. The Guineveres had our own strategy. We'd often select priests stationed side by side, so we could shoot each other glances, make cross-eyed faces at one another to ensure we weren't taking it too seriously.

"The Sick Ward makes *me* feel sick," Ginny had confessed to her priest, an old man with a half crown of hair. She stood with one leg crossed over the other; her knees were white from dryness. Ginny was always cold.

"Mrs. Martin must have been pretty once, but now she's plain ugly," Gwen confessed. "Is ugliness a sin?" she asked, licking her lips, then flicked her hair from one shoulder to the other.

"I don't think God is calling me to help the sick," Win had told her priest. She refused to look at him; she said doing so would only lead him to think she cared about what he thought. "He'd rather me do extra kitchen duty."

My priest had soft, wrinkled skin that looked like crumpled paper smoothed out again. "My worst fear is being like them," I had confessed. By which I meant alone.

We were each told to say twenty-five Our Fathers and ten Hail Marys and abstain from dessert, an easy task since we rarely had dessert anyway, which showed just how little these priests knew about our lives at the convent.

Certainly, some of the convalescents were livelier than others. Mr. Macker, for example, could do magic tricks with an old coin he kept tucked in the pocket of his bed shirt. He pulled the coin out of one of our ears and presented it to us, his hand shaking, a gummy smile flashing across his face.

"Why, you don't say," he said, and he examined the coin quizzically. "Could probably barely hear with that thing in there."

Mr. Macker kept a photo by his bed of a woman holding a poodle, and we could only presume this to be Mrs. Macker. The photo looked aged, yellowed a bit and faded, but you could still see the woman well enough. Whoever she was, she was pretty, curled brown hair clipped back in barrettes and a yellow ribbon tied around her waist. She half knelt in the photo, and her arms wrapped themselves around the dog. The Guineveres suspected Mr. Macker missed Mrs. Macker deeply, but he didn't always remember that he did, not even with the photo right in front of him. "My doctor said to take two of you and *not* call him in the morning," he said to us at least once a week.

"Oh, Mr. Macker," we replied. We no longer blushed when he said this.

"Which two?" asked Gwen.

"Any two," Mr. Macker said, and he patted the tufts of hair on his otherwise bald head.

"Both at once?" Gwen said, winking toward the old man. Later, in the Bunk Room, she explained to us in hushed tones what a threesome was. "Think about it," Gwen said. The other Guineveres sat in silence for a few moments, our eyes tick-tocking back and forth, our faces scrunched in puzzlement.

"How does that even work?" I asked after a few minutes, and Ginny and Win burst out laughing. "What?" I said, but they only doubled over, joined by Gwen this time, until they were all breathless.

Even though we liked Mr. Macker well enough, we didn't want to take care of him. We felt awkward when we had to change his gown; we didn't think this proper. We'd pull the sheets back to reveal his thin, bony legs, so white they were startling. His stomach poofed out, and his back arched forward so dramatically that his shoulder blades popped out like little wings, as if he were a disheveled old angel. He kept his fist shut, holding his prized coin in his hand.

"I won't do it," said Gwen, quiet so Mr. Macker couldn't hear her. "I have dignity."

"But Sister Connie said," I reminded her.

"I'll tell her I did it, then," said Gwen. "A dirty shirt won't kill him, you know. And if it did . . ."

"Thou shalt not lie," I said. I believed in the Ten

Commandments, and besides, The Guineveres made a pact to always tell the truth. At least to each other.

"Thou shalt not tattle," she replied, pinching her cheeks for rouge.

Win sighed. "Poor old man."

"I'm glad I'm not him," Ginny said.

"At least we're not old," Gwen said. "At least we've got our youth." She stood back, played with her ponytail, twirling it around her finger. She clenched her jaw and pouted her lips. She called this her starlet look. Gwen believed one day she'd be discovered by a talent agent and whisked off to a movie studio to begin immediate filming. That's when her new life would really begin.

"I'll do it," I said. And I did. I crept into the Back Room, tiptoeing past Ebbie, who looked sophisticated even when gathering soiled bed-sheets, past Sister Madga, who was sorting pills, and past the old men and women whose breathing made gurgling noises, as though they were underwater. I opened the storage room where they kept the bed shirts, right next to the door Sister Connie expressly forbade us from opening, the one we tried to open once, but it was locked. The Guineveres suspected the door led to a dungeon where they flogged the misbehaving old folks or locked up girls like us, girls who'd tried to run away or who'd done something worse than running away, though we couldn't think of what that might be. When I returned to the Front Room, poor Mr. Macker kept his eyes to the ceiling.

"I'm sorry," he said. I helped him into his new shirt, but I didn't say anything in return, just worked as quickly as I could without looking. I didn't want him to feel embarrassed, not like The Guineveres did when we undressed in the Bunk Room, turning our backs to hide our bodies.

The next day was Mail Distribution Day, the low point of our weekly routine. Mail Distribution took place every Tuesday, after Morning Instruction in the classroom. The classroom itself was stuffy and rectangular, containing few decorations, aside from some framed photos of Jesus and Mary and some saints, and a sign that hung above the blackboard that read humbly in truth. Our desks were nailed to the floor so that the rows would remain meticulously even, and our books and Bibles were stored neatly on the metal racks beneath our seats. Sister Fran's large desk stood at the head of the classroom, though she rarely sat down at it. Instead, she stood leaning against the blackboard, and when she'd turn around to write out assignments or notes, we'd notice a chalk line across her back. We called this Sister Fran's Other Ruler because it seemed to measure about the same length as the one she often held in her hand as she lectured.

Usually when the bell rang, indicating the end of

Morning Instruction, girls bounded out of their seats and lined up for lunch. On Mail Distribution Day, however, we remained seated. Sister Fran walked ceremoniously up and down the rows, silently setting mail on the desks of the girls who received something. The Specials almost always greedily fingered fat envelopes stuffed with letters. Sometimes they even dug into small packages of gifts, or hard candies that Sister Fran made them share at lunch. "What one receives, we all receive," Sister Fran said, though we knew this wasn't true. Even The Sads got mail from time to time, short missives from guilty relatives who wished the girls' lives had turned out differently. Not surprisingly, whenever a Sad received a letter, her face became a mess of hands and hair as she quietly sobbed.

"There, there," Sister Fran would console her, offering a handkerchief. "God favors a grateful heart. Be thankful you've received tidings at all. Not everyone is so lucky."

We knew she was referring to us. The Guineveres never received letters from home, not a word from a single relative who claimed to have missed us. Maybe they misplaced our address or moved or the letters got lost or stolen or consumed in a fire at a post office. We stopped trying to rationalize the reasons. It did us no good. Win and Gwen claimed they didn't care. What would they want to learn from home anyway, they said. They weren't going back. Not ever. But Ginny and I, we always held out hope.

"Anything today?" Ginny asked as Sister Fran walked down her row, passing her desk without stopping. What she wouldn't give for a letter from her dad, even a short note with one of his funny cartoon drawings. She received one once, when she first arrived, but that was years ago. In the drawing, a man held a bouquet of balloons in each hand, and as he lifted off the ground, dust clouds kicked around his dangling feet. Ginny thought maybe her father had been trying to tell her something, a subliminal message passed through his pencil strokes. *"Hang on tight. XO,"* his note read. She taped it above her bunk, and she looked at it every night before Lights Out.

Sister Fran backpedaled to Ginny's desk. "I'm sorry, dear. Not today," she said. She squeezed Ginny's shoulder.

"And for me?" I asked. My mom sent me a series of cryptic postcards once, about three months after I arrived, before I ever even met The Guineveres. On them were passages from the Bible. "Happy shall they be who take your little ones and dash them against the rock," one said. "And I will make them eat the flesh of their sons and the flesh of their daughters," read another. She signed her name, but nothing else. I asked Sister Fran about the passages, and she assured me that they spoke to faith and obedience. Still, the postcards scared me, despite the fact that I was happy to hear from my mom and know she was okay.

"I'm sorry, dear. None for you, either. Maybe next time." Sister Fran offered The Guineveres conciliatory glances as we spread our palms on the smooth surface of our desks. We looked out the window, to the sky, the way Ebbie always did. We waited while the other girls read and reread their mail, and then we lined up for lunch.

That evening we were allowed Rec Time for watching the filmstrips the Sisters screened against the white wall of the Rec Room. Most of these filmstrips were educational, about animals and plants, where they lived, how they grew. Time-lapse photos showed flowers budding, then blooming, then shrinking again. Others had names like "Danger and Dignity," "A Guide to Good Grooming," and "The Perils of Pants," and these were the ones that bored us the most. During this hour, The Guineveres sulked in the Bunk Room. Ginny wrote to her dad. I worked on a letter to my mom. Win and Gwen sat on the floor beneath us and played with each other's hair.

"Oh, quit that," Gwen said, looking up at us. "You both look so serious. You know you won't hear back." She flung a hairband in our direction, and it hit Ginny on the forehead.

"Ouch."

"Come on," Gwen said. "I'm just trying to

71

help." She stood up and grabbed my notebook and turned to a new page, and together we composed a fake letter home, a note to convince our parents to come get us, take us away from Sister Fran and the Sick Ward and the dying convalescents.

Gwen sat down on the bed beside me. "Dearest Parents," she said as she began to write. She clicked her tongue and bit into the end of the pencil with her front teeth before going on. "I write to inform you of the peculiar habits of Sister Fran, a most devoted abbess, and a woman I deeply admire. This evening, while she was praying her nightly devotional, I kept hearing her breathlessly shout, 'Sweet Jesus! Sweet Jesus!' I heard some bumping and crashing, and even some grunting, so she must have been praying vigorously. When she opened her door, none other than Father James walked out, adjusting his collar. Imagine my pleasure to learn he's just as devoted as she. I truly hope someday I can dedicate my life to such an enduring and most pleasurable cause. It's so very good to see men and women of the cloth working so closely together. Practically on top of one another."

Gwen stopped, handed her pencil to Ginny, who continued, "But I do worry if I'm doing enough for my spiritual life, as I know you want me to develop as a good Christian girl. Recently I read about Agatha of Sicily, whose breasts were cut off after she refused a suitor, and in turn she was made a saint. I'm writing to tell you that I plan to amputate my boobs. I've not developed much in the way of fullness, but at least if I'm not made a saint, I'll no longer have to invest in a bra." Ginny held out the pad of paper for Win to take.

"Well, that's rather violent," Win said.

"I was trying to be convincing," Ginny said.

Win shook her head, propped the notebook on her knees, and contributed to the letter: "Despite these atrocities that I may or may not decide to commit to my body"—and here she paused to eye Ginny disapprovingly—"I want you to know that I'm in good hands. Just the other day, Sister Claire accidentally put Epsom salt in the vegetable broth. It gave us all the runs, but I have to say, the soup never tasted better. Flavorful, actually."

The Guineveres laughed.

"How positively crass," said Gwen.

It came down to my turn, so I took back my notebook and my pencil, and I wrote, "Please come back. I'd rather be with you, even if you think I'm better off here. I know you said you'd always be with me in spirit, but that's what Sister Fran says about the Holy Ghost and angels and saints. I feel awfully alone for a room so crowded with invisible people." I looked up when I finished writing to see three faces devoid of expression, then three fake, exaggerated yawns.

"But that's not funny," Win said. "That's true."

The Guineveres didn't want to hear the truth. The

truth bored them. Maybe the truth *was* boring. "Write about how you fell madly in love with Mr. Macker instead."

"Say that you had a threesome, once you figured out how it worked," Ginny added. They all three giggled, but I didn't think it was funny at all.

"Tell them you're studying a new language and that you're learning to speak in tongues," Gwen added. She then explained she had once gone with her cousins to a Pentecostal revival where congregants spoke in tongues, calling out like wild animals. She described how they'd writhed on the floor, kicking their legs and arms as if they were doing the backstroke in invisible water.

"It was kind of"—she looked side to side to make sure a Sister wasn't in the room—"sexual."

"Not everything is sexual," we said.

"*Body* language? They didn't even use real words." And then she imitated what she had seen, throwing herself on the floor of the Bunk Room, pumping her hips and moaning monosyllabic sounds until Lottie Barzetti and the rest of The Specials came over to see about the fuss.

"What are you *doing?*" Lottie asked. She wore glasses, dark-rimmed, cat eye–shaped ones that, coupled with her floppy bangs, made her resemble a puppet.

"She's speaking in tongues," Win said flatly.

"What's she saying?" Lottie was younger than us, but had lived at the convent longer than anyone else, a fact that made us resent her even more. When her parents wrote her letters, she'd stand in the middle of the Bunk Room and read them aloud to the rest of the girls in an affected, authoritative voice, proselytizing as though Sister Fran had put her in charge. Her parents were missionaries, and their letters sounded like sermons. They bragged about the difficulty of their work and of their perseverance, and they begged Lottie to do the same: to work hard, to persevere. Once she turned eighteen, Lottie left the convent, and I later learned she died in a car accident in South America, where she, too, then worked as a missionary. She was only twenty-three. All these years later, I still feel badly for the way The Guineveres treated her. She didn't deserve that fate.

"She's saying God knows what you do when nobody's looking," Win replied. Win had naturally wavy hair that grew frizzy between Wash Days, and she had a habit of spitting on her hands to smooth it down, as she did now.

Lottie's nose crinkled as she tried to keep the glasses in place, and she folded her arms over her chest. "That's sinful," she said. "To pretend to talk to God like that."

Win stepped close to her, hunched down a little so she was nose to nose with Lottie. Then she removed Lottie's glasses so she could get a better look. "He *knows*."

"He knows about you, too," Lottie muttered in defense, then swiped her glasses back from Win. "He's omniscient." She took a few steps backward until she ran into a bunk. Win moved closer, The Guineveres on her back like birds in formation.

"But you know what the difference is?" Win asked. She moved so close to Lottie she could feel her breath, then went right ahead and answered her own question. "*I* don't care." Lottie twisted her face in abhorrence.

"You're just sore because you never get mail," chimed Shirley. She stepped forward to wedge herself between Win and Lottie. Shirley had auburn hair that she wore in a short bob, and white teeth that were perfect squares. She was angular and tall, and there was a stillness to her that suggested extreme restraint. "I feel kind of sorry for you."

Win would have lunged for Shirley, no doubt, but at that moment we heard Sister Fran's whistle. "Lights Out!" she yelled. The lights flickered three times, the fifteen-minute warning. As the other girls began to fill the Bunk Room, it grew quiet, save for the squeaking of the beds as the girls climbed into their bunks, gathering their night-gowns and toothbrushes from the baskets that hung from metal bed frames. Some girls, like Dorrie Sue and Nan, had decorated the wall above their pillows with photos of family or prayer cards. Some of The Poor Girls decorated with flowers from the courtyard that they'd dried by pressing into books. Lottie hung the letters from her parents above her bed. Reggie decorated her space with a photo of a man she claimed was her father, but nobody believed her because he looked too handsome. Sister Fran usually didn't say anything about these spaces, unless something caught her eye that she deemed particularly improper, like the time one of The Delinquents hung a drawing of Joan of Arc burning at the stake, her eyeballs popping from her sockets, hanging there by little curlicue springs. Sister Fran simply ripped it down herself during Morning Roll without saying a word.

The Guineveres waited our turn in the Wash Room until four sinks opened up, and we scrubbed our teeth until they were minty. Gwen brushed her hair, and Ginny splashed her face, and then I divided the butter that we'd secreted from dinner, and we rubbed it into our rough elbows and through our hair. Gwen glossed her lips with it, and Win smeared some on the dark circles beneath her eyes. When Jeanette and Polly, the last of the other girls, finally left the Wash Room, Win mouthed to the rest of us, "Follow me," and she gathered several handfuls of toilet paper from the bathroom stall, urging us to do the same. The Guineveres ran the toilet paper beneath the faucet and balled it into our fists. We walked casually back to the Bunk Room, hiding our hands in the fabric of our nightgowns. While Lottie gabbed with Dorrie Sue, we located Lottie's bed, pulled back her covers, and emptied the contents of our hands.

We were required to sit atop our bunks for Evensong for as long as Sister Fran stood in the doorway, illuminated by the single light above her head. "Pleasant dreams, my girls," she said finally, once we finished with prayer. "May the angels keep you." She pulled the chain to extinguish the light, then darkness. At that moment everyone shimmied beneath their covers, but above the shuffling and screeching of bed frames we heard Lottie whimper.

"Someone's wet my bed!" she said.

"You wet your bed?" one of The Delinquents asked from the dark, and the room exploded with laughter.

"My bed is wet!" Lottie said. "And no, I didn't do it."

"The Guineveres did it," Barbara said. Her parents, we'd heard, had died in a house fire on Christmas Eve. Snippets of every girl's Revival Story drifted through the Bunk Room or Rec Room—those occasionally Sisterless spaces—at some time or another. These stories found ways to tell themselves, even against our wishes. Stories are like that; they seek to unravel. Nobody wanted to be the most pitiable girl in the convent, so The Guineveres found it was better to tell our own stories than to leave them to the whispers of the other girls.

Our eyes adjusted to the darkness, and we could see Lottie kneeling atop her bunk, collecting wet wads from beneath her covers. Her bed frame moaned with each movement of her body, a singular noise made louder by the quiet.

"You're making an awful lot of commotion up there," Gwen said.

"And you wonder why your parents want nothing to do with you?" Shirley snapped. Her parents, we'd heard, ran a coffee plantation on another continent. They were wealthy people, and from time to time they sent Shirley money, even though she didn't have anywhere to spend it. During chapel, she'd make a show of putting it in the collection basket, laying it two-handedly atop the other donations left by the girls: coins, drawings, hair ribbons. Someone had even once donated a pair of socks because Sister Fran insisted that each of us could find excesses in our lives, if only we looked harder. "Leave her alone," Shirley said.

"Are you making love up there?" Gwen continued. "Maybe to Saint Fiacre?" she asked. The room heaved a collective gasp because we'd recently learned from the library's copy of *Lives of the Saints* that Fiacre was the patron saint of sexually transmitted diseases.

"That's not funny," Lottie said.

"I thought you were saving yourself for marriage," Gwen said.

"We all know that *you're* not," Shirley said. The other girls didn't even try to conceal their laughter, bravery coming to them in the cover of dark.

"I'd be careful if I were you," Win's voice warned from the other end of the room, and at that everyone *oohed* and *aahed,* and then grew quiet again.

"Why are you Guineveres so mean?" Polly finally said. She came from a big family. Her father was dead, and her mother didn't make enough money as a hotel maid to support all her kids. When Polly came to the convent, her hair had thinned to the point that her scalp showed, earning her the nickname Polly-Polly Ping-Pong. "None of us wants to be here."

Silence washed over the room, and one by one, everybody fell asleep. Except The Guineveres. The Guineveres let Polly's words sink in until our stomachs grew heavy. The Guineveres felt guilty, but we didn't know how else to express our pain. The Guineveres cried ourselves to sleep, as we did some nights, knowing the only thing we had in the world was each other.

In the morning, just as the sun was coming up, Sister Fran woke us, as she always did, with the zip of the whistle she wore around her neck. We clambered off our beds for roll. Unless we were on kitchen duty, we were given fifteen short minutes to make our beds, brush our hair and teeth, and dress for the day. While we scrambled to get ready, Sister Fran walked up and down the aisle of bunks like a drill sergeant, making sure everything was in good order: beds made, nightgowns folded.

"Hurry up, girls. Vanity does not prevent the lamb from slaughter," she'd say nearly every morning, which we took to mean we were all doomed from the start.

And that's how time moved on at the convent; days dropped away from the calendar like baby teeth. We'd rise; we'd eat; we'd pray; we'd learn. We were marching toward our destinies, but it didn't feel like marching. It felt like slogging, like stalling, like drowning. Every afternoon, we'd find ourselves in the Sick Ward again, checking the pulses of old folks who were barely there, wiping dribbling food off the chins of those who were, and reading passages from Bibles with spines so creased that pages sometimes slipped out. Our uniforms began to take on the sickly odor of the Ward, but Sister Fran wouldn't let us wash them except on Saturday. "God does not make exceptions," she explained. "Can you imagine if the Ten Commandments were called the Ten Suggestions?" Her lips pressed together in their usual way, and her eyes widened so she looked like she'd just been pinched on her bottom, which we couldn't imagine was any pastier than the rest of her.

Soon the summer faded and the days grew cooler. Sister Fran brought out our wool sweaters, smelling of mothballs, from the storage closet. I had outgrown mine since last year; the sleeves were too short. I didn't bother to tell Sister Fran. Instead, Ginny swapped sweaters with me, since hers fit a little too big.

Years later, when she had moved to the South, married for a second time, and had three small children, Ginny kept that sweater folded in a small drawer in the bureau next to her bed. She said she pulled it out and tried it on from time to time. It still fit. A little big in the arms, even.

"Why have you kept it after all this time?" I asked her. We hadn't seen each other in years. Over the phone her voice hadn't changed—full of angst that had no language, but was vocal all the same. The convent days had been difficult for all of us, for her especially. She'd always been fragile, and even now that Ginny was an adult with kids of her own, I wanted to protect her.

"I thought I might give it to my daughter someday," she said. "Tell her the story of the time her mother lived far, far away, like a princess in a big stone castle."

"Like four princesses," I said.

"And they all lived happily ever after," she said.

Then there was silence, and I knew what she was thinking. By then we had our own lives. Some of us had been through marriages and children, death and divorce. We'd been hurt, and we'd hurt others; we loved and were loved. Yet sometimes, when we were looking in the mirror, staring back at the grown women we'd become, we still saw those skinny-legged girls in wool uniform skirts, still felt the draft of the convent right down to our bones.

Ginny's Revival

After the accident, they told me Dad was a bad seed, but I didn't believe it. And Sister Fran didn't, either. I asked her once if she thought people were born either all good or all bad, and she reminded me of the gift of free will, that we all have the capacity to choose to be either good or evil. She told me God grants us choices.

I choose to love my dad, then, despite everything. I love him more than anyone in the world. I've always known that deep down inside, we're two of the same soul. Maybe two of the same seed, too. He's an artist, and that's what I want to be someday, which is what makes us extra sensitive, this artist gene we both share. We both worry too much and we keep things bottled up, and that's why we feel bad a lot, physically feel bad, like our stomachs flipped or our throats dried out. Artists are supposed to be tortured; they need pain in order to create, and I'm going to make something wild and beautiful someday, just you see.

My dad and I have more than just the artist gene in common. We both have a cowlick that you can only see when we pull back our hair. We have the same hands, too, slender fingers squared off at the tips like they've been flattened. I remember when

I was little he'd sit me in his lap and let me dip my finger into the beer he drank out of a frosted mug. I liked the taste of it, unlike anything I'd ever tried. It smelled like bread, and it tickled my tongue and felt warm going down, fizzy like a pop. If I was lucky, he'd let me fetch him another one, and I'd proudly retrieve the can from the refrigerator and then another frosty mug from the freezer. Dad taught me that if you poured with the glass at an angle, you wouldn't get that foam that sometimes looks like the flattops some of the boys at school wore.

Dad's a painter. During the day he went to work painting houses. Dad said a monkey could paint a house, so long as it knew how to hold a brush, and that a monkey might be better at it, too, since their arms don't ever get tired. At night, when he'd come home in stained overalls, he'd stay in the garage until dinner, then change his clothes and go back out after we ate. The garage was his studio. He'd cleared out half of it, and set up some easels with canvases along the wall, and it was there he did his *real* painting. I loved sitting in the garage with him when he'd let me. It smelled like gasoline and turpentine out there. Dad looked serene in these moments, like the fumes were going to his head and making his muscles relax so you couldn't see the worry that usually penetrated his face in the form of wrinkles around his eyes. I was usually not allowed to watch Dad paint, only prep the canvases or mix his palette. He kept his work covered with old drop cloths because he didn't want anybody to see his paintings before they were finished. The magic of art is not witnessing all the work that goes into it, he told me, though sometimes I peeked beneath the covers when he wasn't around. A few times I found some paintings of naked ladies. They weren't totally naked but naked enough that I didn't want Dad to know I had stolen a look.

They weren't all paintings of naked ladies, though. Most of the paintings were these cartoonish portraits that were supposed to mean something else. One was a picture of this angular man holding up some barrels that hung over his head by strings. The man's face grimaced, his lips were diamond shaped, and his tongue was a red triangle inside his mouth. Dad told me the painting was supposed to represent the weight of the world.

"What's the weight of the world?" I asked, wondering how you could ever measure something like that, unless you took a piece of it and multiplied it like we did with math problems at school.

"It's a metaphor, for when you feel like nothing is going your way, or if you've got troubles and nothing seems to work right—that's the weight of the world," he explained. "It feels heavy."

I didn't quite understand, and he told me that he hoped I never would.

Mom rarely came out into Dad's studio. She didn't think he should waste time with his "finger painting," which is what she called it sometimes. I don't think she intended to sound so mean. I remember once, way back when I was just small—smaller, even, than when Dad would let me taste on his beer—Mom agreed to allow Dad to paint her portrait. After dinner, every night for what seemed like a million weeks, Mom would sit on this upturned metal milk crate in the garage. She'd put on lipstick and do up her hair for the occasion. Mom was never one to leave the house without makeup, and she certainly didn't intend to be immortalized without makeup, either. Me and my brother would sit down cross-legged in the studio with them, volleying our heads back and forth, watching Mom unnaturally posed like she had frozen through solid and watching Dad's arms glide with each brushstroke he made.

One night he finally sighed and dramatically blotted the canvas, then, announcing he was finished, turned the easel for us to see his work.

"What do you think?" he asked. His arms were braced on the easel, and I noticed his fingers were tipped dark from blending paint.

Mom's smile dropped as she stood face-to-face with the portrait of herself. "Why am I not wearing lipstick?" she asked. "Why the messy hair and the hollow cheeks?"

"It's your essence," he said. "It's not you. It's

the essence of you," he tried to explain. Mom glowered in his direction. "That's how it works," Dad explained. "Your essence is universal, not specific."

Mom seemed confused, or disappointed. "My essence looks sick with pale lips," she said, then went inside and refused to sit for him ever again.

Dad painted me once, too. Night after night I sat on that milk crate, watching his eyebrows furrow and unfurrow. His freckles could have been paint splatters; they made his face look dirty, and I wondered why I had never thought about the way everything is really just a series of dots or lines or curves, shapes that could be copied with brushstrokes if you were a painter, like my dad. He saw the world twice, once in real life, and once on his canvas. It's a kind of double vision, being an artist. When Dad finished with my portrait, he said, "Ta-da," and he turned his easel. On the canvas, he'd painted someone who looked just like me—freckles, red hair—lying in a field of flowers. My eyes were closed, and I was smiling in my sleep.

"You're Dorothy in a field of poppies," he said.

"Is that my essence?" I asked.

Dad nodded.

"But wasn't the field of poppies created by the witch to stop Dorothy from getting to that old wizard?" I asked, knowing the scene from my favorite book. I'd read it at least a dozen times, and the cover was so beaten that Dad fixed it with some tape he brought home from work.

"Yes—but she was happy at that moment, despite the witch's spell. She was dreaming that she was dreaming," he said. "That's you," he added. "The world needs dreamers."

I didn't care what the painting meant. I loved it, and I told him so.

Aside from a few potluck picnics and a couple of visits to relatives around the holidays, we never really did much as a family. My brother ran around with his friends, and when he was home, like at dinner, he'd talk about wanting to go off to college once he graduated high school, maybe become an engineer or an architect.

"Do something practical, something professional," Mom said one night in front of everyone at the table. "Choose a dignified career. For chrissakes, don't end up like your father," she said, by which she meant, I guess, a dreamer, a dreamer like me. Dad set down his fork, politely took his plate from the table, and placed it in the sink. He didn't eat dinner with us much after that.

I never really heard Mom and Dad fight much. Or, I guess I should correct that and say Dad never fought back with Mom. I often heard Mom lay into Dad, saying things like she wished she'd married someone who understood how the world worked, how it *really* worked. She'd mention some guy named Jonathan Andrew who went to divinity school, then became president of some university with his fancy degree, and who asked her once to be his wife, but she had politely declined. At least that's what she claimed. I thought it was funny that Jonathan Andrew went to school to become divine, like divineness was something that could come from a book. Mom said she didn't ever grow up dreaming of being poor and stuck, but she guessed dreams were just something that we did at night to entertain us while we sleep away our real lives. She'd tell Dad that grown men should be providing for their families better—they shouldn't be dawdling in the garage, wasting time and paychecks on silly pictures. Mom would stand mid-rant in the kitchen, fisted hands raised, her face contorted with a sneer, but if someone walked into the room, like me or my brother, she'd immediately turn into Mom again. "What would you like for dinner, sweetheart?" she'd ask, the anger leaving her face and the crow's-feet at her eyes disappearing into her skin.

"Just be nice to him," I'd say to her when I'd catch her yelling at Dad.

"I'm nice," she said. "*I'm* the nice one. You don't know the definition of nice," she'd say, talking to me but looking at him.

"Maybe I should go to divinity school to learn," he'd say.

"They wouldn't even let you in," she'd reply.

Dad began working longer hours, and he'd

come home from work smelling like paint, but too exhausted to spend any time in his studio. He stopped drinking beer and began drinking whiskey. He'd hold a cube of ice in his big hand and crush it by hitting it with a spoon, drop it with the flick of his wrist into a short glass, then pour the whiskey right over it. I could predict Dad's moods by what he was drinking.

For her part, Mom would sometimes disappear for hours at a time. She said she had joined a crafting group at the YMCA, but she never came home with any crafts that I ever saw. Sometimes she wasn't home yet when I returned from school. She'd eventually appear, dressed in her Sunday clothes, which is what she called her nicest dresses, even though we rarely went to church. She smelled different, too.

And then one day I understood. I came home from school for an early release, and when I couldn't find Mom, I went to her bedroom. The smell hit me first when I opened the door: a light scent of sweat and outside and chili spices. I saw Mom sitting on the edge of the unmade bed with some man I'd never seen before. His dark hair stood up in the back, as though he'd rubbed his head with a balloon to create static, like I some-times did. Beneath his nose, a mustache looked like twin peaks of a mountain.

"Guinevere," Mom said nervously, then cleared her throat. "This is my friend Danny. He was just here to inspect the gutters for those birds that keep building nests outside my window. You remember those birds from last year, don't you, Guinevere?" She spoke slowly; her eyelids fluttered. She applied lipstick, casually, but I noticed her hands shaking and her hosiery lying like snakeskins on the carpet.

Danny fumbled as he tied his shoes, clearly in a hurry to leave. Guess those gutters would have to wait. Mom saw him off, then found me in my room, sketching in my notebook, trying to make sense of what I'd just seen. "Let's not tell Dad about Danny. I wanted to clear those gutters out as a surprise," she said, smoothing her hair with a comb.

I should have told Dad, but I never said a word. I don't know why. I wanted to, but I couldn't get the words out when I tried. I thought maybe I could leave him an anonymous note, or call the house from a pay phone down the street and disguise my voice, or simply will the information to him through concentrated thought like Dorothy does when she says "There's no place like home." But I couldn't. I didn't. It's all my fault, and I still feel guilty about it.

A few weeks later, as my mom was making breakfast for my brother and me, measuring out pancake batter and pouring it onto the griddle with a sizzle, she mentioned to us she might be home a little late again that night.

"Craft class?" I asked, staring at my half-eaten stack of pancakes drowning in syrup that made swirly shapes at the edges.

"Craft class," she said, licking her finger.

"Maybe I can take an art class at the YMCA," I said. I wanted to be an artist, just like Dad, even though I wasn't sure if I had the talent. Sometimes the way I saw things in my head didn't match up to how I put them down on paper when I'd sketch in my notebook. That's the way it is with me. I have all these feelings and it's hard to get them out right. It's difficult to say exactly what I mean. Sometimes I just *feel* what I mean. But you can't paint a feeling, can you?

"Maybe," she said.

"Really?" I said.

"We'll talk about it after school."

But after school everything had changed. I knew this as soon as my bus turned the corner to my street. I saw a blur of reds and blues and whites, lights coming from the tops of cars parked in my driveway. When the bus came to a stop, I leaped down, my feet not touching a single step. Dad stood off to one side, whispering with a police officer. His hands were cuffed in front of him. His head hung low like his neck was a hinge.

"Where's Mom?" I asked. Dad wouldn't look up at me, and another police officer came up behind me and pulled me down the driveway and into the back of his car.

"Just sit here, sweetie," he said to me. "What's your name?"

"Guinevere," I said. "Where's my mom?"

"Just stay put right here." He shut the car door. I tried to open it, but it was locked.

Soon some paramedics rolled out a stretcher. A man was covered with a sheet to his neck. I saw his mustache, those twin peaks of hair, and I knew I'd seen this man before. He was Danny. He'd cleaned Mom's gutters, and I didn't tell Dad about it.

"Let me out," I started to yell, pawing at the window with the meat of my palms. The police officer turned and walked toward me, but behind him I could see another stretcher being led from the house, this one completely covered with a sheet that looked like one of Dad's drop cloths, all red dappled. I knew it was Mom. Knew it because I could see her light blue housecoat sticking out from under the sheet, dragging on the ground as they rolled the stretcher that sounded like roller skate wheels against the concrete.

The police led Dad to the back of their cruiser. "I'm sorry," he mouthed. He was looking at me now, behind the glass of the police car, my forehead pressed against the window. He brought his cuffed hands to his face in fists, and I noticed they were stained, from paint or from blood. Maybe both. It didn't matter. The officer ducked Dad's head inside the door, then shut it behind him. *I'm sorry, too,* I wanted to tell him. *I'm sorry, too.* Dad sat face forward, motionless, as still as he'd told me to sit while he was painting my portrait in the garage.

My brother and I stayed at our aunt's house that night. My aunt said people are either born good or born bad, and that Dad was a bad seed just waiting to burst. My brother and I didn't speak. Dad never came home. Mom's funeral—I don't want to talk about it. I'd rather paint a picture of it someday that shows how I still loved my dad, how I loved my mom, too, how I felt responsible and sick and sad and lonely and afraid, like I was a blend of paints, all the colors at once, that ended up a putrid shade of brown.

Not long after the funeral, my aunt took us to see Dad in jail; she waited in the car while my brother and I went inside, emptying our pockets to show we didn't have anything in them. We sat uncomfortably quiet for a while in the cafeteria, then talked about school and the weather. There were other inmates there; other families, too. We didn't have much to talk about, really. What was there to say? Words can't do anything at times like those anyway, other than fill your ears with noise. When we were getting ready to leave, I asked him if he had been painting, drawing at the very least. I remember his eyes. They looked like wet pennies, gleaming with sadness so heavy that I could feel it in my chest.

"I've lost my inspiration, sweetheart," he said.

"Maybe you'll find it again," I said.

Dad paused, then took my hand in his and squeezed it. "Maybe," he said.

A few days later, my aunt told me that I'd be going somewhere to stay for a while. She said my brother would be going somewhere, too, but I later learned he stayed with her so he could finish off his last year of high school. After that, I'm sure he moved far away, but I haven't spoken to him since. I guess he didn't want to be reminded of his old life and all that—maybe that's why he didn't write—and what else would I do but remind him?

My aunt and I drove in silence, not talking, except when she kept bringing up stories about when I was a baby. When I was a baby I used to cry all through the night, and the only thing that would console me was when someone walked me up and down our front porch, bouncing me in their arms. "You liked to be under the stars," my aunt said, but I didn't remember that.

My aunt slowed the car down as we eased past this church, and she craned her neck, squinting to see something. Then we pulled down a steep drive, lined by a fence on either side. I saw the stone building ahead, big as a castle and almost as pretty, except it was kind of scary because there were lots of windows, and the blinds were all closed like they were hiding something inside. This was what I imagined divinity school to look like.

In a way, I guess it was a divinity school.

Our galoshes squished on the marble foyer as we entered, a loud squeak each time I took a step, so I tried to stand still. "My name is Sister Frances Nazarene," said the woman who stood there to greet us. She was the palest person I'd ever seen, and at first I thought she might have been a ghost. She held out her arms as though an invisible bundle of logs rested there. "But you may call me Sister Fran." I turned toward my aunt, but I knew. I knew. She kissed me. She left. I didn't say a word to her, not even good-bye. I didn't ask her about my brother. I didn't ask her if she'd come back for me. I already knew the answer.

"The joy of God is the innocent," Sister Fran said, turning to me once the door was shut. She opened a vial of oil, and she dabbed me on the forehead, drawing a cross with her thumb. I began to hyperventilate, the first asthma attack I'd ever had, and it left me feeling dizzy.

Sister Fran flexed her cheeks into a smile. "There, there," she said, putting her hand on my shoulder. "God has plans for you." She removed her hand and walked to a side closet, from which she produced a mop and a bucket. She pointed to the marble floor, smeared muddy with footprints from my galoshes. "And his first plan is for you to clean your mess," she said, tsking and handing me the mop. I took it, and as my hand touched the handle, I thought of Dad's old painting, the man with the grimaced face, the barrels hanging overhead. At that moment, I opened my mouth to protest, but I stopped myself. Something clicked—not audible, but inside me. I thought of his face, twisted and angular, his tongue, red like a tiny fire in his mouth. The mop felt heavy in my hands, not like a mop at all. Like the weight of the world.

Sacrifice

T he first week of October, just before a supper of baked cauliflower and boiled potatoes— we remembered the meal was all white, the color of purity—Sister Fran blew her whistle to call everyone in the cafeteria to attention. We had not yet said Grace, so every girl instinctively drew her hands into prayer and, unhinging her neck, bowed her head in repose. But Sister Fran trilled her whistle again. "We shall say our blessing in a moment, girls. First, an announcement." We raised our heads. Sister Fran paced the length of the serving table, where steam rose from food in curlicues that seemed to be spelling something in cursive. A message from God, we thought as we recounted this moment later in the Bunk Room. Sister Fran hesitated, then covered her mouth with her hand like a flesh-colored beard.

"A group of young men, soldiers, will be arriving here shortly to recover in the con-valescent wing," she said. "They've been injured in the War." She walked down the aisle of tables now, past The Sads whose spines bent like C's, so that Sister Fran tapped their backs to tell them to straighten up into a proper posture. "All of us at the Sisters of the Supreme Adoration have been called to be part of the War Effort," she said. She continued walking, marching, rather, as though this discussion of the War had altered her stride, militarized it. She finally came to a halt in front of The Guineveres' table. We pulled back our shoulders and stiffened our abdomens. "This means all of us," she said. She swiveled and marched again toward the serving buffet.

Remember, we were only young girls then, and the War, so far away, didn't seem to concern us. Gwen's dad had once fought in a war, but she didn't know much about it except that a picture of him in his army uniform hung on the wall of their living room. And now when Sister Fran uttered the word "war," only three letters long but with a heft that echoed off the high ceilings of the cafeteria, the same way it did when she said the word "God," we were still relatively impassive. Instead, we wondered who these young men might be. Gwen kicked us under the table, hardly able to contain her smile that threatened to flip inside out and swallow her face entirely.

"Soldiers," she mouthed. The tips of her ears burned red with excitement.

They arrived late the next afternoon. The Guineveres sat on break in the courtyard, chilly in our thin gray sweaters. Ebbie Beaumont hugged her knees in her usual spot across the way from us, but instead of gazing up toward the sky, all of us watched the bus pull up behind the gate. We would have mistaken it for a school bus, except it was white and had a faded red cross etched on its side, paint peeling away like pencil shavings. Three sober-faced men hopped out. They wore beige uniforms, and Sisters Connie and Magda scurried out from the convent to unlock the gate for them. The five of them spoke in low tones, in a series of nods and hand gestures. One of the men handed Sister Connie a crumpled stack of papers, and she pointed toward the door that led to the Sick Ward. When they opened the back of the bus and pulled the first young boy out on a stretcher, both Sister Connie and Sister Magda lowered their heads and motioned the sign of the cross. Ebbie looked at us and shrugged her shoulders. We shrugged ours back. One by one the soldiers were carried inside.

These were not strapping soldiers in crisp metal-pinned suits or in field camouflage, as we immediately imagined when Sister Fran first mentioned them, not the clean-cut boys we'd dreamed of as we drifted off to sleep. Instead, they were the kind who had fought in battles, who had suffered injuries so severe they were in comas. They were the kind with body parts wrapped in gauze or in plaster. The kind whose wounds were so deep you could smell it on them, even outside in the courtyard, a dusty metallic scent that made us take such short breaths we felt woozy.

"Ebbie," Sister Connie called, motioning her toward the entrance to the Sick Ward. Ebbie stood, wiped the back of her skirt, took in one last dose of the sky. Then she joined Sister Connie, who put her arm around the girl and whispered something, though we couldn't hear what.

Even though our break had gone long, The Guineveres didn't move from our benches in the courtyard. Ginny pulled at her socks, and Win picked up a handful of gravel, flicking the pieces one by one onto the path below. When two of the men carried the last soldier inside, the third reached into the back of the bus and pulled out five duffel bags, olive drab and shaped like sausages.

"My dad had one like that," Gwen said, so we knew they were government issued. The outsides of each were marked in chalky white, a long series of numbers separated by dashes. The man dropped them on the ground in front of him, heedless of breakable contents, and dust kicked up like smoke. He looked at his watch, then around for the other officers, but they had disappeared inside, so he sat on the edge of the bumper drawing circles in the dirt.

"We can help you, sir," Gwen hollered from our bench. The uniformed man stood at attention, looking surprised, as though he hadn't even noticed us. As though the female form had startled him. He checked his watch again, tapped his foot anxiously, then nodded. We followed Gwen to the courtyard's gate, the one that usually remained locked, a threshold to another world.

Up close, we could see the officer's deep-rutted scar that lined the side of his face, from his neck to his chin. It was raised and red, shaped like a hook, like a crooked finger pointing toward his nose. He angled his face away from us, and we tried not to stare. The Guineveres were not impolite.

"Thank you for your service," Gwen said. She stood square in front of him, one hand resting on her hip.

The rest of us echoed her sentiments. "Yes, thank you," we said, despite the fact that we wanted to ask him about his scar, how he got it, or if it hurt. His posture was that of a telephone pole, and for a moment we thought he was going to salute us. Instead, he tugged at the brim of his hat the way a cowboy might.

"Uniforms. Personal effects," he said, gesturing toward the canvas duffels at his feet. Perhaps military men didn't speak in full sentences, or perhaps we made him nervous. Either way, we took his gesture as acceptance of our help. We each picked up a bag. They weren't particularly heavy. Win, the strongest of us, carried two, one slung over each shoulder, and from behind, as we walked back to the Sick Ward, it looked like she had sprouted a set of tubular wings.

In the Back Room, we saw the five soldiers already cocooned in their beds. Sister Connie and Sister Magda and Ebbie all tended to them, making sure their sheets were properly tucked, their pillows adequately fluffed. The old folks gawked toward them with slack jaws. We may have gawked, too, even if we tried our best not to. They looked so out of place with their scars and their bandages, with their lanky, youthful bodies and thick hair. Usually we took pleasure in stories of people less fortunate than ourselves— that's why we liked the tales of the saints, that's true—but there was nothing we liked about seeing these soldiers who had already brought with them a peculiar smell to the room, a scent both sour and sweet and ferrous all the same.

"What's wrong with them?" Ginny whispered. We didn't know, and we weren't sure we wanted to.

"Will we have to take care of them?" Win said. "I didn't sign up for this."

"Nobody signed up for this," I said.

"Where should we put these?" Gwen finally asked Sister Magda. Magda was short and round, and always wore a worried expression on her face, which caused permanent wrinkles on her forehead, three perfectly parallel squiggle lines. Her complexion was dark, and on occasion she muttered to herself in a different language. "It's their personal effects and uniforms. The officer asked for our help."

"Sister Connie?" Sister Magda called out. "Their personal effects and uniforms?"

"Just find a place," Sister Connie huffed. She was signing some papers now, directing the uniformed men toward the front of the Sick Ward, where Sister Fran waited to greet them.

The Guineveres were instructed to stow the duffels in the storage closet, and as we passed the soldiers' beds, we got a closer look at them. One had a bandaged face, covered almost entirely. A shock of blond hair and a pair of soft, pillowy lips were the only things that distinguished him from a mummy. Another was missing an arm; he had small scabs on his face that made it look like he had freckles. There was a big, stocky one, too. His legs were bound separately in two huge casts held together with a bar that extended from knee to knee. One of the soldiers was missing three fingers: his pinkie, his ring finger, and his middle finger, so his hand looked permanently shaped into a gun. The final one was not bandaged at all. Aside from the few cuts on his face and deep purple bruises beneath his eyes, he looked, not healthy, certainly, but not unwell. His eyelids were shiny like wax.

"His injuries are probably internal," Ginny whispered.

"And that makes him the sickest of all," Gwen added.

"What are their names?" we asked Sister Connie. On the clipboards at the end of each bed she'd written a number where a name should have been listed, a number that corresponded with the last two digits listed on each of the duffels.

"Nobody knows," she said. "That's why they're here." She took their pulses, nodded as she counted the beats in her head, then jotted notes on the clipboards.

"But what about their dog tags?" Gwen asked. She had seen her father's dog tags, which he'd kept hung on his bedpost long after he left the army. On them, in raised block letters, was listed his name, her mom's name, and an address she didn't recognize, since they'd moved so many times. In the bottom right-hand corner was stamped a *C,* and when she asked him what this stood for, he told her Catholic, though she'd never known him to go to church. "For your mother's peace of mind," he had explained.

"No dog tags. No identification," Sister Connie said. She didn't look up, didn't convey the slightest hint that she might have felt sorry for the soldiers. "It sometimes happens this way, unfortunately."

"They're in a coma, girls," Sister Magda reminded us, as though this fact weren't obvious. "That's very serious."

"And we must help the helpless," Sister Connie interjected. Sister Connie was no older than Sister Magda, but she was the captain of the Sick Ward. She was the kind of woman who claimed to hate being in charge, but at the same time, enjoyed exerting her authority. If she hadn't been a nun, one might have described her as brassy. "It's part of the War Effort. We must all do our part, and this is ours. Nursing is a vital and noble occupation, girls. Especially now. Not everyone has the stomach for it." Sister Magda nodded.

The Guineveres didn't have the stomach for it, not like Ebbie, who tended to them unfazed, her expression not revealing a hint of repulsion. When she leaned over their beds, her bare arms skimmed the bodies of the soldiers, and she didn't rush immediately to wash her hands, as we might have. Though I hate to admit it, even now all these years later, at first those soldiers revolted us. We wanted nothing to do with them. Their seeping gauze made us uncomfortable, as did their missing limbs; their motionless faces made us think of funerals, of the gray pallor of some of our grand-parents whom we'd seen buried in coffins far beneath the ground.

"Maybe they'll wake up," one of us said. We tied aprons over our uniforms, filled basins half-way with water, and carried them sloshing to the beds of the soldiers. We grimaced as we pressed the dampened rags onto their hands and their necks, to their foreheads or any skin exposed to air. Sister Connie's oft-repeated dictum: Blessed are the pure of heart and the free of dirt and bacteria.

"Hopefully they'll wake up," the rest of us said,

sour-faced, dropping our rags into the water, where they landed with plunks. We wiped our hands on our aprons. We listened to our stomachs grumble. We waited for Sister Connie to release us from our duties.

A couple of weeks later, one *did* wake up. No. 14, according to his charts, the one with the missing fingers. He awoke in the middle of the night, calling out for help in a brittle voice. He woke most of the old folks, too, who began yelling for help themselves, as though they were all trapped on a capsized ship. No. 14 half dragged himself out of bed, but he couldn't control his limbs, which had already begun to atrophy. During Checks Sister Magda found him upside down, draped like a blanket over the foot of the bed, his head tipped backward, his mouth still contorted in the shape of a scream.

His name was Jack Murr. He went by Junior. That's all we learned of him, mostly because he was too stunned to talk. He couldn't convey much else, couldn't tell Sister Connie where he was from, and couldn't identify the other soldiers in the ward. Sister Connie had brought him a blank sheet of paper, a clipboard, and a pencil, and he'd written his name, barely legible, in shaky block letters. When asked if the other soldiers were his friends, he shook his head slowly, then closed his eyes and tears welled up beneath them. The Guineveres watched him from a measured distance while we were on Sick Ward duty, while we emptied bedpans, changed sheets, or read the daily passage from the Bible to the dull-eyed old folks who cared to listen. Junior would lie propped up in bed, his lids half drooped like midday window shades, his mouth slack from the constant drip of morphine he received. Sometimes he'd run his good hand over the bandaged nubs where his fingers once were, his lips silently counting his missing digits. On occasion, Sister Magda and Ebbie would help him sit up in bed or stand with assistance, his legs quivering beneath him. Gwen swore that once, while Ebbie was changing his bed shirt, he broadened his chest and mouthed "hello" over Ebbie's shoulder and in her direction, but the other Guineveres didn't believe this. "Do you think I'm prettier than Ebbie is?" she asked.

Sister Fran took to the phone in her office, and only a day later she had located Junior's family. By the end of the week they were there, two spindly parents weeping over their son's bed as if they had seen the image of Jesus Himself. His mother wore a thin brown dress, patterned with leaves that could have been mistaken for upended fish. Her eyes were deep pits, and she smelled thickly of cigarettes. "They said you were gone. They said you were gone," she kept repeating, rocking at the edge of his bed, peppering his face with wet kisses that left behind smears of red lipstick that could have resembled blood had we not known better. And yet, there he was, her injured, shell-shocked son, right before her very eyes. They were ready to take him home.

Home. We thought of our own homes as we watched the scene unfold from our hands and knees, scrubbing the floor of the Sick Ward. Our sleeves were rolled up to our elbows, and our hair was pulled back by the same kind of rags we were using to spot clean. Our own parents knew exactly where we were. Our mothers didn't weep joyously over us, soaking our skin with grateful tears. Our fathers didn't stand with bent heads, like the statue of a withered Eve after her banishment from paradise.

"I'd give three fingers to go home, too," Gwen whispered. She leaned back on her haunches and tucked her fingers into her palm, mimicking the soldier's missing digits.

"Don't be mean," replied Ginny. "It's more than that."

"He sacrificed," I said. "They all did."

"It must be nice," Win said. And we knew what she meant. We were happy for the soldier, true, but we felt sorry for ourselves. We wanted to go home. We wanted our parents to come get us. Because we had sacrificed, too, we felt. We had sacrificed, too.

Junior's father tried to help him out of bed, but he didn't have a good grip, and his son fell limp like a sack of flour, his arms above his head. Sister Magda took over, expertly hooking her arms beneath his armpits and easing him into a wheelchair that Ebbie held in place. Then Ebbie swung the chair around and wheeled him out of the Sick Ward. Sisters Connie and Magda walked ahead with Junior's duffel, his parents following. Junior's mother turned back every now and then to kiss her boy or to whisper something into his ear.

The Guineveres formed a convoy behind Ebbie. We'd never seen anybody leave the Sick Ward before. At the door, Ebbie turned to face us, then struggled to ease the wheelchair, back wheels first, through the raised doorframe. Her bangs had grown just past her brows, and every so often she'd blow them out of her face with a puff of air. Junior didn't make a sound as his wheelchair landed with two small thuds on the graveled ground of the courtyard. Ebbie gazed toward the sky, then leaned her long arm in to shut the door. She smiled at us in this moment, the corners of her mouth betraying her otherwise inscrutable expression. And then, for the first time, she spoke to us. "You know, don't worry so much about not getting letters," she said. "They never say anything important anyway. Who needs parents, really? You'll be fine." The door closed and clicked. Then silence.

We didn't know it at the time, but we would

never see Ebbie again after that. She'd been sent home with Junior and his family, who couldn't afford to hire any help and who refused to send him off to yet another institution now that they had found him. Sister Fran might have called it Christian Charity, but The Guineveres raged silently in our loafers, scrunched our toes until they ached. "Nurses are indispensable on the home front, girls. You're learning invaluable skills," Sister Connie said that afternoon when Ebbie left.

Yet we were incensed. We didn't know why. "She's not eighteen yet," we said in a fit of pique, as though this explanation would somehow force Ebbie's return. "Rules are rules." On the day any girl turned eighteen, she was released into the world with a change of clothes and lunch in a paper satchel. But not a day before.

"Just a few months shy. And anyhow, we must make exceptions during times like these," Sister Connie said, scratching something onto the clipboard attached to one of her patients' beds. "She's part of the War Effort. We all are."

"Will she stay with Junior until he recovers?" one of us asked.

"He's a long way from that." She set down her clipboard. "God willing, though, he'll overcome this earthly obstacle. We are but bodies that contain souls, and the soul is the most important part." Sister Connie must have noticed the look of dejection on our faces: pouted lips, droopy eyelids, arms crossed at our chests. "We should be thankful for these boys fighting over there so that we can live peaceful lives right here. Next time you can't sleep, count your blessings instead of sheep." She handed us a stack of clean pillow-cases and instructed us to begin changing the beds.

We certainly didn't feel thankful for these injured boys, nor for Ebbie's absence, the effect of which only seemed to double our workload. In addition to our usual duties, Sister Connie taught us how to monitor blood pressure by pumping an armband full of air, and how to administer pills, then check to be sure the old folks had swallowed them. Nothing felt more punitive than seeing the pink slug of an old person's tongue wagging in his mouth.

We slumped in the pew during Wednesday's chapel service, Sister Lucrecia's organ a pained cat's meow. These masses were long and tedious, though much different from the masses some of us had been to in our Unholy Lives. For one, some of those services had been said in Latin, a language none of us understood anyway, and for two, no women were ever allowed on the altar, not even to deliver the gifts. We always thought this was odd—that grown women couldn't step foot past the altar rail, while young boys could. That we were commanded to recite the Hail Mary, but if

Mary were present, in flesh and blood, she'd be required to stare at some old priest's balding head or sit on a pew so hard, her bottom numbed. Meanwhile, altar boys pranced around the altar at will, as though being born with male bits entitled them to light candles and carry crosses and help the priest prepare communion. It all seemed unfair. Especially to Mary.

At the convent, however, the Sisters helped Father James prepare the Liturgy. They gave readings and assisted with the bearing of the gifts and stood behind Father James as he blessed the sacrament. The presence of women on the chapel's altar might have seemed progressive, except for the fact that the Sisters didn't dare impugn the sanctity of the convent with the presence of young, red-blooded testosterone. They were guarding their territory, more than anything, exerting authority over their small, protected domain. At least, that's what The Guineveres guessed.

Sister Fran read from Psalms about the power of miracles, her voice echoing off the high rafters, inflected with such gravity that we looked upward to see if we could actually see them, her words, hanging from the ceiling like hooked meat. Father James followed this up with a Gospel reading about Jesus healing a blind man. When he spoke, his eyelashes fluttered in a way Gwen often described as "boyishly charming," and if he hadn't been a priest, we might have agreed.

During his homily, Father James stood behind the pulpit, clinging to the edges of it with white-knuckled hands to steady himself.

"Girls!" he said in an impassioned voice, as a general might say "Charge!" to his commanding company. "This week, one of the young soldiers in the convalescent wing awoke from his comatose slumber. This boy who doctors predicted would never walk or talk again. This boy who was far from home, who served his country, who was grievously injured in the War. This boy over whom we prayed—over whom I prayed. This boy who was beyond hope, all hope for hope. We prayed. We asked God for a miracle. He awoke." Father James paused here, either for dramatic effect or to take a breath. His face was red, and he breathed heavily, as though he'd just climbed some stairs. He surveyed the chapel, the bored girls who sat on pews before him. Perhaps we looked in need of a pep talk. "There are no coincidences, girls, only miracles. Always miracles. You must simply look for them. You must trust that they'll happen."

Father James went on about the War, about the War Effort, about our part in it, et cetera, et cetera, but we heard nothing else of it. Gwen nearly fell asleep. Win's stomach rumbled. Ginny and I squeezed our hands together, tighter than we did during the Lord's Prayer.

Then, after chapel, in the cafeteria, as we awaited

our turn for warm beet salad and creamed onions, the Bunsen burner caught fire. Sister Margaret ran for an extinguisher. The spray contained the flames from spreading, but lunch was ruined, a foamy wet mess. Instead, we were served a frozen ziti casserole, a meal option usually reserved as a Friday reward after a week when no girl received a JUG.

"A miracle!" Ginny exclaimed, scrunching her freckled nose. She forked three layers of ziti and took a bite.

"There are no coincidences," Win said, ballooning her cheeks with pasta. We were always on the verge of hunger at the convent, so when we were served something we liked, we ate as much of it as we could.

Coincidence or not, during Morning Roll the next day, Sister Fran misplaced her whistle. Instead of the shrill, high-pitched zip, she resorted to clapping her hands together for an alarm. By Morning Instruction she had located it, but the whistle-less wake-up call, followed by a whistle-free breakfast, seemed luxurious to us. And, as Win noted, it didn't at all impact our ability to form perfectly straight single-file lines.

Three days later during Morning Instruction, another coincidence: A particularly fierce storm caused a power outage. We heard a clap of thunder, then complete darkness. Nobody moved from her desk, where we had been bent over our Bibles reading about Ruth and Naomi. Sister Fran was quick to light candles, but the smoke alarm sounded. She was visibly flustered. In an unusual move, she dismissed us early to the Rec Room, just in time for the power to hum back to life.

In the Sick Ward later that day it was Ginny who first pointed out that maybe miracles really *do* happen, and maybe Father James was right, and maybe The Guineveres had overlooked the obvious in our most pitiful of states. "There are four boys left in the Sick Ward," she said. "There are four of us."

"And?" Win said.

"Maybe they'll wake up if we pray for them," she said, helping Gwen tie on her apron, which clearly hadn't been washed since last week. It was stiff with dirt and dried water.

"If we're to believe Father James," Win added.

"They'll wake up for *us,*" Ginny said. She took a thirsty gulp from one of the old folks' water glasses, and moisture clung to the soft hairs of her upper lip. "And then . . ."

"And then we'll go home with them. As their nurses. Like Ebbie did," Gwen said, finishing Ginny's line of reasoning.

"It's our way out," Ginny said. "It's our only way out."

We stood in silence for a moment, taking in this idea. We bit the insides of our cheeks. We nodded our heads, thinking.

"But none of us is eighteen," I said after a while.

"That doesn't matter. Think about it. The War. Sister Connie herself said there is a great need for nurses right now, and we're *practically* nurses," Ginny said. "Plus, they let Ebbie go."

"We'll be part of the War Effort," Win said. "We must all do our part."

"Brilliant," Gwen said. "And for the record, I don't plan to be a nurse, *for real,* when I get out of here."

"Yes, we know," Win said. "A secretary."

"That's right," Gwen said. "A secretary."

And so it was agreed: If we could wake the soldiers through the power of prayer, through the power of sheer will, or anything else we could think of, we'd go home as their nurses, just like Ebbie. Surely Sister Fran would make another exception during times like these—war times— and none of the other girls had received training in the Sick Ward. None of them knew the proper method for changing sheets or disinfecting bed-pans or administering pills or monitoring vitals. We'd dedicate ourselves doubly to the cause. We'd learn more. And once out in the world, we'd convince the soldiers' families to let us stay with them forever or we'd run away or we'd find our own parents or . . . It wouldn't matter; we'd be free. Freedom would give us options to choose our own destiny that had nothing to do with the stone walls of the convent or the Sisters in their somber regalia or the Sick Ward full of bodily fluids we preferred not to name.

"I wonder what my mom would think of me being a nurse," I said.

"I'm going to visit my dad," Ginny declared.

"And then what?" Gwen asked. She had no desire to go back home, and she told us so, though she didn't say why. She believed we should stick to our original plan, the one foiled only months prior: find our way to the city and eventually marry executives.

"We have to trust it will happen," I said. "That's the only way miracles work."

"It will. I already believe it," Ginny said. She gestured the sign of the cross for good measure, and so we all did the same.

Win assured us she had expertise in waking people up from deep slumbers. She'd found her mom, after all, passed out on several occasions, and she'd revived her with a few staple tricks. "They can't stay sleeping forever," she assured us. "Their comas will eventually wear off."

"Just like Junior," Gwen said.

"Just like Junior," we agreed.

For the first time in months, we felt excitement, *real* excitement, as if a hummingbird lived inside our chests. The moment the bell rang, signaling the end of Afternoon Instruction, we raced to the Sick Ward for our service. We crept into the Back Room with its drawn window shades, the muted quiet commanding reverence. We measured the vitals of those sleeping soldiers; we read to them; we watched them for the slightest sign of bodily change. We clasped our hands tight, prayed as hard as we could, clenched our eyes until we got headaches.

We read to them from the Bible in voices so loud that Sister Connie instructed us to hush. When she wasn't looking, we pricked their toes with sewing needles or flicked their faces with our fingers. Upon Win's urging, we dunked their hands simultaneously in two bins of water: one warm and one cold. Win said she'd heard if you did this to a sleeping person, they'd wet their bed, which would surely wake them up. But nothing.

We could hardly contain ourselves when Sister Magda came by for Checks. She sometimes had to remind us that there were other patients in the ward and to circulate our attentions. *The soldiers need us,* we'd reason with her. *They need our prayers.* Maybe that's all we wanted back then— to feel needed. Maybe that's the ordinary angst of teenage girls, the desire to believe their existences are worth something.

What we didn't know yet was how much we'd come to need these boys. We didn't know yet how these wounded soldiers would undo us, or that they would unravel us, one by one. That's the power of prayer, the risk of it, too: You never know how God will answer. At nights in the Bunk

Room, before Lights Out and after we swapped out our uniforms for nightgowns, The Guineveres would link our hands together, rest our eyes, and pray for a miracle. For four miracles, in fact. We wanted out. We wanted to find our way back home, wherever that would lead us.

All Saints'

Gwen was the first to stake claim to one of the soldiers. It was All Saints' Day, a holy day of obligation, and after mass in the chapel, while the other girls were given Rec Time, The Guineveres were required to serve our daily JUG penance in the Sick Ward. Not that we cared. We were hanging Thanksgiving decorations: figurines of long-limbed pilgrims and Indians; plastic cornucopia we set on the front tables, despite the gripes from the old folks that they took up too much space. Thanksgiving was one of the few secular holidays that Sister Fran acknowledged, Halloween passing by without as much as one jack-o'-lantern.

Yet All Saints' Day, she told us, was her favorite holiday of them all, for it celebrated every saint, known and unknown, and the communion between the faithful living and departed. "The saints surround us, my girls," she said during Morning Instruction, pointing to the framed photos of saints that hung around the room, "intervening on our behalf. They are in constant communion with us, even if our human eyes can't pay witness." Sister Fran pointed her index finger toward the ceiling and made lasso motions with it, and as she did this she beamed. Half-cocked eyelids scanned the room, certain we'd see Saint Vitus, who protects against oversleeping. "Isn't that wonderful, girls? To know that we are never alone?" Sister Fran radiated, her translucent skin nearly glowing like a saint's might.

In the week leading up to All Saints' Day, Sister Fran made games of our math problems: "If there are ten thousand and two hundred saints, but only eighty-three percent have feast days, how many other saints are unknown, forgotten, or as-of-yet undiscovered?" or "If Saint Anne had to travel three hundred miles twice a day to find suitable husbands for those who prayed to her, how many miles would she travel over the course of a year?" Saint Anne was one of Gwen's favorite saints. "Saint Anne, Saint Anne, find me a man," she'd sing in the Wash Room at night as she twirled in her nightgown. For our history lesson, Sister Fran made dittos of bingo cards, each square containing a name. From the front of the room, she called out clues from a hamper that she'd fashioned from a rolling pin and a Crisco can. "Be hopeful you never have to call upon me, for I am the patron saint of dysentery," she read, trying her best to suppress a grin. She reminded us that there's a saint responsible for every possible area of the human experience, even impolite ones.

Maybe it was this idea that prompted Gwen to argue that The Guineveres should all be responsible for one soldier each, that such a delineation of order would eliminate confusion, should it come to that. "Can you imagine if there were no patron saints? It'd get mightily confusing, don't you think? If we lost something, we couldn't just pray 'Tony, Tony, turn around.' Instead we'd have a crowd of ten thousand breathing down our necks. We should focus our talents, like the saints did," she said, further explaining that if we each took responsibility for a soldier, we could provide adequate prayers and attention to each. "Besides, we need to know who will go home with whom." After we finished setting up the decorations, we followed her to the Back Room with our dust rags in hand. "What if only one wakes up?" Gwen questioned. "What if he only needs one nurse at home? Which of us would go?"

We hadn't considered the logistics, instead imagining that one day they'd all pop awake at the same time, like four Lazaruses simultaneously arising from the dead. We dropped our rags in the soiled linen bin, and we washed our hands at the sink, taking care to scrub beneath our fingernails as Sister Connie instructed.

"She has a reasonable point," Win said. She dried her hands on her apron, tugged down her skirt.

"Whichever of us gets out first will come back for the others. Right?" Ginny asked.

"Right," we said.

Gwen, of course, had already picked. "This is

my boy," Gwen said, leading us to one of the soldiers' beds, where she plunked down so hard he bounced twice. It was late afternoon. Sister Connie had left to check on the old folks' supper, and Sister Magda busied herself taking inventory in the storage closet. We could hear her counting in a foreign language. Outside, the day was cloudy, an endless dirty sheeted sky. "I've already decided. You three can fight over the others." She twisted her body to get closer to her boy; her legs splayed in different directions, but her knees still touched, as Sister Fran instructed. "Your chastity, girls, begins with the knees," she'd warn.

Gwen had selected the soldier whose clipboard read "No. 63"—the last two digits of that long string of numbers found on his duffel—the boy with the bandaged face. His lips were visible, dry and powdery, and Gwen dabbed at them with a rag she'd dampened with water. Whoever had bandaged him cut eye slits in the shape of half circles and poked smaller holes near his nose that allowed him to breathe. Other than that we couldn't tell what he looked like, save his skin that was tanned on his neck and his hands. Gwen thought there was something romantic about the fact that she couldn't yet see his face, like the Man in the Iron Mask, or Zorro, or the Frog King. "Boys with obscured identities tend to be the most handsome in the end," she explained. "And the richest." She ran her fingertips through hair that grew like a fern from the top of his head.

"Who do you think he is?" one of us asked.

"I'll find out when he wakes up," she said. "I bet he lives in a huge house, an estate even. I bet I'll have my own room right next to his."

At the thought of this, our new homes, the rest of us scrambled toward Our Boys, for that's what we called them from that point. Our Boys, Our Boys, as though to claim were to possess. We fought over who got to pick next, and Ginny, after a particularly fierce game of Roshambo where she threw three rocks in a row, won the honor. She chose the one whose clipboard read "No. 25," the one with the scabbed face. She said even if the scabs scarred, they'd probably just look like freckles. "I have freckles, you know," she said, as though we'd never taken notice. "My dad had freckles, too." Here her eyes turned downward. "*Has* freckles," she corrected herself. Her Boy had a thin, aquiline nose, dark, bushy brows, and his face was patched with hair because someone had tried to shave around his injuries. "He seems sensitive," she said. "Not brutish like your normal soldier. Maybe he comes from a family of artisans. I wouldn't even care if they lived in an apartment."

"They're not all brutish," Win said. The two of us then had a thumb war to see who'd pick next, and she beat me easily, nearly crushing my hand in the process. Despite her claims, she selected the most boorish-looking soldier of the bunch, "No. 93," according to his clipboard, the one with the broken, bandaged legs raised in a traction splint. His casts were as thick as tree trunks around the thighs, and his hands were big enough to crush a human skull. He still had traces of dirt deep beneath his fingernails. Or maybe it was blood. "Apartment living isn't so bad. I'd take a tenement house to here, anyway."

I didn't tell them that I'd never lived in a house, not once, had only ever lived in rented rooms, or worse. There were some things I couldn't tell The Guineveres, not even if I wanted to. They wouldn't understand. "I don't care where he lives," I said. I was the last to pick, so in some ways My Boy chose me. "No. 22," the one with no visible injuries, except dark circles beneath his pitted eyes. He had brown hair, parted and combed to the side. His mouth curved, two pink peaks with a plump lower lip. His forehead scrunched a bit, set with lines, little seismic waves that I imagined traveled throughout his body to his soul that was still very much awake. I sat down beside him, half thinking he might startle and open his eyes, but he didn't. Of course he didn't.

Yet something strange happened in that moment as I claimed him as My Boy: Deep inside me, something moved, almost imperceptible at first, like a small fish in the darkest part of the ocean. Then it swelled through my stomach, as though I had swallowed a whale, whole. I felt a longing to keep him safe, to protect him. For the first time in my life, I could claim someone as mine. "Don't worry. I'm here," I said to him. I'd never sat so close to a boy before, had never felt one's breath on my skin, the way it left both warmth and moisture, which reminded me of a summer day. "Wake up," I whispered. "So we can go home."

Our proprietary relationships made Our Boys seem more human to us, their wounds less repugnant. We no longer held our breaths when we were near them, nor adjusted their bedsheets with pinched fingers. The Guineveres began wondering about Our Boys in the most general sense: what kinds of sights they had seen in battle, if they'd been afraid, how they had received their injuries. We wouldn't have wanted to know the answers to most of these questions. We wouldn't have wanted to know about blood and mud and marches with rucksacks slung on their backs and blisters inside their boots. Or about days camped out in ditches, with rain so heavy the world felt like it was ending. Instead, while they slept, we gazed at them with awe and curiosity, believing that our destinies lay in these beds somehow, in these sleeping soldiers covered with thin blankets.

Sister Fran spoke frequently of the War Effort, which meant we were occasionally asked to do an additional chore that seemed unrelated to war altogether. In the Rec Room, Sister Margaret had set up a basket of yarn and needles, and some, like The Specials and The Poor Girls, spent their Rec Time knitting scarves and socks to send overseas. But not The Guineveres. We had more important work to do, a higher purpose than knitting.

During Rec Time, The Guineveres dangled upside down from our bunks, our hair spreading out like fans, speculating about Our Boys, or, if not about Our Boys, about where we'd go to live, how we'd convince their families to let us stay, even after Our Boys recovered. We'd be the daughters they never had, or, if they had daughters, we'd behave even better than their biological ones. We'd never leave our dirty clothes on the floor or our shoes in the hallway, as our parents complained in our Unholy Lives. We wouldn't take liberties with our freedom. We'd clean all of the dishes after dinner and do exactly as they said, even if it meant being quiet all the time.

"My mother always told me I gave her a headache," Win said. "Pfft. *She* gave *me* a headache, if you want to know the truth. Heck, she gave herself headaches. But I was never allowed to say so. I don't even think she liked me."

"I know exactly what you mean," said Gwen.

"They liked you. They *have* to like you," I said. "They don't have a choice."

"They have a choice," Win said.

"I feel guilty that I don't miss my mom," Ginny

said. "I mean, I do, but when I think of home I don't think of her anymore. I think of my dad. I think of how happy I made him, how he painted me as Dorothy in a field of poppies, how he said that's my universal essence. That's the part I like to remember."

"What about you?" Win asked me. "What do you like to remember?"

Blood rushed to my head, so I pulled myself up from the bunk and swung my body around. "I don't know. All of it, I guess. My mom never meant to hurt me."

"Keep telling yourself that," Gwen said. "Maybe you'll eventually believe it."

"In our new homes, of course, nursing Our Boys back to health will be top priority," Ginny said, summersaulting off the bunk. She stood and shook her head to steady her balance, then straightened her skirt, which had twisted on her waist. "But we'll have to be careful. If they recover too quickly, they'll just send us back."

"I'm never coming back," one of us muttered.

Maybe it was all of us.

During mealtimes, we brainstormed ideas for getting Our Boys to wake, plans we executed with no success: We smuggled ice into the Sick Ward and slipped it beneath their bed shirts; we burned their fingertips with matches. "You have to hold the flame steady for at least three seconds," Win instructed. But nothing. Recently, Lottie had come down with laryngitis and lost her voice for a week. She couldn't read the letters from her parents out loud in the Bunk Room. She couldn't sing at mass or volunteer to lead Grace in the cafeteria. We counted this among the abounding miracles, and we had faith that Our Boys would snap out of their comas if we kept on praying.

When we checked on Our Boys during Sick Ward duty, their pulses beat strong; their vitals were stable. They even seemed to listen when we read to them from the Bible, their faces relaxed, save the occasional muscle tic. The Guineveres believed it'd only be a matter of time. Junior had awoken, after all, so we didn't believe we were hoping in vain. But even if we were, isn't that what a miracle is? Isn't that why you pray for one—because you've run out of options?

While eating fruited gelatin at dinner in the cafeteria, we bragged of the smallest hints of bodily movement, proof that each of Our Boys was the closest to wakefulness.

"His lips pucker when I come near him, like he wants me to kiss him," said Gwen, proudly stuffing a forkful of dinner in her mouth.

"That's just because his lips are swollen," replied Win.

"I think it'd be weird to kiss him if he wasn't awake to kiss you back," Ginny said. "Don't you think?"

"The body wants what the body wants," Gwen

said. She leaned in and whispered so the other girls wouldn't hear her. Or worse, Sister Fran. "Haven't you heard of a wet dream?" Win and Ginny covered their faces with their napkins.

"What's a wet dream?" I finally asked. I imagined it probably wasn't a dream about being submerged in water, a dream I sometimes had since coming to the convent. In this dream I was drowning in a river; my mother was missing, and I frantically searched for her. The water kept pulling me under. I'd come up gasping for air. A bridge hovered above me, and beyond that only black sky. Nobody could hear me when I called for help. But I knew this wasn't the wet dream they were talking about, and The Guineveres confirmed this. They burst into suppressed fits of laughter, and Win squirted milk through her nose.

"*That's* a wet dream, Vere," Gwen said, pointing now to Win, who was wiping her upper lip. Ginny could hardly contain herself, either; she wiggled like a nesting bird trying to hatch an egg.

Sister Fran craned her neck toward us when she noticed the commotion. To this day, I swear that woman had a sixth sense, or compound vision like a fly. She stood from her table and walked toward us. The Guineveres all raised a forkful of gelatin to our mouths.

"The joyful will inherit the earth, girls. But the giddy shall not. What manner of foolishness is this?"

The Guineveres chewed slowly, each waiting for the others to say something.

"I'm waiting."

"I was teaching my friends something I learned in school once, Sister Fran," Gwen said. She set down her fork and folded her hands like a good girl.

"And what, pray tell, is that?"

"About nocturnal animals."

"That's very kind of you to instill such knowledge." Sister Fran tried to dislodge a piece of gelatin with her tongue. As she did this, her open mouth revealed teeth the shape of gravestones, yellowed near the gums.

"But I was wondering, Sister. Do nocturnal animals sleepwalk during the day?"

"What a silly question, girl." Sister Fran placed her hands on her hips, our only indication that she had a waist beneath her billowy habit.

"What I mean is, don't some animals do things in their sleep that they may not remember? Like a bear. Mustn't a bear relieve himself when he's hibernating?"

"This is not appropriate dinner conversation. Or conversation, period." Sister Fran's lips snarled, and she took a few deep breaths. Up close, one could see veins beneath her gossamer skin. "You will say twenty extra Hail Marys at Lights Out."

"Yes, Sister," Gwen said.

"All of you."

"Yes, Sister," The Guineveres said.

"And God will know if you've not completed them," she said.

"Yes, Sister."

When Sister Fran returned to her own dinner, Ginny leaned in to the rest of us. "I don't know about wet dreams, but mine's eyelids flicker when he's asleep. I think he's trying to tap something in Morse code," she said.

"What do you think he's saying?" asked Win.

"Well, I need to learn Morse code."

"Mine senses I'm there," I said.

"How do you know?" asked Ginny. She loved this game more than the rest of us.

"Because his face squints up like this," I said, shutting my eyes and wrinkling up my face.

"That's just a wince of pain," Gwen said.

"He hums beneath his breath. Only I can hear it when I'm close to him," I said, wanting to believe Our Boys would wake soon. It was almost Thanksgiving. I'd been at the convent more than three years by then, and yet another holiday season would pass without my mother. They say the missing will fade, but not for me. I'd never get used to being without her. Despite the days that melted into weeks and months and years, I still held out hope that I'd hear from her. I still wanted to know she was okay. Yet Mail Distribution Days came and went, and nothing.

But we had Our Boys to think of now. Destiny

had brought them to us so that they could bring us home. Their eyes zigzagged in their sleep, hidden beneath sealed lids; their faces seized involuntarily. Sometimes they'd sweat through their sheets, and we'd have to freshen their linens before Wash Day, an exception the Sisters made only for those in the Sick Ward. Sister Connie taught us how to change the fluids on their IV drips. We prayed. Gwen bit Her Boy on the flesh of his arm. Nothing, not even a subtle shift in his vitals. Nurses had special aptitude for patience, Sister Magda told us. We waited. And we waited. Ginny plugged Her Boy's nose and scratched his chest with the metal comb that was used for lice. Nothing. We waited some more. The War Effort required extraordinary perseverance, but we were up to the task. The Guineveres were a unified home front.

A few days before our monthly penance service, we had our usual conversation about what to confess. We huddled on the floor next to Gwen's bunk, and we flipped through the most recent *National Geographic* borrowed from the library. The glossy pages popped with color. We paused when we came to a photo of a man and a woman looking out onto a beach where a crimson-colored mountain jutted out into the water. That's where we wanted to live someday, on a coast where it would feel like we'd arrived at the edge of the world. But for now, we began the process of examining our lives for some semblance of sin.

Confession was awkward. We never knew what to say. The days leading up to it, we racked our brains or sometimes acted poorly toward the other girls—yanked their hair or hid their shoes—just so we'd have something to admit. Other times, we'd simply revert to our "Sister Fran Sin" and confess to the priest that we had somehow disrespected our venerated abbess. We'd detail the faces we made behind her back during Morning Instruction, or the impure thoughts we had when doing so, while she turned around to write the name of that day's saint on the chalkboard. Or we'd describe how we'd ridicule her pet parrot that she kept caged in her office. The bird's name was Pretty, but we called it Ugly. On occasion she'd bring the bird to class and perch it on her hand to show us how it could say the phrase "God doesn't make junk." Then it'd take off, fly across the room, swooping down only inches from our heads. Sister Fran nodded contentedly when Ugly returned to her finger. "God doesn't make junk. God doesn't make junk," it'd say. "That's right," Sister Fran would reply in turn. "God doesn't make junk." We hated that bird.

"What should we confess this time?" Ginny asked as we sprawled on the floor before Lights Out, our toes all touching. Dredging up another confession was a tedious task. Once Ginny confessed that she scratched herself across the face and blamed Shirley for doing it; Gwen confessed that she hid the key to the sanitary closet because she knew it was Irene's time of the month, and she wanted to embarrass her. Win once confessed to peeking through the curtains in the bathroom during bath time, "just to see what Noreen looked like." I confessed to calling Reggie a liar when she told me her dad was a general in the War.

"Let's all confess the same thing," Gwen said.

"What?"

"We covet our neighbors' wives," Win said. And we all laughed, lying there on the cold floor of the Bunk Room, draped across one another so we couldn't tell whose limbs were whose, even though we were scolded by Sister Fran when she caught us lying like this.

"The Flesh, girls. The Flesh," Sister Fran would say, lightly slapping us.

"It's comfortable," we'd say.

"Heaven is comfortable," she'd reply.

The Guineveres wanted to confess something that was true—this was our undoing. We were naïve enough to think that, all else aside, confessions must come from our hearts, and as soon as we uttered our penances, we'd be absolved of our sins. We still believed in a world that was honest and fair. If there really was a God above us, he'd know we were lying, and we didn't want to chance it. Convent life had made us superstitious that way, suspicious even of our doubts. Afraid.

"Let's say we don't honor our mothers and fathers," I said.

"Boring," they sang.

"We'll have to *do* something first so we have something to confess," Gwen said.

It was then determined that we'd kiss Our Boys.

This was Gwen's idea. After all, she was the one who claimed Her Boy made smooching faces toward her as she sat at his bedside. Win reasoned that it might stir a biological reaction that would wake them once and for all, and Ginny held the romantic notion that perhaps all they needed was a kiss, like in *Snow White* or *Sleeping Beauty*. "Both those fairy tales are about comatose women, if you really stop to think about it. And don't both those stories end with the princess going home with the man who kissed her? We're not reinventing the wheel, my friends."

After lunch the next day, we raced to the Sick Ward. We claimed Our Boys and then our Bibles from the Holy Cabinet, registered vitals, sat with ankles crossed, and pretended to be reading from the Good Book. When Sisters Connie and Magda both exited the room, that's when we were supposed to go through with it—offer our lips up to Our Boys.

During the penance service Sister Lucrecia's organ wailed again, signaling the start of confession. The chapel itself was a small space with a high, slanted ceiling that came to a point. Rows of pews extended from the altar, set so close together we felt cramped, overwarm. It wasn't unusual for a girl to pass out during mass from the heat, and if she did, Sister Fran would have her sit in the last row of pews and hang her head between her knees. The only way one could leave chapel during service was if she vomited, as Irene had done several times in the past year alone. She was known for her weak stomach.

About midway through the penance ritual, The Guineveres lined up, circled the chapel, and selected the priests to whom we would confess. The priests motioned the sign of the cross over our heads, then detail by detail we told our Fathers we had sinned.

"I kissed a boy," Ginny confessed. I knew she had gone through with it—knew they all leaned over the beds of Their Boys with puckered lips. But their kisses held no fairy tale magic; none of Our Boys awoke.

"I made out with a boy," Gwen confessed.

"I tried to kiss a boy," Win confessed. She had told us about it in the Bunk Room, how his lips felt too cold to go on with it for very long.

"I thought about kissing a boy," I confessed.

"Chicken," The Guineveres said when we shared our confessions. I tried. I really did. I hovered over him for a good five minutes, just watching him breathe in and out. I touched his face. I squeezed his warm hands. I composed myself, took short, nervous breaths. His eyes fluttered; his nose wiggled, just barely, as though he were lightly sniffing flowers. And when I scanned the length of his body, tucked beneath covers, right where his legs met his torso, the sheet was tented. A thick, ghostly finger pointed toward the ceiling. My face grew hot; my whole body, too. I felt like a match, struck, like Saint Agnes of Rome, who was burned alive, fire lapping her skin as she prayed for salvation. I squeezed my eyes shut, then opened them again, and there it still was, a phoenix trying to rise from his groin.

It's not that I didn't know what it was. *I knew.* But I'd never seen it before—*this.* Not up close. Not from a distance, either. I wondered if My Boy was having a wet dream, and if it was called a wet dream because you should throw water on it to douse it. I thought maybe I should try to push it down, but I couldn't will myself to touch it. Every time I got close to the bed my hands shook like one of the old men in the Sick Ward who had the tremors. In the end, I did what I thought best, what My Boy would have wanted from me: I walked away. I gave My Boy some privacy.

But I didn't tell The Guineveres about this. Not then, and not when they grilled me on the floor of the Bunk Room about why I didn't kiss My Boy.

I was nervous, I explained to them. That was the truth.

"Don't you want him to wake up?" Ginny asked. "Don't you want to get out of this place?" Oh, I did. I did. He was moving closer to me, to wakefulness. I'd be the first to go home. I wanted to tell them about the sign from My Boy, about how his body reacted, but I was embarrassed. For myself. For him.

"Of course," I said. Then I changed the subject. "What does it feel like?" I asked. I had never kissed a boy before, never had the opportunity, really. The few boys I knew in my Unholy Life knew who my mother was, and they stayed away.

"It felt like pressing my lips against two dead slugs, to be honest," Win said. "I've kissed someone before, and it didn't feel like that. Of course, the person I kissed wasn't in a coma."

"I liked it enough, but his lips were dry. He's not the best kisser," said Ginny. "But that's not the point."

Gwen claimed Her Boy kissed her back. She said they locked in a passionate embrace; she'd felt his tongue on her own, and his hand just barely moved to the small of her back, reaching for the bottom of her uniform skirt.

"Thou shall not lie," I muttered.

"Thou shall not neglect Thy Boy," Gwen said. "Men are snakes." She smiled with lips that she'd reddened with raspberries. I could smell them on her breath.

"I . . . I just don't know how," I admitted. We were still sitting on the floor of the Bunk Room, the cold stinging our bare skin.

"Practice makes perfect," Gwen said. She pulled her hand into a fist and began kissing it with dramatic smacking noises. "Mmmmwah! Mmmmmwah!"

"Don't be stupid," Ginny said. "It's not the same."

"Okay," Gwen said, and she leaned forward and kissed me on the mouth, a strong, quick kiss that left my lips vibrating.

"Stop," I said, pulling away. Gwen leaned back on her hands and laughed, her face to the ceiling so I could see the ridges on the roof of her mouth and the little mounds on the undersides of her teeth.

"Now you've got your first kiss out of the way. Your second won't make you feel as nervous," she said.

"Leave her alone," Win said. She was always defending me—still would, to this day.

"What? I was just trying to help. Do you want one, too?" Gwen said. "I've got plenty to go around." At this, she perched on all fours and crawled toward Win, moving in close till their noses were practically touching. "Is this what you want?" Gwen asked.

"Stop it," I said. This time I was defending Win.

Gwen ignored me, kept her eyes fixed on Win. "Why didn't you like kissing Your Boy?" She puckered her lips, made a series of kissing noises. "Is something wrong with you?"

"I'm not afraid of you," Win said.

"Then prove it," Gwen said. Nobody said anything, but then again, nobody knew what to say. Gwen came to her knees, placed her arms on Win's shoulders, squared herself. "Just one little kiss."

"Fine," Win said. She squinted her eyes just barely, just enough to show a subtle hint of anger, and to let Gwen know that she wasn't going to back down. She unballed her fists, then wrapped her arms around Gwen's neck and, squeezing her hard, planted a kiss smack on her mouth. "Oh, Gwen, Gwen!" Win said, dramatically, her voice three octaves higher than normal. "I've never felt this way in my entire life. Thank you. Thank you. I will never wash these lips again." And at this, The Guineveres all began to laugh until our flanks ached.

A few days later, with The Guineveres prodding me on, I bent over My Boy, squeezed my eyes tight, and presented my kiss-shaped lips as an offering. He didn't wake up.

But I felt guilty after that, and I thought of confessing what I'd done to Sister Fran or Father James. It's not that I didn't want to kiss him—I

143

did. More than anything I wanted him to awake. I remember how my head buzzed as we made contact. I felt his body twitch, as if a shock of electricity had run up his spine. His lips were warm, damp. My Boy took my breath away, sucked it right into his dream world, his sleep world, where it radiated light, illuminating beams of fire like a sacred heart.

Thanksgiving

We awoke to the sound of rain on Thanksgiving Day. After breakfast, we shuffled to the chapel, through the corridor with its windows so drafty we felt damp. Outside, the rain fell in bars; the whole world was a prison cell. During the service, incense rose up to the rafters, then hung there like a mist. Saints stared at us through the stained-glass windows with sober downturned faces, clutching books or staffs or hands to their chests. Sister Lucrecia's organ howled, as if the keys lamented being touched. The Guineveres sat in the fifth pew, worrying the hems of our skirts. Our JUG in the Sick Ward would be over the next day, and we felt sick ourselves. No miracles. No reviving Boys. No hope for a better life on the outside.

We turned our thoughts to Thanksgivings past, to our memories of sitting around white-clothed tables, some of us at least, the way we ate too much turkey and dressing and corn pudding and pearled onions and creamed spinach, then sat around talking about how much we had eaten. Inside the convent, gluttony was a sin, but outside, gluttony was the purpose of the holiday, the whole point. Didn't the Sisters understand how the world operated? We looked to Sister Fran, whose head was bent, whose eyes winced as though prayer were painful. This was a woman who had not known excess. Her skin was too tight around the bones of her cheeks, giving her a skeletal appearance. When we knelt, the cushioned kneelers made soft flatulent noises, which sometimes made us laugh—but today was not a laughing kind of day. Today we were reminded of home.

During the sermon, Father James addressed us from the pulpit. He steadied himself with his hands as he leaned forward. He blinked hard, clicked his tongue, then paused for several moments before he spoke.

"Girls," he finally said. "Today is Thanksgiving. We celebrate. We celebrate you." Father James slurred his words and tottered a bit from side to side as he aimed his index finger in our direction. Spit bubbles formed at the corners of his mouth, and his cheeks flushed red, but not from embarrassment or cold. Packed inside the pew, The Guineveres nudged each other with our knees.

"He's in his cups," Win mouthed. We nodded.

"For everything there is a season, girls. A time for every matter under heaven. A time to be born and a time not to be born. A time to plant and a time to . . . pull up weeds. You must get rid of weeds or they'll choke the garden. Have you ever seen tomatoes grown among dandelions? There's a reason for that. There's a time for cleaning and preening and succeeding. A season for loving. A season for baseball and a season for . . . uh . . ." Father James paused, swallowed. Sister Fran puckered her lips, twisted her neck in concern, but her expression remained placid because she was not one to emote. Father James sidestepped away from the pulpit but lost his balance a bit and, thinking better of it, returned to his position, the pulpit between him and the rest of us. He composed himself and continued. "A time to keep quiet and a time to keep very quiet," he whispered. "A time for war." Here he lowered his head, and we thought he might have fallen asleep.

But after a minute of awkward silence, he jolted and peered up. "Girls, I want you to know that today we celebrate all that we have and all that we don't. And sometimes it's the not having that serves us best. Sometimes, in fact, it's exactly what God wants and exactly what we need. We need to be protected so we can protect others. This is not a weakness, girls," and here, Father James seemed to draw out the *s*'s like *z*'s, but he didn't stop. "You are lucky to be here. You think life's hard, but it's not. There is hell and there is war. The two are difficult to distinguish, but hopefully you'll never know the sting of either. That's why you need to be good girls. The world is a mysterious place, full of times. An abundance of times. Times. War times. Peace times. Sometimes it is difficult to figure out exactly what time. As you sit here today, ask yourself: What time is it?"

Father James paused and checked his watch, his eyes drooping as if on the cusp of a nap, and Sister Lucrecia took this as her cue to sound the organ. The Guineveres snorted under our breaths, trying to withhold our laughter. But really we were thinking this: What was the plan for us? What was the plan for Our Boys? Did our families miss us this Thanksgiving? Did their families miss them? We tried to imagine ourselves sitting beside them, a banquet of food splayed out in front of us. Their mothers wore pearls; their fathers smoked pipes; their grandparents had kind, warm faces, the way grandparents did. We all sat together, crowded around one enormous table decorated with flowers and gourds, with dripping candles lit just for the occasion. It was Thanksgiving, and all eyes turned to us in thanks. We'd taken such good care of Their Boys during a difficult stretch. The War. The injuries. They were so far from home. Thank goodness for us.

Our reverie lasted through communion, as we proceeded toward the altar and as Father James clumsily placed holy wafers on our tongues. We pretended these cardboard discs tasted like turkey dinner, homemade, like the gratitude of four families who had come together to celebrate Our Boys. As we waited for the succulence to dissolve on our tongues, for the sweet taste of pumpkin pie to fade from our mouths, it occurred to us what time it was for Our Boys. It was their time of need, and we would nurse them through it. That's what you do during difficult times: You stand by those who need you the most. You don't abandon them, don't just leave them alone to suffer. We grew angry again with our parents, and, at the same moment, we grew calm. There in the chapel, as we listened to the closing prayers, we believed to the core of our beings that our lives would be perfect if only Our Boys would wake up.

After mass, we single-filed to the Rec Room while the Sisters prepared our real Thanksgiving meal in the kitchen. No doubt, it would be some tasteless fare: globs of runny potatoes; stiff, dry dressing. The Sisters weren't known for their culinary skills, perhaps, as Gwen once suggested, because they never had to woo a man with them.

Jeanette and Polly and the rest of The Poor Girls had volunteered to help Sister Claire in the kitchen; they seemed to have an overattachment to food, but what did we care? It was no business of ours. The older girls retired to the Bunk Room for naps, and The Delinquents followed them, wishing they were older themselves. The Specials worked on their knitting in the corner, proud to be part of the War Effort, especially on a holiday. "The War Effort takes no days off," they insisted. The rest of us lounged listlessly around the Rec Room, listening to the radio.

The radio was made of wood with a large dial

and metal knobs that the Sisters usually removed so we couldn't turn it on. But today was a holiday, and, as Sister Fran claimed, holidays should feel *special,* even for girls like us. She permitted us radio time during Christmas and New Year, and she also made such allowances during Rec Time on the day before any girl turned eighteen. Perhaps she wanted to send whoever it was off into the world with memories of her leniency. Or perhaps she thought the radio would offer a glimpse into the outside world, now changed. For us, we'd come to associate the radio not with connection but with loss.

Sister Margaret had tuned the radio to a Thanksgiving Day parade. The tinny radio voice described the floats, not ones like at the Sisters' annual festival, but real floats that actually floated, led by men and women in costumes. We could hear drumbeats in the background, the occasional clash of a cymbal. Wherever the parade was located, it was raining there, too, because the man on the radio kept saying it was coming down like cats and dogs. We kept trying to picture what that'd be like—for cats and dogs to literally fall out of the sky in a biblical sort of way, like frogs. We were imagining these animals falling from the sky, landing, like cats do, on all four paws when the reporter introduced another man who'd just returned from the War. Our ears perked up, holding on to his every word. Win yelled for everyone to shush, and the room grew quiet.

"There's no place like home this Thanksgiving," the radio voice said. "I'm sure that's how you're feeling today, thankful to be back on your own soil."

A younger-sounding voice replied, "Yes, sir. It's good to be home."

"What did you miss the most?"

"I missed my family," the young man said. "And spaghetti. I missed spaghetti. With meatballs."

The two shared a laugh; then the voices went quiet for a minute, observing a moment of silence. We could hear trumpets playing in the background, some clapping and whistling. We tried to imagine what the parade must look like with all this rain. Everyone must have been wet, their hair slicked to their foreheads, their clothes clinging to their bodies, the way Father James looked after emerging from the dunking booth.

The radio announcer came back on. He suddenly sounded very far away. "Thanks for your service," he said. "And to the rest of you: Come home safely."

At that moment, Sister Margaret turned down the radio. "You're in for a special treat, girls," she said. Sister Margaret was in charge of supervising our Rec Time. She walked over to where she had spread out brown packing paper on the Ping-Pong table, along with some paint and small canvases. Ginny's face lit up, though she was trying to remain cool. We all hold ideas of who we are, images of ourselves that may or may not be accurate: Gwen was pretty; Win was tough; I was faithful. But Ginny's was more specific: She was creative, a painter—an artist—and she considered herself one even long into adulthood when it became apparent that she wasn't, when all she had to show for her art was some finger paintings her children had hung on her fridge. "We'll be sure your paintings are sent overseas," Sister Margaret said. "It's part of the War Effort. We must all do what we can. And a pretty portrait would go a long way toward raising spirits, don't you think?"

Sister Margaret was the youngest of the Sisters and also the kindest. After dinner in the cafeteria, she often walked around asking if we'd had enough. On occasion, she'd slip us pieces of hard candy, little strawberry-shaped ones that we'd tuck into our cheeks and let dissolve slowly like communion. Her eyes were set far apart, and her pupils were misaligned, but she was pretty in her own way. Though she wore her habit, we could see her brown hair and a bobby pin that had fallen out of place. A loose curl hung from her forehead, making her seem more human somehow. Beneath her habit Sister Margaret was just like us, a girl who pinned her hair.

"Does God approve of war?" Shirley asked.

Shirley had the posture of someone rich, perfectly straight, as if her spine were fashioned from a golden rod. We were all standing around the Ping-Pong table now, watching Sister Margaret set up the painting station.

"If it's warranted, if you're fighting to preserve the good, like we are, then yes. In a world full of evil, war is inevitable. We are born to struggle. Just think of Eden," Sister Margaret said. She pried the lids off the paint canisters with a butter knife.

"But there wasn't a war in the Garden of Eden," Nan said. The Guineveres felt sorry for Nan because her face was covered with acne, but this didn't stop us from disliking her. She was a Special, after all, and so probably deserved it.

"Oh, but there was," Sister Margaret advised. "The struggle between good and evil is a war indeed. We're always fighting it. That's a never-ending battle, and you'll wage it until your death."

"So, then, you're saying God approves of war," Gwen said. She stood with her hands intertwined behind her back, her head cocked to the side. She seemed genuinely concerned, though she could easily fake such expressions. Such was her nature, a quality that unsettled us all because we never knew when she acted out of sincerity.

Sister Margaret set down the butter knife and carefully placed the paint lids in a bucket. Then she began to organize the brushes. "Well, He doesn't approve of it, per se, but recognizes its necessity. In the Bible, He authorizes war to protect the faithful from their enemies or to punish those who disobey Him."

"If He protects the faithful, then why didn't He protect the soldiers in the Sick Ward?" Ginny asked. She picked up a dry brush and began dotting the freckles on her arm with it.

"Oh, girls. I shouldn't get into this. This is Sister Fran's domain. I don't want to overstep my bounds."

"If they're on the side of the good, our side, God should have protected them," Ginny pressed.

"It's not our place to say what God should do. War is a human initiative and will necessarily involve some human casualties. It's an unfortunate reality. However, think of all the lives that wars have saved in the history of time." Admittedly, we didn't know much about war, or its history.

"What about 'Thou shalt not kill'?" Barbara chimed in. We called her Barbaric behind her back because of the permanent scowl on her face. "Wouldn't soldiers have to break one of the Ten Commandments in a war?"

"That would make every soldier a sinner," Lottie said. She squinted as she said this, then pushed her glasses up the bridge of her nose.

"My dad killed people in the War, but he's not a sinner," Reggie interjected. "He's a general, and he has a very important job." She rubbed her neck as if lathering it with soap. "He's a good person. You'll see when he comes back for me. He said I could invite you all to my welcome-home party, but only if Sister Fran says it's okay. Do you think Sister Fran will say it's okay?"

"Take this up with Sister Fran, girls," Sister Margaret said. "I've said too much already. War is complicated, that much I know."

At that point we didn't understand what was so complicated about it. There was good and there was evil, just like in the Garden of Eden. There were Our Boys and there were those who had fought against them. How I wish I could still render the world so clearly in black and white.

"Just remember what Father James said during today's sermon," she added.

"But we'd need clocks to figure out what time it is," Shirley said, and the room filled with giggles that summersaulted through the air, then stopped just as abruptly as they'd started.

Sister Margaret grew serious. "No," she said. "You're lucky to be here, that's what he said, and you should be thankful. It *is* Thanksgiving, after all." With that she lifted the hem of her skirt, swung around, and walked out of the room. "I expect to see some of your paintings after dinner. Make them cheerful," she called from the hallway, her voice bouncing off the walls.

Left to our own devices, The Guineveres

commandeered the painting area, readied our canvas, and mixed colors together to create a morose shade that reflected our mood. We didn't say much, didn't talk about what we'd do once we could no longer see Our Boys during Sick Ward duty, which concluded the next day. Instead, we worked with one palette, each taking a turn making brushstrokes on the empty canvas until it was completely covered in dark paint, like a sickly night sky without stars.

"We'll call it *Blind Leading Blind*," one of us said when we stepped back.

"They always wind up in the dark," another Guinevere added.

A group of older girls went up to the Bunk Room, and we claimed their spot, picking at the jigsaw puzzle they'd left unfinished on the coffee table. We knew the puzzle by heart now. It was an image of the Sistine Chapel, only the pieces of Adam's manhood were missing, his nipples, too, so it could never be finished. We weren't sure if these pieces were lost or if the Sisters had claimed them in an act of censorship. However, what the Sisters didn't realize was this: What we conjured up in our imaginations was far more graphic than any single puzzle piece could have depicted.

"Missing: the first phallus of humankind," Win said, pointing her index finger to where Adam's genitalia would have been, as if she were marking a spot on a map. She was trying to ease our self-pity, our hopelessness, our anger about being so far from home on a holiday.

"Why do priests need one anyway?" Gwen said. "They're not supposed to use it."

"Adam wasn't a priest," I said.

"Well, they need it to pee," Ginny said matter-of-factly. She had pulled up her sleeve and was rubbing at the dried paint on her skin, trying to remove it. "There's a time for everything, even for going to the bathroom."

"I wish we were allowed to wear watches," I said, then spread out on the couch. "My mom gave me a watch, but Sister Fran took it away."

"She takes everything away," Ginny said. "She'd take the sun out of the sky if she could."

"But this watch was special." I didn't tell them what my mom said when she gave it to me, that the watch held powers, special ones that would protect me. I didn't tell them a lot of things about my mom, not only because I thought they wouldn't understand, but because I wasn't sure I even did.

"Well, I don't need a watch to tell me it's Vere's time," Gwen said. "I saw her dip into the sanitary closet," she sang. My face grew hot, ashamed of my body or of my biology, or both. Gwen was right, and they all knew it. I covered my face with a pancaked throw pillow. "What? It's no big deal. I like getting my period. It's a woman's truest suffering."

"Like how all the saints suffered. Like how artists suffer for their art," Ginny said.

"Well, that's a bit dramatic," Win replied. "It's so embarrassing, really. Down *there?* I'd rather have a nosebleed."

"Like that wouldn't be obvious," Gwen said. "Besides, what's there to be embarrassed about? Menarche is a point of pride. It means you're a woman."

"We're not women yet," I said, hoping to shift the conversation. I sat up and crossed my legs, placed the pillow on my lap.

"That's what the Sisters want you to believe, with all their 'girls' this and 'girls' that," Gwen said. "In some countries, you'd be married off by now; you'd have a baby or maybe even two. Just because you want to remain a virgin your whole life . . ."

"That's not true," I replied, but maybe it was. The thought of intercourse terrified me, and the fact that I referred to it as "intercourse" was likely proof of that.

"I want to have a baby with My Boy someday," Ginny said. And we all turned, looked at her with surprise. "What?" She smiled. "I love him."

We would have responded to Ginny, but in that moment Reggie came up to admire our progress with the puzzle. "Can I help?" she asked. Reggie wanted so badly to be part of our group, but that was as impossible as a camel passing through the eye of a needle. She often followed us around the courtyard during our constitutional walks or chose the sink next to ours in the Wash Room at night. During chapel she sometimes tried to squeeze into our pew, but we widened our postures, spread our legs indecently so as to take up as much space as possible.

"We're already done with it," one of us said.

"Oh. Well, maybe I'll paint a picture to send to my dad. He really is a general in the War," she said. "And he really is coming back to take me home. He said so."

We didn't believe her, and as if sensing this she added, "He is."

"If that's the case, why don't you write him," Gwen said. "Write him and see if he'll tell us who those soldiers in the Sick Ward are. If generals are so important, then surely he can do that."

"Okay," she said.

"And if he can answer that," Win added, "*then* we'll believe you."

"Will you come to my party?" Reggie asked, her eyes brightening. "If Sister Fran lets you?"

"If Sister Fran lets us," one of us said, even though we knew she wouldn't. Girls were strictly forbidden from leaving the convent until the day they turned eighteen. With the exception, of course, of Ebbie. But there was the War to consider.

Reggie skipped off to join Lottie, Dorrie Sue, Shirley, and Nan. They'd abandoned their knitting projects on the couch. So much for the War Effort. Now they giggled as they danced to the music that played from the radio. Their arms swung in the air, and their feet shuffled against the tile floor, making chirping sounds. They held their arms upward and allowed themselves to be spun by invisible dance partners who clearly stood taller than they did, since they peered toward the tin ceiling as they did this.

The Guineveres reclined on the couch and shot them menacing looks. Win grunted audibly through a closed mouth, which came out like a growl. The Specials were acting special again.

"What?" Lottie kept saying as she twirled in the arms of her imaginary man.

"What?" Gwen repeated in a high-pitched baby voice.

"Just because you're not happy doesn't mean we can't be," said Shirley, whose shoes looked new, so we wondered if her wealthy parents had anything to do with it. Special Shirley and her special shoes.

"Who says we're not happy?" Ginny said. She scowled defensively.

"Fine, you're happy," Lottie said. She fiddled with her glasses again. They covered nearly a third of her face.

"Happiness is boring," Gwen said. "Happiness means you've stopped trying."

"I feel sorry for you, then," Lottie said.

"No wonder your parents threw you away," Shirley added.

At this, Win hurled herself from the couch and grabbed a mound of Shirley's hair before we had time to stop her. Shirley bent forward at a ninety-degree angle, and we pried Win's hand off, knuckle by knuckle. "It's not worth it," one of us said to her. We walked back to the Ping-Pong table, where we brought out a new canvas. We began painting again, this time a field of grass, some trees in the distance.

"I really do love My Boy," Ginny said mid-stroke. "I can't help it. It just happened one day. Love is like that. You can't control it." She dabbed four quick red spots to create a patch of flowers. And then at the top, near what should have been the sky, she drew some hearts raining down from the horizon.

Maybe it was the fact that it was Thanksgiving. Maybe it was the fact that we were stuck far from home and wished we were almost anywhere else on earth than here. Maybe it was that Sick Ward duty ended the following day, and Our Boys still slumbered, so far from wakefulness that leaving the convent seemed like an impossibility.

Or maybe it was simply the way Ginny looked, her red hair pulled back, her small arm shaking as she blotted paint, her calves too thin to even hold up the socks that had slouched down around her ankles. She was pitiful and she was angsty, and yet she was a reflection of all of us. Maybe love isn't too far a cry from suffering. Maybe that's why we fell in love with Our Boys, or why, at first, we said we did. Because we wanted our suffering to be useful; we wanted it to lead us to a greater good.

"I love My Boy, too," Gwen said.

"Me, too," I said.

"Of course," Win said.

"And I want to have a baby," Gwen said.

"After we're married," I said.

"And after he gets a job as an executive," Gwen said.

"Yes," we all agreed. "Yes! Yes!" And suddenly Thanksgiving didn't seem so depressing any-more because we were together and we were in love, and what more could we ask for on a rainy Thursday than that?

Saint Cecelia

FEAST DAY: NOVEMBER 22

Beneath her silken gowns, Saint Cecelia wore a sackcloth so rough it chafed her skin when she moved. She fasted often and prayed to the angels above, kneeling so the coarseness of her clothing burned her knees. Her knuckles grew red from pressing her hands together in such fervent devotion. "Oh, save me from the flesh," she'd pray.

Her parents had different ideas, instead giving her in marriage to a young pagan named Valerian. Their wedding did not lack for indulgence or festivity. Lyrists played while the bride and groom danced with such grace it seemed as if their feet never touched the ground. None of the guests returned home having the slightest idea that the bride was unwilling. After all, Valerian came from an aristocratic family. Besides, Cecelia had no choice in the matter.

When the last of the guests had left and the servant laid white sheets on their bed, the couple retired to their wedding chamber.

"Oh, dearest Valerian," Cecelia said. "I must confess." She was shaking; sweat formed at the small of her back.

"My beauty," he said, moving in close to touch her dark hair, pinned back with a wreath of flowers. Cecelia had never seen such hunger in the eyes of a man not in want of food.

"Our vows are invalid," she admitted. "I'm already wed to an angel." Here she felt her face grow hot; she slanted her eyes toward the floor, where her servant had set her slippers beside the bed. The thought of undressing, even if only her stockings, made her nervous. "He stands here beside me now, in fact."

Valerian moved toward his beautiful wife. "I see no angel," he declared, wondering if she'd sipped from too many chalices of wine.

"He's here beside me," she said, turning and looking up past her shoulder, pointing to what seemed to be the wall behind her. "He guards my maidenhood," she said.

He looked at her in disbelief. Her father had told him she was a docile creature. He'd expected obedience. "You're my wife; I shall touch you if I will," he said, indignant. Then he softened, figuring this a case of bedroom terror. The poor girl had never been alone with a man. Not like *that*.

"I'm warning you: Great harm will come to you if you touch me. If you respect my virginity, he shall leave you alone," she said, then pointed to the angel by her side, but Valerian saw only an empty wall, some candelabras, the fireplace now settling to dim embers.

"I'm not to touch you?" he asked in disbelief. He was certain this was an excuse—perhaps she was shy. Modesty is an admirable quality in a woman, but it is not the only admirable quality. "It shall only hurt at first," he explained.

Cecelia grimaced.

"Show me your angel," he said.

"You must first get baptized," she said. "Then you can see him."

Valerian, a kindhearted boy, went off to find a bishop to baptize him, if only to appease his wife. He suspected he'd return and then, knowing what lengths he had gone to for her pleasure, would be rewarded with pleasure of his own. Yet when he returned to Cecelia, he saw him with his own eyes: a giant angel with flaming wings. The crude-looking angel quickly produced two crowns of roses from behind his back, and he placed them on their heads. Valerian was woozy from shock, Cecelia woozy from prayer. They fell asleep fully clothed, their marriage never consummated.

The two spent the next year preaching their faith far and wide, converting thousands of the disinherited to the path of grace. They worked side by side, sometimes clasping hands as they raised them before crowds of people. Valerian's hand felt warm in her own. Once, after a stint in the river where they'd seen hundreds of bodies fall into the water and rise again reborn, Valerian raised her hand to his lips and gently kissed it.

This was the only kiss they ever shared, and she felt a buzzing in her body, all the way down to her unspeakable regions. Afterward, she clung to his strong forearm as they walked through the crowded city, bustling with throngs of the unblessed.

Their work was dangerous, however. Their ruler was a godless man, a tyrant. When Valerian wouldn't recant his faith, he was slain, and Cecelia, heartbroken but still defiant, found herself arrested, thrown into a windowless cellar with gray walls of cold stone. Her fiery-winged angel flapped his wings in protest, but he could not speak in a language the unfaithful could hear.

Cecelia refused to renounce her faith, for what could she disavow? Could she reject her heart, or the blood running through her veins? And so she was sentenced to die by suffocation, barricaded into her own bathroom. As fires burned around her, she stood in the corner of the darkened room, pressed between a wall and her soaking tub, where she used to pray for hours as her fingertips pruned. She thought about her life, her sweet Valerian who never touched her but once to kiss her hand. He had been a decent man; she might have truly married him in a different life. Outside, her tormenters fed the furnace ten times the normal fuel. Fires were set outside her window. She could smell the thick smoke, but it didn't affect her senses.

In fact, her pores didn't excrete one drop of sweat. When she grew bored, she prayed—or she thought of her parents, her poor Valerian who would have made a handsome lover. Why had he kissed her knuckles that day? Why had she felt a jolt of energy course through her whole hand, her arm, through to her stomach, and farther down, too? Down *there*. She thought about her body, which did not belong to her, so she laid herself out on the floor as if on a funeral pyre, and she waited.

After a few days, her tormentors realized their death sentence had not worked. Instead, they resorted to a hatchet. They led Cecelia outside, placed her thin neck upon a boulder. The stone felt cold on her cheek and her ear. The world looked different sideways; everything had sharper edges.

She knew her death was near. Her body was not her body. Her angel sat next to her, but he did nothing. He tucked his wings into his armpits, and he lowered his eyes. Her tormentor raised his hatchet high above his head and brought it down upon Cecelia, once, twice, three times. Cecelia felt her neck grow cold. Her shoulders became wet, but her heart went on beating.

Crowds of people flocked to see the beautiful, maimed maiden. They remembered her from the river, looking on as they were dunked and blessed. They soaked up her blood with their napkins and sponges while she sang beautiful hymns to them in a voice as clear as a harp.

She bled for three days, after which the world became lighter, colors fading into the sky. First went the blues, then the reds, then the greens, then everything looked black and white. She saw her angel. His wings were no longer engulfed in flames. He was a young man now, and he was holding her, and they were flying up, up. She felt herself rising. She sang her beautiful hymns in a voice that sounded odd, like an untuned instrument. She couldn't recognize it as her own, though she felt the vibrating of her chest, the thumping of her heart within. She was rising and singing, rising and singing, and as she floated up high, cradled by her angel, so high she could see only the tops of the heads of the people below, her vision tunneled, and there she saw her sweet Valerian on their wedding night those years ago, his face filled with splendor, his cheeks plump and ruddy. They were dancing together, twirling to the music.

"Sing with me," he said, his eyes wet like ink, his face glowing with youth and excitement. "Sing with me, dear," he said, his smile so broad she thought she might be consumed by it.

So she sang. With her whole heart, she sang.

Advent

The day after Thanksgiving, Sister Fran called us into her office. We knew what the visit was about. The end of our JUG. Our progress report. Another lecture. A warning to be good.

As soon as we reached the threshold of the room, we were hit by the smell of holy oil mixed with the scent of cedar chips that lined her parrot's cage. Sister Fran sat with two fingers pressed to her lips. Her whistle rested on the desk in front of her, where she'd been cleaning it with silver polish.

"Sit down, girls," Sister Fran said. Gwen and Win sat down on the two wooden chairs, and Ginny and I took a seat on the small bench off to the side, near Pretty's cage. The bird occasionally squawked and tossed a seed between the bars.

The walls of the office were otherwise bare except for a small cross that hung in the corner, and we tried to avoid looking in its direction. We once heard that if you looked at a crucifix with a heart full of sin, your eyes could burn out of their sockets. Although we knew this probably wasn't true, we couldn't help holding on to such super-stitions—and other ones, too: like if you didn't cross yourself with holy water at church the devil could get into your heart, or if you went to bed

169

without saying a prayer and you died in your sleep, you'd be relegated to purgatory forever.

"As you are aware, girls, your Justice Under God has officially concluded. I want you to know, on behalf of Father James and myself, we were very satisfied with your diligence. I can only describe your progress as touched by grace." Sister Fran did not have an accent, a point we often debated, though she clenched her jaw as she spoke, and her voice was so high, so silvery, it seemed that she did. Sister Connie once bragged that Sister Fran came from wealth and pointed out that she'd given it all up to become a nun, as though proving to us the purity of her intentions. None of The Guineveres came from money—though we weren't as poor as The Poor Girls—and so we supposed that wealth gave one a monied accent, which wasn't really an accent at all.

"We're happy to continue—" Ginny started to say, but Sister Fran interrupted her to remind her that she wasn't asked to speak.

"The season of Advent is nearly upon us, girls. Do you remember the meaning of the word 'advent'?" She looked at us, one by one. Gwen raised her hand, and Sister Fran nodded toward her.

"It means 'a coming,' Sister," she said.

We'd learned this during our Morning Instruction only a few days prior. Sister Fran stood at the front of the room, pointing to where she had written on the chalkboard *Advent=a coming.* "Say it three times, girls," she said. "The rule of three: It takes a trinity of repetitions to commit a fact to memory."

"Yes," Sister Fran said, pleased with Gwen's answer. "Indeed it does." She placed both her hands on the desk in front of her. Veins popped out like little blue rivers, and her raised knuckles were small, rocky islands.

"It also means 'an arrival,'" Sister Fran said, though she hadn't mentioned this part during our instruction session. "The season asks us to wait in celebration of the First Advent and in hopeful anticipation of the Second." We nodded, uncertain why she was giving us this lesson yet again. We were tired of lessons. To us, Advent meant lighting a few extra candles, hanging a wreath, and attending additional church services in the long lead-up to Christmas. In our Unholy Lives, some of us used to make chain links out of construction paper to help with the countdown to the holiday, but Sister Fran found the idea too secular for the sanctity of the occasion. Instead, she let us decorate the Rec Room with cardboard ornaments, each containing a scripture of the day. "Father James and I, seeing how dutifully you executed your responsibilities with the con- valescents, believe you have been called to a life of service. Destined for acts of selflessness and servitude like Saint Bernadette or Saint Veronica. We applaud you on the completion of your JUG, and we hope that you've been filled with the grace of the Holy Spirit. It seems you've reformed your wayward behavior. Your itch, shall we say, to leave the convent. You've impressed us, girls. And now, we believe your call has been extended, beyond your original JUG. What I am saying, girls, is this . . ." Here she scanned each of us, moving her eyes up and down our uniformed bodies, in the habit of examining us for dress code violations. "You've been chosen to act as altar servers."

We furrowed our brows and widened our eyes, which may have looked similar to our Holy Constipation look, but it was merely a look of confusion. Holy Confusion. Girls weren't allowed to be servers—that's why they were called altar *boys.*

Sister Fran continued, "Ordinarily, such an overt disregard of sacred tradition would be blasphemous; however, with so many boys called away to fight, these are extraordinary times, and we have an extraordinary need. Father James insists the doctrine of Our Creator evolves with the needs of His people. We're all a part of the War Effort, girls, and we must lend our skills and talents where needed. We mustn't keep them under a bushel basket, as the Bible tells us. Don't you agree?" The Guineveres wanted to stop her here to inform her that we were already contributing to the War Effort. No, not knitting scarves to send overseas, as the other girls did during their Rec Time. Our contribution was larger than that: waking Our Boys, going home with them. It's true, no Lazarus-style miracles had occurred, but we were willing to wait. *This* was our duty and our obligation. *This* was our contribution. We wanted to be nurses, not altar girls, for altar girls couldn't leave the convent to care for wounded soldiers, to accustom them to their new lives, the way Ebbie Beaumont had.

But, of course, we couldn't tell her that. Instead, we simply nodded our heads again. "And you, young ladies, will be among the first female altar servers in the entire country." Sister Fran smiled, the corners of her mouth poking upward. "Oh, isn't this wonderful, girls? What an advancement! What an opportunity!"

We remained still in our seats, trying to grow excited, too, if only for Sister Fran's sake. We had to admit that, although Sister Fran more often terrified us than not, we still craved her praise. She was, after all, our de facto parent, and what girl doesn't seek such approval? But how could we hope for a miracle, how could we tend to Our Boys in the Sick Ward if we couldn't even see them? And what should happen if they woke up without us? Who would go home with them then?

Win raised her hand, and Sister Fran acknowledged her with a hard blink. "What are our duties as altar girls, Sister?" she asked.

"It's an altar *server,* not an altar *girl.* There's no such thing as an altar girl," she corrected. "Father James will provide you with adequate training." She explained to us that we'd be serving during Sunday service in the parish church, as well as here during our weekly services for the convalescents. Our hearts quickened as she spoke these words. On Wednesdays, before our all-girl service in the chapel, Father James said a mass in the Sick Ward because the old folks were either too ill or too weak to attend Sunday's celebration. However, we'd never seen it. Usually during this time, we were praying, pencils poised, for the blessed release from our Morning Instruction.

We didn't ask another question after that. Getting out of Morning Instruction, spending Wednesdays in the Sick Ward service with Our Boys, leaving the convent to go to the church in town, even if it was just right up the hill: now *those* were ideas that excited us. Our eyes lifted to the tin ceiling of Sister Fran's office, and we imagined ourselves standing gloriously at the altar, beams of light raining down from above. Maybe God could hear our prayers better from an altar, and maybe that had been the problem all along, one of volume. It must be difficult to discern discrete requests among so many girls chattering in prayer.

"After your *incident* this summer, I had to pray for guidance on this matter. Father James is certain you've reformed. And I'm certain that God forgives even the lambs who stray from the path, but only once they're back with the flock. Be mindful of this, girls—and be careful what you do with such liberties. That is all. You may go."

The Guineveres single-filed out of Sister Fran's office, but as soon as we rounded the corridor, out of earshot, we burst into squeals of delight. Linking arms, we jumped up and down, our toes touching and leaving the ground with perfect synchronization.

"Altar girls!" we said, light-headed from exhilaration. All was not lost. Our Boys could still awake to us, to The Guineveres who, at that moment, loved them more than anything in the world.

Years later, at a dinner party with the man she was supposed to marry, Win sat across the table from a woman bragging about winning the Butter Bean Beauty Pageant in her youth. The woman wore lipstick too bright for her complexion, and her voice had a southern accent that only seemed to highlight her insincerity. Win took a too-large gulp of her wine, turned to her, said, "I've never participated in a pageant, but I was one of the very first female altar servers." She took another long slug from her glass. "In the entire country." A smile spread across Win's face as she said this, but then she looked up at the man she was supposed to marry, who was shaking his head at her in disapproval, and an emptiness sank into Win that she hadn't felt in years. "Oh, how nice," the southern woman said, turning stiffly to her husband. "She was an altar girl."

"Altar *server,*" Win corrected. "There's no such thing as an altar girl." She lifted her wine to her mouth, finishing the glass as she blinked back tears. She wasn't even sure why she was crying. I guess it was a mix of reasons.

Win never did marry that man, and she said it was the one thing in life she never regretted. That her choice had finally set her free.

The next morning, Sister Fran walked us up the steep graveled driveway for our first training session. Father James waited for us outside. He led us past the front entrance of the church with its broad, sweeping archways and into a side door leading to the rectory.

I can't explain it now, but back then, when we took our first steps into that rectory, we felt an advent in the truest sense of the word: We felt something coming—an arrival of some sort—though we didn't know what. Father James brought us into his office, shut the door, and motioned to a table where an assortment of pastries was laid out on a silver platter. A glass pitcher of the orangest juice we'd ever seen dripped beads of sweat down its belly.

"Well, you can't train on an empty stomach, now can you?" Father James said, and he picked up a pastry and bit into it. Small crumbs tumbled down his face.

We thought this might be a test at first—like the temptation of Christ—so we hesitated, looking at one another with uncertainty. Holy Confusion.

"Go on," he said, and he took another bite, then licked his thumb.

Gwen stepped forward, plucked a pastry from the tray, and sank her teeth into the cap of a cheese crown. She smiled, and we could see cushions of dough packed around her gums.

"Atta girl," Father James said. He stuffed the rest of the pastry into his mouth, then smiled with plump pink cheeks.

At that point, three more hungry hands grabbed for pastries, and we all stood eating until our fingers were sticky and our stomachs were full. We washed the pastries down with orange juice that tasted sour from the sugar that buzzed in our mouths.

After we ate, Father James led us back out of his office and through a hallway that connected the rectory to the church. We walked through the main foyer, with its gray-white marble floor and its statues of saints lined up like a greeting committee, and into a side room.

Unlike the church itself, this room was unadorned. It had a dull brown carpet and a leather couch along the wall. It smelled of woody incense in there and other scents that were not immediately recognizable, but we knew them simply as church smells.

"This is the vestry," Father James explained. "On the days you serve, you'll come to the vestry first. You can find a cassock that fits you in here," he said as he opened a closet. Two racks of identical white robes hung neatly on hangers. "These are worn *over* your clothing, of course," he said and cleared his throat so as to remind us not to remove our clothes. "Go ahead, try one on."

We sorted through the closet, but many of the robes were too big in the arms, and the hems dragged on the floor as we paced.

"These cassocks were not intended to be worn by . . ." Father James cleared his throat again and rubbed his large hands together as if he were soaping them. "By people of your size and stature, girls, but we must make do," he said, and as he spoke we could smell the faint hint of alcohol on his breath. "They slip on *over* your clothing," he reiterated as he turned his back toward us despite his instructions. Perhaps he felt it indecent to watch us dress in any fashion. "Let us pray that our young fellows return safely," he muttered with his back to us.

We quickly found what appeared to be the smallest robes, and we slipped them on over our heads, mussing our hair in the process. They were baggy on us, and stiff, but Father James showed us how to cinch the rope belt in a way that drew up the hem so at least we wouldn't trip on the material. "Altar boys!" Win exclaimed when we looked in the mirror, and we all laughed. Father James told us there'd be none of that kind of tomfoolery, so we stopped and swapped out our laughter for church faces.

It's peculiar: For all our church instruction, we rarely thought about the symbolism of our actions during any given chapel service. We sat when we were told to sit, knelt when instructed to do so. When it was time, we melted communion wafers that tasted like cardboard on our tongues, yet we hardly stopped to consider why we were doing it. After Father James's scolding, however, we took our training seriously. We were shown where the processional candle was kept, how to hold the liturgical Bible during the ceremony so Father James could read from it. We all practiced the correct way to hold the large wooden cross and how to light and properly swing the incense jar, so the smoke didn't blow in just one direction. Afterward, he showed us how to carefully gather the linens, the chalice, and the missal from the credence table, the items he used to help him bless the sacrament, then how to pour a small pitcher of water into a glass bowl so he could wash his hands before the rite of Eucharist. After that we were to help him gather the bread and wine from the gift bearers and place them on the altar. This is when he'd consecrate the bread and wine into the body and blood of Christ. Transubstantiation, he explained to us, and we thought about that, really thought about what it meant to consume flesh and drink blood. It would have seemed cannibalistic if the ceremony itself weren't so solemn and beautiful.

"You are part of the flock now, girls. Stand up straight. Sing with your full voices. No giggling. No whispering. No sound-making of any kind. If you must sneeze, turn your head away from the altar. Above all, try to enjoy the service. This is a celebration, after all," Father James said.

Our first celebration was the following morning, the first Sunday of Advent.

"What if I forget what I'm supposed to do?" questioned Ginny. We were in the cafeteria, taking timid sips of water. Church canon dictated we fast before mass so the host wouldn't mingle in our stomachs, digesting in unholy unison. Not that it mattered. We couldn't have eaten anyway. "What if I have an asthma attack?" In the winter, Ginny's freckles faded, lending her a clear complexion, but also drawing attention to the small scabs along her hairline from where she sometimes nervously pulled her hair from the roots. "I've never been onstage before."

"It's not a stage. It's an altar," Win said.

"Nobody is there to look at us," I told her.

180

"Speak for yourself," Gwen said. She lifted her chin and smoothed her hair.

When it was time, Sister Fran walked us up the hill to the church. Even today, all these years later, that walk had to have been the single coldest moment I can ever recall. Our uniform skirts hit our numbed knees; our calves turned grayish-purple from the chill. We pressed our sweaters closer to our bodies, but the wind just seemed to zip through our clothes, and our teeth rattled like loose bones.

Sister Fran led us to the rectory door before leaving us with the vague warning, "Remember, girls. God sees all."

Father James was sitting in the vestry when we arrived, making some notes in a steno pad. He wore a dark purple frock, and a thin sheen of sweat glistened above his lips. He didn't look up at us when we entered, didn't say good morning or offer us pastries this time, so we made our way to the closet, found our robes, and got dressed. We soon heard the shuffle of feet through the closed door, and the low drone of the organ music sounded our cue. Father James stood and handed Gwen the processional candle, Win the large wooden cross, Ginny the Bible, and me the metal incense holder.

We proceeded to the foyer, our shoes clacking on the marble floor. Father James looked straight ahead—his eyes sad, the way some of our parents' eyes had looked when they dropped us off at the convent: guilty and remorseful, but something else, too, some sort of kindness or softness that both confused us and brought us to silence.

Father James opened the door to the main church with a brisk shove of his arm, and suddenly it was like seeing a world of color again. Like Dorothy when she enters Oz, Ginny told us later. The lights were bright, and the prayer candles flickered and danced as we walked down the aisle. The pews were a sea of reds and blues, greens and purples; parishioners packed together in rows so that their clothing blended like a patchwork quilt. I swung the incense, trying my best not to knock it into my shins. When we reached the altar rail, we all bowed simultaneously, and just at that moment, a cloud of incense smoke caught me in the face, and my tears magnified my vision. We took a deep breath as we stepped up onto the altar, and for the first time The Guineveres stood where before there had been only boys.

The church looked so different from this vantage point. We hadn't really anticipated all the people, despite what Father James had told us. Sunday mass was busier than ever these days, he explained, because the pastor of the parish the next county over had been called away as a war chaplain. To us, however, it was a strange feeling to have lived so long in a convent, secluded from the rest of the world, only to find ourselves on a stage—an altar—with a hundred sets of eyes staring at us as though we were on display. We thought that we'd feel powerful, special because we were the only girls allowed up there on the altar, but we didn't. We tried to sit up straight. We tried to stand with our shoulders back, with dignity, with the Lord, but we became suddenly and fully aware of our own self-consciousness, of our awkward, growing bodies hidden beneath our robes.

As Father James read the opening prayer, we could see many of the parishioners sneak glances at us. We scanned the crowd for girls our own age, and we scrutinized them, as much as they scrutinized us. Their eyebrows arched with curiosity; their heads tilted. They wore patterned scarves over their heads, white gloves, pearls, high-waist dresses with butterflied collars. We grew embarrassed of our rough unmanicured hands, of our sackcloth outfits, of our scratchy uniforms beneath. We knew what they must have been thinking. We beat them to it. One of them whispered to another, and we were certain it was about us. Our faces burned, and we wished we could melt away, like Lot's wife or, as Ginny might say, like the Wicked Witch of the West after she'd been doused with water. Win tried everything in her power to keep her arms at her sides and not cross them in front of her chest, a habit of hers, but in doing so she only looked jittery. Gwen gazed directly out over the parishioners at some unknown point in the distance, her face blanker than I'd ever seen it.

For the petitions, a parishioner in a brown suit walked up to the pulpit from the third pew. He adjusted his pencil-thin tie, unfolded a piece of paper from his breast pocket, and began to rattle off the petitions one by one in a low, monotone voice.

"For the Holy Catholic Church. For our pope and bishop, and all priests and deacons, we pray to the Lord," he said.

Lord Hear Our Prayer, the congregants refrained.

"That Advent be a time of reflection, that it be filled with prayer, repentance, and love, we pray to the Lord," he said. Sweat beads patterned his forehead. He wiped his brow with a handkerchief.

Lord Hear Our Prayer.

"For those who have died, especially David Banyon, William Smith Jr., Johnathan Townsend, Matthew Saunders, George Payton Goodwin III, James McCallihan, and Mark Collins. May we be ever mindful and thankful for their service to God and to country." The lector looked up and out at the parishioners. The Guineveres eyed one another. This was a list of the local boys who had recently died in the War.

Lord Hear Our Prayer, refrained the congregation. We heard a few sobs from the pews. A woman in thick-framed glasses nearly collapsed into the arms of her husband, who helped her take a seat.

"For Peter Drexel, currently missing in action. May he be found and safely returned." Here, the man paused to look toward a couple sitting in the front pew—Peter's parents—agony plastered on their faces in the form of hollow eyes and sleep deprivation. Mr. Drexel swung his arm around Mrs. Drexel's shoulder and pulled her in close. Her mascara was smeared. A single tear streaked down her face. "We pray to the Lord," the man said.

Lord Hear Our Prayer.

"And for our own needs and intentions that we silently recall in our hearts . . ." The lector paused for a few moments, and The Guineveres' thoughts immediately returned to Our Boys in the Sick Ward. *Please let them wake up,* we silently begged. *Please let us be there when it happens. Please let us go home. Please, please, please, please.* "We pray to the Lord."

Lord Hear Our Prayer, the congregation boomed, The Guineveres loudest of them all, despite the fact that we thought the refrain was all wrong. We wanted the Lord to do more than just hear our prayer. We wanted Him to answer it.

In the vestry after mass, we neatly hung our cassocks and put away all of the items we'd used in the service. As we did this, we could hear Father James down the hall, talking to Peter Drexel's parents. We caught only snippets. *Missing in action. No response to our letters. Nobody can tell us anything,* the Drexels' voices said. *You must keep the faith. You must trust God has a larger plan. Miracles do happen,* we heard Father James respond. Silence followed, which we assumed meant they were praying.

We weren't sure if we should head back to the convent or not, but we were hungry, and it was nearing lunch. When Father James still hadn't shown up in the vestry after what felt like a rosary's worth of time, we walked back to his office and opened the door. He was leaning back in his desk chair with his eyes closed, his collar removed, and his shirt gapping at the top to reveal dark coils of hair on his chest. A bottle of wine sat on his desk, an empty glass, too, still coated with liquid.

"Father?" one of us asked.

Startled, Father James popped his eyes open. He looked down at the bottle, and then toward us, before quickly sliding the wine beneath the desk like a little boy hiding a toad from his mother. It was too late, of course. We'd already seen it.

The Guineveres weren't so naïve as to be surprised at the sight of an adult drinking alcohol. But Father James wasn't an adult. He was a priest. Sure, we'd seen him tipsy before, but not up close like this. Besides, it was barely past noon on a Sunday.

"Even in God's house, one should knock before entering," he said. His face was rouged. When he spoke, it sounded like he balanced marbles on his tongue.

"Sorry, Father," one of us said, and we all hung our heads because that's what he probably expected us to do.

Father James mumbled something, but we couldn't quite make out what, then poured himself another glass of wine, his hands shaking as he did so. We stood there quietly, a wall of schoolgirls in front of his desk, not knowing what to do.

Father James leaned forward, looked up at us like a dog might, which is not to say that he was pleading, but that he seemed so unguarded to us at the moment. Or maybe we'd just caught him by surprise. "Proverbs tells us: 'Give wine to those who are bitter of heart. Let him drink and forget his poverty, and remember his misery no more.' We could use that advice, especially these days." He lifted his glass up in the air, jiggered it a bit, then knocked it back in three heavy swallows.

"Can we try some, then, since the Bible says it's okay?" Gwen asked, and we elbowed her. We didn't want to get into trouble. She stared at him brazenly with those blue eyes of hers, as though communicating to him some secret.

Father James set down his glass and, hesitating, lifted the bottle from his desk. Then he corked it and placed it in his drawer. "Do you need anything else, girls?" he asked.

We shook our heads.

"Then you may be excused." Father James leaned back in his seat again, which protested his weight with a shrill meow. We could see the beginnings of whiskers beneath his chin, and the way the light bounced off his cheeks made his skin appear to sparkle.

We were just about out the door when Ginny turned and asked in her delicate voice, "Where is Peter Drexel?"

Father James rubbed circles around his eyes, then cradled his face in his hands. "MIA, I'm afraid. Nobody knows," he said. He buttoned his shirt to the top and began affixing his collar.

"Like the soldiers in the convalescent wing?" I asked.

"No, not quite like them," he said. "There are a lot of Peter Drexels in the War, I'm afraid. And frankly, I'm not sure whose fate is worse: Peter's or those boys down there." Here, waved his hand in the direction of the window and downhill, toward the convent. As he did this, he knocked over a carving of a wooden monk. Win bent down to pick it up.

"Well, they were brave to have gone in the first place," Ginny said. "Peter Drexel willingly sacrificed his life. Some men have been made saints for lesser reasons."

"Well, we don't know the fate of Peter Drexel yet. But not everyone goes to war willingly. Not all men volunteer. Some are forced to go, you know." He removed a handkerchief from his shirt pocket and blew his nose.

"Wouldn't that make it more of a sacrifice? If you don't want to do something, but you go ahead and do it because it's right?" one of us said.

"It depends on what's in your heart," he answered. "But we must always keep the faith, girls. Mustn't we?"

"Yes," we said. "We must have faith."

"And, girls," Father James said as we turned, now halfway out the door. "Excellent job today. I never had a doubt. Not like that old rube Thomas." His mouth crooked into what we could only assume was a boozy smile.

We took our time walking back to the convent. Sister Fran stood in the foyer when we arrived, awaiting our return. We only nodded when she asked us if the mass went well and if we enjoyed our role as altar servers.

"Very good, girls. Very good," she said.

We joined the rest of the girls in the cafeteria for lunch. We didn't notice The Specials glowering at us as we filled our trays or The Sads who slumped disconsolately over their bowls or The

Poor Girls who had eaten so quickly their trays were already empty. We couldn't be bothered by the rest of the girls, who would have appeared positively jejune had we turned to notice.

"Poor Peter Drexel," Ginny said. She stirred her steaming bowl filled with a murky brown liquid. She might have begun to cry.

"They know his name, but not where he is. We know where Our Boys are, but not their names. *Our* parents know exactly where *we* are. *And* they know our names. Could the universe play a crueler trick than that?" Win said. She rubbed at the dark shadows beneath her eyes.

"Do you think Our Boys volunteered for the War? Do you think they wanted to go?" I asked. We all blinked, and it felt like we were blinking underwater.

"They volunteered," Ginny said. "I know it."

"How are you so sure?" Win asked.

"Because I'd hate to imagine it any other way," she answered.

"Did you see Mr. and Mrs. Drexel? The grief on their faces?" Gwen said. "I've seen that look before. It's a look of desperation. And you know what desperate people do?"

"What?" one of us asked.

"Anything. Anything at all." She took a sip of water, smacked her lips, and exhaled loudly. "Maybe we've been going about this in the wrong manner," she said. "We can't wait around forever for a miracle to happen. It's tedious, and anyhow, there's another way out."

"What way is that?" the rest of us asked. At that moment, behind us, Reggie "accidentally" dropped her tray, and Sister Fran blew her whistle. This was the second time Reggie had dropped her tray this week, and she'd probably be given a JUG for it. The Guineveres swore she just did it for attention.

After the commotion settled, Gwen went on. "We'll find out Our Boys' identities, their names, who they are. Then we can locate their parents, who'd be so incredibly grateful for our efforts that they'd let us come home with them. Even if they never wake up."

"They'll wake up," I said.

"Look, they haven't woken up yet. We're running out of options," Gwen said. "And time. Do you want to wait until you're eighteen? Do you really want to waste away here? I, for one, am not willing to sacrifice my youth."

"Go home with them as nurses?" Ginny asked. "We're altar girls now."

"We're practically nurses. You're missing the point. None of the other girls have been trained in the Sick Ward. They wouldn't know the first thing about a blood pressure gauge or how to change sheets with a patient still in the bed without tossing them over the side. We didn't just forget those skills because we became altar girls, you know. You can be more than one thing at once."

"Sister Connie was right. Nursing skills are mighty useful," Win said.

"We're part of the War Effort," I added.

"And there's a great need for nurses during wartime," Gwen said.

"Even if we can figure out who they are, it doesn't mean their parents will let us come home," Ginny said. "Especially if Our Boys haven't woken up yet." She stirred and restirred the contents of her bowl, even though by now it had gone cold.

Gwen plucked a stray hair from between her eyebrows with her fingernails. "Just look at the Drexels," she said. "Do those seem like people who would turn away the very individuals who located their son for them? Wouldn't the parents of missing soldiers, more than anyone, understand the plight of a poor orphan so far from home?" We thought of Mrs. Drexel in the front pew of the church. She looked gaunt from worry, haggard, unkempt. Her hair was matted, unwashed for days. Her nose was red, raw from crying. Her prayer hands were clasped bone-white tight. Mr. Drexel, too, with his sunken cheeks, with his eyes that screwed into slits of grief, as though the world didn't pain him as much if he took in only a little bit at a time. "They're desperate," Gwen said again. "And desperate people do all sorts of things you wouldn't expect. How do you think we wound up here in the first place?"

"But how will we do it?" I asked. "How will we find out their identities when we don't know anything about them?"

"I have an idea," Gwen said. She pinched her cheeks for blush, then grinned.

The Guineveres didn't say a word. We didn't have to. By now we could communicate through blinks and nods and raised eyebrows—through telepathy. Gwen brought her pinky to the center of the table, and we all hooked fingers.

"I'm still counting on them to wake up," Ginny said.

"They will," Gwen said, "but at least we have a secondary plan. God helps those who help themselves."

We agreed.

Then we slurped our lentil soup breathlessly. The world was opening up for us. We felt sharp. We felt focused. We'd never been hungrier in our lives.

Communion

The Guineveres woke up Monday morning groggy from restlessness. It seemed a dry, hazy murk had settled around us. We clamored to the Wash Room and took sips from the faucets, pausing between breaths to splash water on our faces. But even the water couldn't wake us completely. At breakfast we fidgeted in our skirts, scratching our dry skin, leaving white marks like the trail of an airplane in the sky. We buttoned and unbuttoned the cuffs of our sleeves just to have something to do. Poor Ginny fared worse than the rest of us, the lack of sleep manifesting itself as nausea that hit her each time she attempted to raise a bite of squash casserole to her mouth.

"You should eat something," Win said. The Guineveres handed Ginny our bread.

"Two more days," Ginny said, articulating what nobody had yet spoken, perhaps the real reason for our uneasiness. She pinched off a small piece of bread and allowed it to dissolve in her mouth. Two more days until the Wednesday mass in the Sick Ward. Two more days until we could see Our Boys.

"We'd better get used to waiting as military wives," Ginny said.

"Who said anything about being a military wife?" Win said.

In the classroom the next day during Morning Instruction, we stared up at Sister Fran's nativity scene mobile that, when it shifted unbalanced, twirled the wise men like they were pirouetting. We hunched in our desks, pretending to take notes. Sister Fran's heels clicked as she paced the front of the chalkboard. She pointed with her ruler to the name of the day's saint: Saint Bibiana.

"She endured her suffering joyously, as should we all," Sister Fran explained, slowing her strides. She sometimes lectured with her eyes closed, the faintest hint of a grin sweeping across her face. We swore in these moments that Sister Fran was the happiest we'd ever seen her, that if the Rapture came, she'd be sucked right into the sky, her arms and legs pumping with jubilation. Saint Bibiana's father was tortured to death, her mother beheaded. Her sister died at the feet of the ruler who'd persecuted them, and Bibiana, upon whom forced starvation had no effect, was put under the care of a wicked woman who tried to seduce her. "Eventually, they tied her to a pillar. She was beaten to death. And with each blow of the executioner's lead pummel, she cried out in ecstasy. Isn't that wonderful, girls? That she could endure the pains of this life with such elation? That she turned her despair into euphoria, knowing what awaited her in heaven? That is the true beauty of Saint Bibiana, a quality we must strive to emulate. How might we all endeavor to do the same?" This was not posed as a rhetorical question. Sister Fran opened her eyes and examined her bored pupils for an answer. Only Lottie raised a hand.

"Could we give up our Sunday supper and instead have a dance lesson?" she said in all earnestness. A few of The Specials clapped in agreement, but the rest of us groused. If anyone could suffer joyously, it was Lottie, and I often thought of this later, when I learned that she'd died. I imagined her smiling as she careened off the road. Perhaps she moaned in ecstasy as she was thrown through her windshield, landing in a gravel pit a few yards away. Lottie would never fully grow out of her baby-fatted cheeks; she'd never marry; she'd never have kids. Instead, she'd remain in our memories a young, earnest, and faithful girl. Although Lottie and I never became close—not like The Guineveres—I still suffered a loss when she died. We all did. Call it the camaraderie of heartbreak or the shared trauma of growing up. I was sad to learn the news.

"We could consider that a possibility," Sister Fran said. "But I don't see much usefulness in dancing. Perhaps knitting instead. Let there be utility even in our recreation, and besides, the War Effort can always use socks." Soon the bell sounded, but we remained in our seats because it was Mail Distribution.

The radiator hummed while we waited. Sister Fran removed a stack of mail from a satchel beneath her desk. With three weeks till Christmas, we were anxious—guardedly hopeful—for some word from home. Even a card signed only with our parents' names.

"Anything?" Ginny asked Sister Fran when she paused beside her desk. Sister Fran pretended to shuffle through envelopes, scrutinizing the names of addressees. Her nose wiggled. She clicked her tongue for show.

"It doesn't look like anything has arrived this week, dear." She patted the top of Ginny's head. "I'm sorry."

"For me?" I asked. I already knew the answer, and Sister Fran didn't even pretend.

"Not this time," she said. "Perhaps you should write another letter," she suggested, then placed her arm warmly around my shoulder. "Better to give than receive. That's an excellent policy to remember, don't you think? Something therapeutic in letter writing, like baring one's soul. The benefit is yours just by writing it." She walked ahead to finish doling out the mail. That week, Shirley received a box of Christmas decorations that she promised to hang in the Bunk Room. Dorrie Sue opened her envelope to discover a silk handkerchief, folded into a tiny square. Nan got a Christmas card that, to her delight, chimed "Silent Night" when she opened it. The Sads cried again into their short, apologetic letters. The Delinquents and the older girls held their notebooks to their chests, ready for Sister Fran to dismiss them. The Guineveres, we bit the inside of our lips. We blinked. We swallowed. We tried to act nonchalant, like secretaries on a smoke break.

Later that day, we traced the perimeter of the courtyard during our constitutional walk. The geraniums had long since died inside the shoe planters, their purple heads languishing over the laces. The cold stung our eyeballs; our noses leaked. We could hear the strained warbles of birds overhead.

"I bet Our Boys' parents would write them letters," Ginny said.

"If they knew where they were," Win said.

"Do you think their parents assume that they're dead?" I asked.

"Do you think our parents assume we are?" Gwen said.

"I'm not sure they'd care," Win said.

"Look at the Drexels. They care," Ginny said.

"They care too much," Win said. "And it's killing them."

"There's a danger in caring too much," Gwen said. She was looking toward the sky, the way Ebbie used to do, but there were no planes up there today. Only gray.

To our great relief, Wednesday finally arrived. The mass in the Sick Ward overlapped with Morning Instruction, so Sister Fran made us dittos of the day's lesson so we wouldn't fall behind. We tucked these papers inside our notebooks, stored them beneath our desks, then tried to hide our pure giddiness as we excused ourselves. Father James waited for us in the Sick Ward, still dressed in his lay clothes. He directed us to relocate all the tables to the side of the room, so the old folks could line up in rows facing the makeshift altar at the front. Win carried the chairs two at a time over her head while Gwen leaned up against the wall, counting.

"We need three more," she said.

"Don't worry about helping," Win said and rolled her eyes.

"I won't."

Ginny pushed the tables with her arms in front of her, so she looked like Sisyphus, minus the hill. I lined the chairs up into rows and lowered the window shades to prevent the sun from directly hitting the room.

After we were finished, Father James provided us with robes he said we could keep in the Sick Ward, for future use, and Sister Connie instructed us to change in the storage room. The storage room itself was dimly lit with one overhead bulb, and it was lined with shelves packed with linens and bed shirts, stacks of metal bedpans, glass jars filled with medicine, huge rolls of gauze and boxes of cotton balls, and other medical supplies. She cleared a space on the shelf for us to store our cassocks, next to a Bible and a small processional cross. As we pulled the stiff robes over our heads, we spotted Our Boys' duffels wedged beneath the bottom-most shelf. The numbers, written in white, were facing out, so we could make out whose was whose. "There's My Boy's," Ginny said, pointing.

Once we were ready, we met Father James at the entrance to the Front Room. Those old folks who could walk with the help of a cane or a walker ambled toward the chairs now lined in rows. The Guineveres passed out hymnals while Sister Magda widened the door to the Back Room so that those who were too weak or unable—Our Boys included in this number—could hear the service from their beds.

Although we had already served our first mass as altar girls, we didn't feel much more confident in what we were doing. Our muscle memories had not kicked in yet, plus the process was different here in the Sick Ward. First, it wasn't a church. Second, there was no official processional; we simply walked from the back of the room to the front. Father James asked Ginny to carry the Bible and Win to carry the small cross, and the rest of us walked with our hands folded at our stomachs. No organ music played, there was no tabernacle, and Father James had already blessed the host, so we skipped the bearing of the gifts. Father James kept mass short: only the first reading, then the Gospel, then the homily. No second reading. No petitions. The old folks sang hymns in muffled, unenthused voices; some slumped forward in their chairs, their muscles tired from sitting so long. During communion, Father James walked from person to person, and the old folks opened their mouths as though a doctor had instructed them, "Say ahhhh." A few looked like wrinkled children forced to take medicine, and others chewed the host with their dentures, despite the fact that they were supposed to let it dissolve on their tongues. Once Father James had administered to everyone in the Front Room, he motioned for us to follow him to the Back Room. Our eyes scanned the dimness for Our Boys, and when we saw them a wave of warmth washed over us.

Father James walked to the bedside of the closest patient, Mrs. Martin. Mrs. Martin had what Sister Connie had told us was a terminal illness. Some days she was awake, and other days she was not. Thin tufts of hair grew out of her freckled head, and her chin melted into her neck. Win held what we called the Holy Crumb Tray beneath her wilting mouth; Ginny held the bowl of hosts; Gwen stood by with the chalice of wine. Father James picked up a wafer from the bowl, broke off a small piece, dipped it into the chalice, then motioned to me to pry open the mouth of Mrs. Martin. I pinched her nose and squeezed her chin, then tugged just gently enough so her lips parted. Father James muttered his blessing, then rested the host atop her tongue.

"Amen," The Guineveres said without prompting.

Next we moved over to Miss Oatley, whose dentures rested on her bedside table. Her mouth hung ajar, revealing oversized baby gums, so thankfully I didn't have to pry it open in order for her to receive communion. Touching the old folks' faces, even to feed them the host, twisted my stomach, which is exactly what guilt feels like: heavy, as if one had eaten a handful of pebbles, swallowed them whole.

Father James administered communion to every old person in the room, but he did not offer it to Our Boys. Instead, he stopped at the side of each of their beds and prayed a blessing, extending his hand close to their heads like a cook checking the temperature of a stove burner. We asked him about it at the conclusion of the service.

"We have no way of knowing their faith," Father James said.

"But Sister Fran said taking communion gives us eternal life. Couldn't you give it to them just to be on the safe side?" Ginny asked.

"Even if we knew their faith," Father James

explained, "we have no way of knowing if they're in a state of grace or if they've given confession since their last mortal sin. And they've certainly not been observing the Eucharistic fast," Father James said, pointing to their feeding bags, IVs connected by tubes to their forearms. "It is my duty as a priest to administer under the strictest of guidelines, and I take these duties seriously."

After mass, we helped rearrange the Front Room again, and we put away the service items, the hymnbooks, the candles, the bowl, and chalice. Father James left, Sister Connie went to check on lunch, and we were free again to change. Inside the storage room, as we folded our robes and finger-combed our static-heightened hair, Gwen began tugging Her Boy's duffel—the one marked with the long string of numbers ending| in 63—out from the space beneath the shelf where it had been wedged.

"Well," she said to us. "Aren't you going to get yours?"

"We'll get in trouble," I said.

"We're already in trouble," she said.

"Is now the time for this?" Win asked.

"Now is precisely the time for this. It's their personal effects. How else do you expect to learn anything about them? Do you think the Comatose Soldier Fairy will appear?"

Ginny began dragging out Her Boy's duffel and even managed to unclip the closure strap.

We didn't know what we should expect to find. Nothing like dog tags or birth certificates would be inside them; otherwise they'd have names listed on the outside and not simply a number.

"One at a time," Win said. "So we can each see. We need all of our eyeballs if we're going to figure out who they are. We've got to work together." Win was always so reasonable, so levelheaded. That's why it surprised me years later to learn that she struggled with alcohol, just like her mother. Seems to me she would have had the foresight to resist it, but I know now from her stories, from all that she lost—her friends, her jobs—that addiction is stronger than willpower. It runs through one's blood.

Gwen demanded to go first. She unstrapped the canvas. On top was a pressed uniform: khaki pants, khaki shirt, a hat that resembled what a line cook would wear, also khaki, some boots. She pulled out a pair of white boxer shorts, tugged at the elastic, and waved them in a hula-like fashion. The Guineveres covered our faces in embarrassment.

"Show some decency," one of us said.

"Hurry up," another one of us said.

From the bottom of the bag, she pulled out a box. It was light, made of green-tinged metal. She pinched the clasp on the front, and the box emitted a shallow creak as she lifted the lid on its hinge.

"What's in it? What's in it?" Ginny said. A clue about one of Our Boys was a clue about all of them.

Gwen reached inside the box. "Comb," she said, pulling it out and setting it on the floor in front of her. "Sugar packet. Chiclets. Matches." She sorted through the box some more, then pulled out two postcards. "These," she said. The postcards were identical. The front pictured blue-green water, rocky hills covered with trees, an inlet with some fishing boats.

"Read them!" one of us said.

"Blank," Gwen said, and she held up the first one to show us, its corners bent and frayed from where it'd been stuffed into his pocket. On the second postcard, Gwen's Boy had only just begun to write something. His handwriting was boxy and crooked, as though his hands were shaking when he wrote it. "Dear M—," Gwen read. "This postcard reminded me of home. If you are reading this . . ." She stopped, flipped the card over again to inspect the front once more.

"If you are reading this . . . what?" Ginny said. She grabbed the postcard out of Gwen's hand.

"That's all it says."

"Who is M?" I wondered out loud.

"It could be his mom," Win said.

"Or a girl back home," Gwen said. She pulled from the box a small photograph and flashed it in our direction. A picture of a young woman, tight brown curls, a small, curved nose like the beak of a bird. " 'Love, Marjorie P.,' it says."

"Could be his sister," Win said.

"And this?" Gwen said. She now held out the flat of her hand on which sat a ring, a thin gold band with some nick marks on it.

"Could be . . . ," Win said, but even she couldn't wager a guess.

"Do you think he's married?" I asked. Ginny handed a postcard to me, and I analyzed it. Craggy shores. Small, rippled waves. Rock formations that arose from the water like humpbacks. It was like no place that I'd ever seen, though I'd never been to the ocean.

"Engaged," Ginny said.

"He may never have gone through with it," Gwen said. "In fact, I'm certain that he hasn't. Not yet, anyway. I mean, look at Marjorie P. Does she look like the marriageable type?" We shook our heads. Loyalty to The Guineveres meant agreeing, even when you didn't.

"Clues, anyway," Ginny said. "You know what his home looks like. There's a Marjorie P. there."

"And just how do you suggest we locate Marjorie P.?" Win said.

"And what will we do if we find her?" Gwen asked. She placed his ring on her wedding finger. Her lips puckered. She already felt territorial.

"All finished? My turn," Ginny said. Her

patience was wearing thin, and she began to lift items out of Her Boy's bag. Standard uniform. Another metal box. She licked her lips and opened it, quickly rummaging through the contents. "Comb, of course."

"Good grooming is essential. Even during wartime," Gwen said. Win cracked the door to the storage room to check for Sister Connie.

"Gum. Playing cards. Some sort of meshy material. And this," Ginny said. Between her forefinger and thumb she held an hourglass. She handed it to me, and I watched the small granules slip through the narrowed neck. "And this," she said. Now she held out a box, about the size of her palm. The outside was shellacked with a painting of a snake encircling itself, eating its own tail. She shook it, and we could hear a soft sifting noise. "Something's inside." The box rattled as she pulled at the lid.

Finally, she dumped the contents into her trembling palm, and we circled in front of her.

"What is it?" one of us asked. Whatever she held was brown, mottled with spots, shriveled, and folding in at the edges.

"A fig?" someone suggested. We all touched it, and it felt hard.

"Could it be medicinal?" someone asked. "An exotic mushroom or something?"

"A piece of leather?"

"A lucky talisman," Ginny said. She gently

closed her fist around it, as if cupping a firefly, the kind we watched at night from the window of the Bunk Room. She rifled through the box some more, with her eyes closed this time. She was trying to memorize the contents by heart.

Win had already begun opening Her Boy's duffel. She skipped removing his uniform and dug down for the box she knew she'd find at the bottom of the bag. She sat on her heels, knees together, box balanced on her lap. She unlatched the lever and swung open the lid. "Comb," she said, and with the flick of her wrist she pulled it out of the box as quickly as she placed it back in.

"The sign of a gentleman," said Gwen.

"What else?" I said.

"He smokes." She held up a miniature pack of cigarettes, the cherry-red package crumpled and flattened.

"I'll take one of those," Gwen said.

"You don't smoke," Ginny said.

"It's an attractive addiction. Light my cigarette, darling," she said, and she held two fingers to her lips, an imaginary cigarette tucked between them.

"There's no such thing as an attractive addiction," Win said.

From the box, Win soon produced a small wooden paddle, no bigger than half a ruler in size. Atop it sat a brown speckled horse, and atop that a cowboy with a wide-brimmed hat. The horse's hooves were mounted to the paddle by elastic strings, and when she manipulated the two buttons on the sides of it, she could move the horse in different directions. Push both buttons at once, the horse crouched down. Only one at a time and in succession and he appeared to be galloping. Win laughed in simple amusement.

"Juvenile," Gwen said. She still wore Her Boy's ring, which was several sizes too big for her. She hadn't put it away with the rest of his belongings, explaining we should each keep one memento by which to remember Our Boys.

"Could he have been a cowboy?" I asked. "Lived out west? Maybe they all live out west as ranchers or herders."

"Executives, remember?" Gwen said. "How many times do I have to explain this?"

Finally, then, it was my turn. I unclasped the hook, and I reached my hand past his uniform, and just as I felt the cool metal on my fingertips, we heard Sister Connie. "Girls! For goodness sake, are you still changing?" she hollered.

The Guineveres' bodies went rigid, as if steel had been poured through our veins. "Almost finished, Sister!" someone yelled. We scrambled to shove the duffels back in their rightful places beneath the shelf.

"Here we are," we said, popping out of the storage room a few minutes later.

"Hurry up or you'll be late," Sister Connie said. "You know how Sister Fran values punctuality."

We peeked at Our Boys once more, sent silent intentions aimed at their hearts. "Saint Adrian will watch over them," I whispered. He was the patron saint of soldiers, a fact we learned during our All Saints' bingo lesson.

"But don't forget what happened to Saint Adrian," Gwen said. She turned toward me. "His limbs were cut off one by one."

"And then his head," Ginny said.

"And then his head," Gwen repeated. Gwen traced a line with her index finger on my neck.

"Who's the patron saint of the patron saints?" Win asked. She knew how to defray tensions, a skill that would help her in her later life when she'd really need it. It's not that Win didn't care what others thought of her—it's that she cared too deeply. Once, when she talked to me from her home out west, she told me she'd finally discovered the key to happiness in life. *"Care less,"* she said, putting equal emphasis on each word. This was after she left the man she was supposed to marry, and after she quit drinking, but before she opened her bakery. Maybe this was her way of telling me that sometimes you just have to let go. I've tried to take the suggestion to heart. Sometimes in the mornings while I'm lying in bed, I breathe in and out slowly, in and out. *Let. Go. Let. Go.* It hasn't come easily to me.

We heaved a heavy sigh toward Our Boys, then left to find the rest of the girls, who were still finishing up Morning Instruction. Sister Fran stood writing at the board when we arrived, a chalky line across her back from where she'd leaned up against it. "Take your seat, girls," Sister Fran said to us without turning around. Her parrot, Ugly, was in the classroom today, which meant we were having morality lessons. "Say 'God doesn't make junk,' Pretty," Sister Fran commanded the bird as she picked it up. It adjusted its wings and sidestepped along her slender forearm.

The bird squawked unintelligible noises, a string of vowel sounds.

"God doesn't make junk," Sister Fran repeated, kissing the air. In her other hand she held a thin biscuit the color of a communion wafer, and the bird lunged toward the treat. "No, no, Pretty," Sister Fran said, bringing the bird toward her, nose to beak.

"Dear me, where's my whistle," the bird sang. "Dear me, where's my whistle."

The room filled with laughter. The Guineveres took our seats, picked up our pencils, and copied down the day's lesson plans. Sister Fran lectured on the history of the Advent wreath: Purple candles signify penance, and the pink candle signifies joy, she explained. Each candle represents a thousand years and shows just how long humanity had to wait for Our Savior, and just how lucky we were when He finally was born on

Christmas morning to save us all. The Guineveres nodded. We pretended to take notes. But instead, we took Sister Fran's suggestion and scribbled out letters.

Ginny wrote on a new page of her notebook she had titled "Advent" in large block letters as a decoy. "I'll think about you every time I look at your Lucky Talisman. I'll keep it hidden in my shirt, and at night I'll keep it beneath my pillow. But I'm not sure how lucky it was if you were injured so badly. Maybe it saved your life, though. Maybe you could have died. What do you think happens to us when we die?" Ginny tapped her pencil to the tip of her nose.

"If you're actually reading this letter . . . that means you're awake," Gwen wrote in her notebook. "And that means I need some answers: Do you think I'm prettier than Marjorie P.?"

"Someday I'd like to move out west," Win wrote to Her Boy. "And ride horses. I've never been on a horse before. Have you? It seems like 'out west' is another way of saying somewhere better than here. At least that's how I think of it. But if that's the case, then almost everywhere is out west."

I stared at the blank page of my notebook and doodled some hearts and some stars, and an angel with feathery hair. I knew almost nothing about My Boy. I tapped my pencil to my teeth. Beneath Ginny's desk she rubbed Her Boy's mysterious object, her Lucky Talisman that she hoped would bring her luck. Win had stuffed the small wooden toy inside her waistband. She bloused her shirt out to obscure the lump, and I wouldn't have even known it was there, except for the fact that she kept touching it. Gwen discreetly pulled Her Boy's ring from her bra, then tucked it in the cave of her fist. I looked on in envy. They each had something of Their Boys to hold.

"I just want to go home," I wrote in my notebook. But we had no homes, so we had to find out who Our Boys were. We'd learn their names, their hometowns. We'd track down their parents, and they'd wake up, just like Junior did. And the end of our story would be like a fairy tale, I assured myself. It would not be like a saint's life, which almost always ended in suffering, no matter how joyous. I gazed up at the nativity mobile above Sister Fran's desk. Those foam wise men spun and spun. One's mouth was agape in wonder—or in pain. It's hard to tell the two apart.

Win's Revival

My mother said we were going for a ride, and I didn't think to ask why she was shoving Grandfather's old trunk into the back of the car. "Help me, Guinevere," she said, so I did as I was told, because I always did as I was told, especially since my incident at school.

My mother held one end, and I grabbed the other, gripped its metal edges, and angled it into the car. The trunk was heavy; it smelled of mothballs, and its leather peeled in places, flipped up like browned rose petals. Grandfather usually kept the trunk in his closet—he'd brought it over with him from the Old Country—and sometimes I found it as good a place as any to sit and hide, the closet door cracked just enough so it wasn't too stuffy. I loved that old trunk. Its leather warmed quickly, and it was wide enough so I could lie across it, my legs hanging to the floor, to where Grandfather kept his shoes. In these moments, I'd run my hands along its edges and imagine its history. I wondered what it was like in the Old Country or if it was a better place than here, more fitting, somehow, for people like me.

My mother had been avoiding me since my incident, still sleeping at breakfast, and gone until after I had cleared the dinner plates. She had dark eyes, big bones, and a sharp nose like Grandfather, like me, which had the effect of conveying sternness, even when she was in the best of moods. When she glowered, however, she could inspire fear, the heart-racing kind, so I'd been hiding out on Grandfather's trunk for hours just to be safe, doing homework or sleeping or practicing piano on the cardboard cutout of a keyboard, since we couldn't afford the real thing. Whenever I did see my mother, she cried. I believed it was my fault, and I felt badly, really badly, because more than anything I wanted my mother to be happy. Sister Fran might say that's proof of putting others before yourself, which is virtuous. But I didn't feel virtuous. I felt alone.

We'd moved in with my grandparents since my father "went away," and I knew my mother felt lonely, too. She couldn't handle it when I made much noise, dragged my feet on the linoleum, chugged my Coca-Cola too loudly, or accidentally burped from too many bubbles. "Please, Guinevere," she'd say, lighting a cigarette and pouring herself another vodka. She wore lipstick, which stuck to the rim of the glass in greasy, fish-shaped marks. "You'll never get a man that way."

What did I want a man for, besides? I wasn't even fifteen. The boys in my class wore fuzz on their chins; their posture was unbalanced, tipped forward, as though cell division had proven exhausting. If these were the men my mother was talking about, I'd gladly pass.

Grandmother would rest her warm hands against my cheeks. She didn't talk much—my mother claimed she was "slow"—but I loved her just the same. "Let her be," she'd say, looking at me. "The girl is good."

I did the best I could in school, though I can't say I was happy there. I never excelled in my classes, but I never failed, either. Often I found that what came easy to others didn't come as easily to me. I had to try harder, which didn't seem fair. During gym class, however, I could outrun any of the girls or climb the knotted ropes so quickly that Linda Carol called me a tree witch. I'm not sure where the tree part came from, but I don't think she meant it in a mean way. Linda was the kind of girl you'd call "sturdy"—long, thick arms and legs, and a waist that came in small around her middle. I loved that her last name was a first name, too. She touched up her makeup while standing at her locker between bells, but she could just as easily jump cannonball-style into the school's pool, even after our teacher told her not to because it wasn't ladylike. The feral boys clamored around her in a pack, and as much as I wanted to hate her, I couldn't help but think she was the most beautiful girl I'd ever seen. I found myself staring at her, wondering what it'd be like to be one of the boys who put his arm around her high waist, wondering what'd be like to have Linda's warm body pressed up against my own. I'm not sure where these thoughts came from, but they scared me.

School distracted me from my home life, but things got worse around the holidays. One day I came home and found my mother passed out in the bathroom, her hand still clutched around a vial, tiny white pills spilled out on the floor like a Connect-the-Dots game. I called for Grandfather—he'd know what to do—but nobody was home, so I ran to the neighbors' house, and they called the emergency line. My mother revived with the help of the paramedics, two men dressed in matching white outfits with sorry looks that spread across their faces when they saw me holding my mother's hand. But I never cried. Not once.

Mother was angry with me for a week for calling on the Vogels. Said she could never face them again, so she might as well move somewhere far away where she wouldn't be recognized. I only ever wanted to please my mother, but I felt I could never do anything right.

"I was fine," she said. "I was just tired." She hugged me, which was something she didn't do often, and her fat tears landed on my head. She kissed my cheeks and buried her nose in my hair. I didn't know what to say, so I said nothing, just stood still as a mannequin until she finally let go.

I knew her behaviors related somehow to the

fact that my father "went away." I can't say I was surprised he left, so I'm not sure why anyone else would be. My mother and father fought all the time, except when they were ignoring each other. "Please, Meredith," my father would say. At least he was polite about it. Nobody told me where he had gone, but "away" suggested it wasn't a vacation, and he wouldn't be returning with souvenirs like he did when he had jobs out of town. "Away" meant "not here," and though I was never told, I knew he wasn't coming back. I'd never see him again. But I didn't cry about it.

At night, I heard my mother talk to Grandmother in a drunken whisper, which actually meant she spoke loudly, not whispering at all. "It's all so embarrassing," my mother sobbed one night. "I saw Mona Thomas at the grocery store, and she turned her cart down the cereal aisle to avoid me. Me!" I could tell by her voice that my mother had been drinking. Grandmother, for her part, responded in a kind tone, and my mother cried harder, accusing Grandmother of taking *his* side. I began to imagine a story about my father's new life in a different city: a wife and a kid, a small house just like ours. I wondered if he looked in on his new kid like he used to look in on me at night when he thought I was asleep. I'd keep my eyes closed, playing possum, because if I did, he'd stand there for a while, and I could feel the weight of his shadow above me. If he found me awake, he'd simply shut the door, his footsteps fading down the hallway. Father had never been around much—he was frequently off traveling for his job, though I was never clear what that was, exactly—but those times he was home, he called me names like "kid" and "hon." I liked it when he did that, called me by a nickname. Made me feel like I was special, the same way it did when Linda Carol called me a tree witch, I guess.

My mother appeared to be getting better after what she called her "fainting spell." She began cooking again and even made my favorite dessert twice in one week, banana pudding with vanilla wafers. She brought out the Christmas decorations early—she knew I loved Christmas—and had the tree all trimmed one day when I arrived home from school. The blue lights sparkled at even intervals, and if I squinted while I looked at them, I could pretend I was in a snow globe, like the ones I had seen at the department store where my mother had taken me only a few days earlier for a new pair of shoes.

"Why do I get new shoes in the middle of the year?" I had asked my mother after she flagged down an attendant, a balding man who resembled a weasel, with a long neck and close-set eyes. Usually I got a pair of school shoes in the fall and a pair of sandals in the summer. New shoes were a luxury we could rarely afford. The weasely man returned with a metal foot measure and knelt down on the floor in front of me. He looked up and waited.

My mother ignored my question. "Someday, Guinevere, a man will kneel down before you, and it won't be to measure your feet." My mother may have been drunk; I smelled alcohol only faintly, so it may have been her perfume. I slipped off my loafer and placed my socked foot onto the grid. "Let's hope you say yes," she said. The depart-ment store clerk slid the measure around my foot with the look of a man performing a specialized science.

I was allowed to pick out any shoes I wanted, so I chose a pair of white saddle shoes, like the ones Linda wore to school. Plus, my mother nodded approvingly once the clerk helped me lace them up and asked me to pace across the room to see how they fit. I never wanted to disappoint my mother.

But somehow I did. At school, Linda had called me a tree witch again. This time I wasn't climbing a rope. Her lips were moving in slow motion, forming O's, then parting as she smiled, her tongue resting on her teeth. We were standing in the locker room, the only girls left, and I moved in close to her, so close that I could smell her hair. I had never done anything like that before, had never smelled anything so sweet, not like candy, but like apples and air, like autumn itself. She tucked her hair behind her ears, and I could see her face and a mole that rose from the surface of her neck. I wanted to touch it, that mole, her neck that sloped so gently, like a straight line and a curve all at once.

Linda kept blinking quickly, nervously, like she was thinking the same thing. She had dark eyes, like mine, but hers were round and bright, and I swear they sparkled, even in the dim light of the locker room. Her jawline was straight, and her chin came to a tip, like the point of a heart. Her skin was smooth and even as sand, but lighter than mine. She kept biting her lip, like she was thinking that it was confusing what she was feeling right now, but it was kind of okay, too. She moved in closer to me, or me to her. And we stood there and we stood there. And I thought maybe she was daring me to go first, like when she called me a tree witch and dared me to go higher. So finally I just did it—just pressed my lips against hers, and it was the warmest sensation I ever felt, like my whole body might explode from warmth. Like it'd been dark inside me and someone had finally turned on a light bulb. I buzzed in my limbs, and in other places I didn't know could buzz.

We may have been like that for a second, or maybe minutes. Just kissing and standing and touching each other lightly on the arms and neck. But then Linda pushed me away, hard, with the tips of her fingers. Her expression dropped. She scrunched her shoulders forward and turned her head. "I'm not like you," she said, but her voice didn't sound like when she'd called me a tree witch. There was no kindness to it, just a hard edge that cut me across my chest until I was breathless.

I felt my body grow cold, then hot, and I did the only thing I could. I reeled back, and with all my weight, I punched her. I punched Linda Carol, right in the face. She cupped her nose and blood ran from beneath her hand. And at that point I didn't feel anything, not remorse or regret, not even the usual gut-heaviness I felt when I looked at her.

My mother didn't yell at me when she picked me up from school, suspended for a week. "My daughter . . . the boxer," she said. "I'm so embarrassed." Then, later, Linda's mother called. My mother cradled the phone with her shoulder, a bottle in one hand, a glass in the other. I listened from the stairs, holding the rails like prison bars. "My Guinevere would never do anything of the kind," she said, then waited, slugging back quick gulps of vodka. "I've never heard anything more preposterous in my life." More waiting. More drinking. "Well, if that's the case, blame her father." She slammed down the phone, and it made a high-pitched ding that sounded louder in the silence. My mother wouldn't look at me. But I didn't cry, not even when she turned away from me with a look of disgust and walked into the kitchen.

I spent the next few days hiding from my mother, from my shame. I spent much of my time tucked away, sitting on Grandfather's trunk, keeping up with my homework. Grandfather told me that education was key, that if I stayed in school I could do anything I wanted, anything at all. Not like him. He'd dropped out of school back in the Old Country. Grandfather used to let me sit with him in his workshop while he tinkered with the car, or changed the oil, or built boxes for the chicken coop he had in the backyard. He taught me how to swing a hammer, all the way through the nail so you get the most leverage. Once he let me help him saw down a dying ash tree by the side of the house, showed me how to measure the tree around, how to cut a notch so we'd know which way the tree would fall. Grandfather praised me for catching on so quickly, said that I was smart and strong and that girls like me didn't come along very often. If I couldn't be good like my mother wanted me to be, and if I couldn't be pretty like Linda, I wanted to be smart. And even if school didn't always come easily to me, I convinced myself that if I tried hard enough, everyone would see in me what Grandfather saw. That even if I wasn't book smart, I was still smart in my own way. I liked being called smart. It meant I could figure things out on my own; it meant that I didn't need anyone.

I was sitting on Grandfather's trunk, struggling

over some math problems when I heard the bell ring and then the commotion downstairs. Someone was knocking into things, tipping over lamps and tripping over furniture. I knew it was my mother, and I knew she was drunk again. Grandmother began crying, and Grandfather, who was usually so calm, yelled, "Meredith, please," just like my father used to. Then it grew really quiet. Mother was nowhere to be found at dinner, and Grandmother and Grandfather ate in silence.

"You're a good girl," Grandmother said.

I nodded, took another bite of tuna noodle casserole that had grown cold on my plate. I didn't feel good.

It was only a couple of days later when my mother asked for help shoving Grandfather's old trunk in the back of the car. "We're going for a ride," she said. These were the first words she'd spoken to me since my incident. She wore her winter dress, cream with a red belt, the one she usually reserved for Christmas. At that moment, I would have done anything she asked, so I scrambled to help her. I lifted and heaved that trunk with all my might into the car. I didn't think to ask her why.

Grandfather appeared at the door once the car started up. "Where are you going?" he asked, probing my mother suspiciously. The car was his, after all; my mother just borrowed it. He stood on the porch, leaning up against the rail that I knew to be wobbly. Glancing up at him from this angle, I could see the lines on his face, deep crinkles on his forehead and around his eyes. His white hair looked like wispy clouds that were trying to lift off his head.

"We're just going for a little ride," my mother said. "This girl could use some scenery." Grandfather widened his eyes and cocked his head in a quizzical yet vaguely threatening manner. He called for Grandmother, who came out of the house and stood next to Grandfather on the porch.

"Where you riding to?" Grandmother asked. She stood next to Grandfather and wrapped her arm around him. I wish I had a picture of the two of them standing there like that, my grandmother in her apron, my grandfather in his favorite old checked shirt. But I can tell you, if I did have that picture, it would only make me sad.

"Well, I can't tell you without ruining the holidays, now can I?" Mother said. She rested her hand on my shoulder.

"I just made a blueberry buckle," Grandmother said. Her apron was smeared with dusty flour handprints. "Why don't you come get some while it's still warm?" Grandmother took a step forward, and Grandfather placed his hand on her shoulder. "Come on, Guinevere," she said, waving me out of the car.

I turned to my mother, who was sitting next to me in the driver's seat. Her hands were on the wheel, and she was checking her makeup in the rearview mirror. Eyeliner extended out past her eyelid, like a genie's. I touched the car handle, intending to open the door, but my mother gripped my shoulder, her fingers digging into me. "Not now. We don't have time," she said, then hollered out the car window, "We'll get it later. Keep it warm for us." My mother put the car in reverse and backed out slowly as Grandmother and Grandfather both now walked toward us. Their faces stretched into a look I recognized only in retrospect.

"I love you," I could hear Grandmother say, her voice fading over the sound of the car.

"I love you, too," I said, not realizing it was the last time I'd ever see them.

The sky was slate colored, no sun in sight. Yet, despite this, my mother wore her sunglasses. Tears dribbled from beneath the frames.

"Are you okay?" I asked her. She didn't respond, just faced forward, both hands on the wheel. I turned my head and watched out the window as the trees blurred by us; their leafless limbs were crooked fingers pointing us somewhere. But I didn't know where yet.

After a while, my mother turned on the radio, and we listened to Christmas music, which made me feel kind of sad—the opposite of what Christmas music is supposed to make you feel. My mother kept blotting her eyes with a handkerchief.

"Why'd you do it, Guinevere?" she finally asked. "Tell me what I've done wrong."

"You didn't do anything wrong," I said quietly.

"Tell me I've been a good mother. Tell me I've been good at something," she said.

"You've been a very good mother," I said. And at that point, I really meant it because I didn't know how else I could feel toward her.

"If only your father had been here for you."

We drove for a long time in silence until the road narrowed and we appeared to be in the country. Wherever we were, I had never been there; I knew that much.

"Where are we going?" I finally asked, but she didn't say anything. "I won't do it again," I said. "I'm sorry. I don't know why I did it. But I'm sorry."

My mother placed her gloved hand on my knee and patted it.

Finally, we crested a hill, passed a church, then turned down a long gravel drive, and in the distance I saw this huge stone building, a fortress on the horizon.

"Are we going to church?" I asked, confused. I could see crosses sticking out from the roof, though no signs marked the place. It reminded me of pictures from my history books. I remembered that King Henry VIII lived in one, and he'd killed some of his wives, chopped off their heads.

"We're here," she said.

"Where?" I asked.

My mother didn't say anything.

I could hear the slow crunch of the gravel as my mother parked the car. She paused to take a deep breath, checked her lipstick in the rearview mirror, and opened her door. I got out of the car, too, and followed her as she walked toward the stone building, up a short flight of stairs, through an archway, and to a door rounded at its edges.

The door opened before my mother had the chance to knock.

A set of eyes peered out, and at first I thought these eyes belonged to an old man. When the door opened wider, however, I was surprised to see a nun standing before us. Were we here to volunteer? Was this my punishment? We hadn't been to a church since my father went away. Since long before he went away, and even then only on holidays. But my grandparents did have a crucifix hanging in the house, and every once in a while I saw Grandmother praying to it, her lips muttering something in the language of the Old Country.

"I'm glad to make your acquaintance," Sister Fran said. "Welcome." She took my hand into hers; it felt frail and thin—like fish bones. We stepped into the cold foyer, colder even than the winter day we had just left behind us. The place smelled like a church, like spice-scented smoke that made my throat tickle. Ever since, when I smell incense I think of that moment, standing in the chilly foyer, Sister Fran to one side of me, my mother to the other, like I was being given away at the altar. Or just given away.

"This is Guinevere," my mother said.

"I'm Sister Frances Nazarene," she said to me, now shaking my hand as she held it. "You may call me Sister Fran." She faced my mother. "Do you have her things?"

I turned toward my mother, but she stared down at her feet. She was wearing blue eye shadow, spread evenly from her lashes to her brow. My mother nodded. "Just for a little while." She finally looked up. Her lips were pursed, and her eyes looked like two dark marbles sinking into sand—they were shiny, but she wasn't crying. "Until we get things sorted out." Then she kissed me on the cheek. Her lips were dry.

My mother walked away.

"You can't leave me here!" I shouted. "Come back!"

"We'll have none of that here," Sister Fran said. "Happy are those who long only for their souls. And from what I understand, my girl, we have a lot of work to do." She walked toward a small corner table and picked something up, then stood in front of me. I was too frightened to move. "The joy of God is the innocent," she said. "You shall be washed of your sins." There was a lilt to her voice that sounded like an accent, but it was not—just primness, I later realized. She reached out her thumb and rubbed my forehead with something cold and wet. The liquid dribbled down my face like a tear. But I wasn't crying.

Someone brought in Grandfather's trunk, which was filled with my things. I was given my uniform, asked to remove my new saddle shoes, the ones like Linda Carol wore. "We'll keep them in your trunk," Sister Fran explained. Sister Tabitha showed me to the Bunk Room, where all the girls stared at me with button eyes, wide and unmoving. I sat on my bunk until it was time to eat supper. Nobody said hello to me.

I never cried, though. Not then. Not once.

Baptism

On the third Sunday in Advent, the sole rose-colored candle is lit, Sister Fran explained to us during Morning Instruction that Friday. A miniature replica of an Advent wreath rested on her desk, a circle of pine with four long candles nestled into it. "We call this Sunday Gaudete Sunday, which means to rejoice. Now I want you to repeat this three times. Gaudete," she said.

"Gaudete," the room chanted, three times over.

"Excellent. Now who wants to light the candle today?" Sister Fran asked, holding up a matchstick like a tiny conductor's baton.

Reggie raised her fleshy arm, and when Sister Fran nodded toward her she made her way to the front of the room. Reggie struck the match easily, but it took her a full minute to ignite the candle.

"Come on, Reggie!" cried a voice from the back of the room, one of The Delinquents.

"Shhh!" Sister Fran snapped. "Patience."

Reggie finally got the wick started and stepped back to reveal her handiwork. The flame bounced, but it didn't extinguish. "What are we rejoicing for?" Reggie asked.

"Do not end your sentence in a preposition," Sister Fran said.

"What are we rejoicing for, Sister Fran?" Reggie offered.

Sister Fran clenched her jaw but let Reggie's grammatical inexactitude slide. She was only one person. "Because the wait till Our Savior's birthday is almost over."

"But that'd be like rejoicing that the War is over before it actually ends. Why not just rejoice on Christmas Day, when the wait actually is over?" she asked.

"Silly girl," Sister Fran began, then stopped herself. Reggie annoyed even Sister Fran, a fact she could not fully conceal. There was just something about the girl: her pudginess, her earnestness, her constantly stained shirt, the way she often stood on one foot, scratching her ankle with the other. Later in life, Reggie would become an elementary school teacher, and she'd curry her students' favor by taking them on field trips to amusement parks, petting zoos, and roller rinks. My best guess is that she was trying to regain the friends she had never known in youth, and that realization makes me wish we had all been kinder to her. But kindness toward Reggie was difficult, even for Sister Fran, who closed her eyes and drew in a few deep breaths. "I do not suggest one compare the War to Advent," she said, dismissing Reggie and facing the rest of the classroom. "We're not waiting for the War to arrive. We're waiting for it to end. On Gaudete

Sunday, however, we rejoice in the promise. The hope of our redemption."

The Guineveres were hoping for redemption. For answers. In the library, we crouched between the stacks and pored over geography books, old art books, and topographical maps, trying to locate anything that could provide us information about Our Boys. Gwen skimmed *Spacious Skies: An Aerial View of Our Country* looking for terrain similar to that found on Her Boy's postcard. *This postcard reminded me of home,* he had written. But where was home? Ginny fanned through a copy of *Wonders of Wildlife*, slowing down when she came to the section titled "Rebellious Reptiles." She found pictures of cobras with heads of pharaohs and fat pythons with sharp saws for teeth, but nothing looked like the self-consuming snake on the front of Her Boy's wooden box. Win flipped the pages of *Exploring the West*, and when she found nothing of use, not even any pictures of cowboys, she picked up a copy of *Exploring the Orient.* That's when she nearly shrieked. There on page 117 was a black-and-white sketch depicting a snake devouring itself. Ouroboros, the book called it. An ancient pagan symbol. A sign of cyclicality, of re-creation, of eternal return. At the ending is a new beginning; in death, life.

Nobody knew what to say. Ginny traced circles around the snake's body with her finger. Gwen snapped shut her book, and the small puff of air smelled like wet newspaper.

"Do you think they could be Buddhist or Hindu or . . . *something else?*" I asked. We collectively gasped. The very thought scandalized us. I worried for My Boy and the possible sacrilegious contents of his duffel. Ginny recalled a woman who lived down the street from her in her Unholy Life. She wore a red dot between her eyes, and she smelled like body odor and spices. She never smiled, and sometimes she didn't wear shoes, so Ginny assumed she was a member of a cult. Gwen quickly located a copy of *A Brief Look into Religions and Cults of the World.* The cover was layered in several years of dust, and we crowned Gwen with our bodies as we all tried to glimpse the pages at once. We saw photographs of bearded men in turbans, shrunken human heads attached to the end of stakes, drawings of women with multiple limbs growing out of their torsos like oblong spiders. Despite the fact that we'd found this book in the convent's library, we felt sacrilegious looking at it, especially during Advent. We didn't find anything else about the Ouroboros specifically, but we did see several pictures of serpents.

"Do all serpents represent evil?" Ginny nervously asked. She rubbed her palms; her invisible stigmata wounds flared up again. She had tucked her Lucky Talisman up her sleeve, and we could see it poking out like a little brown tongue.

We spotted an illustration of a snake dangling from the branch of a tree. Beneath the snake, a long-haired woman leaned her back against the trunk, her eyes closed, presumably sleeping, unaware of his forked tongue only inches away, or the fire emanating from his mouth. The caption read, "Idleness is the devil's playground."

We gulped. It was at that very moment we collectively decided that Our Boys needed to be baptized—just in case—and we'd be the ones to do it. We'd once learned during Morning Instruction that the sacrament of baptism need not be administered by priests alone. Sister Fran taught us that the infant mortality rates of the earlier centuries allowed for midwives to baptize babies, just to ensure they'd make it to heaven in the case of illness or defects. To our surprise, church canon dictated that in the case of necessity *anyone* can baptize *anyone,* and if Our Boys didn't demonstrate the specialized case for necessity, The Guineveres didn't know what did. The next time we had the chance, we assured ourselves, we'd baptize Our Boys in water.

"Just in case," I said.

"Yes," The Guineveres agreed. We all breathed the dusty air of the library, heavy with old books and mothballs. "Just in case."

On Gaudete Sunday, just two weeks before

Christmas, the church was brimming with people, standing room only. Along the back wall of the church crowded weary parishioners, two rows deep. Holidays brought out the religion in people. Wars did, too. The combo of both was good for church attendance, and Father James seemed pleased. We could tell he'd been drinking, could smell it on him when he came to the vestry before mass. He put his violet robe on inside out, kept referring to his Bible as his "book." "Where's my book?" he asked us. "I can't go on without my book." We found it for him on the arm of the couch, where he'd set it down before dressing.

Alcohol affects everyone differently. Father James, at times, was a jubilant drunk, upbeat and funny. His step contained an extra bounce. He told us jokes before mass. Bad ones, mostly:

> What do you call a sleepwalking nun?
> *A roamin' Catholic.*

> What do you call incense burning in mass?
> *Holy Smoke.*

> How did Eve ensure Adam wasn't
> cheating on her?
> *She counted his ribs.*

Father James nearly doubled over after he delivered a punch line. His formality all but disappeared, and in these moments we felt a fondness for him. As soon as he joined the processional line, however, his demeanor changed completely. Sternness overtook his body in the form of stiffness, as though he'd sprained his neck. During mass, he wouldn't look us in the eye, as though to do so would give him away. Our demeanor changed, too. We felt so vulnerable up on the altar, so open to judgment from strangers with whom we'd never so much as exchanged a word. If they knew so much about us, knew we were the poor orphan girls from down at the convent, why didn't they offer their help? Why didn't they ask us to tea or invite us to their potluck dinners or encourage their daughters to introduce themselves to us after mass?

The sunken-faced Drexels sat in the first pew, as usual, and when the lector read the petitions and rattled off the list of boys who had recently died in the War—Sam Gordon, Andrew Winnebaker, Simon Hale, Thad Marino—they crossed themselves and nearly stumbled forward from the weight of their bowed heads. We couldn't help thinking of Our Boys at this point, knowing that hearing one's name in church is never a good sign. It means you're sick, dying, or dead. "Don't wait for a hearse to take you to church," Sister Fran would sometimes say.

During the concluding rites, before Father James dismissed the congregation, he offered his announcements. Bake sale for charity. Coat drive for the homeless. And then he paused and nodded toward Mr. and Mrs. Drexel, who at that signal stood and faced the congregation. "As you know, Peter Drexel is missing in action, and we would appreciate your continued prayers for his safe return. The War Effort requires those on the home front to do our part—to do more than our part, as the case may be. I'm here today, along with Mr. and Mrs. Henry Drexel, to ask you to consider contributing to a letter-writing campaign on Peter's behalf. If you're so inclined during this holiday season to help those who are truly in need—as we all should do—please join me in writing to the Veterans Administration, beseeching them to provide the Drexels with information about Peter's whereabouts and more transparency in their efforts to locate him and bring him home. You'll find addresses in today's bulletin. May God bless us all." Mr. and Mrs. Drexel resumed their seats, the organ cued, and we began our processional down the aisle and out the back of the church.

We took our time in the vestry, changing out of our robes. After the last of the congregants said their good-byes, Father James joined us. At first he was silent, and we were afraid we might be scolded. We had forgotten to light the Advent candle, and when Father James made note of it during his homily, referring to it as the flame-that-would-never-extinguish-in-our-hearts before taking notice of its dry, waxy wick, all four of us were caught with a case of the titters we could barely suppress. We laughed so hard, so silently, that Ginny looked to be having an asthma attack. Granted, it wasn't *that* funny, but something struck us about the peculiarity of that moment: the faces of the parishioners pointed reverently toward the Advent wreath, Father James's violet-robed arm bobbing toward the unlit candle, his face slack with disappointment and booze.

Now, in the vestry, Father James scrutinized us, as though trying to read the intentions of our souls. As he did this, he teetered in his vestments, his hands tucked beneath his sleeves. He'd recently dyed his hair black to cover his premature grays; faded dye traced his hairline, and he smelled like furniture polish.

"We're sorry about the candle, Father," Gwen said. We were sitting on the couch, our knees pressed together at the bone.

"You certainly need to be more attuned to such details in the future."

"And the laughing, Father," Ginny said. "We're sorry about that, too."

"This isn't a penance session, girls, though I'm certain church canon is such for a reason. Altar *boys* rarely succumb to fits of giggles. This is the house of God, and though He enjoys mirth, he's prone to earnestness during the service." Father James released a long sigh, and with it a cloud of sour breath. "Such times call for the lowly to step into higher positions, do they not?"

We nodded our heads, then lowered them completely.

Father James stumbled to his closet, the one where he kept his own vestments. He swung open the door and staggered backward a little, knocking into the processional cross that was propped against the wall. He took hold of the cross with one hand to steady himself, but it rocked back and forth on its one wooden leg. At that point, The Guineveres jumped from our seats to help him. We grabbed him beneath the armpits, the way we did with the old folks in the Sick Ward. That's when we noticed the bottle of wine beneath his robe, leaking dark liquid around its crooked cork like the slow dripping of blood down Father James's vestment.

We led Father James to the couch and sat him down. He thanked us by patting our hips, which seemed impious, but could have just been the angle at which we were standing. "Tell me, girls," he said. "Do you believe that God is fair and just? That He's a good guy?"

"A good guy?" we asked.

"A good God," he corrected.

"Yes, Father," said Gwen, licking her lips until they were shiny.

"Yes, Father," the rest of us replied.

"Then you'll know, girls, that there are certain

things God asks us to keep to ourselves—personal sufferings, you may consider it. But personal joys, too, and the sufferings and joys of others. God already knows all—and so He can read even the deepest of our thoughts without our having to say them aloud. Do you understand?"

"We understand, Father," said Gwen. "Don't we, girls?" When she said "girls" she held on to the *s* just like Father James.

"Yes," the rest of us said. "He's omnipotent." We did understand, which is why we didn't feel compelled to tell anyone about Our Boys. How we loved them. How we intended to locate their families and go home with them, finally leaving the convent for good.

"There is no church law governing the taking of wine as a sin," Father James explained. "In fact, the Good Book tells us, 'Drink no longer water, but use a little wine for thy stomach's sake and thine often infirmities.'"

"If it's not a sin, then, can we try some?" Gwen asked. "For our stomach's sake." She batted her eyelashes and wrapped her fingers around the neck of the wine bottle as she sat down beside Father James on the couch. "It just may help us keep these sufferings to ourselves," she said. Without waiting for a response, she raised the bottle to her lips and took a swig. Then she passed the bottle to us.

At first the rest of us didn't know what to do.

We'd never drunk alcohol before, except for sips from the communion chalice, and we weren't really sure that we wanted to. But Gwen kept prodding us on, and to resist would have seemed a betrayal. "Bottoms up," she said. One by one we closed our eyes and lifted the rim to our lips. And, like that, we were baptized in wine.

Still today, I don't drink much, maybe because I can never replicate the euphoria of that first time. There was a bit of magic to it. The warmth from the wine washed over me; it spread down my body, through my stomach, and out to my limbs. It's the closest I've come to feeling aglow with the Holy Spirit. My body melted into a relaxation I can only compare to the deepest meditation. The bottle passed from hand to hand, and each time, bottoms up.

The wine quickly numbed us—a good kind of numb. Our muscles relaxed. We didn't cross our legs as we sat, didn't bother pressing our knees together, and this, to us, was a release. We felt loose and free to speak without first being spoken to, and so we did.

"Father James," asked Gwen as he opened another bottle of wine from his closet and passed it around again, "Did you ever have a girlfriend, before you took your vows?"

Father James blushed. "That isn't the the kind of question you're supposed to ask a priest," he said.

"Sister Fran says there are no stupid questions,"

Win said. She ran her tongue along the underside of her lips as though her mouth were losing feeling, like mine was.

"Okay, I will answer, then. Yes, I did once."

"What happened to her?" we asked.

"What happened to her," he repeated. He looked sidelong as though someone were waiting in the wings, then hummed for a moment and touched the scar on his lip. "What happened is that I decided to join the priesthood. I had a calling. One's vocation is stronger than one's earthly desires, you know. That's why it's considered a sacrifice of the highest blessing."

"Do you think all sacrifice is a blessing?" one of us asked. "Like those soldiers. Or like us."

"Like you?" Father James laughed. "Girls, you haven't sacrificed anything yet. Just wait until you're older, and then you'll see what real sacrifice is."

"We *were* sacrificed," someone said. "By our parents."

"And do you know who else was sacrificed by His parent? Consider yourself in very good company."

"Sister Margaret says God approves of the War," I said.

"Sister Margaret is still learning," he said.

"What did she look like?" we asked. "Your girlfriend?"

"Oh, girls." He sat up and tried to remove his

arms from his robe, but thought better of it and settled back into the couch.

"At least tell us her name," we said.

Father James grinned, then looked out the window as if he were remembering something funny. "I suggest the four of you get back to Sister Fran. These times are not ones in which we'd wish to create unnecessary worry."

"Why do you always say 'these times'?" one of us asked. I'm not sure who; the alcohol had softened us. "Why don't you just say wartime?" Father James shook his head, then passed the bottle, and we drank once again; this time Ginny spilled some down the front of her blouse. Father James handed her his handkerchief.

"There's a time for everything," he said. His body relaxed, and he swept a hand through his hair. "A season for every single activity you can think of under the heavens. And I mean every single activity."

"A time for killing?" we asked.

"And a time to heal," he replied. "Dear girls. One domino falls, the others go." Here he stopped to flick an imaginary domino suspended midair.

"But how long will it last?" one of us asked.

"Nobody knows."

"Do you think they'll find Peter Drexel?"

"I certainly hope so. For his parents' sake, as much as his. The home front can be as brutal as the battlefield."

"If the VA knows where Peter is, why wouldn't they just say so?"

"Maybe they don't know that they know. Lots of information gets lost in a bureaucracy during wartime."

"Do you think the soldiers in the convalescent wing will wake up?" Ginny asked.

"Girls, I've learned not to ask myself questions that only God can answer. It's a futile endeavor."

Ginny curled herself into a ball on her chair. Gwen shut her eyes. Win plucked out strands of hair from her head without flinching. Suddenly we felt very afraid, as if the whole world comprised a tiny point and we were sitting on the edge of it. As if at any moment the room might explode, sending small bits of shrapnel through our hearts. The radiator clicked in the corner. We unbuttoned our sweaters.

"You needn't worry about the War," he said.

"But we want to worry about the War, Father," we said. "We're part of the War Effort."

"Then perhaps the greatest effort of this War will be understanding your place in it. And there is no place for girls like yourselves." Father James burped beneath his breath. "There's a difference between what we want and what we must do. That's why God created both desire and duty." He burped again. "And now you, my dear girls, must return to the convent. *That* is your duty. And it is my desire to send you back."

"At least tell us your girlfriend's name," we said. "Just that one detail."

He paused before he spoke, his smile the shape of an orange slice. "Her name was Guinevere."

"Guinevere?" we said. We couldn't tell if he was being serious. But then he laughed, and then we laughed, too, and soon we were all laughing in the vestry, our torsos bent, our arms crossed over our bellies to contain ourselves.

"Oh, the bounty of Guineveres," Father James said.

"Was she pretty?" we asked.

"Have you ever met a Guinevere who wasn't?" he said.

"Well, some are prettier than others," added Gwen.

"Not in the eyes of God," he said, winking at the rest of us. "Now back to the convent, or Sister Fran will serve my head on a platter for supper."

Our feet felt far away as we walked downhill toward the convent. We didn't feel the chill of the day anymore, only the sun beating down on our backs, warming us like the wine had. The convent appeared oddly beautiful before us, like a dream. Ginny began to cry a little at the sight, and I put my arm around her. The four of us glided down the hill; our toes never seemed to touch the ground.

And I can tell you this: The wine opened up something inside of us, as though new blood had been transfused into our buoyant veins. We changed. I can't say how, exactly, but we changed. A sense of calm washed over us. A sense of purpose, too.

The wind whipped our bare legs, but we hardly noticed it. We walked four across as we neared the bottom of the hill, our fingers intertwined. It was as though this warmth—another's fingers tucked between our knuckles—protected us from cold, if we could just focus on it. Much of happiness, we'd been taught, was really about where we chose to place our attention, and that's where we chose to put our attention, in each other's hands. When we arrived at the grand foyer, and that last burst of wind zipped inside, we didn't even hesitate when we turned toward the Sick Ward instead of toward the cafeteria and the other girls.

The wine had only emboldened us. We felt overwhelmed with the urge to touch Our Boys, squeeze their warm hands, and whisper to them how we knew what it felt like to be sent to a strange place, away from one's family and friends. We wanted to sit on the beds next to them and tell them things only they would understand: We felt alone. We felt afraid. We felt let down. But not with them. With them, we felt—something. Safe. Needed. If only we could figure out who they were. If only they'd wake up.

A small Christmas tree stood in the Front Room of the Sick Ward, decorated with ornaments that we'd made during Morning Instruction the previous week: angels, wise men, stars, and snow-flakes. Sister Fran had given us patterns, the felt fabric, and cotton balls, and she taught us how to sew even stitches. "It is my duty to instill useful domestic skills in each and every one of you," Sister Fran announced, walking up and down the even rows of desks. "You'll need such skills out there in the world, and you'll look back at your convent days as ones of leisure." She handed us each a spool of thread.

Mr. Macker and Miss Oatley were playing a game of checkers at a table near the window. "Oh, oh!" Mr. Macker said as we passed them. "Girls, girls!" he said.

We stopped and turned toward him, but our heads felt detached from our bodies, as though our minds were no longer housed there, but somewhere outside ourselves. Sister Magda came into the room holding a tray of paper cups full of pills. "Need something, girls?" she asked.

"Mr. Macker wants to show us his magic trick," Gwen said, looping her arm around Mr. Macker and bending over his shoulder. Drunk, she was a creature who craved the comfort of touch. "Right, Mr. Macker?"

"We promised him we'd come see his magic trick—didn't we, Mr. Macker?" Win added.

"Very well," said Sister Magda, and she proceeded on her way. "But make it quick. You're not scheduled to be in here, you know. Not without Sister Fran's approval."

Mr. Macker beamed with a squinted face. He smelled like mildew, the way some of the old folks smelled because they sweated through their nightclothes. "These are my girlfriends," he said to Miss Oatley. Mr. Macker couldn't fully round out his *r*'s, an effect of age or illness, we weren't sure. When he spoke he sounded like a child with a speech impediment. "All four of them."

"A little young, if you ask me," Miss Oatley said. Her lips puckered, and she made her move on the checkerboard.

"Just what the doctor ordered," he said. Mr. Macker showed us the coin he held in his hand: gold around the edges, silver in the middle, like a bull's-eye, unlike any kind of coin we recognized. "Now everyone, put out your hands," he said, and he demonstrated, holding his palm up and out, visibly shaking. We did as he said. He touched each of our hands, pressing his thumb into the middle of our palms. Mr. Macker showed us the coin again as he closed his fist around it and appeared to squeeze. He instructed us to close our hands into fists, too. Sister Magda returned from the Back Room and stood over our shoulders. The Guineveres did our best to suck in our breath so she wouldn't smell the alcohol.

Mr. Macker unfolded his hand again to show he was no longer holding the coin. "Who's taken my coin?" he asked. "Was it you?" He motioned to Gwen, and she opened her fists. Nothing. "You?" he said, and pointed to Win. She opened her palms. Nothing. "Could it be you?" he said, and Ginny's fists sprang open to nothing but air. "Then you must have it," he said to me, and I slowly opened up my hands to reveal the tarnished coin in the center of my left palm. I never even suspected it could have been me since I was never chosen for anything.

"Very good," Sister Magda said from behind us, clapping. Mr. Macker's gummy smile looked like an infant's in the way that infants sometimes look like old men.

"Sister Magda," Gwen said, turning on her toes like a ballerina, "can we go visit with the other patients? It's almost Christmas, and we'd like to spread some holiday cheer."

"Why, that'd be lovely, girls," Sister Madga said. "But we're expecting some visitors today."

"Visitors?" we asked, but Sister Magda didn't have the time to answer. Just at that moment, Sister Connie entered the side door, leading in from the cold two weary-looking guests. They were husband and wife, we surmised, by the way they stood so close together as though hewn from the same skin, the way the man touched the small of her back as the woman stepped inside. The husband wore glasses on the tip of his nose. His hairline receded, and he kept nervously touching his bald spot. His wife wore no makeup; her lips were the color of putty. Sister Connie looked somber, serious. "This way," she said, and she led them to the Back Room.

"Are they here to visit a relative?" Win asked.

"They're here for the soldiers," Sister Magda said. Our hearts quickened. Sister Magda crossed herself. "They're hoping one might be their son." Blood drained from The Guineveres. Our buzzes wore off immediately. Sister Madga walked ahead, and Ginny began to hyperventilate.

Years later, when we recalled this moment, Ginny and I discussed our conflicting emotions. By coincidence, it was Gaudete Sunday. We were on the telephone, and I could hear her daughter playing in the background. Ginny told me that once you become a mother, it's like you've been permanently wounded, your insides are always raw. She couldn't imagine what those poor parents must have felt searching for their son. Older now, Ginny admitted to feeling so vulnerable that sometimes she looked at her daughter and physically ached. She said she'd give her life for her little girl, do anything to protect her, which is why having children only brought back the old wounds from her girlhood, made her question everything. I understood this by then. I really did. However, there, in the moment, as we stabilized Ginny and walked to the edge of the Back Room where Our Boys slept, we didn't know how to feel.

For this moment was the culmination of our greatest hope, a chance for one of us to prove herself to be a valuable nurse, a chance for one of us to go home. We watched the man and woman walk slowly through the room. Some of the old folks sat up in their beds. Sister Connie picked up a clipboard. The couple stopped at the foot of Ginny's Boy's bed, examining Her Boy. They shook their heads. Ginny hunched forward, bracing herself on her knees. She steadied her breathing. She fanned herself with her hands. The couple continued. Sister Connie then led them to Gwen's Boy. His face was bandaged, so they couldn't see what he looked like, but the woman pressed her lips to his forehead and stayed in that pose for a moment.

"What's she doing?" Gwen said. She dug her fingernails into the flesh of my upper arm.

"Motherly intuition, I guess," Win said.

The woman stayed in that pose for a moment too long to be comfortable, and we thought she was stuck, as if her lips had frozen to a flagpole. But after a while she stepped back and shook her head.

"Intuition is a pathetic excuse to kiss him," Gwen whispered.

Sister Connie led the couple farther into the room, to the bed of Win's Boy and then to the bed of mine. The woman and her husband took their time—or maybe they were just tired. Their spines curved as though they had twin cases of scoliosis. Eventually they shook their heads. Not their son. Not their boy.

We lowered our heads as they walked past us to avoid looking at them again. I'd like to say it was out of respect, but that would be untrue. The Guineveres were both crestfallen and relieved. Here we were, girls who would have given anything to be saved from life in the convent. And yet we weren't ready to let each other go. Not like this. There was no commandment governing the confusion of teenage girls nor the tempest of emotions that raged inside us at that moment. Sister Connie and Sister Magda followed the couple outside. The Guineveres unlinked our arms and listened to the beeps and coughs and silence of the Sick Ward.

And that's when we took our opportunity to baptize Our Boys. We snuck into the Back Room, and we filled small pill cups with water, and we carried them to the beds of Our Boys. "I baptize you in the name of the Father, the Son, and the Holy Spirit," we said, pausing at each turn to spill a bit of water on their heads. Their hair dampened, and droplets ran down the sides of their faces like tears. Or maybe they really were crying, like us. We wiped our own wet faces, and we smudged damp crosses on their foreheads with our tears. Our Boys were beginning anew again, not like the Ouroboros, that pagan serpent symbol, but like good faithful gentlemen who believed in the cross and the wise men and following stars and the birth of a baby in a manger far away. A baby who would save the world someday. It was almost Christmas. We loved Our Boys more than ever. We were sad, but we rejoiced. We still had hope.

And then we draped our small bodies across their chests. I could feel the breath of My Boy hit the back of my neck with soft bounces. His slumbering noises—the soft, rhythmic in-breath and the hint of a whistle on the out-breath—sang to me a love song. My skin felt hot where his touched mine, and I noticed a light thumping between my legs that would have embarrassed me if not for the remnants of alcohol. I understood why they called it the devil's drink, because if he had been awake, there's no telling what I might have done. I squashed my breasts against him, and I closed my eyes, breathing with My Boy, in and out, until Gwen snapped, "Rise and shine, lovebirds."

I lifted myself slowly from his chest, and at that moment, I saw it again: The bed was tented, right where his groin should have been, standing at attention. Gwen looked at me, and I looked back at her. She said nothing. We stayed trapped in each other's glance for a moment—her with her half-crooked grin, me with eyes of shame for My Boy.

"Don't tell anyone," I whispered. It wasn't his fault, My poor Boy—his body wasn't his.

Gwen stepped closer, tilted her head, and grinned so big I glanced over at Win and Ginny, both prostrated over the beds of Their Boys. I could see her pink gums, the ridged beds of her teeth. "Tell anyone what?" she said. She ran her fingers along the footboard, not taking her eyes off My Boy. But then she did. She locked glances with me. "Tell you what. I won't tell anyone if . . ." She paused, then somehow her smile got wider. "If you touch it."

"Just go away."

"Touch it. Once. We'll consider it practice. Just tap it with the tip of your finger. Then I'll believe you really love him."

"I do love him," I said. At the moment, I felt sick with love. Heavy with it. Nauseous, in fact.

"Well . . ."

I turned toward the bed, toward My Boy. Toward . . . it. I lifted my finger. I took a deep breath. But my hand wouldn't budge, my fingers held back by some invisible force—maybe it was the Holy Spirit. I couldn't do it. I loved My Boy, but I couldn't do it. I felt a heat rising in me, up from my feet to my head. I then began to cry, quiet tears that wobbled down my cheeks.

"Oh, stop it," Gwen said. "Don't be so sensitive. I was just trying to help."

"Don't tell anyone," I said, wiping my eyes dry.

"I won't."

"Promise?"

"I won't tell a soul."

Win hollered, "Let's go!" from where she now stood at the door to the Front Room, and I followed The Guineveres through the Sick Ward, and down the shaded corridor that led back to the other girls, and we blended in with the rest of them.

Years later, when I spoke to Win on the phone, she would admit from her place out west that Gwen had told her what had happened that day we first got drunk and baptized Our Boys, how I looked at My Boy with a cringed, contorted face. How I cried.

"I didn't believe her," Win said gently, all those years later. Her voice had aged from time and from smoking and from drinking too much until she realized she was turning into her mother and so she quit. "You couldn't trust her," she said. "Even though you wanted to."

Win never married, never had kids of her own, but she seemed the most maternal to me. The years had softened her, given her the kind of wisdom and insight you gain only from loss. Maybe this was the same kind of vulnerability that Ginny had described. And maybe you don't have to have a child of your own to feel that.

"But we were The Guineveres," she said. "What choice did we have?"

"Not much, I suppose, but still," I said. I was

embarrassed all these years later, ashamed for My Boy, how his body betrayed him.

It was true; I didn't trust Gwen. There was something dangerous in her face. Sometimes she tipped her head back in laughter, then looked sideways toward an invisible camera, just holding the pose, role-playing herself. Other times she'd penetrate me with those magnetic eyes of hers, so pretty and sad and sincere all at once. I wanted to be overtaken. But I sensed something, too, just beneath the surface, wounds too deep to be seen. Maybe it was her stillness when she whispered, "I won't tell a soul," her tongue coming to rest on her teeth. Maybe it was simply that I wanted to believe her. I wanted to believe her so badly. Back then, I'd have made bread out of stones, if she'd asked me. I'd have eaten it, too.

Saint Irmina and Saint Adela

FEAST DAY: DECEMBER 24

When Irmina and Adela were young, they liked to play games of the imagination in the shade of the garden's walls. Irmina would help her sister Adela braid branches of the white willow tree into headbands, and they'd prance through the courtyard pretending to be pixies or the dancers they'd seen entertaining the court. These girls were princesses by birth. Their mother had died, and their father, the distant Dagobert, traveled frequently to other villages, founding cloisters and abbeys. It was his life's work. They'd heard the stories of their father, a king who ruled with firmness and piety: When he was a child, he was kidnapped, exiled, and threatened, his throne taken from him unjustly. However, these stories did not reflect the father they knew, a burly and bearded man from whom they wanted nothing but affection.

The girls would pick him flowers from the garden—beautiful bouquets of lilacs and daisies—and they'd place these at the foot of his throne when he'd arrive home from his travels. Their father would smell the bouquets, nod toward his daughters, then tell the officers to have the seamstress make his girls beautiful dresses of the finest silk. In their bedchambers, the girls would practice singing melodies, and they'd serenade their father. He'd nod and tell the officers to ask the cook to bake the girls the finest delicacy.

At age fifteen, Irmina was promised in marriage to Count Herman. She was satisfied enough with this selection, even though a young officer of the court, a boy Irmina had known since childhood, professed his love and begged her to be his bride. Irmina resisted his entreaties, wishing only to please her father by marrying the man he'd selected. Herman, though a bit scrawny and with breath that smelled of pickled herring, wore a beard like her father's, and when they would walk in the garden or dance in the great hall, she could feel the coarseness of it when she pressed her cheek against him, which she did often, just for the experience of it.

Not surprisingly, her father had arranged for no expense to be spared for her wedding. The great hall was decorated with holly and ribbons, and rose petals were scattered across the floor. The servants washed the windows, and light shined through so brilliantly that Irmina and Adela had to shield their eyes when they came to check on the progress of the wedding arrangements at midday.

But three days before the wedding, Adela came running into Irmina's bedchamber with bad news.

Count Herman had been pushed off a cliff by the jealous young officer. Adela stood shaking in her gauzy nightclothes as she explained how both men tumbled to their deaths down the rocky precipice and into the choppy waters below. Irmina stayed in bed all day and all night, all day and all night again, scratching her fingernails into the side of her face to see if she could replicate the feeling of her cheek pressed against Herman's.

After a few days, Irmina sought out her father; she wanted to be consoled, wanted him to pull her into his broad chest, stroke her long hair, cradle her like the child she was. She was only fifteen, not so old, after all. She found her father in the stables; he was dressed in his travel cloak, getting ready to head out to yet another village to help establish yet another abbey.

"Can't you stay with me?" Irmina pleaded, her neck craning as she gazed up at him sitting on his white mare. "I need you, Father," she said. "Please stay." Dagobert smiled softly through his grizzled beard and told the officer to get the young girl anything she wanted to help her recover from her grief. He galloped off on his horse, and Irmina listened to the clopping of the horse's hooves until they faded.

Irmina turned to the officer. Her heart was bounding about in her throat; her eyes began to seep tears—not for Count Herman or the young officer, but for her own loneliness. "Tell him I want a convent of my own," she screamed through clenched teeth. She'd never felt more betrayed in her life. "As large as this castle. Larger!"

She hadn't meant it, not really, but when her father returned home a fortnight later, she learned of his plans to build her a convent. She was to become a nun.

The convent was beautiful, of course, large with arched entries and a gabled roof. Irmina tended to the sick, helped the needy, and walked above the steep slopes of the cliffs across the bay from where she used to live. She refused all visitors. Instead, she spent much time alone in her chambers, her forehead resting on folded hands.

Her sister Adela fared only slightly better. She married the man to whom her father had promised her; there was no love. And then her husband died shortly after their union, leaving her alone again. By this time their father had died, too. Adela, now grown into a beautiful young woman of royal blood, had many suitors, but her heart had grown empty from lack of use. The heart is funny in that way: When it keeps on loving, and loving, and loving what isn't there, it becomes attached to the notion that love is the wait itself, the emptiness of it. She did the only thing she knew to do. She followed her sister's devout example; she founded a monastery with her father's inheritance.

Both sisters—Irmina the virgin, Adela the widow—died alone within the walls of their holy palaces. On their deathbeds they both imagined the old willow tree they used to play under, now dry, sagging with the weight of years and weather. But it would bloom again. It always did. That's what faith teaches us: From hopelessness springs hope. From longing, desire.

The Vigil

Sister Fran granted us special permission to serve at the Christmas Eve Midnight Vigil. In fact, she'd come to trust us, a conclusion she arrived at only after Father James reported back to her that we'd served with the faithfulness and ability of even the best altar boys with whom he had worked. "They're but little lambs led back to the flock," he had told her, declaring us fully reformed from our August transgressions. The Guineveres didn't quite know his reasons for such declarations, but we were grateful and accepted his pronouncement all the same. The other girls fell asleep on Christmas Eve with images of Christmas trees bursting at their bases with gifts, but Sister Fran kept telling us to "keep Christ in Christmas," by which she meant: We'd probably only receive what we received every year: an apple, an orange, and a pair of wool socks, knitted by the Sisters themselves.

While the other girls slept, we, The Guineveres, the little lambs, climbed that old hill in total darkness, save the singular beam from the flashlight Sister Fran had lent us. We felt pinned in by the night—no moon or stars cast light upon our path—silenced by the quiet, the murkiness of the late hour. The treading of our feet upon gravel made the only sound, and it seemed we were in a dream. Because the clock in the Rec Room was set fast, and because girls at the convent were not allowed such things as watches, we arrived at the church early. In the vestry, we pulled on our cassocks, trying our best not to muss our hair, and then we looked for Father James in his office to get our processional assignments.

We found him there, his forehead glued to his desk, his fingers wrapped around a half-empty bottle of whiskey. The bottle said Sunny Brook, I remember, because that sounded like a nice place, a place where there was no winter. A place where the streams never froze, where clouds never sagged with the gray weight of snow.

"Father James," we said. One of us put her hands on his shoulder to rouse him. He didn't move, his body dead weight. "Father James," we said again. We could smell booze when he breathed, and for this reason we knew he was alive.

"What should we do?" one of us asked.

"We've got to wake him," said Gwen.

"I know how to do it," Win said. "My mother used to get like this."

If there was one thing we knew, it was this: Should Father James be found drunk, they'd replace him with another priest, maybe one of those who came in to take our monthly confession. Maybe he'd be the old wizardly-looking priest who smelled like fish or the one with a birthmark that covered the side of his face like a hand. And maybe this new one wouldn't be so inclined to let girls on his altar. It's true, the masses were tedious, the cassocks scratchy, and we sometimes felt the pitiful glances of the parishioners pelt our skin till it was tender. But to ascend that hill alone, our voices floating on empty air, not contained within the walls of the convent, bouncing back from the archways so we could hear ourselves speak—this was a luxury. When we climbed, the muscles on the backs of our thighs strained in unfamiliar ways, and we stretched our arms as far up as they could go, like swimmers, made ourselves as tall as possible. We felt powerful in moments like these, as if we weren't embodied creatures, as if we weren't full of sin and guilt and things unholy. We were The Guineveres, and we could do anything we wanted. Anything at all.

"Don't wake him yet," said Gwen. She began to open his desk drawers, searching for something. In his bottom drawer, she found a telephone directory, a recognizable sage green, several inches thick. She handed it to Win.

"What do you want me to do with this?" Win asked. "Smack him with it?"

"Hide it," Gwen said.

"Hide it? Where?"

"Anywhere," Gwen snapped. Then she gently plucked the Sunny Brook from Father James's grip, undoing his fingers like little latches. She hitched up her robe, tucked the bottle inside the waist of her skirt, then dropped the robe again and cinched her belt tighter. "Okay, you may proceed."

"What are you doing?" I asked.

"What does it look like I'm doing?"

"Thou shalt not steal," I said.

"Thou shalt not be a bore," she said.

Win tucked the telephone book into the front of her waistband, then filled a glass from the pitcher of water on Father James's bureau. She proceeded to pour it slowly over his head. "I baptize you in the name of the mother, and the daughter, and the holy spiritess," she joked. Father James rattled his head on the desk, and Win slapped him a few times on his rouged cheeks, leaving finger marks. "Father James," she said. "Father James, you need to wake up."

Father James raised his head and saw us standing around him. He licked his lips shiny again and blinked his eyes. They were bloodshot, unfocused, red as if he'd been crying.

"Father James," Ginny said, "the Midnight Vigil will be starting soon." Ginny fingered the inside of her sleeve, which I knew meant she was checking for her Lucky Talisman.

"We need our assignments," I said. "Is your sermon ready?"

"I can't do it," Father James said. His words

came out garbled, as if he were speaking underwater. "I can't do it," he said again. He rested his elbows on the desk and covered his eyes with his hands. "Do you know what it's like, girls?" he said without lifting his head. "Do you know what it's like, girls, to feel you'll never know the answers? To have to act strong when you are not?" He grunted, or maybe he just cleared his throat.

We stood there for a moment, looking at our feet. Our shoes were identical, but worn out in different places: Ginny's at the front, Win's at the sides, Gwen's in the back from where she often stepped on the heels so she could dangle her shoes from her toe, pretended she was wearing a slip-on.

"Yes, we do know what it's like," one of us said. "We know exactly what it's like." Father James removed his hand from his face. Crow's-feet appeared at the edges of his eyes.

Win retrieved another glass of water, and I placed my hand on his shoulder. He took a few sips from the glass, and we sat in a half circle until one of us said, "Sometimes we don't know the answers, and we must go on all the same." And another of us said, "Because the only unpardonable sin is losing faith." We had paid attention during Morning Instruction.

"So it is," Father James said. "So it is."

It was a blessing that the Midnight Vigil is said in darkness, the church lit only by candlelight. By candlelight, the parishioners could not see Father

267

James's ruddy face or his bleary eyes. They did not notice that Father James's black hair looked disheveled, as if he had just gotten out of bed, or that his nose was runny and his cheeks were streaked with dried tears.

By candlelight, nobody's attention was drawn to the protruding bottle that Gwen balanced in the waistband of her skirt, or to the blocky bulk beneath Win's shirt, covered by their robes. But I could see it. I could see it in the way they moved slowly, their arms held close to their bodies.

Back then, back when I was just a girl, I believed the world was black and white. There were the good and the bad. The faithful and the unfaithful. The sighted and the blind. There was inside the convent and outside. Those who left and those left behind. The world was split in twos, like Noah's Ark, paired off. I know better than that now, and I don't think back on those days as ones of ignorance. Instead, I admire my younger self as a girl who held an infinite amount of hope that we'd make the right choices.

After mass, we didn't see Father James again that night. He never came into the vestry to hang his garments, and his office was empty when we walked by it on our way out the door. It was past one o'clock, far beyond our usual bedtime, but The Guineveres were not tired, were not ready to go back to the Bunk Room and lie on our beds staring up to the dark. Instead, we sat at the top of the hill, the gravel pinching our skin. The moon was high in the sky now, muted behind translucent clouds, but bright enough so we could see the outline of the enormous convent. We felt so small beneath the weight of the building. The moon was a million miles away, the stars even farther. It was Christmas.

Gwen pulled the bottle of whiskey from her waistband, held it to the sky. It was Christmas, even in Sunny Brook.

"To Christmas," Gwen said.

"To Christmas," Win said.

"To Christmas," Ginny said.

"To Christmas," I said. I swallowed a big swig of the whiskey, and I felt the burning rising up through my nose. And like Joan of Arc, I was set on fire.

After we drank to Christmas, we drank to Father James, then to the War, and to Our Boys who had served there. We drank to our loneliness that felt like a disease, to the Jesus Juice we declared we were drinking, to our new socks we'd find in the morning beneath the Christmas tree in the Rec Room, to the rancid plum pudding we'd likely have to choke down during dinner, to Sister Fran and her Holy Constipation look. We drank to a lot of things, until we were no longer cold and the bottle was empty and we were drunk.

Walking down the hill was not so easy this time. Win couldn't hold the flashlight steady, and none of us was able to stop laughing as we clung to each other's clothing in the dark. The night air seemed to propel us forward, and we felt a sense of euphoria that made us believe we could jump into the sky and hang on to the moon if we wanted to. A few stars poked through the canvas above us, and we wondered which of them was the North Star, the guiding light for the three wise men. How'd they know which star to follow? Who was the first person to discover that the stars could lead the way, that they remained fixed in the sky, night after night? We philosophized as we walked, our heads hung back so we could take in deeper breaths. It was nighttime, and it was Christmas, and we were The Guineveres, and life was perfect in that moment, fleeting, which made it all the more beautiful.

Whiskey had a different effect on us than the wine had. We were unsteady yet effervescent, ponderous and bold. We felt desire in places we hadn't before, in parts of our bodies covered by our bathing suits. Our Boys never felt so far away from us, even as we walked toward them.

"Our Boys," one of us moaned.

"Our Boys," the rest of us echoed, our throats to the moon, our voices full of forbidden longing.

We grew silent as we neared the convent. The stone structure blended into the night, and even though we couldn't see the enormity of it in the dark, we could still feel the weight of its shadows.

We entered through the front door, and, like Jonah, we were swallowed whole. That was the spell of the place, the power of it, too. We lost ourselves within those gray walls. Or maybe we gave ourselves over. Later in their lives, long after they left, both Win and Ginny would admit to me that they didn't resent Father James or Sister Fran or the other nuns. They resented the convent itself, as though it were a living, breathing thing capable of such blame.

"Let's be the first to wish them a merry Christmas," one of us said.

We didn't talk further about it. Our love felt boozy, but stronger for it. Win turned off the flashlight because we knew our way by heart. We tried our best to be silent, but the floor felt wobbly, our legs unsteady. We stopped every few moments and bumped into each other, then tried to restrain our laughter beneath a blanket of darkness. For all the years we'd been at the convent, we'd never seen it at night—not like this, not after the last Sister had said her nightly prayers and crawled into bed to dream about whatever a Sister dreams about. About Jesus as her bridegroom. About what it might feel like to have human hands caressing her papery skin.

The small Christmas tree lit the Front Room of the Sick Ward, and by its light we could see that the door to the Back Room stood open, like an inky threshold to another world.

"I want to see what's in the duffel," I said. "My Boy's box. His personal effects. I still haven't looked." I wanted a piece of him to carry around, too. Each of the girls had something of Her Boy, and at night in the Bunk Room, when it was safe, they'd lie on their stomachs and examine their prizes. Ginny rubbed her Lucky Talisman with her finger, memorizing its smooth center, its ridged edges. Win played with her paddle, making the wooden horse gallop and gallop. She vowed to get a cowboy hat someday. Gwen, for her part, had twined dental floss around Her Boy's ring, so it fit properly on her wedding finger. Sometimes she slept that way, careful to remove it in the morning and tuck it beneath her fitted sheet.

We crept to the storage room. Win hid the telephone book beneath our cassocks, and I pulled the metal box from deep within the duffel. It felt light, nearly empty. I opened it. My eyes adjusted. Inside were no cigarettes, no gum or matches. Only one item: a pocket-sized Book of Psalms, a two-dollar bill tucked inside.

"No comb?" Gwen asked.

No comb.

"That's it?" Ginny said. "Nothing else?"

Nothing else.

"Maybe you didn't need to baptize him after all," Gwen said.

"Couldn't have hurt," added Ginny.

"No, couldn't have hurt," I said. I wondered

which psalm was his favorite, which one he'd turn to in his darkest hours.

We stood by the bed of Our Boys. We slid our bodies beneath their covers, and we shared their warmth. We kissed their cheeks and wished them a merry Christmas. We whispered to them stories about ourselves, things we'd tell no one else: the kind of wives we'd be, the kinds of songs we'd sing to our babies when they could not sleep. We told them we loved them from somewhere deeper than our souls. Our love radiated around us like an aura, like halos. God had his plans, and we had ours, and we hoped they were the same. Because we were tired, and we were drunk, and it was Christmas.

I woke up to the sound of Mr. Worlizter coughing. The room held a different light, gray and fuzzy as my eyes came into focus; my head pounded in my teeth. I quickly unfolded myself from the crook of My Boy's arm, where I had been sleeping. He seemed to shift when I stepped out of the bed, but I didn't stay to take note. I scanned the room for the others, but I didn't see The Guineveres. I didn't have time to think about the fact that they had left me behind, or *why* they would do that to me. Now Miss Oatley began to stir, calling out for water, and I didn't even stop to refill her glass. Instead, I raced out of the Sick Ward as quickly as my legs could carry me. The convent went by in a blur—corridor, foyer, hallways, the blacks and whites and grays of the walls and the marble floors. The lights were still out, which was a good thing, but as I passed the kitchen, I could hear the clanging of pots and pans, the swishing of water, which meant some of the Sisters were up already, preparing breakfast. I ran faster, through the Rec Room with its lit Christmas tree, beneath which sat our Christmas packages. I charged up the stairs to the Bunk Room, three at a time.

I was breathless when I arrived. Everyone was still sleeping, and the silence rang in my ears, a high-pitched chorus. I tiptoed down the aisle of bunks to the end of the row and, as quietly as I could, changed into my nightgown, climbed the metal railing, and crawled into bed. I stashed My Boy's Book of Psalms beneath my pillow. The room spun around me, so I closed my eyes. I felt like I was on a raft in the water, tipping back and forth with the tide. I didn't think I could ever sleep again, but I must have, because before I knew it, it was time to rise.

Instead of our usual wake-up call, we arose to a group of Sisters serenading us with Christmas carols. I buried my head in my pillow, but this did nothing to stifle the sound. As they reached my end of the room, I sat up and made movements toward getting out of bed. I looked down at the Sisters—Monica, Claire, Lucrecia, Tabitha. No Sister Fran with her wicked whistle, her declarations about lambs and vanity and cleanliness and diligence.

This detail would come to be an important one. Although we didn't know it at the time—Gwen, Win, and I all grimaced at the sight of one another as we filed to the bathroom to change our clothes and brush our teeth—Sister Fran sat at that moment in her office with Ginny, whom she'd found passed out in the alcove, curled up next to a radiator.

"Why'd you leave me there?" I asked Win and Gwen. I watched them in the Wash Room mirror. My feelings were hurt. They both looked tired. Win's dark circles resembled black eyes. Gwen's normally smooth hair clumped in tangles.

Win shrugged her shoulders. "I don't know," she said. "When I left, everyone was still awake. At the time, I didn't even think of it."

"I barely even remember getting back here. It's not like I left you there on purpose. Animal instinct kicked in," Gwen said. She splashed her face with water. "Survival of the fittest." She began picking through her hair with a comb.

Ginny told us later that she had awoken in bed with Her Boy. It was still dark. Knowing she couldn't stay there, she wandered the hallways, confused. Ginny had a tiny birdlike frame, so it's no surprise that the Sunny Brook hit her the hardest. She couldn't find her way back to the Bunk Room in the dark, but she was cold and so very sleepy. She thought she'd rest for a few minutes—like Dorothy did in that poppy field, she told us—so she found a warm spot to close her eyes. On her way to do morning checks, Sister Magda spotted her there, and when she realized Ginny was too drunk to rouse, she called for Sister Fran.

Ginny woke up on the bench in Sister Fran's office, her double vision finally focusing until she saw Sister Fran hovering above her, her face white with anger. "Now," was all Sister Fran said, meaning she expected Ginny to talk. But Ginny knew better than to incriminate us; she alone took the blame. She did not mention how we'd found Father James passed out in his office prior to the Midnight Vigil, a bottle of Sunny Brook in his hand. Nor did she mention the wine he let The Guineveres have after we served mass. She simply explained how, after the Midnight Vigil, she'd drunk the leftover wine from the chalices when nobody was looking.

"And what of this?" Sister Fran said to her, unfolding from a handkerchief Ginny's Lucky Talisman. Ginny instinctively checked her sleeve. Sure enough, it was gone.

"That's mine," she gasped, and she grabbed for it, but Sister Fran pulled it away. She folded the handkerchief again and set it on her desk.

"Where did you get it?" Sister Fran demanded.

"I found it," she said.

"Where could you possibly have found this?"

"It was in with the soldier's things," she admitted.

"A drunk *and* a thief," she said in disbelief. "Have you learned nothing during your time here? To steal from those unable to defend themselves?"

"I didn't steal," she said. "I was just borrowing it. For luck," she added quietly. She wanted to tell Sister Fran that *she* was defending Her Boy. *She* was looking out for him.

"For luck, girl? For luck? Do you know what sort of perversion this is?"

Ginny shook her head.

"An ear! A human ear!"

Ginny's throat became a desert, dry and filled with sand. She felt an asthma attack coming on. Her stigmata wounds ached. Pains shot through her eyes. Her hands felt filthy, full of death. The room began to fade, tunneling to a pinprick of light. That's the last thing she remembered before she passed out.

Ginny did not show up to open our Christmas packages in the Rec Room. Her gift lay alone beneath the tree, untouched. We could not find her during the Christmas Celebration in the chapel, where Father James preached with a worried look on his face. Her seat stayed empty at lunch, and at Christmas dinner, in the cafeteria decorated with drooping tinsel. Her bunk remained made up, even after the last of the girls had climbed into bed that night, happy bellies full of Christmas ham.

The next day Sister Fran called an emergency all-girl assembly. The topic: Depravity. Everyone filed into the Rec Room and sat cross-legged on the floor, kneecaps touching. Shirley and Lottie sat behind us, and we heard them whispering about Ginny. "Looks like they lost a Guinevere," Lottie said, and Win didn't even turn around to shoot her a menacing look. Instead, we squeezed each other's hands, digging nails into skin. By now, all the girls had noticed her absence.

When everyone was settled, Sister Fran commanded the attention of the room with a zip of her whistle. "Quiet," she said; then she pursed her lips tightly together, and it looked as though she was about to spit. Next to her stood Father James, his nose rosy, his expression sunken.

"Girls," he said. "Indulgence is a sin." He avoided eye contact with The Guineveres, skimmed over our heads as he lectured us. We were told that befogging our minds with the drink of sin was not a vice becoming to girls *like us*—girls brought up in the image of God. "The joy of God is the innocent," he said, and at that, Sister Fran nodded vigorously. Father James nervously fingered the buttons on his cuff and then announced an impromptu penance service to be held after lunch in the chapel. "I encourage you to let God know what he already knows," he said, and he weakly caught our glance, just quickly, with a pleading look. "You have nothing to gain but absolution." Absolution was freedom.

I don't know why we wanted to keep his secret. Perhaps we thought it would somehow save us. Ginny was still nowhere to be found during confession in the chapel. The Guineveres spaced ourselves out from one another. As the music played, and as the other girls lined up to unburden their souls to the old priests who stood around the perimeter of the room like creepy grandfathers, we made our way to Father James, who sat at the open door of the confessional, barely hidden by the penitential grille.

"I stole a whiskey bottle from a drunk priest, and I kept this from Sister Fran," Gwen confessed.

"I slapped a priest. It was to wake him up from too much drink, and I kept this from Sister Fran," Win said.

"I accepted liquor from a person who should not have offered it, and I kept this from Sister Fran," I said.

We were told God forgives even the gravest of sins. We were told that the only unpardonable sin is losing faith. We were told to say ten Hail Marys and twenty-five Our Fathers. We were told to fast and spend the night reflecting on the nature of our sins. We did what Father James instructed because we were good girls. We were very good girls indeed.

Saint Ita

FEAST DAY: JANUARY 15

Saint Ita was known as much for her youthful beauty as for her purity of heart. Her chestnut hair and round hazel eyes attracted the attention of many suitors, and her father, despite knowing her desire to lead a virginal life, promised her to the most noble gentleman who presented himself, hoping to continue the strong line of worthy heirs. Ita resisted; she fasted for three days straight, taking not a morsel of food nor a sip of water. On the third night an angel intervened, appearing to Ita's father in a dream. In the morning he relented, and soon his daughter became a nun.

From that point on, miracles surrounded her. Once, Ita refrained from human fare for months on end, eating only of heavenly food. She'd open her small mouth to the sky, stick out her tongue, and chew what appeared to be air until she claimed she was full. During these months, she kept a healthy glow and sharp attentiveness, suggesting to those around her that she never wanted for sustenance or suffered greatly. On another occasion, she healed a man who had been beheaded for unjust reasons. She held his severed head, oozing a viscous liquid from the neck, and twisted it back onto his limp body until his eyes popped open again. On still another occasion, she brought her own brother-in-law who had been mortally wounded back to life. Upon seeing this miracle, her sister fainted and fell into a state of shock; her eyes remained open, but the woman could not speak, not even to articulate her joy. These acts were no great effort for Ita, no more difficult than dressing in the morning or spraying the garden with the water she'd collected from the well.

Quite frankly, she was *good* at everything. Nearly perfect if, indeed, perfection were an attainable human state. However, perfection alienates. With each miraculous act she performed, it was as though she'd rise, like the thin layer of milk left to warm: separate but a part of the whole. When she'd perform her miracles, the boys at the school she founded—boys who would later become important church leaders—stared at her with wide eyes of wonder. They'd wriggle away when she held them, afraid they'd be turned into toads.

At night, after she prayed, Ita would think of her parents, whose home she'd left all those years ago. She thought of the way her mother washed her in the small lake near their castle. Afterward, she'd float Ita on her back, swishing her gently back and forth in a wavelike motion. With her ears beneath the water, Ita could hear nothing, and this sound of nothingness comforted her somehow. She could see her mother standing above her in the water, looking down with such tenderness. When Ita floated weightlessly, she felt the world could stop, blend colors from the sky and ground, fade away completely, and still she'd be okay.

In these moments, Ita felt a longing, deep inside her, a small pain beneath her ribs. How could she, a woman with tremendous talent, a woman who could resurrect the dead, a woman so kind she once suckled a beetle until it grew as big as a pig, be ruled by the impulses of her body? It was impossible for her to admit that she wanted a child, but she did.

However, she'd taken a vow of chastity, and she certainly couldn't expect an immaculate conception. Even she wasn't capable of such a miracle. She tried to nurture the young boys in her school, but they were wiry and rambunctious, too old by the time they'd arrive at the convent to sit still for a moment of embrace. She thought of her mother—of that floating state—and she prayed at night for a moment, just a moment, in which she could nurse a child, in which she could feel the weight of an infant rest in her arms.

One night, while Ita was dressed in her night-shirt, kneeling before her bed in solemn prayer, she was called by a higher power to stand and cross her arms. Soon, in the crook of her arm, the infant Savior appeared. He was swaddled in a soft, white cloth; wispy hair covered His head, and His breath smelled sweet like buckwheat with honey milk.

Ita bent her head and stared down at the infant Savior, who was looking up at her with clear, innocent eyes that had not yet seen suffering, virgin eyes that had witnessed no pain. She felt the weight and the warmth of His body; she felt air move in and out as He breathed; she felt the rapid beating of His heart on her forearm. She was consumed with a love so powerful, she thought she might combust, explode into a million little pieces that would waft down to the earth like ash.

The infant Savior wriggled in His blanket, then freed His hand and reached toward Ita. She bent her head closer to His face, and He squeezed her nose with His fat baby fingers. Ita held Him closer, overcome with the urge to protect Him, with the desire to keep Him from the suffering she knew He would face. It's terrible to be a mother, Ita thought—to know suffering exists and to feel powerless to stop it. A wave of sadness surged through Ita's body, and she began to sing a lullaby that she composed as she went along: *Infant Jesus, at my breast, Nothing in this world is true, save, oh Tiny Nursling, You.* The baby's eyes grew heavy as she sang. His lids drooped, then fluttered for a moment as He struggled to stay awake. Ita lay back in her bed, the infant Savior resting on her chest. He suckled her breast, and she was surprised to find she was producing milk. It hurt at first, the way His gentle sucking tugged at her nipples, but then she got used to it, and she felt sleepy, so sleepy. She drifted off, and when she awoke a few hours later, He was gone. Her chest felt warm where He'd been resting. He'd left her with a longing so deep, so real, it seemed she had never lived a single day without Him at her bosom. But she'd taken vows, and she couldn't turn back now. For all of Ita's miracles, this much is true: Until she died, she'd feel that pain, recognizable even in her sleep, the tug of her breasts, the throbbing of her glands begging for a mouth to fill.

Ordinary Time

Ginny returned to us a few weeks later, looking scrawnier than ever, pale and shrunken. The Guineveres thought she'd been sent away. Where, exactly, we did not presume to know, and when we asked Sister Tabitha in the cafeteria she simply said, "Sh-sh-she's being well cared for, girls." However, Ginny reported to us that she'd been in the convent the entire time. She had served her JUG on the third floor, in a room overlooking the courtyard. "They called it the Penance Room," she explained, though we'd never heard of it before. The third floor was off-limits to us, an empty floor the Sisters used for storage, from what we gathered, and so we rarely thought of it, never imagined that Ginny had been with us all along. From the Penance Room, Ginny reported, she'd watched the priests arrive the day after Christmas, and she'd worried about the rest of The Guineveres, if we'd gotten in trouble on her account. The old priests huddled together outside like a flock of fat, golden geese. Father James uneasily wrung his hands.

"I thought about opening the window and hollering down 'Judas!' or something," Ginny said. "But I figured I was in enough trouble already." We were sitting in the cafeteria, our plates filled with remnants of buttered noodles and field peas more aptly described as brown slurry. "You going to eat that?" Ginny asked me, pointing to my roll. I shook my head, and she reached for it.

If nothing else, Ginny was hungry. Very hungry. The Sisters had put her on a cleansing diet of some sort, forcing her to eat only broth and water. She was required to follow a regimen of vitamin intake, and every night Sister Connie watched her swallow horse pills to help her sleep. Sister Fran and Sister Tabitha both visited her frequently, assigning her readings from the Bible, which she was asked to reflect upon.

"I told them exactly what they wanted to hear. I was so sorry. I'd never do it again. Please forgive me." Ginny rolled her eyes midbite, then resumed her chewing. "I'd have repented my name just to get out of there."

"Not your name!" The Guineveres said.

"Of course not," Ginny replied.

After the first week or so, she'd been tasked with awful daily chores: scrubbing, bleaching, dusting. One day she was asked to wash all the windows on the third floor. Sister Tabitha had left her with two buckets of water. "One is s-s-soapy and the other clear. S-s-soap with one hand and wipe with the other," Sister Tabitha said, demonstrating. "Idle hands, troubled heart, my dear." The windows were caked with winter grime, and this part Ginny described in arduous detail: how the dirt stained her fingers, and how the water began to smell fishy, like one of the priests. After a while, when she'd dip the sponge in the bucket full of water, it'd come out dirty, no matter how hard she wrung it.

At this point, Ginny went to look for Sister Tabitha, intending to ask her to swap out the buckets with clean soap and water. She walked down the hallway, then down another, checking for signs of the Sister. She found rooms lined with boxes with girls' names scrawled on the side in marker. "I found the one marked with my name, and I looked inside, quickly. I didn't want to get caught. Just my old clothes, mostly. Stuff that would hardly fit me anymore. Depressing." We'd almost forgotten about the belongings that had arrived with us.

"Did you see my grandfather's old trunk?" Win asked. Ginny said she hadn't, but then again, she didn't know what it looked like.

Sister Tabitha was nowhere to be seen, so Ginny kept on down the corridor, past the Penance Room, past an alcove that looked identical to the one she'd passed out in, all the way down to the end of the hallway. One of the doors there was peculiar looking, set back from the others, with a small half-circle vent at the top.

"So I opened it," Ginny said.

"And?" We leaned in. We set down our forks. Sister Fran blew her whistle, which meant we had only ten more minutes. But Ginny took her time; she enjoyed an audience, almost as much as Gwen.

"And," she said, "it was a stairwell." We sat back in our seats, disappointed. "But they weren't like our regular stairs. They were narrow and straight. Dark, too, and stale smelling, like dirty laundry. Reminded me of a secret passageway."

"Probably just a back staircase, for servants or something," Win said.

"Nuns don't have servants," Gwen said. "Nuns *are* the servants. Will you get on with it already?"

Ginny slouched in her chair, injured. "Well, I went down them. I had to knock off cobwebs. I could barely see, and I nearly had an asthma attack. I had to stop to catch my breath, and I about passed out. I'm not sure what kept me going, except the grace of God himself."

"And . . . did you wind up in some secret room with wood paneling and creepy portraits with moving eyes?" Gwen said. "Did you hear organ music played by a ghost?"

"No. When I got to the bottom, I peeked through the crack. I could see Sister Connie in her nurse's uniform," she said, her eyes glinty and shining. "Sister Magda, too. I was inside the Sick Ward. The Back Room. The door Sister Connie told us not to open? It doesn't lead to a dungeon." Ginny smiled. "It leads to Our Boys."

Back then, while sitting in the cafeteria listening

to Ginny relay her story, The Guineveres still believed in a higher purpose. We had to; otherwise we'd have nothing at all. We certainly didn't have friends aside from each other: Lottie and Shirley and Nan and the other Specials, they would barely speak to us, especially since Ginny had been caught drunk in the alcove. To them we were bad influences. Even The Sads and The Poor Girls avoided us during Rec Time, so we usually stewed in the corner alone. Our eighteenth birthdays, still too far in the future to feel real to us, didn't offer much consolation. Besides, where would we go? What would we do? Our only shot at a normal life was with Our Boys.

When Ginny told us about the back stairwell— we called it the Catacombs, after those sacred tunnels beneath Rome—we didn't say a word, didn't have to. By now, The Guineveres could communicate with only quick glances, a secret language. Our hearts rose up in our chests; the buoyancy lifted our postures. What we conveyed to one another through only blinks and the wrinkling of our foreheads was this: We could reach Our Boys anytime we needed them, anytime they needed us. If we took the main stairwell up one flight to the third floor, then we could access the Catacombs down to the Sick Ward, where Our Boys slept. We would not have to risk walking from one end of the convent to the other, wondering if Sister Fran was in her office or

Sister Tabitha on her hands and knees, cleaning the foyer that always glistened with wax.

"Of course, we can't be foolish," said Gwen.

"We must establish some rules," I said. We were girls accustomed to regimen.

"No drinking when we visit them," Ginny said. "Look where that got me."

"Well, you found the Catacombs, didn't you?" Gwen said. "Everything happens for a reason." One of us was always saying that. One of us was always believing it, too.

"But still," Ginny said. "I think it's wise."

"Only at night," Win said, "at least an hour after Lights Out."

"And never on Sundays," I said.

"Why?" Ginny asked.

"Keep the Sabbath holy," I said.

"True," they said.

"Never go alone," someone said. "Only together."

"Only together," the rest of us said. Always together. We grasped hands, forming a crisscross of arms.

"But what about your Lucky Talisman?" Win asked. She didn't use the words "human ear" to describe the gruesome object that Ginny had been toting around in her sleeve. "Does it make you feel differently? About Your Boy?"

Ginny grew serious. "I've had a lot of time to think about it," she said. "In the Penance Room. And what I've come up with is this: I don't know where it came from or how he got it. But if we were all judged based on just one action, called a bad seed for it—I know I wouldn't like that. My dad, he made a mistake when he . . . you know. And I'm not saying he was right. Sometimes you get pinned in a corner and you have no choice. I'm not making excuses, but I guess that's how I feel about My Boy. Maybe the War pushed him in ways we could never understand. Besides, if you love someone, really love him . . ." Her voice trailed off, and her eyes gleamed beneath a layer of mist. She rubbed her palms, her stigmata. In moments like these, we could understand why Ginny considered herself an artist. Her sensitivity was like an open wound that occasionally scabbed over but never healed completely.

"In fact, I've had time to think about a lot of different things. Exile does that to you," Ginny said. When she spoke this time, her diminutive frame sprouted larger, and her grin contained just a hint of the devil. "I've been thinking about Father James."

"What about him?" one of us asked.

"That he's a louse?" We described to Ginny how he'd come to the all-girl assembly to lecture us on drinking, how he wouldn't deign to look at us when he spoke of the sins of depravity.

"He owes us one, don't you think? More than one. After all, he introduced me to the depravity of intoxication in the first place. If he doesn't help us I might be inclined to confess the whole sordid tale to Sister Fran. And there's no telling what she'd do with that information." Ginny grinned.

"How can he possibly help us?" Gwen asked.

"He can take us to the Veterans Administration, that's what he can do. He's a priest. He knows people. He knows *everyone,* practically. They can help us there. I've thought this through."

"But we don't even know where that is," Win said.

"But he does. That's where Peter Drexel's parents are writing—other parishioners, too. The letter-writing campaign? Remember?"

"That sounds like blackmail," I said.

"That's precisely what it is," Ginny said. "But we have no choice. We have to find out who they are. We're the only ones who can help them." Ginny finished the final scoop of Gwen's beans, and Sister Fran blew her whistle again. "They're the only ones who can help us."

"Why can't we just write the VA?" I asked, crumpling my napkin on my tray, pushing out my chair, standing.

"I've lost faith in letters," she said. I understood what she meant. Writing letters felt like shouting in the dark. I'd written my mother faithfully over the years but never heard back. Ginny wrote her father, too. Mail Distribution had come to feel punitive.

"An excellent plan," Gwen said.

"Or our swan song," Win added.

"At least we'd go down fighting," Ginny said. "At least we're doing something. You try living for weeks in the Penance Room. I practically died."

And that is how it was decided that we'd blackmail Father James. Sister Fran expressly forbade any of the girls from leaving the convent, even for day trips, believing such ventures could impede our spiritual growth. "Do you know what lies beyond here, girls? Sin, that's what," she'd say. "You'll be exposed to plenty of that when you're eighteen. I'm liable for each and every one of you until that day." Even when Lottie asked permission to visit a nearby town where an apparition of Mary was known to appear every May, Sister Fran refused to budge. "But there won't be sin if Mary's around," Lottie tried to reason. But rules were rules.

It'd been months since Our Boys arrived, and still no proof that they'd awake. Our own detective work had stalled, and so we believed that the VA was our final hope, our last chance at discovering Our Boys' identities. Maybe, like Father James said, they didn't know what they knew, bureaucracies and all. Someone, some-where must have overlooked a crucial detail of Our Boys: where they'd been found, when, what other units were in the area at the time. Or maybe they could provide us a list of soldiers who, like

Peter Drexel, were MIA. The Guineveres could work backward from this list, narrow it down, one by one. If they had photos on file, even better. Addresses, too.

To expedite the process, we'd bring them new information, all we had gleaned. The Ouroboros. The toy cowboy. Marjorie P. near a rocky place by the shore. We'd show them the postcards, Gwen's prized ring. We'd tell them which one smoked, which had mesh netting, which carried around with him a small Book of Psalms with a two-dollar bill inside. The VA was liable for veterans, after all, responsible for them as Sister Fran was for us. We were certain they could help us help Our Boys. With God all things are possible, especially if you're on the side of the good. That's what The Guineveres believed. And even if we hadn't believed it, we were running out of options.

Ginny was grounded for a month from serving as an altar girl at the church. This was Sister Fran's decision, and Ginny accepted her punishment without complaint. When the rest of us saw Father James on Sunday, he acted nervous in our presence. He fidgeted with his steno pad, pretending to study his sermon. When he joined us in the vestry, he dressed in silence, gave us our assignments, then waited outside the door for us. Since none of the other girls were trained as servers, Father James had to carry the Bible himself during the processional. He held it high, obscuring his face from us completely.

After mass we confronted him with our demands.

"Preposterous," Father James said.

"We just want to help," I explained. We didn't tell him about how we'd kissed Our Boys, or baptized them, or how we'd studied their sleeping bodies, every nuance, every tic. We didn't tell him how we loved them or that when they woke up, we planned to go home with them, make homes with them, marry them someday. Instead, we simply explained that we didn't want these soldiers to be forgotten, for their fighting to have been in vain. They were so far from home; their parents must be worried sick, like the Drexels.

"Sister Fran would never allow it. Do you know how many times in the history of her tenure she's let one of her girls leave the convent? The VA office is several hours away. It'd be an all-day affair."

"Ginny went to the hospital once for an asthma attack," Win reminded him.

"Barring medical emergencies. I could count the times on one hand. In fact, I wouldn't even need hands to count them." Father James put his arms behind his back as though to demonstrate his point.

"What about Ebbie Beaumont?" we asked.

"That was different," he said. "She was almost eighteen. Part of the War Effort."

"*We're* part of the War Effort," I offered.

"And weren't you the one who told us that there are certain things one does not have to confess? Certain things God already knows? Our personal joys and our personal sufferings, too?" Gwen said. She took a seat in one of the cushioned chairs, stretched her back, and crossed her legs at the knees. She smoothed her eyebrows and pinched her cheeks for color. "Now it would be a shame if Sister Fran found out about how Ginny was first introduced to the depravity of alcohol, don't you think? How we've all been exposed to spirits of the unholy kind."

"Indulgence is a sin," Win said.

"And the joy of God is the innocent," I offered.

Father James's lips were poised on the brink of sound, but he remained speechless. He calmly took a seat at his desk. He pulled out a bottle of Sunny Brook. He did not offer us a drink. "I'll see what I can do," he said. He took a slug.

"You'll have to do better than that," said Gwen.

"You shouldn't rely on the Veterans Administration, girls."

"And why not?" Win asked.

"Because it's an institution, just like any other. The bigger it gets, the more it requires to feed itself, the less it serves the people."

We didn't know what he meant. Not quite. "We'll take our chances," Gwen said.

"I'll look into it," he said.

"You'll take us," Gwen said.

"One can't simply saunter up to the VA unannounced. It isn't a church, after all." He capped his Sunny Brook and returned it to his desk, then nodded to the door for us to leave.

As we walked back to the convent, we felt a rush of energy surge around us like a giant wave. The Guineveres were Noah on his ark, all but saved, given one last chance to prove we were worthy of our fate. We hurried to the cafeteria to find Ginny. We whispered our plans to each other. We ate peanut butter and pear sandwiches as though they were a feast. All we could do now was wait.

When we stood on the altar, lighting candles or wiping the chalice, or genuflecting as we received the bread and wine from the gift bearers, we weren't thinking of the body and blood. We weren't thinking about the girls our age who looked upon us with pity from their pews. We weren't thinking about how God could save us. Instead, we thought about Our Boys' families, if they vacationed at the shore, if they had a seashell collection, if their mothers made casseroles. Then we thought about Sister Fran, about how she so easily located Jack Murr's family, and in moments like these we wondered, if that was that simple for her—just a few phone calls to her network of clergy, really—why hadn't she bothered to find our parents, too? Why hadn't she tracked them down, asked them why they never wrote, told them that we're good girls, after all, and maybe they had overlooked that fact?

We decided we'd write our parents again. Win and I both wrote letters to our mothers. Ginny wrote another letter to her dad. Gwen said she didn't feel like writing a letter, that if her parents wanted to find her, they knew good and well where she was. We planned to deliver our letters to Sister Fran on Mail Distribution Day, but after Morning Instruction, as Sister Fran plucked envelopes from her burlap sack, slapping them down on the desks of expectant girls, she stopped beside Ginny. She hovered above her holding a postcard, pinched between the tips of her fingers like a handkerchief. "I believe you have mail today," she said brightly.

"I do?" Ginny said. She stretched her small body as tall as it would go without getting out of her desk, and she pushed her mane of red hair from her face.

"Not just for you, though. For all of you Guineveres."

We turned in our desks to look at each other, then watched as Ginny slowly raised her arm to pluck the postcard from Sister Fran's hand, her eyes full of astonishment, as though she'd just had a vision.

In the cafeteria, while the other girls lined up to fill their trays, we each took our turn holding the postcard. On the outside of it was a photograph of a fountain: a stone woman with arms out-stretched, water pouring from her hands. We could see buildings in the background, men in fedoras, women in long skirts and collared shirts. A small boy in a suit leaned over the water, probably searching for coins. "I told you not to worry about getting letters," it read. "They never say anything important." The handwriting was loose, as if the card had been written on a train. The postcard was from Ebbie Beaumont.

Looking back, I can say this was probably the kindest gesture anyone had made toward us, The Guineveres, since we'd been dropped off at the convent. And even though the postcard didn't say much, didn't ask how we were doing or offer news, or even provide a return address, we had never felt more connected to the world in our lives. Ebbie had managed to leave. She was out there, nursing Jack Murr, Jr., waking up each morning to limitless possibilities. And yet she had taken the time to write us a note.

"It's a sign," Ginny said. We were superstitious. All things were signs. Our plates were full of soggy spinach and buttered bread. We were more determined than ever to find a way out of the convent.

"We'll find Ebbie and thank her in person," Win said. "Soon."

"Maybe she's fallen in love with Junior," Gwen said.

"Probably," I said. "Do you think they'll get married?"

"After a proper courtship," Ginny said. She folded the postcard into a napkin so it wouldn't get dirty. Until she left the convent, she'd consider this one of her prized possessions.

"He'll have to get better first. You can't woo someone from bed," I said.

"That's what you think," said Gwen.

We never did deliver to Sister Fran the letters we'd written for our parents. What good would it have done? Maybe Ebbie was right—nothing important ever comes by mail. Beneath the table, I crumpled the letter I'd written to my mother, which contained mostly a laundry list of questions: "Are you okay? Where are you? Are you taking care of yourself? Are you taking your medicine? Why haven't you come back?" Truth be told, The Guineveres weren't sure if we wanted our parents to come back, because we knew that if they did, we'd have a difficult choice to make: Our Parents or Our Boys. Our past or our future. Our old families or our new ones.

"Do you think the Veterans Administration can tell us anything about Junior?" Win asked. A piece of spinach was lodged in the gap in her front teeth. "We know his name, after all, and maybe he was found with Our Boys. Maybe they were in the same unit or something."

"Maybe," one of us said.

"What if they won't tell us anything because we're not next of kin or because we're not eighteen?" Ginny said.

"Then Father James can sign for us," Gwen answered. She pulled the crust from her bread and ate it. "Or we can just lie."

"I hope they haven't forgotten about Our Boys. I hope they aren't so focused on the War or on finding MIAs like Peter Drexel that they overlook the unknowns right here at home," Win said. "It's easy to willfully forget."

"Yes, just look at our parents. Selective amnesia has served them well," Gwen added.

"What if they have no files, no records? What if they don't know what to do with the information we give them? Or if it takes them a long time to get back to us? What will we do then?" I asked. The Guineveres set down their forks.

"Vere, don't be a doubting Thomas," Ginny said. This was a possibility we couldn't allow ourselves to consider. "Aren't you the one always talking about faith?"

"Yeah, Vere. We need you to keep the faith for all of us," Win said. "If not you, then who? You're like . . . Bathsheba."

"Bathsheba was an adulteress. She had an affair with King David, and her bastard child died because of it," I said.

"She's definitely not Bathsheba," Gwen said.

"Well, not Bathsheba then," Win said. She never

received high marks in church history, a fact that made her hate it even more. "Maybe Esther or someone." She picked at her teeth with her tongue.

If I were Esther, I wanted to say, I'd be saving my people, leading The Guineveres out of our exile. I knew I didn't have that kind of power, and besides, Esther was Jewish. We had to rely on the people at the Veterans Administration, I wanted to say. But I'd learned my lesson, not to depend too heavily on anyone. You'll only be let down. Instead I said, "We have to have faith that the VA can help."

"That's more like it, Esther," Win said.

The days moved slowly in the convent, turning into nights, then mornings. During Instruction we learned about home economics and grammar and basic mathematics, and we tried to think about how we could best apply these skills toward helping Our Boys once we got out. We learned about the seven mortal sins and abstinence and the Divine Office, and these concepts seemed less useful to us. Sister Fran taught us that we were on Ordinary Time, the time of the liturgical year that falls outside of Lent and Advent, Easter and Christmas, penance and celebration. To us, ordinary meant unimportant, meant idle, meant waiting.

In the classroom, Sister Fran leaned up against the chalkboard when she spoke, and when she pivoted to write "Ordinary=Ordinalis=Ordo= Order" in tidy cursive, a line of chalk dust was etched across her lower back, her other ruler. Win reached over her desk and drew her pencil across Shirley's back, and Shirley reeled backward with a fist, only narrowly missing. "Say *ordinalis*, girls. Say it three times."

Ordinalis, ordinalis, ordinalis. Win now flicked tiny flecks of notebook paper into Lottie's hair. Several girls had fallen asleep, their cheeks pressed flush against their desks, their mouths shaped like oysters.

Ordinalis, Latin for "ordinal," which refers to the numbered weeks of Ordinary Time. And *ordo, ordo, ordo*, as Sister Fran made us repeat it, is the Latin stem, meaning "order." Thus, she explained, Ordinary Time reflects the rhythm and order of the church. Vestments worn during this period are green, symbolizing hope and expectant anticipation. "Oh, but it's far from ordinary, girls," Sister Fran said. "It's a season of miracles, of mystery. Now turn to John, chapter two."

During mass that Sunday, Father James read from the Gospel about Jesus turning water into wine at a wedding in Cana. His lips quivered as he read, and his homily was short, a rehash of one we had heard around Christmas. Afterward, we hung our robes in the vestry, waiting on Father James. We'd been patient up until now, good girls, some might say, but we'd met our limits.

Ebbie's postcard had reignited something in us, made us pine for lives where we could be the ones walking around a city fountain, tossing coins inside. The Veterans Administration held the answers for us. We needed a date.

"Ask for proof that he even called. Get the name of the secretary he spoke with," instructed Ginny before we left her at the convent, still serving out the tail end of her punishment. "Threaten to tell Sister Fran again," she said. She was holding our postcard from Ebbie. It had already begun to fray at the edges. "Or the archbishop."

We'd threaten to write to the cardinal on top of that, to the pope, if we must. We paced the room. It was raining outside, but sunny. Lottie Barzetti said that when it rains and shines at the same time it means the devil is getting married, but what did Lottie know? We sharpened our canine teeth with our tongues.

Father James arrived more than half an hour later. Gwen's mouth contorted in ready vitriol. We were going to lay into him—we were—but then we noticed he'd been crying. He settled onto the couch and placed his head in his hands. Tentative and stunned, Gwen and Win sat down beside him; I knelt at his feet.

Father James inhaled a long, audible breath. "My brother. He's dead," he finally said. We thought he meant another priest at first, a fellow clergyman. We were used to hearing the terms brother and sister in reference to those not really related, except by belief. "He is . . . was . . . seven years younger," Father James said, and we knew he meant his baby brother, his flesh-and-blood brother, the kind of brother with whom he'd grown up, shot marbles, visited fishing holes. "He . . ." Father James's voice broke in half.

"The War?" we asked.

Father James nodded.

"Did they say his name during the petition?" Win asked, though we weren't sure why this mattered. The list continued to grow. This week it contained at least a dozen names.

Father James shook his head.

"A shame," said Gwen. Sometimes she spoke in what we called her starlet voice, a voice so soft, so breathy, it seemed you could gather it in your hands and put it in your pocket. She spoke like this when she acted out for us in the Bunk Room the monthly confession she planned to give. "I do declare that I hid my peas in my shoes, dear Father," she'd say, fanning herself. "And for that I am truly sorry."

"He went into the service, and I . . . I went to the seminary," Father James said. His words were drawn out as if his tongue were swollen. He'd clearly been drinking. "I didn't want to fight. I don't believe in it. I told him to join the seminary, too. It's not a bad life. Better than some. But he wouldn't listen. I told him not to fight. I was older than him. I should have protected him. I should have . . ."

"There, there," Gwen said, and she placed her hand on Father James's chest, leaned into him and rested her head on his shoulder. Her eyes drifted back and forth, sweeping across Father James's body. Win and I swapped puzzled glances. If Sister Fran were there, she'd have said, "The Flesh, girls. The Flesh."

A lot of what we knew about war, in general, we had read in textbooks, back in our Unholy Lives. But nothing we'd learned in those books taught us what to say to Father James, who at this moment slouched forward on the couch in the vestry, hanging his head in grief.

"We're sorry," Win said.

"What happened?" I asked, but as soon as I asked it, I wished I hadn't. He died in the War, that's all I needed to know.

"He was all the family I had." Father James, with his face turned downward, with his eyes red-rimmed and puffy, appeared fragile in this moment, so vulnerable, like a little boy. The Guineveres had to remind ourselves that he wasn't *that* old—not much older than Our Boys, in fact. Authority veils itself as age. As wisdom, too. People are so willing to follow those who claim to have answers.

"Everything happens for a reason," I said.

"He should have joined the seminary, like me. I knew it was coming. The War. I knew we'd be protected here. They couldn't draft us, and we wouldn't have to enlist," Father James said. "It's not that I don't believe in God—I do. I do. But I wanted . . . I knew I wouldn't have to fight this way. The home front needs fighters, too."

"We understand," Gwen said, and I'm pretty sure she meant this. The Guineveres saw ourselves as the protectors of Our Boys, even though we stood to gain in the process. In a way, I guess you could say that we all understood the costs of freedom, the effort and agony one must sustain to earn it. Gwen nuzzled into Father James again, rubbing her ear against his shoulder as though she had an itch she was trying to scratch. Then she reached for his hands resting in his lap and intertwined her fingers into his. Father James relaxed his body.

"He wouldn't listen. My brother wanted to be a hero, and now . . . Maybe I'm the cowardly one." At this point he began to sob.

The Guineveres had never witnessed a grown man crying. Back then, men didn't cry. Now, when I talk to Ginny on the phone, she tells me stories of her son, of how coddled young boys are these days, how they wear their hair long and sleep in their parents' beds and talk about their *feelings* in school, as though their feelings had anything to do with their education. In the convent, however, outward displays of emotion were discouraged as the hysterics of young girls. "Above All, Restraint" could have been the guiding motto of the Sisters. Therefore, paying witness to Father James as he wept, taking such deep breaths we thought he might be choking, unnerved us, as if the universe had turned upside down.

We blinked in the face of his revelation. It was true, I'd later learn, that he'd joined the priesthood to avoid the draft. Did this make him a coward or a con man? A man of morals who let nothing stand between himself and what he believed? Better or worse than a young soldier who carried around with him a human ear? Or men who killed? We weren't sure, but we didn't need to be. In that moment, Father James was more like us, more human and demanding of compassion than we ever could have imagined. We couldn't bring up to him our visit to the Veterans Administration. At least not then, not while he was grieving.

Did Our Boys believe they were fighting for a worthy cause, we wondered as we walked back down the hill, to Sister Fran who was waiting to ensure we hadn't drunk the remnants from the chalices. And what about our parents? Had they thought they were doing something good by leaving us here? Had they thought we'd be better off somehow, enriched by the Sisters and their monastic life? We didn't think so. But how could we know? How could we tell? At lunch The Guineveres picked at our egg salad sandwiches and wondered if Our Boys had ever killed anyone in the War, and if they had, were they worried for their souls?

We were young still, didn't know that some questions should never be asked, that we wouldn't have wanted to know the answers anyway. Years later, Ginny and Win would both report that they'd shudder when people asked them *why* they had lived in a convent as girls. It didn't seem fair that *they* were the ones left answering such questions, they both complained. Sometimes they'd lie and tell whoever had asked that they were considering monastic life for themselves, that it was a trial run that didn't pan out in the end because the food wasn't very good. But their straight-lipped expressions gave them away. You can't rid yourself of that kind of pain completely, no matter how brave you are, or how good, no matter how far down you bury your memories. Memories are like that, like mustard seeds, tiny at first, but eventually the largest tree in all of the garden.

Involuntary Doubt

I t had been weeks since Ginny had discovered the Catacombs. The Guineveres waited out the Sisters, until they had stopped scrutinizing her so closely, expecting a relapse. We bided our time, growing outwardly devout. We volunteered to wake up early to serve on breakfast duty, and we boiled the oatmeal with the diligence of Saint Juliana ministering to the sick. During Morning Instruction, we studied the hardest, paid the closest attention, raised all four of our hands to answer Sister Fran's questions about Genesis and Exodus and the Flood.

"Adam's rib," we answered.

"Original sin," we answered.

"Two of every species," we answered.

"Moses on the Mount," we answered.

Correct, four times over.

Later, while Sister Fran taught us biology lessons about the creation of the world, about amoebas and dinosaurs and Adam and Eve, she explained to us the difference between obstinate and involuntary doubt. "Obstinate doubt is the denial of truth, girls, and it's a sin. But involuntary doubt, on the other hand, is hesitation of belief or the anxiety caused by the obscurity of faith. Now when I say that God created the world in seven days, you may find such a magnificent feat nearly impossible through the lens of human rationality, for what human do you know who could accomplish such an extraordinary coup? Anybody? Anybody?"

"My dad is a construction worker, and he worked a lot of overtime," one of The Delinquents said, and the room burst into laughter.

Sister Fran raised her whistle to her lips, but everyone hushed before she even had time to blow it. "Involuntary doubt speaks to our humanity."

Lottie was taking such vigorous notes that her glasses slid down to the tip of her nose, and she looked like an old librarian. She raised her hand. "Does that mean, Sister, that doubt is not a sin?"

"Only if it's involuntary, dear. You see, girls, there's room for doubt, even in the faithful."

I raised my hand, and Sister Fran acknowledged me with a hard blink. "How do you know, Sister? How do you know if your doubt is voluntary or involuntary?"

Sister Fran paused for a moment, thinking. "That's an excellent question, and we shall take it up during tomorrow's instruction. For now, I want to turn to our math lessons. Does anybody here know how to calculate the mean sum of all the hours in forty days and forty nights—the length of the upcoming liturgical season of Lent?" As if on cue, every girl bent over her desk, scratching out calculations in her notebook.

Did The Guineveres begin to doubt? We did. Did we believe it was a sin? We did not. Our doubt was involuntary, brought on by the fear that we'd be stuck at the convent forever, or until we were eighteen, which was practically the same thing to us. We were afraid Father James would let us down, like everyone else. We found it increasingly difficult to imagine our futures, to believe that the VA would have answers.

During chapel, and despite our doubts, we closed our eyes the tightest, clasped our prayer hands until our fingers hurt. We didn't know how we'd find our homes, but we had to believe that we would. We dreamed of Our Boys, imagining the way their eyes would flutter as they kissed us. Imagining our wedding days, the vows we'd take. *We do. I do.* With our heads bent and swaying, we looked rapturous, inebriated with the Holy Spirit. Sister Fran called us "good girls" when we lined up to leave the chapel, though we didn't feel like good girls. We felt lonely. We felt afraid.

Finally, one night, after Lights Out, we stared into the darkness, waiting for an hour to pass. We'd grown fairly skilled in measuring time by instinct. We prayed the rosary three times, our Our Fathers and our Hail Marys and Glory Bes, to tick away the time. Soon enough, we gathered in the corridor outside the Bunk Room, and we made our way to the third floor. The moon was out, shining through the windows, the same ones that Ginny had cleaned a month ago, the light making our path more visible. We passed several open doors, passed the room that held boxes marked with our names, passed shadows that looked like they might spring to life and capture us. We traipsed along, holding on to one another, dressed in our white nightgowns that revealed our bony ankles and bare feet. We tried not to be scared, tried to think about what Sister Fran had taught us about channeling our fears into the Lord, letting Him take the brunt of the burden. He wanted to bear it.

The four of us had to push up against one another as we filed down the narrow staircase. It was almost total darkness, but we could smell each other's hair, the sickly floral scent of our shampoo, the same one used on the old ladies in the Sick Ward. We could feel each other's hot breath on our necks. Our bodies trembled as we slowly descended, an energy pulsing through us that I could only explain as love. At the bottom of the stairwell, we all stopped, bumping into one another in the process. We'd arrived. One of us opened the door, and our eyes adjusted to the dark.

We found Our Boys sleeping where they always slept, blankets tugged up to their necks. We talked to them in whispers. Some of us cried. Some of us clung to their chests just to feel them breathe, to make sure they were alive. We weren't sure how long we were there—longer than the duration of Morning Prayer, for sure. We gathered by the stairwell door and composed ourselves, but when Win wrapped her fingers around the knob and pulled, we heard only the thud of resistance. The door was locked.

"I guess it only opens one way," Ginny said sheepishly.

"Now what?" one of us said. We grew nervous, and it came through as gulps and heavy breathing.

"Well, only one way back," Win said. "May as well do it." Win never allowed her emotions to overtake her, not like the rest of us. While the rest of us bent over the bedsides of Our Boys talking or weeping, I sometimes caught her simply sitting on the edge of the bed, not saying a word.

"Great," Gwen said. I could practically hear her eyes roll.

"No point in crying about it," Win said.

"Wait a second," Gwen said, and she crept into the storage room. She materialized a few moments later with the hidden telephone book beneath her armpit like a clutch.

"What are you doing?" one of us asked.

"Just go," Gwen said. She could not be bothered with questions.

We crept into the Front Room, the moon casting bar-shaped shadows onto the floor of the lobby. Win led the way, and the rest of us followed close behind.

"Nurse, Nurse," we heard one of the old women say, and we stopped in our tracks and stood as still as statues. "Nurse," she said again, her voice a loud whisper. We didn't know the name of the woman; she'd arrived after Our Boys. "Can I have a sip of water, please? I don't feel well." The voice was frail and scratchy, deep for a woman's.

"What do we do?" Ginny whispered.

"Leave," Gwen said.

But I walked over to where the water pitchers were kept, and I found one that was full. I made my way to the bedside of the old woman. "Here you go," I said, filling her glass.

"You're not a nurse," she said. She took the glass in both her hands, but had a hard time putting the straw in her mouth, so I helped her.

"No," I said.

"Why are you here?"

"Same reason as you," I said.

"You're sick?"

"I'm waiting."

"Thank you," the woman said, motioning for me to take the glass; she'd had enough. "Waiting for what?"

"Hurry up," Gwen snapped. "We don't have all night for small talk."

"To go home," I said. I set down the glass and rejoined The Guineveres as we started for the door again. But at that moment, we heard footsteps, so we retreated to the Back Room. Sister Connie. Checks.

We hurried to the far end of the room and

crouched in the corner, behind the supply cabinet, where we waited, squeezing each other's hands for reassurance. We heard a few noises from the Front Room, some muffled conversation. We were sure the old woman was telling Sister Connie that she'd just seen four girls in nightgowns. Soon Sister Connie appeared in the Back Room. She didn't make a sound, just methodically walked down the aisle of beds toward us, stopping to adjust pillows or straighten blankets. She appeared tired, even in the dark; the circles under her eyes were black crescents. We stiffened as she made her way closer to us, and just as she was about to get to the end of the row of beds, My Boy groaned in his sleep, catching her attention. He saved us, My Boy did. Sister Connie turned around and away. The Guineveres breathed relief.

She stood at the foot of My Boy's bed. "Again," she said, tsk-tsking, then picked up his clipboard and made some notes. "You must be having unpleasant dreams, Number Twenty-two." She stood for a moment watching him, as I sometimes did, and then she turned and headed for the door.

The Guineveres didn't move, didn't chance it, just continued crouching until our legs tingled. After a while we stood up, shook out our limbs, said good-bye to Our Boys once more, and tip-toed right out of the Sick Ward and back through the convent.

However, we didn't head to the Bunk Room immediately. Gwen demanded that we stop in Sister Fran's office first. "We have a phone call to make," she said, holding up the phone book.

"But it's in the middle of the night," I said.

"But it's in the middle of the night," she mocked. "It's only the middle of the night at the convent. Most civilized people don't go to bed when we do. In fact, I used to stay up till midnight in my Unholy Life. Even on school nights."

Sister Fran's office door stood slightly ajar, and Gwen nudged it open with her foot. We half expected to see Sister Fran inside, like a crypt keeper. Instead, her chair was empty, her desk cleared, except for her whistle. To our relief, Pretty's cage was empty, too.

"So this is where she keeps it at night," Win said. She picked up the whistle and hung it around her neck. The Guineveres always imagined that she slept with it resting on her lips, ready to blow it at a moment's notice. "I feel more powerful already." Win put it to her mouth, but she didn't dare blow it.

"What are we doing here?" Ginny asked. Gwen turned on the desk lamp.

"Turn that off," I said.

"We're calling Junior," she said. She set the telephone book on Sister Fran's desk and began thumbing through it. "He's been home for months. Maybe he remembers something, now that he's recovered. He might be able to give us information about Our Boys, or else Ebbie can. I'm sure she can get it out of him."

"We don't even know if he's listed," Win said. She unwrapped the whistle cord from around her neck and placed it back on the desk exactly as she'd found it. "Maybe he lives in a different city. Maybe he moved."

"Look, do you want to get out of here or don't you?" Gwen said. "Because I can't be dragging around dead weight. And besides, do you have any better ideas? Just wait for Father James to take us to the VA, or until we're eighteen perhaps? Get some radio privileges and be sent on our merry way? I don't know about you, but I'm not waiting that long. Look at Ebbie. She didn't."

We knew that to get ahold of Junior, we'd have to look up his dad, but there was no J. Murr in the phone directory, only an L. Murr and a T. Murr. Gwen picked up the phone and dialed the first number without hesitation. She let it ring a dozen times, shaking her head. No answer. With the second number, she had better luck. A miracle is how The Guineveres might have described it. We gathered around the phone. Gwen tilted the receiver toward us, explained to the man who answered that she was an old friend of Junior's, from the War, and that she was trying to contact him with some important information, and, well, would he happen to know how to locate him? The man on the other end went quiet for a moment. "You should talk to his father," he said.

"His father?" Gwen replied.

"Yes, his father. My cousin. Here, let me get you that number," he said. Gwen found a pen in Sister Fran's top drawer. She had no paper, so she jotted the number down on her hand.

She hung up the phone, then immediately picked it up again and dialed the operator. Win peeked out the door to make sure nobody was coming. We all got quiet and listened; the silence made a sound of its own.

The phone rang several times before someone answered. It was a woman's voice this time, all crackly and full of sleep. "Yes, may I speak to Jack Murr, please," Gwen said. She twisted the phone cord around her finger and sat down at the desk, imagining herself a secretary at some office in the city.

"My husband's not here," she said.

"Junior, ma'am. I was hoping to speak to your son."

The line went quiet. Gwen tapped the receiver. "Are you there?" she asked.

"Who is this?" the woman asked. "Are you from the newspaper?"

"No, ma'am. I'm an old friend of his. From the War," she lied, just as she'd rehearsed.

"There are no women in the war," the woman said.

"A nurse. I was a nurse. I *am* a nurse."

"Are you friends with that Ebbie girl?"

"Yes, yes I am. May I speak with her?"

"She's gone." The Guineveres poked each other with glances. Concern? Jealousy? Maybe a little of each.

"Yes, well, Ebbie's a friend of mine, but I was really hoping to talk to Junior about his recovery time at the Sisters of the Supreme Adoration. I was hoping he could tell us—me—about some soldiers who were there with him."

The line went quiet again, but soon we could hear a sound, like the whistle of a teakettle, only lower, full of grit. "It was an accident," the woman said. "My poor Junior. It was an accident. I don't care what they say, and don't listen to what you read in the papers. The papers are full of lies. I'm telling you he didn't mean to do it. It was an accident."

Gwen stood up at the desk. "Is he in trouble?"

"He's dead," the woman said, and as soon as she spoke the words, she slammed down the phone. The line returned to the hum of the dial tone.

Gwen placed the receiver back on the cradle. Our throats felt tight, restrictive. Ginny began wheezing and cradling her palms again.

"What kind of accident do you think he had?" I said.

"Vere, you idiot. He didn't have an *accident,*" Gwen said.

I understood what she meant, but I refused to believe it. Obstinate doubt. Total denial. Why would anyone weather the worst of the storm—the War, loss, injury—only to give up on the other side, just when things were about to get better? That's how I saw it back then: illogical.

"Why do you think he did it?" Ginny asked.

We didn't know how to answer, so we sat quietly in Sister Fran's office, listening to the sounds of the convent at night, the click of the radiators, the creaks of old plaster. Finally, Win said, "Maybe he was afraid nobody would ever understand, that he'd have to live the rest of his life trying to explain it." After all these years, I think Win was right. It wasn't just the sights he'd seen in the War, or his injuries. It was the fact that he'd be forced to stare into the void for the rest of his life, wondering if he'd ever again do anything of value, if his life would ever again have meaning. The War was like that, even for us on the home front: horrible and scary, unspeakable even, but it was real, and there was something to that.

"But what about Our Boys?" someone asked.

"They'll be different."

"How do you know?"

"Because *we* understand," someone said. We heard a rustle outside Sister Fran's window, a gust of wind, the clacking of branches.

"Poor Ebbie," Ginny said after a while.

"She got out, didn't she?" Gwen said. "That's what she wanted."

"But maybe what she wanted changed," I said. "That can happen. She's probably grieving somewhere. In the city." I thought of her postcard. Men and women on their way to work. The boy leaning over the fountain. Somehow the scene seemed sad to me now.

"Well, if she's in the city, she's lucky," Gwen said. "Luckier than us."

"I don't consider that lucky," Ginny said. "Losing someone you love. Especially like that."

"Do you think she was there when it happened?" Win asked.

"I've never seen a dead person," I said, but as soon as the words left my mouth I regretted them.

"I have," Ginny said. But we already knew.

Instead of speaking anymore, we each took turns paging through the telephone directory, checking for our parents' names. None was listed. It felt as though they never existed at all. We had no proof of it. Win turned off the lamp, and we sat there in the dark for a long time. We could hear Ginny whimpering. We could hear an owl outside the window, somewhere in the distance. "Who? Who?" it said over and over, as though we held the answers. We didn't. We thought we heard Sister Magda's familiar footsteps down the hall. Finally, we decided it was time to go.

This is the part of the story where we should have been caught, but we weren't. If we'd been found, and punished, I'd probably be telling a different story. A better one? I doubt that. A couple of us would have been spared some pain, but there was no escaping all of it.

During Rec Time the next day, the older girls blasted the radio from the corner. One of them would turn eighteen tomorrow, and so the radio privileges were restored by the Sisters as her send-off into the world. The girl kept tuning the stations, ratcheting the dial back and forth, as though trying to tune into Earth frequencies from a planet far away. The Specials had taken over the Ping-Pong table. Lottie and Nan competed against Shirley and Dorrie Sue, who swatted at the ball like the summer flies that sometimes made their way into the cafeteria in the warmer months. A few of The Poor Girls had strapped roller skates to their shoes, the ones Sister Fran said were donated by some of the parishioners from the church when they learned we had little in the way of recreational equipment.

The Guineveres eased our bodies onto the floor, then arranged ourselves like fallen dominos and made cushions of each other, since all of the couches were already taken. The fabric of our skirts chafed our winter skin, scaly from the loud old radiators that sucked moisture right out of the air. Above us, the fluorescent lights flickered, and we pretended to watch a filmstrip on the ceiling, one in which we imagined Our Boys in the War. Only, in this filmstrip, time progressed backward: Bullets were sucked out of Our Boys' limbs, and explosions condensed to a single point on the horizon. Our Boys stood up from their crouching position, and they turned toward the sun, their uniforms unsoiled, the fear extinguished from their faces.

The Guineveres prayed we could reverse time for Our Boys, to protect them, to save them from their own fates here in the convent. But if we could, if we really had the power, like God Himself whose own son could walk on water, His toes never even getting wet, we'd never have met them. We'd never get the chance to go home. And in this way, we were relieved that we couldn't do anything about time or about the War or about the injuries Our Boys had sustained.

Our very next thought might have naturally progressed to feelings of guilt, but instead Reggie appeared above us, hovering like a chubby angel without wings.

"My dad finally wrote back," Reggie said. Noreen trailed behind her like a shadow. "I got it on Tuesday. Remember, you told me to write him. Because he's a general?"

"Your dad's not a general in the War," Win said, though she didn't take her eyes from the ceiling. Reggie appeared like an inkblot on her periphery. "You probably don't even have a dad."

"His picture's on my bunk. You've seen it," she said and turned to Noreen, who nodded vigorously but remained mute. "See."

"What did he say?" I asked. I was as skeptical of Reggie as the others. She always fibbed. She once told us she was related to the pope. But The Guineveres were desperate for information—anything at all—and we were willing to hear what she had to say, just in case.

Reggie scratched her scalp as though she were shampooing it, and tiny flakes of dry skin drifted to her shoulders. "He said lots of soldiers go missing. It's not unusual. But they never leave anyone behind. That's a rule of the War or something." The Guineveres offered no response, just listened to the static sounds coming from the ever-tuning radio. If that were the case, where was Peter Drexel?

"That's it?" Gwen huffed. "That's all you could get from your dad, the War general?"

"It was a short letter, actually," Reggie responded. "But he said the War will make the world a safer place. I guess that makes those soldiers heroes. Are they still in a coma?"

We didn't like the word "coma," preferring

"sleeping" instead. "Is the world dangerous now?" I asked.

Reggie shrugged her shoulders. "I don't know."

"Can we read it?" one of us asked. "Your letter?"

"I have a stamp collection at home from all over the world. My dad has been to thirty-seven countries. Thirty-eight, actually, if you count our own. I'll show them to you when you come over for my welcome-home party. That is, if Sister Fran lets you come."

At that moment, Sister Fran charged into the room blowing her whistle, signaling to us for supper. The radio silenced, the skating stopped, the Ping-Pong ball dropped to the floor with a quickening tap, and we all lined up in single file to march. We could barely eat our macaroni-and-mayonnaise salad, our stomachs already too full of doubt. And we weren't sure which kind.

A few days later: confession. We welcomed its arrival. The other girls bowed their heads, conjuring up courage. Nobody enjoyed confession. How could you? It's like taking off your clothes in front of a stranger who is fully dressed. A peep show of the soul. This time, The Guineveres refused to participate.

Near the end of the service, after most of the girls had been given their blessings, we lined up in Father James's queue.

"When are we going to the Veterans

Administration?" we asked, four times over. Our bodies shook, so we crossed our arms to still ourselves. We couldn't stop thinking about Junior, wondering what his last thoughts were as he departed this world, wondering if his soul went up or down. We had to save Our Boys; we had to save ourselves.

"Soon," he said. Father James fidgeted beneath his robe, shifted from one foot to another. We could see his shoes poking out. "The Thursday after next. I'll tell Sister Fran I need you for an in-service." He held his hand over our bowed heads, and we pretended to take his blessing. Ginny faked weeping, Win exaggeratedly swayed her body, and Gwen placed her hand over her heart, but she was really just feeling for Her Boy's ring in her bra.

"Amen," we each said, our doubts subsiding, but not completely. Back in the pew, The Guineveres held hands as we kneeled, as we prayed. We were ordinary girls and it was still Ordinary Time, but we were certain, more certain than the stars in the sky or oxygen or heaven, that something extraordinary awaited us. Our fingers interlaced. We squeezed and released. If only we'd known to be careful what you pray for. It just might come true.

Saint Agatha

FEAST DAY: FEBRUARY 5

To her parents' dismay, young Agatha refused to marry. This despite the string of suitors who often lined their receiving room, waiting for a glance of the willful maiden with a reputation for beauty. *Oh, silly girl,* the gentlemen would say to each other as they leaned back, smoked their pipes, and admired her supple breasts with animal hunger. *Give her time.* But time only bound her more fervently to her Lord. The thought of a man's touch made her stomach roil, and she prayed to Him for protection from suffering.

But it was His will for poor Agatha to suffer. Soon a local prefect, Quintian, heard of the maiden who refused all advances, and he sought the young woman for himself. His desire wasn't born of love or of money—or even of sexual longing—but of ego, pure and simple. A lowborn man, Quintian was greedy for power, greedy to claim that which other men couldn't. He collected maidens like trophies, and Agatha would make an excellent prize. When he learned of the maiden's Christian faith, outlawed in those times, he sent for her, then offered a simple proposition: either himself or prison. It was blackmail, he knew, but what did he care? He was sure he'd bed her by the night's end. He imagined her round bosom, her firm bottom, and his mouth watered at the very thought of it.

Faced with such options, Agatha chose imprisonment. Quintian fumed and ordered her to a brothel, a wretched one that even he wouldn't frequent. Nightly she was subjected to violations of the crudest kind, but nightly she called upon her Lord for protection. *I am your sheep,* she'd pray. As she felt men, wild as wolves, try to climb atop her, her body glowed with a brilliant light. The men flew off her, propelled by some unseen force, thudding against walls and falling unconscious to the floor. In this way, Agatha remained untouched, a maiden till the very end.

After some months, Agatha was called again to Quintian. She stood before him dirty and barefoot. Her dress was in tatters, and her skin was smeared with dirt and with excrement. Still, his mouth watered at the sight of this beauty. He imagined her wide hips and the small of her back and her belly button that would look like a tiny pinhole in the dark of his chamber. He offered her one more chance: himself or prison. He was certain she'd choose him this time.

She remembered the brothel, all those rough hands upon her skin, not delicate like a woman's. The stink of the men caused her to retch, a biological impulse. If only she had been born into a different body. "Prison," she spat out, a faithful girl, but an obstinate one.

And so he sent her to prison, a damp and putrid place reserved for hardened criminals, for those who had murdered and pillaged, raped and robbed. There she prayed to her Lord, *See my heart and know my desires.* Her knees dug into the dirt; a shackle dug into her neck. She felt her soul pulling away, rising up, sucked out through her mouth and her eyes, as if she were being embalmed.

And that was the moment the torturers arrived with a sword, and gave her one more chance to renounce her faith. But she didn't speak, didn't utter a word, didn't even scream when the masked man raised his sword and brought it down fast upon her chest. He sheared off her breasts, now two bloodied mounds in the dirt of the prison floor.

Then the torturer handed her a platter and placed upon it her breasts, nipples to the sky like bells waiting to be rung. *Walk,* he said. And she did as instructed, out the prison door and into the sunlight. With the platter held in front of her, she felt like a serving girl, and maybe she was one. *Here's my maidenhood,* she shouted. *It's here on this platter.* Her breasts jiggled a bit as she walked, and even Agatha had to admit, they were admirable breasts; she'd never seen them from such an angle. She continued through the town, past a gloating Quintian, past the brothel, past the home where she was raised, where at night, in her room, she'd pray for a different life. The gentlemen who'd called her a silly girl were there; they averted their eyes, disgusted by such a sight. Agatha held the plate above her head, her wounds weeping blood.

She had never felt freer in her life.

Lent

In preparation for the upcoming Lenten Season, Sister Fran required us to strip our Bunk Room of any excesses. Gwen was forced to take down her glossy magazine cutouts, and Win had to hand over her domino set that she'd carved out of soap. We used to play dominoes together in the Rec Room—Win was the best, her spatial logic serving her well in such moments—but we had no use for such games now. Instead, we spent our Rec Time talking about the depths of love, of the things a woman must do to procure it. Maybe we were just growing up. We believed that without Our Boys we had nothing; we *were* nothing. And each day we didn't know their identities, each day they didn't wake up, meant we were further from our futures together. We all had our vision of what these futures looked like. Ginny said she wanted to live in a house in the country, raise some chickens.

"Why chickens?" Win asked. "My grandfather had chickens, and I can assure you they're filthy creatures." We were leaning against the wall outside the Rec Room, where we were supposed to be observing quiet time. Even though Lent was still more than a week away, the Sisters had already taken away our Ping-Pong table, our puzzles, our records, even the knitting box for the War Effort, suggesting we fill the time with reflection instead.

"Why not?" Ginny said, adding, "Animals bring us closer to our universal nature. And besides, I want to paint landscapes." She still had dreams of going to art school and hoped that Her Boy could find a job nearby.

"He may have to commute to the city for work," Gwen reminded Ginny. "Do you really want his suit stinking of a chicken coop?"

"I'll raise the chickens myself, if I have to." Her Boy's Lucky Talisman had made her less squeamish. "An artistic life won't be an easy one."

Gwen had begun to craft a future where she and Her Boy eloped, then moved to the other side of the country, where he got a job as an executive at one of the big movie studios. It was there, while working as his secretary, that she'd be discovered by a famous director.

"What if he doesn't want you to work?" I asked.

"I'd tell him to pound sand," Win said. "Nobody's going to tell me *anything* once I get out of here."

"I'll become a model, then. That's not *really* work. You just sit around getting pictures taken."

"You'd really want people ogling you all day?" Ginny asked. "Wouldn't you rather make the art?"

"I'd rather *be* the art, thank you."

"I want to build something," Win said. "But not any of this art stuff."

"Like a carpenter?" one of us asked.

Win nodded.

"Whoever heard of a woman working as a carpenter?" Gwen said. "It's hardly practical. What, will you put down your hammer to pull a beef roast out of the oven? That's hardly appropriate."

"Who says I'll be cooking at all?"

"I want to cook. Every night for My Boy. We'll have dinner together like a family," I said. "At six o'clock sharp."

"But what do you want to *do?*" Win asked.

"What do you mean?"

"What do you want to do *besides* cook? With your life?"

"I want to be his wife," I said. To be honest, I didn't know. I'd been at the convent for more than three and a half years now, four if you rounded up, as I did, and my vision of the future was mired in the memories of the girl I was when I first arrived. What would *she* have wanted to do, I tried to ask myself. *She* would have wanted to stay near her mother. Settle into a house. Grow a garden. But none of these ideas would interest The Guineveres, who believed I should have greater ambitions.

Soon we heard Sister Fran's whistle, which signaled it was almost Lights Out. Lent, Sister

Fran had explained to us during Morning Instruction, was a time for sacrifice. But The Guineveres already felt we'd sacrificed plenty. During Lent we would not be allowed to wear our hair in braids or watch filmstrips or spend time in the courtyard, not even for constitutional walks. The Adoring Sisters would fast every Friday, and, thus, so would we. Our Rec Time would be revoked, and we'd be required to go to bed early so we could meditate in prayer. All the other girls complained in whispers, but not The Guineveres. When the other girls slept, we'd find our way to the third floor, then down to the first. By now we knew to prop the door open with a folded pillowcase so we wouldn't get locked out again. Our Boys always waited for us there, silent as the color white.

Did we feel guilty about our indiscretions, about our deceit, about our lies? We did. I did. We knew Sister Fran would have lectured to us about the sins of the Flesh, about dignity, about the virtues of good girls. So we told ourselves it was what God wanted. Our Boys were scared; they were lonely; they were far from home. We wondered about their favorite song or their favorite meal. We wondered if they drank coffee in the morning, and if so, if they took it black. We wondered what they'd seen in the War; what they'd been thinking the moment they were injured. Had they been afraid? Because we were afraid sometimes. Had they believed in what they were fighting for? We believed in them, and we believed they'd come for us. They were our only hope. So, guilt, did we feel it? Yes. But we were willing to bear it.

True to his word, Father James sent Sister Fran a note, requesting The Guineveres' attendance for an in-service at the church. He told her we'd need a bit more training for the Lenten masses. For good measure, he claimed that a deacon was coming in from a nearby county with another set of altar servers so they could combine efforts. He'd even asked for Ginny's punishment to be commuted, and Sister Fran agreed. Then, on Wednesday, after Lights Out, we snuck down to the Sick Ward again, and we crept into the storage room. There, we double-checked the numbers on Our Boys' duffels, we gathered essential items from their personal effects, and we kissed their foreheads, believing that the next time we saw them we'd know their names and everything would change.

When we walked up the hill on Thursday morning, air slipped beneath our skirts. We felt alive. Ginny windmilled her arms. Win rolled her head in circles around her neck. Gwen stopped to do a few deep knee bends. "We must keep our physiques for Our Boys," she said. "These are supposed to be the best days of our lives." It was not yet Lent. Our bodies felt like our bodies still. We were happy to use them.

Later in life, Ginny would claim that walking up the hill on that afternoon was akin to walking down the aisle when she eventually married. She knew that at the end of it an entirely different life awaited her. Her first marriage ended in divorce, and she always claimed the best part of that marriage was walking down the aisle toward her groom. In those few moments, she felt the possibility of happiness; her hopes had not yet winnowed into solitude, even if it was just a lie.

The Guineveres all believed our lives would change once Father James took us to the VA office. We believed that the path we trudged up that hill was leading us to our futures far away from the convent that loomed behind us, had we cared to look. But we didn't look. We swung our arms as we imagined Our Boys did on their marches overseas. Ginny played the role of drill sergeant. "Onward!" she cried. We focused on the church at the top of the hill, on our destiny, on Father James's car parked in the grassy lot that was just beginning to green after a long winter.

"I get to sit up in the front," Gwen said.

"Why you?" Win asked.

"Because I called it."

"This was my idea," Ginny said.

"You can have it on the way back."

This sounded fair to everyone.

When we reached the top, we caught our breath. "Ready?" Win said. She held open the door.

This would be our first time leaving the convent in years. And even if we knew we'd be gone only for the day, the moment felt profound to us. Ginny rubbed her palms; Gwen ran her fingers over her brows to smooth them down. Our minds were far away, on thoughts of our new lives, but our legs carried us through the rectory to Father James's office, where we found the lights on but the room empty.

"He's probably gone to the bathroom," I offered.

"Why does nobody ever pee in the Bible when there's so much water and wine?" Win joked.

We took seats and we waited, crossing our legs first in one direction, then another. We stood and straightened our uniforms. We wished it were closer to Wash Day. Win had braided our hair for the occasion, then pinned the braid to the side of our heads. The Guineveres had wanted to look sophisticated.

"How long does it take to drive there?" Ginny asked. Nobody answered. Everywhere seemed far away.

"I hope he has a radio," Gwen said. "Otherwise it will be a long drive." She picked up a letter opener shaped like a pointed cross from Father James's desk and pretended to stab herself with it.

We double-triple checked to be sure we had everything. I had written down the long string of numbers from Our Boys' duffel bags, along with their date of arrival, and each of The Guineveres had hidden on her body the personal effects of Her Boy. Ginny couldn't find a way to hide Her Boy's wooden box, so she'd drawn a sketch of the Ouroboros on a piece of notebook paper. Her pencil marks were decisive and thick. She really did have talent as an artist.

After some time had passed, we decided to hunt for Father James in the vestry. No sign of him there, either. We grew concerned, but Father James was not known for his punctuality, not like Sister Fran. We made our way through the hallway to the main church. Inside, some prayer candles were lit, wax melting to nubs. You're supposed to donate money to light one of the candles, but The Guineveres didn't have a penny to our names. We hoped God would forgive us. *Please help us figure out who they are,* we prayed, each lighting a candle in honor of Our Boys. *Please help us find a way out, find a way home. Hear the silent intentions in our hearts. Hear our prayers. Hear our prayers.* The candle flames bounced and flicked. They shrank and grew and shrank again, and it struck us that the flames were contained by their wick, but reliant on it all the same. Bound to a candle, fire was a thing of beauty; unrestrained, a destructive force.

We were thinking this very thought when we heard something crash in one of the confessional booths. "Hello," Win said. She slid open the slatted door. There was Father James, face down, passed out on the bench, his feet dangling over the ledge. His bottle of Sunny Brook lay smashed beneath him, the shards shaped like puzzle pieces.

"Get up," Win said, and she kicked the underside of the bench with a force so heavy that Father James's head popped up, then met the wood with a thud. "Get up!" she yelled, her voice echoing off the sacred walls of the church, so it sounded like all four of us had said it.

"Is he alive?" I asked.

"Of course he's alive," Ginny said.

"He's too much of a coward to be dead," Gwen added.

We looked to each other, from Guinevere to Guinevere, trying to decide what to do. And, as though someone had counted to three, soon we were all on top of him, vultures on prey. We pecked with fingers, pinched with nails, burrowed into his back with quick jabs of our elbows. We even drew blood. Win took the dish of holy water from outside the booth and splashed it on his face. We slapped him. We kicked him. We tried to roll him over, but the dead weight was too much for us. Father James was limp-limbed. Out cold.

We couldn't go on forever with our battering. It was as useful as waking Our Boys. Our hands were tired. Our arms were sore. Father James began to snore. Despondent, we took a seat in the first pew. We wanted to tell someone, but there was nobody to tell, not a soul in the world we could trust with our secrets, except Our Boys. But if they were capable of helping, if they were awake, we wouldn't need Father James in the first place.

We screamed through clenched teeth. Our throats went raw. The sound bounced off the ceiling, as if a hundred girls were wailing. We were a hundred Guineveres now. An army. We kicked our legs. Win batted the back of the pew with a hymnal until its spine broke. Ginny pulled at her hair. Gwen cursed. And soon we all cursed there, in that church. Sent every blasphemous phrase we could think of up to the rafters. I won't repeat them here. That would do no good, and I'd hate to be remembered for that.

"We can take his car," Ginny suggested after we'd calmed down some. "We can go on our own."

None of us had driven a car before. "We don't even know how to drive. Or where it is," Win said. She wrapped her arm around Ginny and begged her not to cry.

Ginny obeyed this command. She was too stunned anyway. Her face was oddly composed. Her eyes beheld the altar with a look of tragic disappointment. "Then we can visit my dad. I've been there once. We can stop and ask for directions," she said. At this, she stood up, and we followed her as she marched back to Father James's office. We watched as she scoured the room, sliding out every drawer and upturning every stack of paper. "I know the keys are here somewhere," she said. She opened the cabinets on his bureau, even dug through the pockets of Father James's jacket hanging on the coat rack. "They're here somewhere. They're here somewhere."

"Ginny, they're not here," one of us said after a while.

"Well, I'm not going to give up!" she yelled. Her braid had come undone, and she ran her fingers through her hair. The other Guineveres would later admit, there in Father James's office, Ginny's skirt twisted halfway around her waist, her palms held out as though they actually dripped blood, she already looked unhinged.

"Ginny, we'll try again. He'll take us again. Another time." I think these words came from Win. In fact, I'm certain they did.

"They're here. I know they're here," she repeated. Then she sat down atop Father James's desk while she scrawled out a note in big bubbly letters. *You can't hide forever,* it read. But even if Father James could have responded, it'd be too late for Ginny, too late for her happy ending.

We didn't return to the convent immediately. I'm not sure why. I suppose a small part of us held out hope that Father James might wake up and come get us, but he never did. Besides, going back to the convent meant creating a new set of questions—Why had we returned so early? What did we learn?—and we didn't have the energy to answer them. The Guineveres weren't liars. Win stretched out on Father James's couch and took a nap. Ginny found some paper and drew somber sketches. Gwen went through Father James's desk drawers for booze but couldn't find any, and then she spun and spun in Father James's chair. We found some stale cookies in his bureau, and we ate them. We opened the window, and took off our shoes. We tried to hold on to the freedom of the afternoon, but we should have known that we couldn't.

We never learned what became of Father James, if he awoke himself from his stupor, or if someone found him passed out in the confessional booth. Either way, he went on a mysterious hiatus. A substitute priest filled in for him at Sunday's mass. He was the one who smelled like fish, and he didn't seem to take kindly to girls on his altar. When we asked him, he brusquely explained that Father James had been called away, and then he turned his back to us as we dressed for mass in silence.

The official start of Lent, and still no sign of Father James. During Ash Wednesday's service in the Sick Ward, a different priest presided over the service, this time the old one who stood with the help of a walker, much like some of the old folks in the Sick Ward. "Remember thou art dust and to dust thou shalt return," he repeated again and again. He gripped his walker with one hand, and with the other he smudged the silky black ash onto the foreheads of the convalescents, fat, finger-painted crosses that made the old folks resemble chimney sweeps. When Mr. Macker received his ashes, he touched his forehead and looked at his hand in confusion as though he had discovered blood on his fingertips. We helped the priest administer ashes to those old folks strong enough to sit in the Front Room, then made our way to the Back Room to greet the bedridden. Immediately our eyes found Our Boys. Mine's lips were parted; his hands were folded on his chest, as though in prayer, and I could see his fingernails needed clipping. He'd lost some weight since he'd been here, but it brought out the shape of his face, his strong jawbone. He looked lovelier somehow, lighter, too. If there is a God, I thought to myself, then hear my prayers and bring him back to me. *Hear my prayers. Hear my prayers,* I'd chant in my head.

I was so busy praying that I hadn't realized Ginny was crying, or rather, unsuccessfully attempting to restrain the tears that formed in her eyes. When I turned, I realized why: Her Boy's bed was empty, stripped down to the bare mattress that was sunken in the middle, imprinted with the weight of a ghost. We assumed the worst. After mass, we huddled with her in the bathroom. Ginny let her tears flow this time and buried her face in her hands. She looked up at us; her ashes had smeared across her forehead, so that she looked dirty, almost feral. We didn't know how to comfort her—didn't know what to say. She was weeping so loudly, then gasping for breath so long, so deep, I thought she might pass out.

"It's not your fault," we told her. Sometimes miracles don't happen, and God never has to offer up an explanation. That's the benefit of being God, I suppose.

"I loved him," Ginny said, taking in a series of quick breaths.

"We know you did," we told her. "You loved him as best you could."

"But . . . but . . . but . . . ," she sobbed, wiping her nose on my shoulder as I held her. Black ash transferred to my blouse.

"He's in a better place," I said.

"You don't know that," she said, and she sobbed harder. "I'll never love anyone again." Her tiny body shook, and I hugged her gently, afraid if I held her too tight I'd crush her fragile bones. "Never."

"Everything happens for a reason," one of us said, though at this point, I'm not sure any of us really believed it.

She stopped crying for a bit and sucked snot through her nose. She rocked herself forward and backward, then said quietly, "He was the only one I could talk to." Her voice was empty, fragile like a teacup. "Even though I knew he wasn't really there."

I agreed there were certain things we couldn't say to anyone else, not out loud. Certain things we couldn't even confess to each other, to The Guineveres, even though we promised not to keep secrets. Private things. Feelings we'd stuffed inside so long, pushed down so far, crumpled inside us like little wads of paper. We didn't know how to smooth them out. But I had to believe, I *did* believe—for my own sake, perhaps—that Ginny hadn't lost faith in Her Boy.

"He was there," I said, stroking her wild hair. "He was there all along."

We all felt Ginny's loss lodge itself in our stomachs till we felt sick, like we'd eaten too much of Sister Claire's plum pudding. What one Guinevere felt, we all felt; what one of us lost, we all lost.

"He suddenly made a turn for the worse," Sister Fran told us when we saw her in the cafeteria. "Such a shame—and so young. But, on the bright side, he'll no longer suffer. God called him home. You never know the time or the place, girls. You know what I say about not waiting for a hearse."

"Yes, we know," we said.

"Can we do something for him, Sister? Something to memorialize him? The War Effort?" I asked. Ginny poked her sweet potato with a faraway look in her eyes. She'd lost the one thing that gave her hope; she'd lost her reason to believe.

"That might be a fine idea, girls. Perhaps a mass in his honor."

"Not a mass," I said. I was thinking of something else.

Later that afternoon, during what would've been Rec Time if not for Lent, Sister Fran gave us permission to visit the Sick Ward. The place felt different somehow, hazy and moody, but calm. The sun peeked through the windows, casting the room in an orange-red glow, as if the whole Ward were on fire. Maybe the whole world, too. Sister Connie showed us to the duffel of Ginny's Boy, though we already knew where it was. We retrieved a pair of his boots from it and handed the bag back to her. She nodded to dismiss us.

The boots were heavy, with thick, cleated rubber soles caked with mud. The tops were made of leather and canvas, and small brass eyelets lined the arches. Ginny carried them to the courtyard, one in each hand, balanced on the tips of her small fingers. The Guineveres followed behind her, a somber processional. We wore handkerchiefs tied over our hair like scarves for respect, but the wind attempted to tear them away. The day was cloudless but cold. Our skirts whipped around our legs. Our faces felt pricked by a hundred small needles. Ginny was on her knees, digging through the soil with her hands.

She carefully filled each boot, patting down the soil with her fist. Dirt streaked her cheekbones from where she occasionally stopped to wipe her tears. Or maybe it was just the wind hitting her eyes. Nobody spoke. Nobody had to say a word. Ginny filled the boot with a small packet of seeds Sister Fran had given us. The Guineveres helped her locate a spot, rearranging some of the Sisters' old shoes to make room. It wasn't spring yet, so no flowers had budded, but in a month or two, this whole row of planters would sprout to life, and Ginny's Boy would be among them.

That evening, we were all uneasy, wondering if Our Boys would be taken from us, too. *You never know the time or the place,* Sister Fran had told us. *He suddenly made a turn for the worse.* We were on edge, anxious and scared. Gwen coiled in her bed, Her Boy's ring on her finger. Win tried to give Ginny Her Boy's wooden horse, but she refused to accept it. The Bunk Room air tasted of urgency. Lights Out couldn't come quickly enough. We had to see them, had to hold their hands and tell them how much they meant to us, how we loved them, and how they gave our lives meaning. Nobody could love them better than us. Not more than us, either. If only we could convince them to stay.

Later that night, we made the quiet trek up to

the third floor and then down to the Sick Ward in the dark. By now, we knew our way by heart; we didn't jump at the shadows or cling to one another so tightly.

Ginny came with us, too. She couldn't bear being alone. When we arrived, she made her way to Her Boy's bed, where we could hear her weeping in the dark. I knelt by My Boy, squeezed his hand, and tried to convey to him, through prayer, through telepathy, through sheer will that I was there, and he wouldn't have to be alone. I squeezed his hand harder as I prayed; it was large and bony, and I could feel small bumps where I knew some scars to be. As I prayed to God—or to whoever would listen—not to take My Boy from me, I felt his hand squeeze back, just lightly, but I felt it nonetheless. My heart quickened, and I rested my forehead on his palm, as if I were receiving a blessing.

Later, in the stairwell, Gwen reported to us that she crawled beneath the covers, pressed her body against Her Boy, then placed his bandaged hand up her shirt.

"You let him go up your shirt?" Win said, and I couldn't tell if her voice was full of disgust or delight.

"Yes! Yes!" Gwen was smiling so big, so toothily, that there was no mystery to her at all. She described the way she'd cupped his hand around her breast, squeezed a little bit so he knew what he was holding.

"Would you do that for Your Boys?" she asked. "For the War Effort?"

"I don't have anything for him to grab," Win said. "Just these two mosquito bites." And she smoothed down her nightgown over her chest to reveal her round breasts, the size of grapefruits.

"My dad used to paint pictures of naked ladies. They had these big breasts that almost looked like another set of eyes," Ginny said quietly. "Sometimes I'd stare at them, thinking that's what I'd grow up to be when I got older. Now I don't know what I'll grow up to be."

"Why do women want large chests?" Win asked. "I don't get it. They just get in the way," she said, looking down at her own ample bosom. "I can barely see my feet!"

"Who cares about seeing your feet?" Gwen said. "It's not about your feet."

"Well, you've got to walk, don't you?"

"You're awfully quiet," Gwen said, now looking at me. "Would you let Your Boy go up your shirt? Because once he goes up, he must come . . ."

"Down!" Win said.

"And you know what happens when he touches your button, don't you?" Gwen said.

"It's not actually a button," Win explained. "But I know what happens."

"Pleasure. Exploding pleasure that makes you feel like you're on fire."

"Not actually on fire," Win said.

"An orgasm," Gwen said. "It's why people have sex."

"And for babies," Win clarified. "Procreation. Populating humanity."

"Don't you want to have an orgasm?" Gwen asked. She leaned backward against the wall and crossed her arms, waiting for my answer.

I stood there in my thin nightgown, exposed; my legs felt weak, as if my knees were made of water. "I don't know," I said. In truth, I didn't. The thought of being naked around a boy made me wriggle with discomfort. I didn't understand the thrill, how someone could take off her clothes without embarrassment. And why would I want to feel like I was on fire? It sounded painful, quite frankly. "Modesty is attractive, too," I said.

"Sister Fran is modest," Win said. "But she's not attractive."

"This is stupid," Ginny said. "Who cares?"

"Freezer," Gwen said, explaining that a freezer freezes up when it comes down to physical affection. A freezer doesn't know how to show love.

I thought about this as I lay in bed that night, staring at moonlight from between the window slats. I didn't want to be a freezer. I needed to be ready to show My Boy love. Beneath my covers, I touched my own body. I slipped my hand up my nightgown and ran it over the smooth, sloping skin of my breasts. I squeezed and pinched just to see what it would feel like. At first nothing happened, but then I imagined My Boy, and slowly my breasts changed shape. My nipples tingled and hardened, as if I were cold, and a surge of electricity whooshed through me, *down there.* I felt ashamed.

If God truly saw all, then He saw me doing that, there in the darkness beneath my covers. My body stiffened at the thought. I straightened my nightgown, and I felt the great weight of guilt bearing down on me until I fell asleep.

Confessions were taken the next week. Still no sign of Father James.

"I was immodest with a boy once, and I don't regret it. But he's gone now, and I think I love him and hate him all at once," Ginny said to her old priest as The Guineveres lined up behind her.

"I tried to kiss a boy again. I mean, really kiss him," Win confessed. "I didn't like it, and I'm not sure I ever will. Are you supposed to feel something more? Because I didn't feel anything at all, and it tasted awful."

"I went to second base with a boy," Gwen confessed to the priest. His pockmarked skin indicated he'd had acne in his youth. "Do you need me to explain?" she asked amidst the background of Sister Lucrecia's organ music. "Because I can." She didn't blink, and neither did the priest, just faced off in a great battle of stone face.

"I'm a freezer," I told the Father. When he asked what I meant, I said, "I need to love better." The old man tilted his head. "And I . . ." I paused, thinking of that night in the Bunk Room when I'd allowed my hands to touch my own body, to know its curves in the dark just to see what it would feel like.

"Yes?" he said, his eyes watering, his jaw locked, restraining a yawn of boredom.

"Never mind."

"God already knows."

"I know. Never mind."

A few days later, Sister Fran called an all-school meeting, the topic: The Flesh. Though Father James's flock of priests could not break the bonds of confessional confidentiality, it had leaked out that some of the girls had exhibited promiscuous behaviors likely to incur penalty in the afterlife.

"We cannot tolerate sins of the Flesh," Sister Fran said, her cheeks sunken in and her skin grayed for want of meat and sleep. Maybe for want of flesh, too. "Your bodies are temples," she said, leaning in and scanning all of the girls sitting, knees pressed, on the floor of the Rec Room. Everyone looked around, trying to spot the harlots among us. "I may not know who you are, but your maker does," she said, as she pointed toward the ceiling, and the black fabric of her sleeve fell back to reveal a thin, pale arm. Her wrists looked like chicken bones. "And He's the one who matters."

Holy Week: It was torturous. We were all required to observe the Sisters' vow of silence. In the cafeteria, the clinking of forks was unbearable. During Morning Instruction, Sister Fran wrote out directions on the board that we were to read select passages from *The Lives of the Saints* and write a five-paragraph essay about what these saints had in common. Saint Basilissa was beheaded for refusing to marry Pompeius, a Roman patrician. Saint Macrina the Younger died an untouched maiden after she refused all her suitors. Saint Cecilia married, but she convinced her husband to let her remain a virgin. I wrote an essay about the virtues of abstinence. Gwen wrote about holding out for the right man.

On Holy Thursday the sky was purple-green. Holy Thursday celebrated the Last Supper, and we, too, felt something stirring inside of us, as if a wait were coming to an end. We visited the Sick Ward that night. We waited until after Sister Tabitha came around for Checks. We wanted to wish Our Boys a happy Easter. Easter marked the resurrection of Jesus, how he rose from the dead. And even though The Guineveres found this creepy and kind of gruesome, like a ghoul or a zombie, it was a new beginning, and this notion felt romantic to us. Our Boys would help us start anew as well, provide us with our final Revival Story, and perhaps our truest one.

When we stepped into the Sick Ward, we each went to our separate beds. I crept up slowly behind My Boy, then placed my palm to his face. That's when it happened: He awoke. His eyes darted back and forth, confused, like a man looking for something he'd lost.

I didn't speak, didn't say anything. I couldn't. I removed my hand from his face and took a step back and tried to catch my breath.

"Are you an angel?" His voice was rough, strained. "Am I dead?" He blinked groggily, from sleep or from morphine, and then he grabbed my wrist.

The touch of his hand startled me, and I stepped back, nervous. Although I'd played out this scene in my head a thousand times—My Boy waking—I didn't know what to say to him. I looked down at the floor, at my feet, then reached for him, our fingers finding each other, intertwining like prayer hands.

"You're not dead," I managed to stammer. "You're alive. You're right here with me. I've been taking care of you," I said, touching him, aware of my clammy hands, my damp underarms. My limbs tingled; my mouth went dry. I tried to think what The Guineveres would say. My heart bounded around my chest like a clumsy wasp, looking for escape. I poured him a glass of water from his bedside table, then fed him small sips, though he resisted.

"You've been taking care of me?" he said, the water smoothing out his voice.

"Yes," I said. My mouth felt so dry.

"What happened?"

I swallowed hard. I moved closer to him so he could see my face better, so I could see his. It was then I saw that The Guineveres had gathered around, arms linked, to watch. Their mouths were open in astonishment, and they were waving me on. "Say something," I saw Ginny mouth.

"I . . . I think you were hurt. You *were* hurt. In the War," I said, searching for words.

He paused as though he was trying to remember something, his eyes moving back and forth like a typewriter. He weakly adjusted his arm; his wrist dangled over the edge of his bed. Win nudged me closer, so I placed my clammy hand on top of his. "What's your name?" he asked.

I blinked blankly, dumbstruck. I can't say why. I've revisited this moment again and again, and each time I try to will myself to say something coherent, something profound, something so he'd know how much I loved him. But I always fail. The truth was, I couldn't speak. My tongue was a weight in my mouth, and I could barely lift it, not even to say my name.

"It's Guinevere," Gwen finally said.

My Boy struggled to keep his eyes open; oh, how he tried. He blinked rapidly to ward off sleep, but his eyes shut like little window shades, and like that, he was gone.

In those days, the only way I understood love was through longing. I hadn't the slightest notion of what romantic love looked like. I'd never been in love, not like this, never kissed a boy who kissed me back. I knew that love hurt sometimes, badly. And that's the only way I can explain what I felt right then, as My Boy rested his weary eyes: I felt pain.

I stood for a few moments in the darkness, until I felt movement behind me.

"Do you think he's healed?" Ginny asked. "Do you think your prayers have been answered? We'll have to say good-bye to you soon, too."

My Boy had returned for me. My Boy had come to take me home.

"You're lucky," Ginny said.

"He has risen!" Win said.

"Don't get your hopes up," Gwen said, not in a mean way, just matter-of-fact. And she was right. By Good Friday, he'd slipped back into his soundless slumber, locked away again in his living tomb.

I cried during the mass—cried afterward, too.

We never did tell Sisters Connie or Magda. Perhaps I was afraid they'd find his family, send him somewhere far away. Without me. Home. In hindsight, that may have been a mistake, for who knows what Sister Connie might have done to help My Boy? Who knows how things might have turned out? Yet who's to say a different ending would have been a better one? The universe has a plan, I must believe, and there's no regretting the past. You can only march forward.

At the time, however, marching forward felt like trudging through quicksand. "He wanted to know my name," I cried. My head was buried in Win's lap. The Guineveres were sitting on Ginny's bed in the Bunk Room; on the wall above us we could see tape marks from where some sketches of hers had been hung, one of a night sky crowded with stars, and another of a green pasture that we knew was a field of poppies.

"Well, at least you have that," Ginny said. "I don't have anything."

"But I didn't ask him his." He'd made me so nervous I'd neglected the simplest question of them all, one that could help me piece together his identity, figure out who he was. I kept running the conversation over and over in my head. *What's your name? What's your name?* His voice had been low, full of gravel, full of sleep.

"You don't have to know his name to love him," Win said.

"But what if I never find out? What if he never comes back?"

"Just keep waiting," Gwen said. Her calves were resting on the top of the mattress. She'd removed her shoes and socks, but we could still see squiggly lines indented into her skin. "What else are you going to do?"

"I've got to have faith," I reminded myself.

"I didn't say anything about faith," Gwen said.

"Then what?" I asked. Win handed me another tissue, then kicked Gwen with her heel.

"Just seems we do a lot of waiting—for our parents, for Our Boys, for the Sisters, for Father James, for our eighteenth birthdays. This whole place is a goddamn purgatory."

"Don't talk like that," I said. Then, "What's that even supposed to mean?"

"I know what she means," said Ginny.

"It takes faith," I said. That's what all the waiting had seemed like to me, a test of some sort.

"Then where are our parents? Where are signs from God that this all isn't some stupid joke? The War Effort. Pfft. What do we even know about the War?" Gwen curled herself into a ball on the floor. Her eyes closed, and her face went slack for a moment, so still that we thought she had fallen asleep. Win nudged her with her foot, and Gwen's eyes sprang open. They were glassy and wet with tears she'd willed back into their ducts. "Of course, I don't mean anything about Your Boy. I'm sure he'll wake up again. Really."

"He'll be back to take you home," Win said reassuringly. "Just don't forget about us."

That night when the other girls were asleep, I closed my eyes and again slipped my hand under my nightgown. I ran my fingers up and down my body, imagining it was My Boy touching me. I tried not to shift in my bunk and make noise, even as I sank my fingers into the moist darkness, searching for the button that would set me on fire. I didn't want to be a freezer. I didn't want to be alone, either. *My name is Guinevere. My name is Guinevere. My name is Guinevere. My name is Guinevere.*

What's yours?

My Boy, hear my prayer.

Easter

The morning before Easter, Holy Saturday, Ginny's bed was empty. Sister Fran said nothing of this during Morning Roll after she woke us with the shrill squeal of her whistle, slapping the bunk rails with her hand as she patrolled the room. "Laziness is just a half a hair away from sloth, girls, a cardinal sin, indeed," she said. The moaning of bed coils filled the room as girls propped themselves up, swung their legs around to dangle over the edges of their beds. Sister Fran marched all the way to the window, then turned around and came to stop at Ginny's bunk. Her sheets and blankets were twisted and thrown to the side, her pillow still dented as though a phantom head rested there. "Good lambs are not idle lambs, nor do they stray," Sister Fran muttered, trilling her whistle once more.

The Guineveres stood by our bunks during Morning Roll, probing each other for answers. We shrugged our shoulders and shook our heads. When Sister Fran called our names, we barely managed to stutter "here," and when we did, she eyed us suspiciously, trying to read the intentions of our souls.

Despite the fact it was Holy Saturday, it was still a Saturday, which meant Wash Day. The Sisters observed Wash Day with the dedication of any of their rituals. Sister Claire, who wore a white smock on these days, rolled a large, thundering bin into the Bunk Room, and without prompting, the girls bundled their bed linens, along with their uniforms, and handed them over to be counted. "We're missing a set," Sister Claire announced when the last of the girls had dropped her wash into the bin.

"It's Ginny's," one of The Delinquents said, and she turned to point to the only bed not stripped to the mattress. Everybody stared for a moment, not knowing what to do, and Sister Claire herself seemed startled by the glitch in her normally seamless routine. She squeezed her face and hummed "hmm" several times over until Sister Fran said, "This is not an apparition, for goodness sake, but dirty sheets!" The girls all giggled, but The Guineveres panicked as she gathered Ginny's wash.

"Do you think she's okay?" The Guineveres finally asked when we found ourselves alone at breakfast. We were eating applesauce, and even though it was warm and smelled of wet newspaper, we gobbled every bite. Our stomachs creaked like rusted hinges, and a day of fasting stretched out before us. We wouldn't eat again until supper, and then only some broth and bread, since Lent meant scarcity.

"Maybe she ran away," Win said. She licked her

spoon, then thinking better of it, licked her hand and smoothed down her bangs.

"She wouldn't go without us," Gwen said. "She'd want an audience for that. You know, the artist thing and all." Gwen took the last bite from her bread plate and, sitting erect, placed it on her head.

"What are you doing?" Win asked.

"I'm practicing my posture," she said, carefully tucking her hair behind her ears without moving her shoulders or her neck. "You should be able to balance anything on your head if you're sitting properly." Gwen's hair was straight and fine; when it got greasy between Wash Days, it simply shined.

"Could she be sick?" I asked. "We need to do something."

"Like what? And wouldn't Sister Fran have said something if she were sick?" Win replied. "Told us to report our symptoms at once?" Win was right; usually when one of us got sick, the Sisters made an announcement of it, demanded that those with even the slightest symptoms, a sniffle or a tickle in the throat, gargle with salt water. The Sisters believed salt water cured almost anything.

"Maybe she's in the Penance Room again," Gwen said.

"Maybe," Win replied.

"We certainly don't want to associate ourselves

with whatever kind of trouble she's gotten herself into this time," Gwen said.

"But we're The Guineveres," I said. They didn't respond, just stirred and restirred what remained in their bowls. "I'm worried," I said, and this time the other Guineveres agreed. We knew we couldn't do anything with our worry, though, so Win suggested we just put it away.

After breakfast, we sluggishly filed to the Wash Room to wait our turn for the fifteen-minute soak we were each allotted. "God does not mean for bath time to be a form of entertainment, girls," Sister Fran would say, reminding us to scrub the backs of our necks and behind our ears. "Washing is labor. Labor is its own reward."

The Wash Room looked like a hospital, like the Sick Ward. Sterile. Industrial. A place that made us feel uncomfortable about the fact that we were embodied creatures, and it was in here, in this white room, where we felt the most shame. The floor felt like ice cubes against our bare feet, and the pungent smell of bleach stung our noses. A plastic curtain hung around each tub, so we could maintain our modesty while we bathed. We undressed in private, and during this time, for fifteen brief minutes, we were alone with our bodies, all smooth skin and curves and hair matted between our legs. We'd step out of our clothing, and we'd remove our undergarments, hanging them over the curtain rod where they'd be collected for the wash. The steamy air felt foreign against our naked skin, coating our bodies in a thin sheen and creating sweat mustaches. We pressed our arms to our breasts, held them close to us as if they might fall away. We tried to avert our own eyes from our flesh, but we couldn't, even when we tried. Especially when we tried. This time was our only chance to peek down at ourselves, at our bodies, tight and rounded, strange and distorted, still changing with age.

Afterward we'd share notes. "Are nipples supposed to be oval shaped or round?" one of us would ask, or, "Is it normal if one boob is bigger than the other?" or "Are they supposed to be pointy?" or "Is your hair *down there* the same color as your hair up top?" We didn't know, and we certainly didn't dare ask Sister Fran such questions. We could only guess and reassure each other that we were, indeed, normal.

Usually, we bathed in silence, save for the clack-clacking of Sister Fran's shoes on the tile as she snaked her way around the room. However, today Sister Fran spoke to us, her voice fading in and out as she paced between the rows of tubs. "You know, girls, your body is a temple." We'd heard this lecture before—we knew it by rote. God lived in us, in this temple. And to destroy the temple is to destroy He who lives there. Water splashed. Bodies squeaked against the porcelain as girls adjusted in tubs.

"God has loaned you these bodies, girls, like a book from the library. Do you write in the book you borrow? No. Do you place that book face-down and break the spine? I think not. You're gentle with the book you borrow—you treat it better than you'd treat your own because you know it is not yours. We must not grow too fond of the book, for we know we must return it. But, still, this doesn't prevent you from using the book, reading it, so to speak, as long as you do so with care.

"Do you see, girls, your body is this library book. You must remain unattached to it, for your own sake. You don't want a fine for ill-treating this property. You must resist your own desires to do as you feel, dog-earing pages or pencil-lining passages, for texts have value, just like bodies." Sister Fran paused to consider what she'd just said, and girls took the opportunity to dip and dunk their washrags, then wring them out.

Sister Fran continued. "Now, girls, this is also why we fast during the Lenten Season. There is grace in deprivation; hunger reminds us that self-denial is holy; fasting—this abstinence—purifies our bodies. It's just as you'll clean your tub before another girl takes her bath; the tub is not yours, just a vessel you use to clean yourself. Such is the body. One sacrifice opens the door to even greater sacrifices. When we deny our bodies, we become closer to our own souls, and, thus, closer to that which the Heavenly Father intended. Do you understand, girls? Do you understand sacrifice?" she asked.

"Yes, Sister," a chorus of voices responded.

"Good," she said. "Your time is up. Now, out, before you prune your skin." We quickly stood, wrapped ourselves in towels, and dressed in the clean uniforms Sister Claire had placed over the curtain rod while we were washing.

But The Guineveres didn't fully understand such sacrifice—not quite yet, not then, as we emerged from the Wash Room with wet hair, hungry, and looking with guarded hope for our friend. To us, sacrifice meant tedium, meant hunger, meant boredom. Our Boys had sacrificed much for the War, but was it worth it for them, their sacrifices? Could even they see that their bodies weren't their bodies, merely books on loan? Would they be fined for the damage they'd caused themselves, the injuries that had been brought upon them? Or, like Junior, the damage he'd brought upon himself? We wanted to ask Sister Fran, but as with our other questions, we didn't dare. Instead, The Guineveres single-filed to the chapel for prayer, our hair still damp, our spirits low, our minds wavering between Our Boys in the Sick Ward and our friend who, like Peter Drexel, was MIA.

We continued to worry about Ginny the next day, as The Guineveres stood at the altar, donned in robes for the Easter celebration. Father James had returned from his mysterious leave of absence, and he'd greeted us in the processional line with a nod. We wouldn't look at him. Years later he'd admit to me what he felt in this moment was guilt. He'd had no intention of further defying the rules of the convent. But it was more than that: He was ashamed.

During the mass, the sea of vibrant pastels, pinks and greens and yellows and oranges, looked surreal to us somehow, as if spring had sprouted inside after a long, slate-colored winter. In the fourth pew, we spotted a soldier in his uniform: blue coat with pins and stripes, with big brass buttons that looked recently polished. We liked to imagine Our Boys in a uniform like this one, or like those uniforms stuffed inside their duffels, which they'd wear again someday on the day we married, their fathers giving us away, their mothers weeping tears of joy. But the soldier in the fourth pew didn't look joyful; his church face was wooden. When the congregation refrained "Thanks be to God" after the second reading, his lips didn't move.

Father James's homily praised rebirth, renewal. He said we were all given second chances. He said today was a day to begin anew. His hair looked freshly colored again to cover his grays; we could see a dark line of dye and smell chemicals, still astringent, when he bent to kiss the Bible before reading the Gospel. Ginny used to be the one assigned to hold the Bible, but this time it was Gwen. She looked past him when he bowed, refusing to accept his apologetic glances. The organ blasted upbeat melodies, so different from the somber dirges of Lent, but even the music did little to lift our hearts, sagging with worry for Ginny.

When the petitions were read, the lector rattled off another list of soldiers taken by the War. Walter Lawson. Raleigh Tucker. Larry Miller. Colin Whiting. Martin McDonald. Jerry Scott. Nicolas Gardner. Billy Gibson. Ronnie Buchanan. Alvin Silva. *Lord Hear Our Prayer.* Another petition was lifted up for Peter Drexel, poor missing Peter Drexel, and his parents appeared as sickly apparitions in the first pew. *Lord Hear Our Prayer.* Mr. Drexel had gone completely gray, even in the beard. Mrs. Drexel's clothes hung off her body. She was barely a body at all.

In the vestry after mass, Father James greeted us for the first time in weeks. We didn't speak, not even when he handed each of us a pile of egg-shaped chocolates. We unwrapped them from their colored foils. We popped them in our mouths without a sound. We became stone statues as we savored the way the chocolate melted on our tongues, the sugar immediately rushing to our heads.

"I'm sorry, girls," Father James said. "I'm truly

sorry. Even I have flaws. Especially so, perhaps. But I cannot take you off the grounds. That's a violation of—"

"Where's Ginny?" Gwen interrupted. We had more pressing concerns than the Veterans Administration at the moment. The Guineveres stood motionless, save for our tongues in our mouths, slithering over chocolate. We couldn't help ourselves.

Father James stood with his back to us, looking out the window. He withdrew a flask from his jacket, took a quick swig, then tucked it back into his coat pocket and turned around to face us. "If there were something more I could do, I would," he said. Here, he examined Gwen with guilt, his eyes cast downward as though he lacked for distance vision.

"We can see you drinking," Gwen said. "You're not hiding it very well."

Father James sat down on the couch, removed the flask from his pocket again, and took a long draw, looking directly at Gwen as he did this. "Better to keep one's sins in plain sight?" he said to her.

"I thought drinking wasn't a sin, Father," she said.

"Where is she?" Win asked. Her face contained a challenge; her sharp nose pointed toward Father James.

"She's in the Penance Room," he said.

"Why?" I asked. I always seemed to be the one asking why.

"Because they found her in the middle of the night, sleeping in the convalescent ward, in the empty bed of one of the soldiers who'd been there. The one who died," Father James explained. He blushed a little when he told us how Ginny had been naked, her nightgown slung over the edge of the bed. Her arms were outstretched and her legs touched at the ankle, a human cross. When Sisters Connie and Magda tried to wake her, Ginny became violent, scratching at their skin like an angry cat, ranting madly about loving Her Boy, cursing them for taking poor care of him. She clung to the mattress and kicked her legs like pistons, and then, finally, after several attempts to calm her down, Sister Connie sedated her with drugs. "They thought she must be under the influence of drink again," he said. "Or emotionally disturbed. She's been through a lot in her life, you know," Father James said.

"We know," The Guineveres said defensively. We knew everything about each other. Of course we knew, and we resented his even mentioning it.

"Poor boy," Father James said, and his voice trailed off, probably because he was thinking of his dead brother at this point.

Poor Ginny.

"Was she?" he asked. "Was she drunk again?"

"No," Gwen said, then sat down beside Father

James, removed the flask from his hand, and took a drink from it.

"How do you know?" he asked.

"We only drink with you, Father," she said. She moved closer to him until their legs were touching; her skirt rested just above her knees. I noticed a scar the shape of a snake on it. One end came to a point.

"I don't think that's wise," he said, reaching for the flask. "I've taken some regrettable liberties."

"I won't tell. Will you?" she asked, glancing in our direction before taking another sip.

"No," we said.

"It's the least you could do, Father," Gwen said. "Just a sip."

"A sip *each*," Gwen replied, then handed Win the flask. When she was finished she passed it to me, and even though I didn't want to drink, I thought I should, to show my solidarity.

"What will happen to her?" I asked, noticing the flask circling the room once more, eyeing it until it returned to me, and I reluctantly drank again.

"She'll probably stay there for a penance period, I imagine," he said. "They are worried about her mental state." He took a long drink himself, then wiped the mouth of the flask with a handkerchief the way he wiped the communion chalice during mass. "That soldier. He was comatose. Dead, for all intents and purposes. What on earth would make her believe . . ."

We stopped him from finishing his sentence. We became balls of fire, fury, seething with emotions we didn't know how to name, with passions we didn't know where to place. Of course we believed in Our Boys. What else could we believe?

"Are you a doctor now?" Gwen shouted, startling even us. She pushed herself away from Father James and stood. Her nose twitched, and she glowered at him without moving her head. "Did you go to medical school to be extra sure to avoid the War? Is that where you've been? Hiding? Some people are braver than that, those soldiers included."

"You can love someone you can't see," Win said, picking up steam. She stood now, too. Her arms became rods at her sides, her fists little balls. "Isn't that what we're taught? Isn't this what your golden book says? Unfortunately there is no commandment for hypocrites."

"Or for people who break their promises." I said. At this, I rose. My jaw tensed. My mouth watered. My head felt filled with cement, my heart, too. "If Ginny loved that soldier, she loved that soldier. Who are you to tell us what love is? How do you know what it looks like? We happen to know it isn't leaving, just up and leaving, when someone needs you the most." What did Father James know about Our Boys?

At least they were here. They'd never disappointed us. If the Sisters taught us about miracles and faith, about the rewards of dedication and hope, about overcoming doubt, then we had to believe we'd go home with them. We *did* believe it.

"Girls, girls. Calm down. I'm sorry. For everything. You must believe me." Father James stood, tucked the flask back in his pocket. He closed his eyes and shook his head. He couldn't look at us. "Like it or not, you are wards of Sister Fran, and I cannot take you to the Veterans Administration without her consent, not even for the sake of those poor soldiers."

It was too late for apologies. We were beyond that point. We'd begin our own letter-writing campaign to the Veterans Administration if we had to. We'd get Reggie's father to do the same. Maybe he really was a general in the War. And if not, we'd find another way. The Guineveres were enterprising. The Guineveres always had a plan. The Guineveres linked arms and rotated ourselves like a herky-jerky chorus line. We exited the room.

We walked back down the hill, seething in silence, each of us dwelling in her imagination, where Our Boys were shrouded in the day's golden light, pulling us close to their chests. When we heard birds chirp, it was Our Boys laughing. The day's warmth was their breath on our faces as they leaned in to kiss us. Gwen plucked Her Boy's ring from her bra, and she placed it on her hand, the gold glinting in the sunlight. "Marjorie P. has nothing on me," she muttered.

We didn't see Ginny until she stepped out of the shadow of the convent's recessed entrance, where she'd been hiding. Her hair was in tangles, and dark crescents hung beneath her eyes. She wasn't wearing her uniform, and she looked like a wild woodland creature in her overly large gown from which her arms hung like atrophied paws.

"What happened to you?" the three of us asked, our voices indistinguishable, our mouths still warm from alcohol.

Ginny stumbled forward, looked around nervously, then motioned toward some high hedges. "We're running away," Ginny said. "Today. Right now." Salty white trails ran down her face; her eyes were red, puffy. "I mean it." We knew she did.

We moved toward her in a half circle, watching our balance as we stepped. Father James's whiskey made daylight settle heavy on our eyes. We steadied ourselves on Ginny and embraced her, clasping her hands with our own, smoothing down her hair, petting her face until she told us to stop it.

"I've thought about it," she said, pulling away. "It's Easter. Plenty of people out, plenty of cars on the road. We'll tell them we've been visiting family," she said. "We'll tell them Our Boys are soldiers. There's a war—they'll help us. They'll help us if they know about Our Boys. We're part of the War Effort." We stepped closer to her again, and she instinctively stepped back. Her twiggy legs looked so fragile beneath her gown, and we could tell she felt tired by the way she leaned herself against the gray stone of the convent.

"Ginny," we said, "we tried that already."

"We tried once," she said. "Only once." She growled, balled her fists, then slowly opened them like an Easter lily blooming. "I'm not going back," she said. And here she gritted her teeth, bared them, and made feral noises, shaking her head back and forth as if a bee were trapped inside. She dropped to her knees and in frenzied motions yanked at the shrubs, trying to dislodge them from their roots. When she realized she couldn't, that she wasn't strong enough, tiny Ginny, she dug up a handful of dirt and began smearing it into her face, like one of those beautiful saints trying to mar her beauty with lye. We didn't do anything, just stood there and watched her do it, watched her rub and scrub as if she were cleaning herself. When she looked up at us, her face streaked with dirt, her eyebrows furrowed in pain, her body bent in an unnatural position, we felt helpless. We loved Ginny, but we knew we couldn't save her.

Years later, when we would recall this scene together during one of our phone calls, Ginny would laugh at her brazenness, calling it a relic of her youth. She's long since settled down, married and remarried, borne three girls and a boy. She likes to joke that they are just like we were then, foolhardy and sensitive, in control of everything and nothing, full of wonder and fear. I know she's a good mother. She never went to art school, but in some ways, I guess, you could say her family is her art. She's created something, a life for herself, even if it is different from her girl-hood dreams.

But in that moment, as Ginny stood slowly in that gown, like one of the convalescents, her face contorted in a recognizable sadness, she couldn't have been further from laughter. She propped herself against the wall, rested her forehead there, and said, "We can leave now, during the chapel service."

None of us spoke, hoping some other voice would sculpt the air into words. We wanted to leave, we did. But we didn't. We couldn't. We wouldn't. We didn't have homes to return to, didn't have families who would stand in the doorway with arms open toward us, welcoming us in. We didn't have parents who would give us advice, or who wanted to see us off into our futures. We had nobody. Maybe our answer would have been different if we hadn't been drinking, but the drinking made us pine for Our Boys in a way that felt like a rush of madness might escape our chests. They were all that we had, and we couldn't leave them, even if we wanted to.

"We're not going," we said. We were looking sideways, all of us. We didn't dare meet Ginny's eyes.

"They're practically dead," she said, her voice wavering. She was trying to keep quiet, still worried about getting caught. She lowered her voice to a whisper. "They're practically dead, and you pretend like they're not. You pretend like they care. Well, I've got news for you: They don't." Her face winced as she said this; she grabbed her hair at its roots and pulled, wanting to inflict more pain on her body so it wouldn't hurt so much on the inside. "They don't even know we're there," she said. "And if they did . . ." She stopped. She cried soundlessly, cinched her face and widened her mouth so it looked like she was choking on air.

We stood there for a while, quiet as prayer. Nobody knew what to say. We rubbed circles on Ginny's back, bony through her flimsy gown. I gave her my sweater. Win gave her some socks. Gwen gave her a ponytail holder, and we finger-combed her hair to settle it down a bit. We huddled together, hugging tightly, like a real family does.

And then we said good-bye. We watched Ginny

scramble up the hill toward the church, then disappear beyond our sight. The three of us stood side by side, holding hands so tightly our fingers became numb. After we were sure she wouldn't return, we turned inside and found our way to the chapel. We fidgeted in our Easter bonnets that dug into the undersides of our chins. We hated ourselves for not joining Ginny, who by now had made it beyond the church, beyond the houses that dotted the town until the road branched in several directions. And it occurred to us, there, as we rested the weight of our bodies on the back of the pew, that *this* was sacrifice. We leaned into the dwindling effects of the whiskey that made us drowsy, woozy with love. We crossed our fingers beneath our hymnals, and we prayed in a way that could only be described as authentic. Rapturous, even. *Boys, hear our prayers.*

Of course, they found Ginny by evening. No cars had stopped to rescue her. Nobody had asked her about the War Effort. She appeared rather out of place, one can only imagine, a dirty pixie girl in a long, ill-fitting gown, only socks on her feet. Sister Tabitha found her wandering alone on the side of the road and brought her back to the convent by the time the stars had dotted the sky. Shortly thereafter, Sister Fran sent her away. We didn't see Ginny again, not even to say good-bye.

For a long time, we could only imagine where Ginny had gone. In our minds it was somewhere worse, somewhere stricter: perhaps a hermitage where she'd be forced to live a life of solitary silence, in a room overlooking a jagged cliffside. Or maybe some sort of prison for wayward youth. Win speculated that she was transferred to a boarding school somewhere in the wilderness. "There are convents everywhere, even in the wilderness," Win reasoned.

Later Ginny wrote me, and I learned the truth: She returned home, or to what was left of it. She went to live with her elderly grandmother, her father's mother, who was too sick to pay her much mind. Ginny cooked her meals and cared for her the best she could. When her grandmother smiled in thanks, Ginny saw her father somewhere beneath that wizened face, and this made her feel close to him still, somehow. They never talked about him—he'd died in prison, before Ginny ever had a chance to see him again—but the poor woman kept his artwork on her walls. When her grandmother died, Ginny packed up some of her father's old paintings, including the portrait he'd made of her as Dorothy in the field of poppies. When she looked at that painting, she still very much saw herself as the young redheaded girl sitting on a milk carton in her garage. She remembered watching her father's freckled face behind the canvas, the arching of his eyebrows as he smiled and painted. She'd been happy in that moment.

Shortly after the funeral, Ginny moved far away. She got an apartment, and she hung her portrait on the wall. I'm not sure if she was better off with her grandmother or not. Or with us in the convent. I guess there's no point in wondering now, is there? Because Ginny turned out just fine.

After all we'd experienced in our lives, Ginny's departure was our first true loss. Or maybe it's just that we hadn't thought we could hurt more than we had, but we did. We felt stunned, as if someone had ripped off a leg and expected us to keep on walking.

But we didn't know Ginny's fate yet, not during Easter mass. Instead, we clasped our hands and pressed them together until our biceps strained. *Boys, hear our prayers.* Sister Fran observed our reverence, pursed her lips, forming wrinkles that looked like stitches. After a thorough examination, she nodded at us in approval. "Good girls," she mouthed, but she didn't know this: The Guineveres were falling apart.

Gwen's Revival

Daddy said I was the prettiest girl in the world, and he would know because he traveled all over before he married my mom. He was in the army. We used to have a picture of him as a young man in uniform hanging in our living room. He looked like a movie star. The photo had been tinged pink to highlight his cheeks, ruddy with youth. His hat just barely tipped sideways, and the most handsome smile I've ever seen spread across his face, like he could be either a devil or an angel. I know he's had lots of women; he was married once, too, before my mom, a fact she never liked to discuss. I bet you he could have had anyone, because he's a charmer—that's where I get it. We can just look at people in a certain sort of way, like we're burning holes through their skin, right down to their bare bones. Believe it or not, people like to be exposed for what they are. I guess it's sort of like confession in that way; there's a freedom to it.

I have two older sisters, but Daddy said the day I was born it was like the world opened up and swallowed him whole. He knew I was special. But even so, I wasn't supposed to tell anyone about the gifts he'd sometimes bring me or the drives we'd take together, where we'd park out at some overlook and hold hands and just talk, the two of us. I'd curl up against him, make a nest of his armpit, and sometimes we wouldn't even say anything; we'd just look out at the town, tiny from where we sat. One day, after we'd been sitting in the car for a while, Daddy gave me a little gift box and told me to open it. It wasn't my birthday or anything, and I asked him the occasion. He told me it was simply because I was the prettiest girl in the world. I never got tired of hearing that.

Inside that box was another box, and inside that one a ring sat wedged between two satin cushions. The band was thin, gold, with three tiny opals set inside of it. The opal is my birthstone, and Daddy told me to keep it in a special place where nobody would find it, especially not my mom or my sisters because then they'd wonder why they didn't get one, too. *It'll be our little secret,* Daddy said, and he told me I could wear it as often as I liked when I turned eighteen. For a long time, I kept the ring in a slit Daddy had cut into the side of my mattress. He said that way I could keep it right there with me when I slept. He called it my Princess Pea.

My mom never did like the attention that Daddy showed me. Sometimes I'd curl up with him on the couch at night while he read the paper, just rest my head on his chest so I could hear his heart-beat, feel the gentle rise and fall of his stomach beneath me. Lying on Daddy's chest felt like I was floating out on a raft in the water, and I liked that sensation. Daddy would run his fingers through my hair. *My beautiful little Blondie,* he'd call me. One day, when my mom found me this way, she made me go to my room, and from there I could hear my mom yell, and though I couldn't make out what she was saying, I knew exactly what it was about.

If you really want to know what I think, I think my mom was jealous of me. See, she used to be pretty, like me, but years had aged her, grayed her hair and widened her hips. She wore these big formless shifts to cover up her growing figure, and she'd be just as likely to wear lipstick as she would be to take a rocket to outer space. In the mornings, she'd sit in the darkened den smoking her cigarettes, just one after another, her hands shaky as she flicked her lighter. This is probably the image I'll hold in my mind when I think of my mom: her dried feet stuffed into slippers, her ankles so white they practically glowed in the dark. Spirals of smoke looked like they could be spelling out something in the air, and if that were true it probably said, *Stay Out.* We knew better than to mess with my mom in the mornings.

Sometimes, before the school bus came, I'd ask Daddy to braid my hair, and he'd try his best. I had to teach him once, how you drag one piece over the middle piece, until it becomes the middle, then you pull another piece over, like they're all taking turns. Daddy would sit in a chair behind mine, tell me my hair smelled like the blackberry patch where he used to work when he was my age, only that my hair was much softer than those prickly bushes. His fingers grazed my skin, and sometimes he'd trace the outline of my neck with his thumb and forefinger, like he was measuring the width. Whenever Daddy did my hair, it came out a little crooked, but I didn't care. He told me I was the prettiest girl in the world and gave me a ring that I could wear as often as I liked when I turned eighteen.

One day, when I got home from school, my mom and Daddy were sitting at the kitchen table, and it wasn't even close to suppertime. My mom didn't wait for me and my sisters to sit down. "We're moving," she said abruptly. She had a wrinkle above her lip that looked like a mustache, and when she looked down, a roll of fat extended from her chin like some thick bubbling liquid. Once, Daddy gave me a photo of her when she was younger, and she looked like a movie star, too—just like Daddy did in his photo. In the picture, her hair was pulled away from her face, and big curls fell over her shoulder like she was in a shampoo advertisement. She was leaning back, resting on her hands, and even though the picture was black and white, I could tell her lips were red. I wished that version of my mom in the picture could have been my real mom, but it wasn't. My real mom sat at the table before us, her large body spilling out over the chair, her lips the color of morning biscuits. "Did you hear me? I said we are moving," she said, this time more forcefully.

My sisters started crying, but not me. "Why?" I asked.

If her eyes could have been released from their sockets, they might have turned into attack dogs. "Ask your father why," she said, but this time in a singsongy sort of voice that held anger on the edge of it.

Daddy stared down at the table, pretending to read something that wasn't there.

"Is this true, Daddy?" I asked.

He nodded. "Yes, I'm afraid it is."

"Ask his secretary why," my mom interjected. "Or her husband, for that matter."

We moved two weeks later.

As we were packing, my sisters told me that Daddy had an affair, and that's why we had to move, and I told them no way did I believe that for a minute. Not a second. But I did believe it, and I have to admit it hurt my feelings, that news did. I felt betrayed, not for my mom, but for myself. I don't know why. On moving day, I took my ring out from its hiding place in my mattress, and I tucked it into my shoe for safekeeping. I liked the way it felt digging into my heel. A Princess Pea.

Daddy said I had a mind that ticks like a clock, constantly moving. I did well in school, even when I didn't try. But the kids in my new school didn't like clock-ticking minds or pretty girls, or new girls for that matter. In the cafeteria on that first day, I held my tray and scanned the room, then finally sat off in the corner by myself picking at my lunch. After a while a group of boys came up to my table.

"So, who are you?" one of them asked. He wore glasses, and his hair was slicked back, rounded out at the front. From behind him I saw a group of girls across the way, rolling their eyes and scoffing in my direction. I caught one of their glances, smirked, then turned to the boy in front of me. "Well, that depends," I said, and I smiled without showing my teeth, in a way I know reveals a dimple. "Who's asking?" I batted my eyes. The boy nervously fidgeted with his sleeves, and his face turned pink in the cheeks. "It's Guinevere," I finally said, and I extended my hand to shake his.

When Daddy got home from work that night, he made his favorite drink. Then he sat me on his lap and tucked my hair behind my ears, said he liked it when he could see my face better. He wrapped his arm around me like a belt, and I told him about my day, about sitting in the cafeteria, about the mean looks from the girls, about the boys who were nice to me. Daddy leaned in close to me; he smelled like sweat and like whiskey, but I didn't mind. He told me not to trust those boys. Said all men are snakes, they slither in the grass, and they bite you on the ankles. Then he pinched my sides until I wriggled off his lap.

"Are you a snake, Daddy?" I asked.

He laughed in one short breath, like a sneeze, and poured himself another drink. He was wearing his undershirt, and I could see rings of sweat that had dried in half circles beneath his arms. "Sometimes a man can't help what a man is," he said. Then he turned around and looked at me like he was looking at something else. "You look just like your mother when she was young," he said, no segue, no nothing. "You know that?" Daddy looked up and down my whole body as if his eyeballs were rolling across my skin. And just as he was about to say something, my mom came in and told us supper was on the table and to hurry before it went cold.

My first day at school signaled what was to come, I learned. The girls would push up against me in the hallways or whisper insults beneath their breath as I walked past them down the halls, but I tried not to let it worry me. They were just jealous, and what did I need them for, anyway? Were they the ones who passed me notes between classes or offered to carry my books? Were they the ones who invited me to dances or asked me to meet them behind the baseball diamond after school?

Three boys, in particular, began to pay me the most attention, leaning against the lockers when I gathered my belongings at the end of the day. They were older than me by a couple of years, and they all sort of looked the same, except one had darker hair than the other two and was a little bit shorter. The two blond ones were cousins, and they had a dusting of freckles across their faces that made them look sick, with the measles or something. All of them had the same squinty look, like they needed glasses. Still, I didn't complain about the company, especially since I didn't have any other friends. They all three told me they thought I was the prettiest girl in the school, though I already knew this because that's what Daddy told me all along.

Those girls in the hallway—the ones who told me my lips were so big it'd take an entire tube of lipstick to put on one application, or the ones who pulled the rubber band out on the days Daddy braided my hair, or the ones who quacked like a duck when I walked by because they said my feet angled out with each step—they sneered as they walked by, clutching their books to themselves like they were trying to cover something up, probably their tiny chests that hadn't begun to grow, not like mine. As they passed by, I smiled as broadly as I could, laughed until I shook, gestured wildly so they'd know I was just fine without them, just fine with the attention from the boys that they wanted for themselves.

But everything changed on the day I brought to school the ring Daddy had given me, slipped it on my finger once I got on the bus. The other girls asked me where I'd gotten it, asked if one of those three boys had given it to me. "You know, they're just trying to see which one can get you first," they said, but I pretended not to hear, instead thumbing the ring round and round. It was a little too big, and I had wrapped twine through it a few times so it'd fit me better.

That day—the same day I wore Daddy's ring to school—those boys asked me if I wanted to go to Stanley Park after final bell. They gathered around my locker, slung their arms around my shoulder, said it was the shorter one's birthday, and, well, wouldn't it be nice to help him celebrate? At that point, some of those girls, those mean girls, nasty girls, walked by. *Quack, quack,* one of them said. She was the ugliest one of them all; her nose tipped up at the end, which gave her a horsey look. "Why, yes, I'd love to," I said, leaning into those boys, thumbing Daddy's ring. "But I have to catch the bus," I said. "Oh, don't worry about that," they said. "We'll get you home," they said—and they shared a glance that was so short I could have imagined I saw it in the first place. I smiled gratefully, hooked my hands through the cousins' arms, and smirked at those girls as we turned and headed for the door.

We could have walked to Stanley Park, but one of the cousins said we'd take his car instead. "Hate to make a pretty girl like you ruin her shoes in the fields," he said. I thought about how angry my mom would be if I came home with muddied shoes, and I agreed. The boys didn't take the straight way to the park, which was just a few blocks from the school. Instead, they drove down residential streets named after presidents: Lincoln, Garfield, Jefferson, Wilson. One of the freckle-faced twins pulled a bottle of bourbon out from under his seat and passed it around. I took a long swig but began to cough, and everyone laughed, even me.

We finally pulled into the park; I saw some other kids from school sitting on the swings, smoking cigarettes. They didn't look up when we drove by, and we kept on driving. "Where are you going?" I asked, Stanley Park fading into a point in the distance. The cousin in the driver's seat said he knew a better place to go. I sat back and looked out the window, watching the presidents' streets go by again: Wilson, Jefferson, Garfield, Lincoln.

It seemed like we drove for a while, but the bourbon had settled into my head, making me feel calm and relaxed. The dark-haired boy next to me sat quietly, gazing out the window, then back to his hands that he wrung in his lap. "Happy birthday," I said to him. "Yeah," he said back. "Yeah, it's happy?" I said, trying to be funny. "Yeah," he said back again in a droll voice.

The car finally came to a stop in a place I didn't recognize. "Everybody out," the driver said. He turned toward the backseat and said, "That means you, birthday boy." We all got out, but there wasn't much to see, except a pair of stone steps that led up to a bridge. "Ladies first," one of the cousins said—not the one who'd been driving—and he put one arm behind his back and extended the other like a waiter balancing a dinner plate in his hand. I began to ascend the stairway. The steps were set unusually far apart, and I was afraid the boys could see up my skirt as I climbed, so I pinched the material at my hips to cut the slack. When I got to the top, I could see a train yard down below. On the far side of the track stood a stack of wooden pallets, and on the side closest to us, some upturned milk crates were set in a circle, centered around an ashy mound. "That's where we're going," one of the boys said, then nudged me from behind. "Let's go back," I said. "I don't like this place." "Oh, don't be a fraidycat," one of the cousins said. "You don't want to ruin someone's birthday, do you?" the other cousin said. "No," I said, but I might have just been thinking it.

My legs felt weak as I climbed down another set of stairs. With every step, I thought my knees might buckle beneath me. Although the sun was shining, the shade of the rail yard felt cold, and I pulled my sweater closer to me, thumbing my ring nervously as I did this. "Now you're going to give our friend his birthday present, aren't you?" the taller of the cousins said when we finally came to a stop. His squinty eyes looked even more squinty in the daytime, out in the sunshine when he actually squinted. "I don't have a present for him," I said. "You're going to give him a kiss," he said. "I want to go home," I said. "Oh, she wants to go home," one cousin said. "To her mommy." I wanted to tell them that my mom was probably at that very moment sitting in her housecoat chain-smoking in the kitchen, like she usually did until supper.

I turned to walk toward the stairs, but someone grabbed my wrist and tugged me back. "Where you going?" the tall twin said. "The birthday boy just wants a kiss from the prettiest girl in the school," he said, this time nicer.

I let out a deep breath, then walked toward the dark-haired boy, who didn't seem particularly eager for a kiss. But I wanted to go home, and I didn't see any other way. He was taller than me, so I had to stand on my tiptoes. I puckered up my lips and planted a peck on his cheek. "There," I said. "Happy birthday." The dark-haired boy didn't react, didn't smile or nod or move from his spot, like his feet were glued in the dirt. "You'll have to do better than that," the shorter one said. His hair was a shade lighter than his cousin's, but they both wore the same crooked grin.

I turned toward the birthday boy, whose face showed no expression. I didn't want to kiss him, but I did. I kissed him right on the lips this time, my own lips suctioning against his like I was sucking blood out of a hangnail. His lips felt hard, moving against my mouth in a chewing motion, as though he wanted to eat me, or something. I'd kissed plenty of boys before, and I can tell you, he was no Casanova. I pulled away quickly, wiped my mouth with the back of my hand, and smiled at him.

The taller cousin moved toward me. "I forgot to tell you it's my birthday, too," he said. And at that point, I knew what there was to know: I was in trouble. The kind of trouble Daddy sometimes warned me about. The bourbon buzz quickly lifted from my head, and I started to walk backward in the direction of the stairs; I felt sick to my stomach.

I don't remember what happened next—or, rather, I do. I was in the dirt, with one of the cousins on top of me, pawing at my shirt, lifting my skirt up over me. "Stop," I kept saying over and over; I was clawing at his shoulders with my fingernails, then my face was in the dirt. I tried to kick my legs, but I knew it was hopeless. So I lay there real still, pretending I was a movie star—like my mother in that glossy old picture of hers, the one Daddy gave me. I stopped resisting, and I let them do what they were doing to me. I wasn't in the dirt of the train yard; I was in a scene from a movie. My hair was pinned up in curls, and I wore makeup, and I was playing the part all movie stars wanted, only the part went to me because I could play it so well.

When they were done, the cousins moved toward the stairs. The dark-haired boy helped me up, and I tried to fix myself, but I was missing two buttons on my shirt. I climbed the stairway with poise, carefully, like I imagine a starlet would do on the set of her movie. I wasn't going to let them see me upset.

It wasn't until we were in the car again, driving past dirty houses and brown square lawns that I realized I'd lost Daddy's ring. That was the moment I began to cry. I tried to wipe away my tears so the boys wouldn't see them.

"Can we go back?" I asked. My voice was shaky.

"She wants to go back," the tall cousin said, laughing.

Daddy was already home from work when I got there. He sat in the study, his drink resting on the arm of the chair. He opened his eyes when I walked in, saw my state, my missing buttons, the dirt on my skirt and beneath my nails. I started to cry. Daddy knocked his drink over, and didn't even bother to pick it up. "I lost my ring, Daddy," I said. "I lost my special ring." Daddy's eyes were bleary, but he pulled me toward his chest, and I folded myself into him. I told him what happened, how some boys had gotten rough. That's all I said—didn't have to give him the details because he knew what I meant. We stood there for a while, just breathing together, until Daddy stepped back, grabbed my shoulders, hard, and kissed me on the mouth. I didn't stop him, didn't know what to do. He was my daddy, after all.

Daddy's kiss wasn't stiff like the birthday boy's; his mouth felt warm, like bathwater, and his lips moved only lightly. I don't know if I kissed him back. I don't. I can't say. I felt like I was in a movie again, only this time I was playing the role of a different woman, one who hurt in all kinds of ways that didn't even have words to describe them. Daddy was crying all of the sudden, and I was standing there, in the study, my clothes dirty and my blouse ripped, and Daddy's tears falling on top of my head like the first big raindrops of a coming storm. "Go change your clothes," he said. "Before your mom sees."

I didn't go to school the next day—or the next. At first my mom kept yelling at me to stop being so lazy, but then she got real quiet around me and hardly spoke a word. The following week, Daddy said we were leaving, just the two of us. I didn't pack many things. Aside from the ring I lost, I didn't have much I cared to take with me. I took a bag of clothes; I brought along with me that old photo of my mother. She was smiling into the camera, her eyes dazzling, her red lips parted slightly, just enough to show a sliver of teeth.

Daddy and I just talked as he drove. He leaned over and put his hand on my leg, resting it there as he spoke. I thought we might drive out to the old lookout, the one we used to go to when we lived across town. But we didn't. Instead we got on a highway, then drove down some winding roads lined with trees already losing their leaves. When we arrived at the convent, his eyes turned downward. He said he was sorry. He said he hoped someday I'd understand. Sometimes a man can't help himself, he said. Sometimes you love something so much you destroy it, he said. He kissed my hand and pressed it into his face. Love's like that, he said.

Daddy walked me up to the door, and Sister Fran was waiting for us in the foyer. I wasn't sad; I didn't know what I felt. The room smelled like bleach, and the marble floor shone, reflecting the light from the chandelier above. I could see my reflection in it. Sister Fran raised her thumb, pressed it on my forehead. "The joy of God is the innocent," she said. "You shall be washed of your sins."

When I turned around again, I watched Daddy walking toward his car, his head hung. He didn't look back, just got in the car and drove away, but that was okay. I knew he was hurting, too.

Sister Fran handed me my uniform, but before she could lead me out of the room, Father James appeared in the foyer, wearing all black, his collar digging into his neck, nicked from where he had shaved.

"Our newest girl," Sister Fran said. "This is Guinevere."

"Another Guinevere?" Father James said, surprised. Sister Fran nodded. Father James had a scar above his lip, shaped like a tiny bone, but he was young and not so bad-looking, after all. He had a strong brow, and a squared-off jaw that could have been handsome had he not been a priest. Right away I caught his eye, and I held his stare, not breaking it even when he extended his arm to greet me. I gripped his hand, his warm, soft hand, and I squeezed it lightly, but clung to that squeeze for just a moment longer than was probably proper. I'll admit to that. Father James blushed. "I'm glad you're here, Guinevere," he said. Of course he was glad. After all, Daddy said I was the prettiest.

The Ascension

It rained for a week straight after Ginny left. Rain soaked the ground, and grass floated like rafts in pools of puddles and mud. The sky was a dirty canopy above us, one long sheet of granite-colored clouds. The Guineveres sat by the Bunk Room window during our free time, watching raindrops start and stop on their downward race toward the sill. We made a game of this, each of us picking which raindrop would beat the others, the winner feeling only mildly less apathetic after victory.

"Want me to braid your hair?" Win asked when boredom overtook us. Her eyes were ringed with dark circles the way they got when she wasn't sleeping well, which had the unfortunate effect of making her look cross.

"Nah," we said. Gwen tried to do a handstand against the wall, and her skirt kept falling downward, revealing her beige underpants and the spidery wisps of hair that crawled out from beneath them.

"Being upside down for too long can cause blindness," I said.

"Good," Gwen said. "Then I won't have to see you two standing there looking at me like that." Little veins bulged out of her reddening forehead.

"You'll be like Saint Lucy," I said.

"Will you stop it with all that saint stuff?" Win said.

We felt a loosening among us, as if a pin had come undone, though we didn't admit it. When The Guineveres were four, we felt solid, like a square, and now, with only three of us, we were a triangle, easily tipped.

And then, just like that, after an interminable week of steady rain, spring popped, first in whites and greens, then followed by yellows and reds and shades in between. The cherry blossoms bloomed in the courtyard, flowers perched like white butterflies on the branches. But cherry trees never stayed in bloom for long; soon enough the petals withered and drifted toward the ground like snow.

We were waiting, but waiting for what? For something, for nothing. Like the Drexels, we soon began our own letter-writing campaign to the Veterans Administration, each of us writing on behalf of Her Boy. Sister Fran agreed to mail the letters, believing our inquiries to be part of the War Effort, but we had to leave out crucial details because, although we didn't know for sure, we believed she read through all our letters before sending. We couldn't ask about Junior's death, or the personal effects we found. Instead, we simply provided a description of Our Boys, their date of arrival, and the long strands of numbers listed on their duffels. In our desperation, we asked Reggie if she'd heard anything else from her dad, any details that might be of use. Reggie shook her head, shrugged her wide shoulders, then went back to stuffing brussels sprouts in her cheeks.

We begged Sister Fran to allow us to volunteer our services in the Sick Ward again, believing our proximity to Our Boys might awaken them. A miracle could yet occur. Our spirits rallied when she agreed. We spent our Rec Time in the Sick Ward, gathering dirty towels and reading from the Bible and carrying basins of water to the bedsides of old folks who needed to wash their hands or their faces. We practiced caution, discretion, never lingering near the bedsides of Our Boys, whose skin we'd casually touch when pretending to straighten their sheets. We'd feel their warmth and catch glimpses of their flickering eyelids that seemed to be the only thing standing between us and them. Gwen guessed that the color of Her Boy's eyes was blue. Win believed Her Boy's eyes to be hazel. I knew the color of My Boy's eyes: greenish gray, like the sky before a storm.

One evening, when Sister Connie had gone to the cafeteria to pick up the dinner cart and Sister Magda was counting out pills into tiny paper cups, we stood around the bed of Gwen's Boy. His face was still bandaged, though the gauze was thinner and no longer seeping. We watched while Gwen pulled his eyelid open with a glide of her index finger. His eye rolled backward, and all we could see was the white part; thin red veins were rivers leading to a larger basin of blood pooled at the corner. Gwen stepped back, appalled, then quickly wiped her hand on her apron.

"We must love despite flaws," Win said.

"Nobody's perfect," I said.

"Perfection is boring," Win said.

Gwen recovered herself with a deep breath, flicked her slick hair from one shoulder to the other. "I'm sure his eyes were beautiful before the War," she said, and we all agreed.

To be careful, we divided our time between the old men and women again, dismayed to find their teeth soaking in glasses set on the bedside tables, startled when they'd moan in crackly voices that sounded like static. There was nothing romantic about the way they stared at us as we read the Bible or the way they pursed their lips for sips of water. When we saw Sister Magda or Sister Connie tending to one of Our Boys, our heads felt hot as teakettles, our breath storms in our mouths. We tried our best to remain calm, but it didn't come easily to us. We were restless. We were in love.

Mr. Macker no longer got out of bed and into his wheelchair. Though we didn't know what was wrong with him, exactly, other than the fact that he was old, we could hear a rattling in his chest when he breathed, and when he spoke, his voice sounded like gurgling water. Sometimes he'd ask in a low voice for one of us to come over and sit with him, and he'd take our hand and he'd squeeze it weakly. "Do you want to do one of your coin tricks?" we asked, picking up his old coin from his bedside table and pressing it into his leathery hands. He looked at us as if he were trying to remember something, though he couldn't think of what. "Do you want to take two of us and not call the doctor in the morning?" we asked. Still he didn't say anything in return, so we sat there awkwardly on the edge of his bed, lumps in our throats like unswallowed food. "Do you want to go home?" we asked.

"Where is that?" he said. His voice was faint, like a record player with no needle.

During confession the following week, we wept as we separately faced the old priest who looked like a bird. His nose sloped forward and tufts of hair were feathers.

"I don't know how to love," Gwen said.

"I hate myself," Win said.

"I question my faith," I said. In addition to my usual prayers, the ones for my mom, I prayed for My Boy to open his eyes again, and yet they remained sealed. His sheet no longer rose where it shouldn't rise. His body no longer shifted in his bed. Every day he felt further away from me, even though I prayed, even though I pleaded.

The next week, following Afternoon Instruction, while the other girls went outside to spend their Rec Time in the garden, now in full bloom with black-eyed Susans and purple hydrangeas, The Guineveres plodded to the Sick Ward for a service hour. The door was locked when we arrived. We knocked, but no answer. We knocked again, this time harder, until our knuckles cracked, the skin split, red rising to the surface. Our Boys were inside, and we were uneasy—and maybe this is what we were waiting for all along, for the worst, for that one day we'd come here and find Our Boys gone, with nothing to show for them but some dirty bedclothes and a sagging mattress. We knocked again, this time with our fists. We pounded and pounded until the lock finally clicked. Sister Connie poked out her head, which due to her height grazed the top of the doorframe, knocking her paper hat askew.

We stepped backward, then tried to move forward, but she blocked us. "You can't come in here, girls. Not today," she said. She gripped the door with one hand and fixed her hat with the other.

"Why not?" we said, alarmed. We tried to look around her, but we couldn't see past the Front Room, where a few old men and women were sitting slumped in wheelchairs. An old box fan whirred behind her. Sunlight spilled through the windows in rectangular shapes.

We feared the unspeakable. *He suddenly made a turn for the worse,* Sister Fran had said once about Ginny's Boy. Our Boys needed us; at this very moment, they needed us. The Guineveres tried to push past her, and she sensed our urgency, our panic.

"Girls, you can't see him. I insist. He needs some peace at this moment," she said. We could see where her white nurse's cap was clipped with bobby pins, her hair greasy at the roots. We didn't budge. "Mr. Macker," she explained. "He's passing, and he needs to do so with dignity. You don't need to see this, not young girls like you. Now go," she said. "Enjoy the afternoon." She closed the door again; our hearts released like fists unfurled. We stood staring at the wood grain of the door, both relieved and upset. Our Boys were fine.

But Mr. Macker wasn't.

Tears filled my eyes. I felt a drop skim my cheek, and my mouth began to quiver, then Win put her hand on my back. Where she touched me, I could feel my heartbeat, right between my shoulder blades.

"It could be worse," Gwen said coolly, playing with her ponytail, twirling it around her finger. It could be one of *them*," she said.

"Don't say that," I said.

"Who would you rather it be?" she asked.

"Nobody."

"Who's Nobody?" she said, her voice all high notes and air. "Is that the gentleman in the second bed over who'd be handsome if not for his rotting teeth?" She cocked her head, flexed her cheeks into a condescending smile.

Win turned toward Gwen with that fiery expression, the kind she usually reserved for Lottie Barzetti or Shirley or another one of The Specials. She scrunched her face until her nose and mouth and eyes came together in a jumble.

"Besides, we're all going to die someday," Gwen said, and she turned and slipped out the side door to join the other girls in the courtyard.

Mr. Macker died a day later.

They say death brings you closer to life. Maybe this is true. I can say Mr. Macker's death made us ache at the thought of losing Our Boys, aches that began in our hearts, then radiated out like an earthquake to all our limbs, out to our fingers and our toes. In a way, I suppose you could say we ached for Mr. Macker, too, though not on the same scale. Our love for him did not radiate, only tickled a little, the kind of tickle you know will go away if you ignore it. We imagined him in a white room, standing free of his wheelchair, younger looking but still old. He'd see the beautiful woman from his photo, and her poodle, too, and they'd smile in recognition. He'd extend his palms, and she'd see that he still had that old coin of his. "Want me to do a magic trick?" he'd ask, by which he meant he still loved her very much.

Only a few days after Mr. Macker died—the Sisters used the word "passed" to make us all feel better about it—we visited Our Boys at night for the first time since Ginny had left. After Lights Out turned the Bunk Room black, and after the slumbering breath from the other girls filled the air, and after we waited for Checks and after we calculated the duration of three rosaries' worth of prayer, we met in the stairwell, like we always did, and made our way to the third floor, like we always did, and crossed the length of the convent to the Catacombs, like we always did, only now we were three instead of four.

"We're like Romeo and Juliet," Gwen said. "Forbidden love, which only makes it more complex."

"Like three Romeos and three Juliets," Win corrected.

"But that would mean we all died," I said, and they both rolled their eyes.

"Don't be so literal," Gwen said.

"But why did she kill herself at the end?" I asked. "Why didn't she just leave the tomb when she discovered he had died?"

"She couldn't live without him," Win said.

"What would *you* do?" Gwen said.

"Well, I wouldn't kill myself," I said. "That's sinful." Gwen looked like she had just vomited in her mouth, but at that moment she pulled open the door to the Sick Ward, and we fell silent with reverence.

The ward smelled different from usual, like bleach and lemons. Moonlight filtered through the open windows. Everything looked softer; shapes lost their edges. We averted our gaze from Mr. Macker's bed, now stripped down to a bare mattress. We didn't want to think of Mr. Macker now. Especially not when we reached the foot of Gwen's Boy's bed. At the sight, we let out a collective gasp that punctured the darkness. His bandages were removed. For the first time we could see his face.

Gwen walked slowly toward his bedside; she raised her hand as if she were going to touch him, but she didn't, and so it looked like she was praying over him, even though I knew she wasn't. I couldn't see her expression, but I imagined what it must have looked like, her top lip curled as if she had eaten onion pie.

With his bandages on, he looked like a normal boy: We could see his eyes, his pillowy lips, the shock of hair that poked out of his bandages like alfalfa sprouts, only blond. But with his bandages off, he was more wounded than we'd imagined him to be, than we could have imagined him to be. Two deep gashes, stitched together, looked like a smile on the left side of his face, and where his nose should have been was a bone bound by withered skin, like a dried apple core.

"We must love them despite their flaws," I said.

"It might heal," Win said optimistically, but I could hear her clear her throat.

Gwen said nothing; her back was to us. She shook, lurching forward and back, propelled by the power of restrained dismay. We stood behind her for a few minutes, until she said, "Go on; I'll be fine." So we left her alone.

Win's Boy's legs were still bandaged together, though they were no longer lifted up in traction. We suspected he was healing nicely. She sat on the bed next to him, her back to his body. She hunched forward and rested her forehead in her hands, her dark hair completely covering her face. I gave them some time alone.

I moved toward My Boy's bed, and I sat down next to him, so close I could feel his breath humid against my skin. He smelled like soap, the same kind we used on Wash Day. Sleep, it's such an intimate act. When we sleep, we accept our vulnerabilities, offer them up to the darkness, bare ourselves whole, exactly as we are. There's no hiding oneself in sleep. We are our truest selves then. And so I felt such intimacy with My Boy in these moments. I watched his eyes flicker, as if he were watching a filmstrip on the inside of his eyelids. I traced the outline of his forehead and nose and lips and chin, feeling a tug inside me with each curve. I felt the gentle rising and falling of his chest, and I pressed my ear to him, resting my head near his heart. I closed my eyes for a while, and I imagined his breath as waves, pulling me in toward him. I prayed in that moment. I prayed hard for My Boy.

And then I opened my eyes and I saw it again: that awful tented sheet. His body responded to mine, and this made me blush. I wasn't sure if it was wrong, this pull in me that both wanted this response and didn't. I wasn't sure if it was sinful, like the Bible said. But it didn't feel that way at that moment, didn't feel shameful like I'd been told. Sister Fran spoke so derisively of the Flesh. The Flesh. "The Flesh" sounds so singular, so solitary. But we were connected, and this couldn't be sinful, what I felt for My Boy. If it were, I'd have admitted right then and there—my body moving up and down in rhythm with My Boy's breathing as I rested on his chest—that I was a sinner.

"Looks like he's up." I sat up to see Gwen standing at the foot of the bed. A smile stretched across her face to reveal her teeth, whiter in the darkness.

She laughed quietly and pointed toward My Boy, to his waist, or below his waist, where the

410

sheet rose like something unholy now that she was looking at it.

My face grew hot, not from embarrassment, but because I realized that Gwen had been watching him, watching us, stealing from me these intimate moments.

"Go away," I said. But she didn't move, just stood there grinning. "Don't look," I said so forcefully I felt my stomach tighten and my neck muscles strain. I turned my body to block her view.

"What?" she said in a hush-hush voice. "I think it's sweet."

"Go away," I said again, swatting my arm toward her, pushing darkness and air. "Leave us alone." And as I stood up and shook the bed, My Boy stirred. His eyes flitted open and closed, as if he had dirt in them and was trying to blink it away. He moaned, not a moan of pain or pleasure, but a moan of sleep.

I gasped, but then became quickly focused, remembering all I had forgotten to say the last time. "What's your name?" I asked him. "It's me again, Guinevere. What's your name?" I reached forward, and I picked up a hand and placed it between mine, then squeezed. Nothing. "Wake up. Please, wake up," I begged him. "Wake up. Please." Still nothing. But I wouldn't stop—how could I? I loved him. Love means we keep trying. Love means never giving up. "It's Guinevere.

Remember me? I've been with you. Wake up. Please. Wake up."

"He's not going to wake," Gwen said softly. She looped her arm in mine and eased me away from the bed.

"I just want to know his name," I said.

"I know," Gwen said.

"I want to go home," I said.

"I know."

Win joined us, and we stood huddled together for a few minutes. Sister Fran reminded us during prayer that wherever two or more are gathered in His name, He is there. However, standing there in the Sick Ward that night, The Guineveres clinging to each other, it felt like we were the only people left in the world, that not even God could hear our silent pleas. Or maybe He just wasn't listening.

The next day was the Feast of the Ascension, the day Jesus was taken up into heaven, a holy day of obligation. During our writing lesson, Sister Fran explained to us that the Ascension was evidence of God's ongoing plan of redemption for us, and she asked us to write a five-paragraph essay explaining what we believed our own redemptive plans to be. "Don't forgot your thesis statement," she instructed. "And clear topic sentences, too. Proverbs tells us that slack habits and sloppy work are as bad as vandalism, so please do not vandalize your essays, girls. Vandalized essays are a disgrace."

The framed photographs of saints gawked at us as we slouched over our desks, staring at the blue lines on the blank page. What we believed, we couldn't write, and what we'd write, we didn't believe. "God has an extraordinary plan for me that I will outline in three parts," I wrote, but my thesis statement was as far as I got. We were excused early to serve the holy day mass in the church.

"Still angry with me, girls?" Father said to us in the vestry after witnessing our glum faces. He offered us a piece of coconut cake a parishioner had baked. We declined.

How could we explain? How could we explain to him all that we felt and all that we'd seen? How could we hope he'd understand our forbidden love, like Romeo and Juliet's? Like three Romeos and three Juliets? Father James had taken vows of celibacy, after all. It wouldn't be worth the breath it'd take to explain it.

"No, Father," we said.

He locked himself in his office while we dressed in the vestry, pulling the cassocks over our heads so that our hair stood on end from the static electricity and we had to spit in our hands and smooth it down. Gwen held the Bible, Win carried the processional cross, and I lit the incense and swung it back and forth, back and forth like a hypnotic pocket watch.

Forty days past Easter Jesus ascended into heaven, and the parishioners' clothes lost their pastel hues. The warm weather already encouraged the women to bare their arms. The girls our age wore linen dresses with hemlines above their knees now. Styles were changing. The world was changing, with or without us in it. Nothing extraordinary occurred during the service, except when Gwen held the Bible up for Father James to kiss before reading the Gospel, I thought I saw her pucker back. Her lips extended just barely—as if she were blowing out a candle.

After mass, when we finished hanging our robes and finger-combed our hair, Father James came in, smelling of whiskey and cologne. He was wearing an ornate purple robe, embellished with a gold trim at the sleeves and hem, and we noticed one of his shoes, shiny as little beetles, had come untied. When he bent over to tie it, he stumbled forward, and we helped him to the couch.

"Oh, girls," he said, leaning back. "Always so helpful." He shimmied his robe up to his hips, then managed to pull it over his head until he became stuck. His shirt rode up a bit, and we could see the dark, downy line of hair that traced a path down from his belly button. We untangled the twisted fabric from his arms and pulled it over his head. Father James smiled mischievously, the scar above his lip widening. He didn't look like a priest at all.

Years later, Father James would not deny being drunk at this moment; it was a tough time, he claimed, for everyone. The War and all. By then, he'd long since given up whiskey, and even swapped out the wine for grape juice in the chalice he used on the sacrament table. God had sent him to the depths of despair—he'd told me those years later—so that he could be brought back again, renewed. Only through absence can we understand presence, he told me, and I understood that by then. I understood it well.

After we hung Father James's garment in his closet, ignoring the empty bottles of wine we saw there, we began quietly backpedaling toward the door. Gwen sat next to Father James on the couch; his eyes were closed, and he was humming the processional tune, something about all the ends of the earth and creatures of the sea.

I tried to motion for Gwen to come on. She leaned back on the couch, her fingers extended as though she were holding an invisible cigarette. We waited. We pointed to invisible watches on our wrists.

But Gwen didn't move from her spot. She sat with her legs crossed, her shoe dangling from the foot she was circling at the ankle. "Go on," she said, her face placid, stiller than I'd ever seen it. "I want to speak with Father James," she said. She blinked. "About my spiritual life. Alone."

We narrowed our eyes, shooting her glances that might have had sound effects, like artillery fire. She didn't budge, except to cross her legs in the other direction and smooth down the pleats of her skirt. Win and I stood skirt to skirt, squeezed into the doorframe together. Father James didn't speak a word, only continued to hum, pretending he didn't notice us.

"I'll be there soon," Gwen said in her breathy movie-star voice. We pitched our thumbs over our shoulders. "What?" she asked, then flashed us those blue eyes of hers, wide and unmoving. She puckered her lips, kissed her hand with a smack, and as she blew it in our direction, her cheeks tightened and her mouth formed a perfect O.

We left her there, Win and I did. Left her sitting cross-legged on that couch. Left her with Father James. Left her knowing we couldn't stop what was about to happen, even if we wanted to. We had Our Boys to think of now. And as they healed and rested—as they moved closer to us— we thought they could wake at any moment. And then we'd go home. It'd been forty days since Easter, and we were full of hope for our own redemption. We wanted to be there when they woke. We wanted to say, "Yes, yes," when they called our names in dry, thirsty voices.

Saint Alice

FEAST DAY: JUNE 15

Even as a child, Alice was frail and had to take extra precautions so as not to catch a cold or otherwise injure her weakened constitution. This was easier said than done for a girl whose heart was ablaze with love, one who always wanted the company of others. Even in Brussels's mild winters, Alice was required to wear no fewer than three overcoats if she wished to join the other children outside. Even then, her small frame shivered as though her blood could do no warming.

At age seven she was delighted to be sent to the nunnery to receive a proper education, for there she knew she'd live in communion with women whose faith was as fervent as her own. On the day she left home, the only tears shed were those from her mother. "Don't cry, Mama," sweet Alice said. "I'll be surrounded by love."

At first this was true. Alice reveled in communal prayers, communal meals, and communal sleeping accommodations in a narrow room lined with cots. The Sisters instructed her in the ways of the spirit and of the intellect, and their young student excelled in both. Not long after arriving, she declared her wish to make the convent her permanent home. She was suited to the monastic life, and the Sisters admired her humility and piety. But most of all, they felt she was touched by the spirit, for even at a young age, she began to perform miracles. Once while she was in the chapel, a gust of wind knocked down the candles, extinguishing them completely. Alice, through prayerful intervention, by channeling the spirit through her own small body, was able to direct the candles to reignite on their own. Even the strictest of the nuns was impressed by this miraculous display of fire, and she permitted Alice to take her vows early, granting her admittance into the Sisterhood.

However, shortly thereafter, Alice contracted leprosy. The heavy-hearted Sisters forced her into isolation, into a small hut they'd erected for her, fifty paces from the convent's walls. At first Alice offered not a complaint, for such freedom of time granted her the liberty to contemplate her favorite subject: the suffering of the Lord. She spent her first days in prayerful meditation, but soon she grew bored.

The monastery's chaplain who came by weekly to offer communion did not help her situation. He'd toss the host inside as though she were a caged beast. This surly man feared contagion, and so furthermore barred her from receiving the chalice. Such denials made Alice lament her fate. More than anything else she desired to be inebriated with blood, to feel it coursing through her veins, warming her in parts unknown. That's when her first vision of the bridegroom appeared. He was handsome, His hair wavy, His beard thick but trimmed, and she couldn't help reaching out to touch it. Already, she was in love. "Where there is part, there is whole," He said, stroking the bones of her face that had divulged her womanhood since her illness.

But Alice didn't feel like part of any whole. She was in pain. She was afraid. Leprosy was merely one of her sufferings. Beyond that: loneliness. To amuse herself, she counted the cracks in the floor or the pieces of straw that comprised the thatch roof. She traced the perimeter of the hut and tallied her paces. She'd crack the door and look up to enumerate the stars that twinkled there, reminding herself that her Bridegroom had once lived under this very sky. After a while, the effects of the disease withered her body. Skin sloughed off in flakes the shapes of crosses, chalices, Bibles, doves. She swept them to the corner, where they piled like snow. Cavernous lesions grew on her skin, and to relieve the pain she packed mud into these wounds. On the days the chaplain came to deliver her Holy Communion, he noticed she'd begun to resemble the crucified Savior: Beneath her gauzy gown, her ribs protruded from her now skeletal frame.

But such bodily impairments didn't deter Alice,

nor her capacity to perform miracles. People far and wide, risking contagion themselves, stopped by her small hut, for they heard she could heal the wounded, cure the sick. And sure enough, the only contagion Alice offered was that of the Holy Spirit. Women brought their colicky babes, who cooed in Alice's arms. The blind who touched her hardened skin witnessed blue skies, the sandy dirt beneath their feet. The maimed—they walked, they skipped, they ran, they danced. Alice could cure anyone. Except herself.

And yet her bridegroom continued to appear to her in visions. He was more like a father now. Old. "My child, I shall never forsake you," He said, pulling her head to His chest.

Limb by limb, Alice's body became paralyzed. She could feel herself fading away, a ghost. Her skin hardened like the bark of a tree. Engorged lumps grew from the sides of her face and down the stretches of her arms and legs. Those seeking miracles stared at her monstrous physique, certain they had met a witch instead of a holy woman. Some turned away in horror. Only her tongue was spared the disease. And with this tongue she often shouted in ecstasy, "Yes! Yes! Yes!" The other Sisters could hear her cry from their windows as they slept on their comfortable cots, their faces hot in the darkness.

Soon Alice lived in permanent darkness. Blindness had stricken her. "Oh, Father, stay with me," she cried. "Don't leave." She didn't know day from night, up from down, suffering from joy. Even her visions began to fade. She thought she felt the touch of hands. Strangers, her bridegroom, her Father, all hungry. For faith. For miracles. For more. But she had nothing left to give. She laid herself down on her cot and waited for her final reward, as a good wife would, as a faithful daughter might. She died at sunrise.

Eternity

Gwen swore to us nothing untoward transpired with Father James after we'd left the vestry. What choice did we have but to believe her? The Guineveres didn't keep secrets from one another. "We just talked," she said that night as we stood in front of the sinks in the Wash Room before Lights Out, averting our eyes from each other's reflections in the mirror. "All very innocent," she declared. She brushed her long blond hair with precision—one hundred strokes from the crown of her head to her roots—then admired her reflection in the mirror, pouting her lips and tweezing her eyebrows with pinched fingers. "Can't two adults have a conversation?"

"You're not an adult," Win said through a mouth full of toothpaste that foamed around her lips as if she were rabid.

"Well, I will be when I'm eighteen, and then nobody can tell me what to do," Gwen replied. She splashed her face with water, and gently slapped her cheeks because she claimed this stimulated blood vessels and provided luster. Then we took out the butter we'd pocketed at dinner and unwrapped it from the napkin. I divided it into three, and we each took our share, applying it to our lips and our hands and the tips of our hair.

"Though I'm sure he *wishes* something happened," Gwen finally added.

"But you're devoted to Your Boy," I said.

"Who'd be awfully disappointed to hear of your coquettish behavior," Win said.

"Yes, I'm devoted to My Boy. My handsome soldier," she said, sighing, cupping her breasts and hiking them up. Gwen slept in her bra because she claimed it aided perkiness. "We will make beautiful babies someday," she said, then smiled at her reflection, satisfied with her nightly regimen. "*After* I'm eighteen."

A week later, eight more soldiers arrived at the Sick Ward, and we knew something big had happened with the War. We learned of their impending arrival from none other than Reggie herself. She heard about it when she'd been sent to Sister Connie for a bandage after slicing her thumb while serving on kitchen duty. Despite her gauze-wrapped hitchhiker's thumb, we didn't believe her.

But then we saw them with our own eyes. They arrived on a school bus, the white one with red crosses. Uniformed men brought out the wounded on stretchers, just like last time, one at a time, like pallbearers carting the dead. The Guineveres watched from the courtyard. We'd pulled our socks down and rolled our sleeves up to afford our skin better access to the sun.

"Maybe they'll recognize Our Boys," I said.

"Maybe they fought together." We agreed it was a possibility that these new soldiers could tell us who Our Boys were. Mail Distribution Days came and went. Still no word from the VA.

"Any cute ones?" Gwen asked, picking the petals off of a black-eyed Susan. Her fair skin was tinged red from the heat, especially across the bridge of her nose. It was early summer. The air smelled like honeysuckle.

"This is real life, you know. This is *their* lives," Win said. She was braiding my hair in two plaits to hide the grease until Wash Day. She ran her fingers along my scalp, yanking a little too firmly. "Would *you* want to be in their places?" she asked.

"Would they want to be in ours?" Gwen said, and she stretched back in the grass.

"At least we have each other," I said. Cicadas rattled, fading in and out in the distance. Nobody said a word until it was time to go inside.

We caught a glimpse of these soldiers a day later when we volunteered our Rec Time to read the Bible to the convalescing patients. The new soldiers were older than Our Boys, our fathers' ages, we guessed. They were all missing parts of themselves—hands, legs, arms, whole swaths of skin that were replaced with pink-hued lines and grooves. Those whose faces weren't bandaged had black eyes the size of baseballs; one soldier's head was shaved, and a line of stitches crisscrossed his skull like a zipper. Their skin looked dirty, but when we looked closer we could see it was just bruised. A soldier with red hair had small scabs we first mistook for measles. All of them slept in a way we recognized immediately. It was an interminable sleep. It was the sleep of Our Boys.

Though these soldiers were wounded fighting to protect us, we certainly didn't feel any safer. Our insular world only felt more dangerous. We observed firsthand the gashes and bruises and scabs and scars, the limblessness, whole sections of the body that should have been there but were gone. We smelled those wounds, like damp laundry that had been left too long, or like sulfur so sour it made our stomachs churn.

Sisters Connie and Magda set up cots in the Front Room of the Sick Ward, and Sisters Tabitha and Margaret were called in to help with the overflow.

We were afraid to go near them at first, afraid of their wounds and their smells and the blank spaces where their limbs should be. We could only wonder if they knew Our Boys, or if they'd ever seen them fighting in bunkers or hiding in foxholes, as we imagined. Did they have families? Wives? Children who missed the sound of their fathers' voices, the heavy footsteps of their boots on the stairs?

Sister Connie wouldn't tell us much, other than

what we already knew: They were gravely injured. The War.

"How long will they be here?" we asked.

"Until they recover . . . or until . . ."

"Until what?" we asked. "Until what?" we demanded.

Our confessions that month came easily. During the service, as Sister Lucrecia's organ bleated like an injured goat, The Guineveres slouched in our pew, kicking the kneelers with the backs of our heels, thinking of those wounded men in the Sick Ward. We watched Lottie confess to the priest beneath the stained-glass window. She closed her eyes when she spoke and tensed her bony body. Most girls, when they confessed, just bowed their heads and spoke quietly, avoiding any eye contact that would make them feel uncomfortable. Reggie, on the other hand, gestured with her hands as she confessed; it looked like she was telling a tall tale as opposed to unburdening her soul. Only later in life did I learn that Reggie's dad really was a general in the War, though he didn't come back for her like she believed. I felt badly for thinking her a liar. Even worse that her father never returned.

After a while, Win excused herself from the pew and selected the priest who stood with the help of a walker. She crossed her arms in front of her to hide her breasts, notably larger than ours, though Gwen liked to claim her own breasts were the perfect handful. "I close my eyes when I walk past the soldiers in the Sick Ward," Win said to the priest. "I pretend I can't see them, and even though their eyes are closed, it makes me feel bad. I try to force myself to look at them, because I know they've done good things. But I can't."

And then my turn. "I know God has a larger plan," I confessed. I selected a younger priest who looked like the statue of Saint Francis minus the animals. "But I don't understand why He'd let that happen to those soldiers. If they're on the side of good—if they're fighting against evil—then it seems to me that God is just mean." My voice grew shaky with anger, and I was aware that other girls were watching me, so I stood straight and tried not to bring attention to myself.

Gwen confessed to Father James. We watched her across the church. Her hands covered her face, and her shoulders shook. She stood beneath the shadow of the giant crucifix, but we could still see she was crying. Real tears, not the fake kind she could sometimes produce on command. Father James reached out and touched her arm, even though that's not what's supposed to happen during confession.

"What'd you confess?" we asked her over our meal of peas and rice after mass.

"I told him I wish they'd never arrived," she said, and she poked at the peas on her plate, rolling the tiny balls with the prongs of her fork.

When she looked up we could see the red rims of her lids, which only made her eyes look more blue.

The Guineveres sank into the rhythm of our own routines. We were nothing if not girls of habit. At Breakfast Prayer, we'd squeeze our eyes shut and plead for Our Boys to wake to us. During Morning Instruction, while we pretended to write down the day's lesson, we drafted letters to the VA again, begging them for help. Then during Rec Time we'd head to the Sick Ward to volunteer. Sister Connie kept us to the Back Room mainly, away from the new soldiers and their limbless, bruised bodies, assigning us instead to tend to the old men and women who waited in their beds, lying on their backs like open-eyed fish. We'd feed Mrs. Martin sips of water while glancing over at Our Boys. She'd grown shriveled in the face, and her chest rattled when she breathed, as if she were sucking water through a straw.

When news came that one of the soldiers in the Front Room had died, Sister Connie asked us to allow time for Consolation Visits. "Human connection is important, especially in times like these." We agreed. We were to sit by the beds of the old men and women and let them talk if they wanted, vent their problems and their worries. Most had no clue about the War, or about the dead soldier from the Front Room. Instead, they prattled on about the weather or talked of the people they used to know in their past lives. Sometimes they'd tell us that we looked like their grandchildren, and if that was the case, we wondered, where were their grandchildren? Why didn't they visit? Why didn't anybody ever visit?

Then, after Lights Out, on our designated days, we saw Our Boys during their Consolation Visits when we snuck back into the Sick Ward. Like we did during our daytime visits with the old folks, we'd let them know we were there, that they could talk to us if they wanted. Gwen would crawl beneath the covers with Her Boy and curve her back against him. We could hear the sound of her legs moving beneath the sheets. Win would sit at the edge of Her Boy's bed, leaning over him, rapt in conversation. In the dark, her thick hair formed a halo of shadow around her head. I'd kiss the rough cheeks of My Boy in certain moments, but other times, we'd just be still together, not asking anything of each other except to stay there like that.

I've since heard it said that a big part of war is waiting, and I can understand why. The nights without Our Boys lasted an eternity. And eternity, as Sister Fran reminded us, has no end. Those nights, I would lie awake in the Bunk Room long after Lights Out, restless, listening to the squeaks and pops as the other girls turned in their sleep. Sometimes, I'd reach beneath my mattress for My Boy's Book of Psalms, thumbing through it for clues, but found nothing, not even one dog-eared page. Other times, I'd rely on my notebook to occupy these lonely hours, rewriting the lives of the saints as I remembered them. Still other times, I'd gaze upon each girl in the Bunk Room—this usually required propping up on my elbows—and I'd try to recall her Revival Story, how she came to live at the convent. I don't know why I wrote these stories down in my notebook, other than consolation.

I was scribbling these stories when I couldn't sleep one night, awakened by the bright moon that slid through the window slats. I didn't want to lie in bed thinking, tempted by thoughts of the Flesh that only made me feel guilty. Instead, I watched Lottie snore. Her parents had recently sent her another letter from overseas, but not the same place Our Boys had been, and she delivered its contents in the Bunk Room like a great orator. Irene slept with a leg hanging over her bunk. Her parents both worked in the coal mines and couldn't afford to keep her. Judy had thrown the blankets over her head. Her mother died in childbirth, and her father drank himself to death. And then my eyes rested upon Gwen's bed. It was empty. I could see the corner of the pillow poking out of her covers like a tongue.

After Morning Roll, we confronted her in the

Wash Room. "Where were you last night?" The Guineveres asked. "Did you visit them? Without us?" We'd grown agitated. Eternity has this effect. The War unsettled us. The waiting, too. There were rules to consider. Nothing felt safe.

"I was in the bathroom," Gwen said, annoyed, shooting us glances that landed like darts on our skin. "What are you, the patron saint of my bowels?" she asked, then lined up for the single-file march to the cafeteria.

We didn't think much of it—didn't have the time to, really. That evening, over a supper of mushroom casserole, Sister Fran called Win to her office. Win hadn't even taken two bites when she set down her spoon. She shrugged her uncertainty and followed Sister Fran. We watched as she strolled through the cafeteria; she nervously smoothed her hair, kinky as we neared Wash Day. Gwen and I took reluctant spoonfuls of the tepid liquid, each bite bitter as it hit the backs of our throats.

Together, we listed all the possible reasons Win could have been called into Sister Fran's office: transgressions, broken rules, ungodly behavior, uniform violations. She hadn't even bothered Shirley with so much as a single spit wad lately. In fact, we couldn't come up with anything that didn't also involve us somehow. And if that was the case, why were we still here eating our dinners?

The truth was, out of all of us, Win had been the most sensible one, the most stable, too. She may have been viewed as tough by the other girls, and, yes, she was angry in her own way. We all were. But more than anyone else, she understood that time would be her way out, and she practiced patience like a saint. She did not get her hopes up when we sent off letters to the VA. She did not cry easily over the bed of Her Boy, like the rest of us. But she was deeply sensitive and awfully wise, and so we had no idea why she could have been called to Sister Fran's office without us.

After our dinner, as we silently single-filed from the cafeteria, we realized what our hearts had never even dared to imagine. There Win stood, in the doorframe of Sister Fran's office, next to a women who looked like an older version of herself, a woman with Win's same aquiline nose and olive skin and dark, frizzy hair. The woman was crying, thick mascara running down her face in streaks. She hugged Win, but Win stood there stiffly, no elbows or knees. Even though we only glimpsed this scene for a moment, we knew this was her mother. We knew this by the way the woman looked at Win with an apologetic, contorted face. We knew this by the way Win fell into the embrace of the woman, rigidly, but not without tenderness. Win didn't see us as we filed past the office. She'd be gone by later that night.

Gwen and I sat on Win's bunk that evening

during Rec Time. Her bed had been stripped down to the bare mattress. I don't know why the Sisters insisted on clearing her bunk so quickly; maybe it was the same reason why we learned it's better to rip a bandage off instead of peeling it away slowly. It hurts either way, but one is faster. The Sisters hadn't yet removed the decorations Win hung above her bed. Nothing ornate—that wasn't her style. Just a couple of clip-outs from an old *National Geographic.* One was an aerial shot of an island sitting in the middle of the ocean. The water was so clear around it you could see the reefs beneath, and way out in the distance, up in the corner of the photo, was a tip of land lined by trees. I couldn't help thinking that's how Win saw us here, that she knew some secret. That, yes, we were stuck on that island, isolated from the rest of the world, but the world *is* out there, after all. We'd eventually make our way back to it. There's no such thing as eternity, not like Sister Fran said. Everything comes to an end, even waiting. Even back then, Win had the wisdom that could lend her that kind of perspective.

But we didn't. At that moment, as Win drove silently with her mother down the highway, Gwen and I could not see the land. We could not even imagine it. We peeled Win's photos off the wall, and we sat hip-to-hip on Win's bunk, too despondent to talk. Win hadn't even said good-bye.

Years later, I'd learn from Win that she had

433

wanted to say good-bye, but she wasn't allowed. Her few belongings were already packed, including her grandfather's old trunk, and Sister Fran had told her that it'd be "best for all of us" if she just left quietly, out the side door that led through the courtyard.

She and her mother went to live in a small apartment over a bakery that wafted cinnamon smells up through the vents. She enjoyed it there, in a place of her own with a window and a view. She'd take long walks alone in the city, and the bakery owner, an older gentleman with a grand-daughter Win's age, gave her scones and strudel cakes whenever she passed by. Win started at a new school, eventually. Made new friends and lost some of her toughness. But as the months wore on, her mother gradually slipped into her old self again. She began drinking, began wearing her housecoat all day long, began looking at Win with those eyes of disgust.

Then one day, her mother left—disappeared, just like that. When Win arrived home from school, she found a note on the kitchen table that simply read, *I'm sorry.* Win was sorry, too, but she was okay. She was almost eighteen, and so the bakery owner hired her, despite the fact that Win never liked to cook. Baking was different, she claimed, more exact. Win continued to live in the apartment until she moved out on the day she was supposed to get married, taking only her grandfather's old trunk with her.

But she didn't get married. She said she couldn't go through with it, that she didn't love the man who'd asked to marry her, that he made her world feel small again, made her feel like she lived on an island, feel like she did those years at the convent. Instead, she dragged the old trunk to the train station, and in her nicest dress she had intended to marry in, she boarded a train that sent her west. She didn't look back.

"I never loved My Boy," she admitted to me years later over the phone. She told me she still had his wooden paddle toy, though. It'd been hidden in her waistband the day her mother came for her, and now she kept it on her mantel. It's funny how we keep such reminders close to us, even if they hurt a little. Maybe that's just what nostalgia is: a willingness to embrace the pain of the past. Win and I spoke often then. She used to call me every other Sunday, until life got too busy. Now we only talk from time to time. But frequency does not determine the depth of friendship. I'm glad for that. No one can ever know you like those with whom you've shared the pangs of your youth.

"I know," I said. Well, I did and I didn't. I wanted to believe we all loved Our Boys with the same ferocity. "But why'd you pretend?"

The line went still for a moment; then she spoke again. "Because I loved The Guineveres," she said. "Besides, weren't we all pretending?"

"Not me," I said.

Win never had any children. I don't know if she wanted them or not. I never asked, and she never told me. She's happy now, and that's the important part.

"Do you still have that old trunk?" I asked.

"I keep it in my bedroom," she told me. By then she was living with Lorraine; the two of them had opened a bakery and built a life together. I've never met Lorraine, but I know she loves Win more than anything, and I know Win loves her, too. But even so, there are things Win can't share with her, not like she can with me. "Lorraine begs me to move it so we can make space for a shoe rack."

"Why don't you?"

"I don't know," she said. She paused, and I could hear her playing with the phone cord, which sounded like the kicking of gravel, a noise I instinctively associate with those uphill marches toward the church. "Because I like it there. Sometimes I sit on it and think." I tried to imagine Win, now grown, lying on that trunk, her long legs right angles at the knees. "Everyone needs a place like that," she said.

I understood what she meant. We cling to the most painful reminders of our youth, our memories or our injuries, perhaps so we can look back to our former selves, console them, and say: Keep going. I know how the story ends.

The Feast of Saints Peter and Paul

Without Ginny and Win, The Guineveres fell into a state of quiet despair. We prayed to God for strength during Morning Prayer—and somehow, by grace or divine inspiration, we remained vigilant and prudent, devout and discreet. While we waited for a response from our letters to the Veterans Administration, we cared for Our Boys as best we could. We looked after Win's boy, too, making sure he was comfortable, his pillow fluffed and his sheets properly tucked. We felt guilty if our eyes strayed over his body for too long, or if we grazed his bare skin as we pulled the blankets to his chest. He wasn't Our Boy, after all.

At the next Penance Service, Gwen and I sat with Reggie wedged between us. As the music played, the girls lined up to give confession. Even with Win gone, nothing had changed. Reggie gesticulated with her hands as she confessed; Lottie closed her eyes per usual; the priests raised their polyester sleeves over the heads of girls to deliver blessings. As I gave confession, I watched Gwen slump forward, her head resting on the pew in front of her. When she got up to give her penance, she slipped out of line, walked a lap around the chapel, then circled back to her seat, and kneeled down again.

"I told the priest that sometimes during Morning Instruction, when Sister Fran brings Pretty, I imagine plucking its feathers off," I reported to Gwen that evening. She was lying on her stomach on the floor, her arms pinned beneath her, so she looked like a fish that had been swept to the shore. "What did you confess?" I asked, even though I knew she hadn't.

"I don't feel well," Gwen said. Her body vibrated lightly, as if she were crying, but she wasn't.

"That's not a sin," I said. "But now you're absolved of it."

"I don't feel well," she said again, and I stroked her back the way my mother used to do when I was small.

Gwen seemed different after that, distant. Though we still sat together at lunch and in chapel, and though I still watched her brush her hair one hundred times in the Wash Room mirror before Lights Out, she turned inward, further away from me than she ever had been. I thought it was something I had done or said, so I tried even harder.

"Want some?" I asked, opening my hand to reveal a pat of butter I had hidden up my sleeve at dinner. Gwen wiped half the square from my hand, but she didn't say thank you or talk about the necessity of good grooming. In fact, she didn't utter a word, just worked the butter through her hair with her fingertips, one strand at a time.

After Tuesday's Morning Instruction, and before we lined up for lunch, Sister Fran readied her burlap sack for Mail Distribution. I looked back toward Gwen, but she was writing in her notebook, not even paying attention as Sister Fran marched the aisles, slapping mail down on the desks of those lucky enough to receive some. I distracted myself by reading over the notes I had taken. During morality lessons, Sister Fran explained to us that the more we give of ourselves, the more we have to give. Our love's like a factory, she said, humming with activity to meet the demand of the orders received. If more love was needed, more was produced. Simple as that. She'd brought Ugly into the classroom for the occasion, and she tried to get the parrot to say "Love in action," but it came out sounding like "Love's a fraction," and the other girls laughed, but not me. I read through my notes, struggling to understand the day's lesson. It didn't make sense, because sometimes it felt like I gave and gave and gave, and soon nothing would be left of me. No love. No action. No factory governed by the simple laws of supply and demand. Nothing but a hollowed-out body.

Sister Fran neared my desk, and for a moment I was certain she had read my mind. I slid down in my chair until my neck rested on the seatback, but Sister Fran clicked her tongue and motioned for me to sit up straight. "A letter for you today," she said. Her sternness diminished, replaced by a grin that revealed her tiny teeth. She laid the envelope down on my desk, as though it contained something fragile, then squeezed my shoulder as she continued down the row. I turned the envelope in my hands to scan the return address, typed in all capital letters. The Veterans Administration.

I swiveled toward Gwen to get her attention. This time she looked up at me, waving a long, rectangular envelope identical to mine. Our eyes gaped in disbelief, our mouths, too. My fingers couldn't work fast enough to peel away the lip of the envelope. I unfolded the letter and flattened it against the surface of my desk. The note was typed on letterhead, a circular seal stamped at the top. I ran my fingers over the indentation in the paper. The letter addressed me as "Miss." I'd never seen that before, not associated with my name, anyhow. It seemed so formal. I took a deep breath and I read:

> Thank you so much for your recent letter to the Veterans Administration. We appreciate the time you took to write. Your inquiry regarding soldier 1097-3845-43-22 has been referred to me for reply.
> We are deeply grateful for the noble

sacrifices of all our veterans, in particular soldier 1097-3845-43-22, who fought valiantly to preserve the freedom we value so dearly. To this date, however, the Veterans Administration has not been able to locate the information you requested.

Please be assured that we are actively trying to identify soldier 1097-3845-43-22. In fact, our top priority is to account for all of our men. We sincerely appreciate your support of our veterans, and we will notify you immediately of any changes to the status of your inquiry.

Sincerely,
Specialist Weatherbee

My heart must have stopped, because the room came to a standstill. They say at the time of our death, life flashes before our eyes and we see scenes of all the moments we've lived and the people we've lived them with. However, I can attest that at this moment, my *future* flashed before me, and this is how I knew I wasn't dying, that maybe, instead, I was being given a second chance. In my future, I see My Boy, his family. We are sitting on a patio drinking lemonade and listening to the radio. I am wearing a gingham dress. The sky is clear. Something warm and heavy squirms on my lap. My Boy laughs loudly, and when he does I can feel his breath on my skin.

I scanned the letter again, scrutinizing every word for any detail I might have missed, any clue. I counted the number of paragraphs: three; the number of sentences: seven, both symbols of perfection in the Bible. *Actively trying. Top priority.* Those were the phrases I kept returning to again and again. My pulse thumped in my temples so it felt like an earthquake had gone through my body. The whole world was shaking. Sister Fran blew her whistle for us to line up for lunch, and I ran to meet Gwen in the back of the room.

"Can you believe it? They wrote back," I said. I spoke quickly, breathlessly. "Our Boys are their top priority. They're going to notify us immediately."

Gwen snapped my letter away from me and handed me her own. I watched as she skimmed the first few lines, her eyelids fluttering, her jaw pulsing. Then I looked down at Gwen's letter that I held in my hands. They addressed her as "Miss," too.

> Thank you so much for your recent letter to the Veterans Administration. We appreciate the time you took to write. Your inquiry regarding soldier 1097-5467-78-63 has been referred to me for reply.
>
> We are deeply grateful for the noble sacrifices of all our veterans, in particular

soldier 1097-5467-78-63, who fought valiantly to preserve the freedom we value so dearly. To this date, however, the Veterans Administration has not been able to locate the information you requested.

Please be assured that we are actively trying to identify soldier 1097-5467-78-63. In fact, our top priority is to account for all of our men. We sincerely appreciate your support of our veterans, and we will notify you immediately of any changes to the status of your inquiry.

The letter was signed by Specialist Weatherbee, just like mine.

Gwen and I finished reading at the same moment, then looked up at each other, squinting as if we'd just crawled out from the dark. She handed my letter to me and took back her own, which she crumpled and threw into the wastebasket.

"They're going to notify us," I said.

Gwen let out a hiss of air. "They didn't even bother to change the wording, Vere. It's a form letter. They don't actually care about Our Boys."

"But he's a specialist," I said, and then I stopped myself. I knew she was right, yet how could I explain that the letter I held in my hands was all the hope I had? That it was the only physical proof that connected me to someone beyond the convent? I was afraid someday I'd disappear completely, not like the saints did, up to heaven. I'd done nothing good. I'd be gone, just gone, vapor floating on clouds. Or worse than that because at least vapor produced rain. That was some sort of future. I, on the other hand, had none.

I folded my letter and shoved it into my shirt pocket. We filed through the cool stone hallways of the convent. We hardly said a word at lunch. Later that night, before Lights Out, I read and reread the letter, a hundred times over, closely, convinced with each reading that the message might be different, convinced I could still find my way home. I fell asleep with it in my hand.

We snuck into the Sick Ward one final time after that, not knowing it'd be our last. Gwen and I walked through the third-floor corridor toward the Catacombs that Ginny had discovered all those months ago. We didn't talk, didn't say much to each other. We held hands as we walked the corridor, two girls who loved Our Boys, two girls who missed our friends, two girls who clung to hope, no matter how futile. We wanted to act as though nothing had changed; we wanted to believe that everything would be okay. Sometimes you have to believe in what you can't see—that's called faith, and we had it still; at least, I think we had it still at that moment as we descended the narrow staircase almost entirely enveloped in dark. When we neared the Sick Ward door, Gwen didn't move, just stood in the blackness not saying a word.

"Let's go," I said. My voice reverberated off the walls of the stairwell.

"You go alone," she said. She sat on the bottom step and tucked her knees to her chin, then rocked back and forth.

I nudged her with my foot from behind. "But Your Boy is waiting," I said.

She sat there unmoving, her body forming a ball when she tucked her head in the space between her arms. "I don't want to see him."

"He needs you, Gwen. Now, more than ever." I touched her warm shoulder, but she shrugged me off.

"I don't know."

"We're part of the War Effort," I said, thinking about what Win would say in this moment, how she could reason with Gwen, reminding her that visiting Our Boys was our civic duty. "When he wakes up, don't you want to be able to tell him that you were here all along? Don't you want to go home with him?"

"It's not that simple, Vere," Gwen said. She stood now and turned, and even though I stood on the step above her, she was taller than me. "I'm not a saint," she said.

"Nobody is."

"You are," she said, her words pushed into my

chest like fingers. I stepped back, injured by her tone. "You make it look so easy."

"Make what look so easy?" I asked.

"Being good," she said. Her voice came out soft. She wasn't being mean-spirited. At least, I don't think she was. "It's hard to live with a saint." She pushed open the door to the Sick Ward where Our Boys waited.

Inside, a humidifier hummed, which usually meant illness. I darted to My Boy's bed, but he appeared okay, and when I touched his forehead I didn't detect a fever. I whispered to him that I was there, right by his side. That I'd always be. I'd never leave him, no matter what. "It's Guinevere," I said to him. "It's Guinevere. It's Guinevere," I kept repeating as though reciting a prayer. I drew my hand through his hair, then down his neck. His skin felt smooth and even, softer than my own, and I kept touching him because he was My Boy to touch.

I leaned over to kiss his forehead, and at that moment I heard Gwen's muted sobs in the dark, high-pitched like the whining of a dog. Afraid she'd wake the others, I went to her, held out my arm to drape her shoulder. But she knocked my hand away, an injured animal pawing at the dark, and I knew better than to try again. I sat down next to her on the bed, and we stayed like that for a while until I felt Gwen lean into me, sinking her head on my shoulder, then finally letting her entire body slink down and rest on my lap. Her hair smelled of soured butter. I didn't say anything, only ran my fingers through it, then rested my palm on the top of her head, praying—if He could hear me—to help ease her suffering. Because if there's anything I'd learned by then, by now, too, it's that suffering doesn't always have a point. Sometimes there's nothing to learn from it.

The next day was the Feast of Saints Peter and Paul. Gwen and I served in the mass, but our eyes were heavy from the long night before. Father James appeared tired, too. The bags under his eyes looked like little canoes that were keeping his eyeballs afloat. He didn't talk to us in the vestry as we dressed. Instead, he sat on the couch with his eyes shut until the music began. To make up for Win's absence, he'd already placed the processional cross in its stand on the altar. He carried the Bible, Gwen held the large candle, and I did my best to evenly distribute the incense smoke as we walked up the aisle.

He opened the mass by reminding us that we were all sinners, that we'd always be sinners; it was our nature. He reminded the parishioners of the sacrifices Saints Peter and Paul had made, the greatest, most selfless sacrifice that anyone could make: their lives. Mr. and Mrs. Drexel nodded their heads slowly throughout opening prayers.

During the homily, Father James stepped away from the pulpit. He stood at the edge of the altar, gesturing with his hands spread like branches of a tree. "What are you willing to give your life for? To whom are you willing to give it?" he asked again and again of the parishioners before him. Mrs. Drexel began to cry onto her husband's shoulder. The missing never eased for her. The missing was part of the War.

During the sermon, Gwen stood in the back corner of the altar, half covered in shadows. I could tell she wasn't even paying attention. Instead, she studied the crucifix perched high above on the wall of the church. Our Savior bared His chest, unclothed from the waist up. His ribs protruded and His muscles flexed with His arms outstretched as they were. I couldn't help feeling sorry for Him up there, blanched with pain, even though He probably felt sorry for me, down here, and even though that's not what I was supposed to feel when I looked at the crucifix.

Father James disrobed in silence after mass, and so did we. He cleared his throat a few times and finally turned toward us, as though he were going to say something, but he stopped himself before any words escaped his lips. He ducked back into the closet, grabbed a bottle of wine, and headed for the door. But before he could get there, Gwen grabbed his sleeve and broke the silence. "Can I have a moment, Father?" she asked.

"Not now," he said. He clasped the wine bottle by its head, turned it upside down like a baton.

"But, Father," she said.

"Not today," he said.

"You said I—" She couldn't finish her sentence before Father James interrupted.

"I said not today, girl. Now that is that," he snapped. His fist became a white, bloodless barnacle around the wine bottle. He released his grip, then tucked the wine beneath his armpit, and he stood for a moment with his eyes aflutter. We thought he might say something more, so we waited. But he didn't. He exited the room without a sound, closing the door to the vestry behind him.

Gwen appeared helpless, standing there in her wool skirt, her skin purple-colored at the knees. She clenched her jaw, and veins popped at her temples. With her index finger, she smoothed down her eyebrows; then she calmly gathered her hair and pulled it to the side.

"Gwen?" I asked.

She said nothing, just smirked with half her mouth. And then, without warning, she swung open the door and bolted. Pumping her arms, she sprinted down the hall, toward Father James's office, her feet sliding on tile as she rounded corners.

He wasn't there. Gwen paced frantically around the room, first sitting on the couch, then bursting toward the sideboard to pour herself a glass of water. She turned in circles as she drank. Finally, she plopped herself in Father James's chair, opened his drawer, and pulled out his bottle of Sunny Brook. Tipping back the bottle, she took a glug and wiped her mouth. Then she rummaged through his drawer some more as if she were digging through sand.

"Come on," I said, checking behind me to make sure nobody was coming. "Let's go." I wished Win were there. She'd have known what to do.

"You go," she said.

"Gwen . . ."

"Go," she said. "I wish you'd just leave already. Nobody wants you here."

I opened my mouth, but no words would come out. My head felt hot; my breath steamed but did not shape sounds. I heard thumping in my ears. Gwen propped her feet on the desk, the way Father James sometimes did. A sticker was stuck to the bottom of her shoe, from one of the younger girls' sticker collections.

"Gwen," I said, moving closer to her. I felt dizzy in this moment; maybe I knew what was coming next.

"Go." Her voice growled, full of venom now. "Please. Leave. I don't want you here." As she said this, her lip curled into a snarl that reminded me of Sister Fran when angry. But Gwen looked so pretty, even now. And that's when she spoke those words. "We're not The Guineveres any-more."

We all have moments that define us, moments

that we can call to mind years later and remember what we felt, what we thought, how the air shifted in the room around us until we felt breathless and we knew nothing in the world could ever be the same. This was that moment for me. Hearing Gwen speak those words, that simple sentence that began with "we" but ended with me standing in front of Father James's mahogany desk, I felt I'd been unplugged from a circuit. My legs became liquid; I could barely stand, so I walked backward, toward the still-open door. I was waiting for Gwen to take back what she'd said, but she didn't. She just sat there smugly with her lips bent and parted, an imitation of a smile.

Years later, after Gwen apologized for everything else, and after I forgave her—what choice did I have?—that one sentence I could never forget. For at that moment, and for the first time since my mother left me here, I came face-to-face with the unutterable truth: I was alone.

Saint Christina the Astonishing

FEAST DAY: JULY 24

The most astonishing saint of them all was Christina, born to a peasant family in 1150. By the age of fifteen, she was orphaned, and by twenty-two she suffered a seizure so severe she was presumed dead. They laid out her brittle body, then carried her to the church in an open coffin for a funeral mass. The church was full of mourners, including her sisters, who wept out of pity for Christina and for themselves. Christina, along with both of their parents, had passed to the hereafter within only a few years of each other, and the sisters had the crushing feeling they were next. The other townsfolk wept, too. Christina may have been a peculiar kind of girl, but she came from good Christian stock, and as with any death, they were reminded of the ephemeral nature of the human condition. They gazed at the gray-pale Christina, wondering about their own fates.

And then, as the priest uttered the Agnus Dei, Christina sat up in her coffin, looked around with wild, animal eyes, then levitated up to the rafters, where she stayed until the last of the townsfolk had fled, their throats raw from screaming.

"Please come down from there," the priest beckoned, enticing her with a morsel of food, a spot of water. He clutched holy water beneath his sleeve. She obeyed the priest, grabbed the water chalice with two fists, and took hungry gulps.

"I could not stand the smell of sinful human flesh," she said, explaining herself. "I had to go up there to escape it," she said, pointing up.

Christina told the priest she hadn't been dead, not at all. Instead, she'd been to hell, where she recognized several folks, then to purgatory, where she recognized even more, and then, finally, to heaven, where she was told she must return to earth to do penance for the sinful, for those stuck below and beyond. "You shall endure many torments, but you shall die from none of these acts," a white-winged angel had told her.

"My life will be so extraordinary that nothing like it will ever been seen," she told the priest, who first checked her forehead for fever and then checked his own.

From this point, Christina found herself fearless, boundless. She crawled into blazing ovens, fire licking her skin, but suffered not a single burn. During the coldest winter months, she'd dash into the river, letting it carry her downstream to the mill, where the wheel whirled around her, scraping her numb, purple-mottled skin. She'd climb trees and perch there in storms, even as the wind lashed her and rain pricked her face.

Christina allowed vicious dogs to lay chase to her, would wrestle them into thorny bushes, and she'd receive not a scar.

Yet she could smell it on them, on others, the scent of sin, spoiled like meat, sickly sweet. Like an old person. Like stagnant water. Like decaying wood. Like waste. She couldn't stand to be indoors, where the smell assaulted her senses, so she slept on rocks and begged for food, and when she couldn't find enough, the heavenly hosts provided. During those times, she could feel her breasts grow heavy, and she'd find a quiet corner where she'd suckle herself, drinking the sweetest, freshest milk she'd ever tasted. Her hair grew wild like a peacock's tail, yet her skin stayed milky white.

From time to time, her sisters, weary of Christina's odd behavior—of the reports from the town that she was again swinging from branches of the tallest tree or rolling through the streets like a human barrel—would chain Christina to her bed. Yet she always found a way to break free, and when she did, she'd run to the forest, whoop-whooping the entire way, like the call of a bird returning to its nest.

Only there, only in the quiet of the forest, the light peeking through the canopy of trees, could she find calm. The shrubs didn't judge her when she broke into gallops or hit herself over the head with a fallen branch. The animals didn't stop to stare when she'd cry out wildly to the heavens, "More! More!" or when she'd bound from tree to tree, swinging her arms like a monkey. Sometimes she felt so much, so deeply, and these outbursts were her only relief, like her skin would explode from the heat of her passions. Other times, Christina felt nothing at all, the even, velvet numbness of intoxication.

There, in the forest, she'd walk barefooted, admiring the texture of bark, the shapes of roots running in and out of the ground like snakes, the mushroom caps that resembled little huts. She didn't want to return to the town, but she knew she must. Her sisters would worry, and she meant them no harm.

At these times, she'd grow quiet, levitate to the sky, and hang there like a cloud or like a white bird, midflight. She didn't know what to do with the powers she'd been given. She hadn't meant to be so astonishing.

The Assumption

The long year wound its way back again, and we were not the same girls. We sweated in the heat of the hazy August sun at the Sisters of the Supreme Adoration's annual festival, where only a year before we'd tried to run away. So much had happened since, and we understood the enormity of heartbreak, the pain that comes from unconditional love. We were tired. The year had exhausted us. Ginny left us; Win was taken; we met Our Boys; we loved Our Boys. We wanted to go home, and yet here we were, still. Again. The old folks were lined up in their wheelchairs with balloons tied to them; they appeared on the verge of an eternal sleep. We thought of Mr. Macker, by now settled into heaven, if such a place existed.

The Sisters scurried about in their pink skirts, creased, no doubt, from being folded and stored since last summer. Sister Tabitha ran the turtle races again—Turtle Downs—and she stuttered out their names through the bullhorn as the creatures ambled dispassionately toward the ends of their lanes. Not much had changed in this year, yet everything had.

Gwen and I worked the concession booth, filling paper bags with popcorn and cotton candy. The booth was constructed of wood with only a small window for ventilation, a little hotbox. Gwen had pulled her hair up, but a few tendrils fell down the back of her slender neck, clinging with dampness. Sister Monica manned the register, and as she stood with her broad back to us, we noticed sweat had rendered her shirt see-through. She wore a thick-strapped beige-colored bra. It surprised us anytime we were reminded of the Sisters' actual bodies—of their having breasts or other attributes of womanhood—because they seemed so androgynous beneath their habits. Our own bras were beige, too, starchy and uncomfortable at the elastic that dug into our backs or beneath our young breasts. I hooked my bra strap with my thumb, eyed Sister Monica, and mouthed "Look" to Gwen. She laughed beneath her breath, which sounded like a hiccup, and then went back to filling boxes with popcorn, her pale lips holding little amusement.

Around midday some girls our age visited the booth, standing in front of the sign that listed prices. We recognized them from church. They wore patterned sundresses and open-toed shoes that strapped around the ankle and revealed red-painted nails. Gwen and I stared at them, wondering what it was like to be on the outside, looking in, looking at us. We suddenly became aware of our wool skirts that itched our thighs, slippery and fragrant with sweat. I looked at Gwen, who'd closed her eyes, and I thought about

Ginny, about Win, about what they'd do at this moment. Ginny would have sucked in her cheeks, made Holy Constipation faces, and Win would have snarled her lip until the girls moved away. But they weren't here—only us—and Gwen sluggishly opened her eyes and pretended not to see them. Their skin glowed in the heat; moisture dampened their upper lips, and when they waved paper fans in front of their faces, the smell of perfume wafted toward us. Their voices projected, clear and excited, unrestrained by sideways glances that told them to speak in quiet tones.

"Now what should we get?" one of them said, sighing as though oppressed by the decision. Her hair was pulled back with a red bow, which she twirled around her finger as she thought about it.

"I can't decide," said another.

"Have one of each," Red Bow said, and she paused, drumming her chubby fingers on her gloss-tinged lips.

I wondered what it was like to live in a world with the freedom to choose. Did you somehow lose yourself, or your focus, when decisions pulled your mind in so many directions? Was it confusing, burdensome, somehow? Father James said that happiness is largely a matter of where you place your attention, and with the oppression of options, where does one place it? I'm not sure I knew at that moment, and I still wonder from time to time, even now, as an adult, if the removal of choice is not a sort of gift, one allowing for supreme focus. In this way, I've come to understand the asceticism of the Sisters, if only obliquely.

"I'll have some cotton candy," Red Bow said. "Blue, not pink."

Gwen handed me the cotton candy, and Sister Monica counted change, dropping it into my hands with her fat fingers. I returned it to the girl, hot with embarrassment, especially when she said "Thank you" in a tone that conveyed she felt sorry for me.

We saw these same girls beneath the shade tent later after Gwen and I finished with our shift. We sat on opposite sides of a table sharing a funnel cake, each pinching at the corners with small nibbles. Gwen's fingernails were chewed to the nubs, unusual for her, jagged and rough, a punishable offense, were Sister Fran to notice. Gwen pushed the rest of the plate toward me, yawned, and, crossing her arms on the table, rested her head on them, her hair gathering like a bird's nest.

"I wonder what they do all day?" we heard one of those girls ask, the one with the red bow again. I wanted to tell her we weren't deaf, not like Saint Mark or Saint René. Gwen raised her head off the table and sat back in her chair, combing her hair with her fingers, her small nose raised just enough in the air to prove that she still had her dignity.

"Are they training to be nuns?" another girl asked.

"I don't think so," said the third. She was the largest, and her dress hugged her hips and her stomach, shaped like a barrel across her torso. "I think their parents just didn't want them anymore."

"Wonder what they did to deserve that?" Red Bow said, biting into a piece of licorice. The corners of her mouth were tinged blue from the cotton candy she had eaten.

Gwen and I pretended we didn't hear. Instead, we watched as Father James slumped over like an old man in his trunks and T-shirt atop the dunking booth. His wet shirt clung irreverently to his nipples, and his rosy face gave him away. "Dear Lord, have mercy," Father James kept yelling, but most of the parishioners didn't have much aim.

"Want to go see Our Boys?" I asked. They were never far from my mind. I fanned myself with our now empty funnel-cake plate.

"Nah," Gwen said. She looked into the distance, past the church perched on the hill above us, past the billowy clouds that filled the sky like powder puffs in a glass jar. She seemed to look right up to the heavens, to where you got to live if you were holy and good and dead. If you were

460

a saint. Later, Gwen and I watched the annual parade make its way toward the church. We moved to the lawn, made a blanket of grass, and surveyed the floats as Sister Tabitha hollered out their names on the bullhorn. Fewer floats marched in the parade this year than last, since the Sisters scrutinized all entries more thoroughly, making sure none of them could hide human contraband. As a result, the floats were smaller, nonspecific, and unimpres-sive: a cross, a star, a garland, some praying hands, and a few formless saints who looked especially short. The Sisters trudged up the hill toward the church, the floats trailing behind them like low-flying kites. One by one, they crested the hill, then disappeared into the shade of the courtyard, beyond our sight.

"Think anyone's inside one?" I asked.

"I hope so," Gwen said. "I hope it's Lottie."

I was on my back in the grass, and when I laughed it felt like the whole sky was shaking.

We talked about our failed attempt last year, how hot it was inside that float, how Sister Monica looked from behind as she tugged us all the way to the courtyard of the church. We laughed as we thought about Sister Fran—how she looked like an angry vulture when she found us hidden inside. Her eyes bulged out of her face and her lips contorted into her Holy Constipation look.

"How do you think she knew we were inside?" I asked.

"Probably because the float was so heavy," Gwen said. "Or maybe because we weren't at the parade." She was sitting on the grass, picking blades, then peeling back the fibers.

"Maybe she's omniscient," I said. "Maybe it came to her like a vision. That can happen, you know. Visions."

"I don't know. It doesn't matter anyhow," she said.

"Maybe not," I said. Then I offered, "It's probably lucky we were caught."

"Lucky?" She scoffed. "You think *we're* lucky?"

"We'd have never met Our Boys," I said. "We'd never get the chance to go home with them." Gwen flicked the blade she was peeling, then lay back in the grass and watched the clouds that formed vague animal shapes above us. She closed her eyes, and I thought she'd fallen asleep, until I heard her voice above the din of the parade.

"Yes, Our Boys," she said, her eyes still closed.

The next day: the Feast of the Assumption, a holy day of obligation. We ate a breakfast of buckwheat and toast, then attended mass in the chapel. Gwen didn't sit by me. A few rows up, she knelt, bent over the pew in front of her as though impaled by it. Her prayer hands were propping up her forehead, and she looked like she was praying, really praying, not just sitting there thinking about something else, like most of us did. Her eyes were shut, and she breathed heavily, and she looked so pretty, like a picture you might find on a prayer card. Only people like Gwen don't wind up on prayer cards.

Yet I wish I could hold that vision of Gwen in my mind: Gwen with fluttering lids, so innocent, so fervent in her prayer, so hurt, so alone, so beautiful because of this. They say everything happens for a reason, but I don't believe it now. I don't know if I ever did. Sometimes things happen that we don't understand, that we'll never understand. Sometimes the people we love invite suffering into our world for no cause at all. But I didn't know that back then, as I admired Gwen from a distance. What I knew—what I believed—was this: Gwen, at that moment, was my friend.

Gwen's secret unraveled later that day. I wasn't the first to know, but I wasn't the last. Some may have suspected all along, I'm sure, but we never spoke publicly of such things as times of the month at the convent. The Sisters left belts and cloths in the sanitary closet, and when necessary, we removed them discreetly. Nobody kept tabs. Why would we think to? We all bore that monthly shame.

Except, now, Gwen.

Her wool skirt no longer fit, so she really couldn't hide her growing stomach much longer.

Her shirt filled out, gaping at the widest point. Lottie Barzetti had seen her dressing for breakfast, attempting to shimmy her uniform around her widening hips. Lottie noticed Gwen's rounded belly, and she ratted to Sister Fran, who pulled Gwen by her collar from the table in the cafeteria. Her gray oatmeal steamed dolefully on her abandoned tray, her spongy fruit half eaten. The cafeteria grew hushed with whispers. I was alone. I felt like Mary Magdalene, only the stones were glances, and the other girls were happy to throw them in my direction. They assumed I was guilty, too, somehow. Complicit.

After breakfast, Sister Tabitha came for me. We walked in silence down the checkered corridor, past alabaster busts of holy saints, past the bronze Stations of the Cross plaques, down the cool, shadowed hallway to Sister Fran's office. The door stood ajar, and I could see Sister Fran holding Gwen by the wrists as she tried to squirm away. Her hair was tangled, and she looked like an unbridled horse. Gwen kept trying to wrangle herself free, but Sister Fran was stronger than she was.

"The Holy Spirit gave it to me," Gwen said, all spitfire and sarcasm. "Just like the Virgin Mary. It can happen."

"You shall not speak sacrilege in this house, ungrateful girl," Sister Fran said, a layer of rage revealed in her voice, years in the making. She swung her arm back and slapped Gwen across her cheek.

Gwen stood there stunned, her long, thin legs bent slightly at the knees as though she were bracing herself for a fall. Her eyes became quarters, round and shiny—wet, but no tears fell. A slap-shaped red mark streaked across her face. Sister Fran wound back to hit Gwen again but stopped herself, softened, and inhaled audibly.

"You must tell me," she said. "You must tell me, girl. God knows already, and soon I shall, too." Her brow furrowed and her eyes sank. For the first time, I noticed how old Sister Fran was—as old as some of the old folks in the Sick Ward—and I felt sorry for her. Her nose crinkled as though she smelled something foul. "Was it Father James? One of the others? Which one?"

"No" was all Gwen managed to stammer; her narrow shoulders crunched forward, and she covered her head with her hands.

"I told him girls should not be altar servers. There are reasons for these rules," Sister Fran grumbled beneath her breath, as if she were chanting a prayer, perhaps to Saint Regis, the patron saint of wayward women. "Father James, laying hands on our innocent lambs . . . ," she said, disgusted. Her upper lip twitched. She looked behind me toward Sister Tabitha. "I knew he had problems, but *this?*"

Sister Tabitha made wordless sounds like the

low whining of heat pipes in winter. "S-s-s-sinful," she said.

"Go get him," Sister Fran said to Sister Tabitha. "Now."

Sister Tabitha stood there for a moment, her mouth agape. She fiddled with the cross pendant that hung around her neck.

"Now!" Sister Fran said again, then turned and slapped Gwen across her cheek, this time lightly and for show. Sister Fran looked like a rabid raccoon in her black-and-white dress, with her lips snarled and thin, her eyes beady and dim. "You will go to chapel, and you will pray until you tell me," she said.

Sister Tabitha turned quickly and left the room, and Gwen stood erect, wiping the tears from her face; her eyes shimmered, so pretty, so magnified, they seemed unreal. "You can't church it out of me," Gwen said, and at this Sister Fran struck her harder than she had yet.

Then Sister Fran swiveled. "You will tell me," she said. Her long, crooked finger extended toward me.

As though propelled by some unseen force, I stumbled forward on wobbly legs. Sister Fran grabbed my forearm and yanked me around next to Gwen. I stood so close I could feel her warm skin against mine, her rapid, audible breath. I reached for her hand and squeezed it. I wanted her to know she wasn't alone.

"Was it Father James?" Sister Fran asked me.

"I don't know, Sister," I said. And I didn't. Not quite yet. I still had faith; it was only just beginning to unwind.

"This will be a *bastard* child," Sister Fran said to nobody in particular. She shook her head and walked in impatient circles.

"Yes, Sister," I said in response.

"Did he . . . did he touch you?" she asked me.

I looked at her blankly, wrung my hands. My mind raced, and I tried to catch up with my thoughts, tried to scan every memory of Father James in the rectory, or in the vestry, or at the back of the church.

"Father James. Did he touch you?" she asked me again.

"No, Sister."

She sighed, relieved, then placed her hand over her eyes as if they ached.

"Did she spend time alone with Father James? Did you ever leave her there alone?"

"Well . . . ," I stuttered. I studied Gwen, but at this point her face was expressionless, as if she were playing her starlet role like she sometimes did. I imagined if she spoke, her voice would sound high-pitched, rhapsodic. I wanted to sink into the floor, melt like candle wax.

"Thou shall not lie," she said.

"She did. We left her behind. We didn't mean to, but . . . ," I stammered, trying to explain how

Win and I abandoned Gwen to Father James, closed the door behind us, even though we knew we shouldn't. I wanted to defend him, but I could only picture Father James's rouged nose, his lip scar more visible when he smiled, his muscular hands that that he sometimes rubbed together as if he were smoothing lotion onto them.

"I knew it," Sister Fran snapped. Her face lifted back to the ceiling, her hands on her ears as though trying to unhear what she'd just heard.

Gwen took that moment to sit down on the bench against the wall. I sat down next to her and put my arm around her like my mother used to do. We must have looked silly sitting that way in Sister Fran's office, and I used to try to imagine that moment, Gwen tucked into the pit of my arm, leaning her body's weight into my chest, her delicate palm resting just below my rib cage. She smelled sweet, I recall, like her berries from breakfast, which she no doubt had rubbed onto her lips, so desperate to wear makeup. I tried to smooth her hair, cooed, "Don't be afraid." I'll admit, it felt good having Gwen rest there in my arms, as if I could care for both of us, as if we were The Guineveres again.

"God knows your shame," Sister Fran said. Pretty chirped from its cage in the corner. "He forgives all, but only if you confess it," she said. Gwen lowered her eyes. That's one thing we always believed: If you confessed your sins, then you'd be set free. The great power of absolution.

"Pretty's so pretty," Pretty squawked, then ruffled its wings.

"Shh," Sister Fran said to the bird.

"God doesn't make junk," Pretty said, and at this Sister Fran rattled the cage to silence the bird.

Soon Sister Tabitha returned with Father James. He was unshaven, his eyelids bloodshot and his hair disheveled. "What's this about?" he said. He saw Gwen and me sitting on the bench, and his body became rigid as an oak tree.

"You," Sister Fran said, more an accusation than answer. "This child . . . this girl. She's . . ." Sister Fran couldn't bring herself to say it, but her lips curled, and I could see revulsion in her face. "With child," she finally spat out. "Tell me if it's your doing."

Father James's face jerked, startled. His eyes rolled around in his sockets like marbles. "Mine?" he bellowed. He uprooted his legs from the floor, walked forward.

"God does not abide fools nor liars. Make not of me one and you the other," Sister Fran replied. "This girl is pregnant. She says it was the Holy Ghost, and I am not inclined to believe that," she said. "Are you?"

Father James said nothing, just slowly turned toward where we were sitting. His face had gone white; his hands shook; he licked his lips nervously. "Is this what you've told them?" he said. I couldn't look at him—not at that moment. I could only imagine him passing us a bottle after mass, his boyish grin inviting us to drink.

"She didn't have to tell me anything," Sister Fran said. "An abomination. That which you do to the least of His people. Young girls! They're here for our protection," she bawled. Then, with a shaking fist, she swiped a stack of papers off her desk, and they fluttered to the ground, wings flapping.

"Preposterous," he said. His voice quavered when he spoke. He placed his hands in his pockets, then immediately withdrew them, held them out the way he did during church, right before we washed them. "That's the truth. Tell her this is the truth, girl," he shouted to Gwen, but she wouldn't look up. "The girl is clearly troubled. Tell her," he said.

"I shall call the archbishop," Sister Fran said. "I have no other choice in the matter."

"Frances—stop. Listen to me. I've done nothing," he said, and this struck me as odd. I'd never heard Sister Fran addressed like that before, not without her title, not with such familiarity.

"You will not tell me what to do," she said. "She is a child. A lamb!"

The room got quiet. Sister Tabitha stood wide-eyed at the door while Sister Fran and Father

James faced off: a nun versus a priest, each devouring the other with glances I could only describe as unholy. They turned toward us sitting on the bench, both with pleading stares. With Holy Consternation.

Gwen untucked herself from my embrace, and where she had been resting quickly grew cold. She rose to her feet, spoke in a broken voice. "It wasn't him," she said.

Father James looked relieved, and he removed a handkerchief from his breast pocket to wipe his forehead.

"Then who? Where have you been?" Sister Fran asked. Gwen leaned against the wall, refusing to say another word.

Sister Fran then turned to me once more. Her face tensed up again, her eyes narrowing. She didn't look like a Frances to me, only a Sister Fran, the only Sister Fran I'd ever known. "Who else did she see? What other . . . men?" she asked, spitting out the word. "Someone you met? Another priest? A parishioner?"

"Nobody," I said.

"Thou shalt not tell a lie," she said.

I felt heady, like I did when I drank church wine or Sunny Brook. My wool skirt itched my legs, and I scratched them. I couldn't think, couldn't do much but peer down at my shoes, toes pointed inward. I was scared for Gwen, but I knew I couldn't protect her.

"There are Our Boys," I said after a long pause.

"Boys? Which boys?" Sister Fran probed, her nose needling the air.

"Our Boys," I said. "Our Boys in the Convalescent Ward. The ones who have been here since last year," I explained, making certain she knew it wasn't the new soldiers, the older ones in the Front Room whom we could barely stand to lay our eyes upon.

For a moment, a smile flitted across her face, as if she might sneeze. As if she had just thought of something funny. "But those soldiers—they're . . . halfway to death."

I clamped my jaw. "No, they're not," I said. Sister Fran ignored me and turned to Gwen again. "They're not dead," I said, this time louder, and at that point Gwen hung her head. She didn't speak—didn't have to.

"Was it one of these boys?" Sister Fran questioned, clearly confused.

"Yes, Sister," she said quietly.

"See, they're not dead," I said again, relieved.

Sister Fran quieted me with a wave. "Which one?" she wanted to know. Gwen covered her mouth, as though that might prevent her from revealing the truth. Then her arms went limp. She looked at me and shook her head, the corners of her mouth bending downward, her bottom lip pouting to reveal fleshy pink. Her blue eyes flashed, and then it hit me. My body froze.

Time slowed at that point. I noticed every drop of perspiration form as a bead beneath my skin, then squeeze out of my pores. I sensed blood surging through each of the four chambers of my heart. In the distance, the church bell rang. I felt, at that moment, what all those saints must have felt at some point, the dissolving of earthly time. I was transcendent. I prayed silently to God, to My Boy, to anyone who would listen, and I waited for Gwen to speak.

"It was Her Boy," she said, finally pointing to me.

Her finger could have been a dagger, like Juliet's. Like Saint Lucy's, who gouged out her own eyes. My vision tunneled; the world contracted to a pinpoint.

And at the end of the pinpoint I beheld Sister Fran's perplexed face.

"The one without any bandages," Gwen clarified for her.

"That's impossible," she said softly. "Sister Tabitha, isn't that impossible?" Sister Tabitha came forward. I rubbed my blurry eyes. I felt lightheaded. I felt sick.

"S-s-s-sinful, but not impossible," she said, flushing. "Anatomically sp-sp-sp-speaking," she finally spat out.

"I'm confessing. I did it," Gwen said. "I'm absolved now because I'm saying I did it." She tried to cry, but no tears came. Instead she looked like she was squinting from sun. "I did it," she said. "Isn't that what you want? My confession. There. Now you have it. I did it."

And then it struck me, appeared like a vision that must have come to some of the saints. I could see it all laid out neatly before me: I thought of My Boy, of his body, of Gwen's steely eyes ogling him. "Men have needs," she had told me. "Men are snakes," she had said. But I couldn't think of it. I shoved it down. I couldn't breathe. My fingers pulsed; they ached. "Maybe it *was* the Holy Spirit," I managed to stammer. "One never knows why or when miracles happen," I said, a line Sister Fran had repeated to us many times before. It was in this way I could convince myself My Boy had done no wrong. He couldn't have. Not to me.

Gwen looked at me, surprised. Her eyes were upside-down frowns that said they were sorry. But it was too late for sorrow to make a difference. I felt sick to my stomach. I wanted to run to the Sick Ward and find My Boy. Ask him: Is it true? Ask him: *Why?* Ask him: Have I not loved you well enough? But Gwen was the one who held the answers, and here she was in front of me now, strained with a pain not localized to a single part of her body. She was beautiful, standing there, her hands crossed over her belly, her legs crossed, too. She was icy and distant and hurt and beautiful, and as much as I wanted to hate her,

I couldn't. It's not what the saints would do. The saints would barrel down into the pain. If their right hand were cut off, they'd offer their left. If that were cut off, too, they'd offer a leg, until limb by limb and piece by piece they were condensed into a tiny sliver. That's what the saints would do: offer themselves.

So I reached out and touched Gwen's stomach, protruding over her unzipped skirt fastened with a hairband. "Forgive this child," I said. They were the only words I could think to speak, the incantation of the priests after confession. I tried to mean it, I did.

But I can tell you now, I suffered as I spoke those words. I suffered. And maybe suffering is the point, its own end. I can't say I regret the way I reacted, that with perspective or time I wish I had lashed out in that moment, that I had shamed Gwen, or unleashed onto her my anger. What good would that have done? We *all* suffered. All of us.

Some years later, when Gwen lived in a city far away, she called me. She'd been divorced three times by then, worked as a secretary at an insurance agency somewhere in the middle of the country. She had begun soul-searching, seeking answers that maybe she'd never find. That old desire for absolution crept up on her, which led her back to me. She wanted to confess to me the details. She wanted me to forgive her. She told me about her secret shame, told me how she'd sneak into the Sick Ward, how she blamed herself, how she hated herself. More than anything else, she hated herself. So she found My Boy, and she—

I stopped her. I forgave her, I said, but I couldn't hear it. I would not let her tell me. I would not bear that story. I would not provide her with absolution.

"You need to forgive yourself," I said. I quickly hung up the phone and sat motionless until it was night, until it was black, and I disappeared into the darkness. Maybe I took the easy way out. Or maybe I just didn't want to know her truth. *My* truth was this: My Boy loved me. He had given me the gifts of faith, and hope, and love. And the greatest of these is love.

My Revival

My mom told me that the difference between superstition and faith is that one produces fear and the other comfort. But I'm not sure I recognize that difference. Because when my mom talked to me about our family's curse, I felt scared more than anything else. You see, she believed the women in my family were cursed to die young. When I asked Sister Fran about it, she reminded me that only God knows the time and the place of our end, but that's not what my mom believed. Her sister and her mom and her grandmother and her great-grandmother, going way back, they all died by age thirty-three, just like Jesus. I didn't know what it was about that age, but Mom told me that's when she'd die, too. She knew it the way she knew when it would rain; she felt it in her bones.

"That's faith," she told me. We were huddled in the back storage room of a church where we'd been staying for a while. The room could only accommodate one cot, so we crowded together on the bed. Mom's long, wiry hair tickled my neck as I lay on my stomach, but I didn't mind. "I'm not afraid to die," Mom said after a while. She believed God called her to higher purposes, and dying young was just one of them. But I was afraid, and I told her so. I didn't ever want to leave her, not even for heaven. She wrapped her arms around me, and her skin smelled like incense because she'd been praying in the chapel.

Some people called Mom fanatical; others called her worse names than that, especially when she'd stand on sidewalks or barefooted in fountains and preach her visions. Strangers stopped to gawk at Mom, whose hair shot up at the roots as if she'd been electrocuted, whose mouth jerked and pulsed as she shouted, sometimes only sounds and spittle leaving her lips. I'd stand with her, but I never spoke a word, just stood to the side as quietly as possible, holding an upturned hat for spare change. Occasionally some nice folks would toss coins inside. I think they felt sorry for me, having to stand there like that while Mom stamped her feet and raised her hands to the sky, shouting out messages she claimed to have received from above.

Yet to me, she was just my mom, eccentric for sure, but I loved her more than anything in the world. "I won't always be here," she'd say, taking my hand in her own. Her fingernails were bitten to nubs; red ridges of puffiness protruded from beneath the nail bed. At night she would rub Vaseline over her fingers, then stick a sock over her hand and sleep that way. "If you acknowledge someone won't be around forever, it won't hurt as much when they're gone, my dear. Because you can't attach yourself to something that wasn't yours to begin with."

"Is that how you felt about my father?" I asked. Mom would give me a look like she'd swallowed a parrot to stop it from talking. We didn't speak about him.

I'd only met him once. We had gone to an apartment in the city and rung a doorbell, and when after a while a tall, clean-shaven man answered, Mom simply said, "This is her." I craned my neck to look up at him, to see if I could recognize myself in his face because I looked nothing like my mom. Her face was round, and mine was long. Her hair was blond, and mine was brown. Her nose was a small angular button, and mine sloped down and broadened at the end. The man at the door appeared to be examining me, too. He squatted down to eye level.

"What's your name?" he asked. His voice sounded dry, but not unkind.

I froze, unable to speak, so I just stood there with fisted hands at my sides, too nervous to move.

"Tell him your name," Mom said to me, but at that the man stood up again, patted me on the head, and asked if we could come back. We never did.

Instead, we moved from place to place a lot, staying in shabby old apartments or hotels or even back rooms of restaurants or shops where Mom sometimes worked for our food. Mom was good at "tending," as she liked to call it. Tending to this, tending to that: cleaning, cooking, sewing, mending, fixing what was broken. On occasion, she'd disappear for hours at a time and reappear all disheveled, her hair tangled and red marks around her lips. I'd ask her where she'd been. "Oh, just tending, my dear. Just tending." And in those instances, my face would grow hot, and I'd realize tending meant whatever Mom needed it to mean.

Mom called her strange habits quirks, but I worried about her. I had to remind her to take her medicine, or else she forgot. Nerve pills, she called them, tiny white dots no larger than a pencil tip. If she didn't take them, she'd sometimes talk to people who weren't even there, have whole conversations with them as if they were sitting right in front of her talking back. "Did you hear that?" she'd ask me, pawing at some invisible flies in the air around her. But I didn't. I wasn't gifted with visions like Mom, so maybe I wasn't gifted with faith.

Once, Mom told this nice shop owner who let us stay in his small storeroom that she knew how the world would end, that everyone's skin would turn purple and peel off and that to save ourselves we must eat raw onions and pray the rosary. Mom would go around eating raw onions as if they were apples, until one day she stopped, saying she thought she'd had enough to act as a vaccine. The shop owner asked us to leave shortly thereafter.

Maybe Mom thought if she kept moving, the curse wouldn't catch up to her. Her own sister died at thirty-three to the hour. At midnight on her birthday, the story goes, my aunt jumped off the same bridge that her mother had fallen from so many years before. Mom said she saw her swan dive to the water's surface that met her sister's body like a solid, not a liquid. "It's just our fate," Mom would tell me. "Fate's not a bad thing. Just means you can let go." Mom's aunt was in a car accident only a week or two before her thirty-third birthday, and my great-grandma died, too, when the family dog caught rabies and then gave it to her. She was thirty-two and three-quarters. Other women in our family went in other ways: food poisoning from improperly canned beans, child-birth, farm accidents, freak accidents, illnesses. Instead of a family tree, Mom kept a list of the dead, like a recipe of some sort, tucked inside her bra.

The year Mom turned thirty-two, we began living in the basements of churches. She said she liked the comfort of Houses of God, because churches amplified our prayers—God could hear them better. She liked to be His houseguest, she joked. And besides, if He went looking for her, He'd know just where to find her. "When in doubt, make it easy on Him," she instructed me with an earnest look on her face, her eyes buried in the depth of her face. During the day, when she wasn't tending, she'd sit in the chapel and light candles, then stare at the flickering light as if she were reading her fortune. "I wonder how it will happen," she'd whisper to herself. I was supposed to be doing the homework she assigned me from whatever books we could find, which usually just involved reading something and telling her about it.

"Maybe it won't," I'd say, hopeful.

"It will, baby. It will," she'd say back. "You've got to have faith." The candlelight danced on my mom's face. The shadows made her jawline disappear into her neck, as if she were already fading. I wanted to hold on to her, so I did.

"Don't worry, baby," she said after a while. "I'll always be with you in here," and when she said this, she tapped her index finger to my chest.

"But what will I do?" I asked.

"What we all do," she said. "Find something to love, and love it." She pulled me close to her. "That's why I have you." When she smiled, shadows bounced on her teeth.

The day before her thirty-third birthday, Mom and I packed up our things and headed to the old bridge where both her sister and mother had died. She promised me she wouldn't jump. She just wanted to be there the moment she was taken since it was a special place to her, as close to a family plot as she could imagine. It'd make her feel closer to them, she said. I did as my mother told me, not knowing if these would be our final hours together.

The bridge sat over the river like a shelf. The railing was made of wood, worn by weather and by years, and Mom pointed out the place where my relatives had gone over. I remember my aunt only from photos. She had light hair like my mom, but wasn't as pretty. Mom and I sat on the ledge, our feet hanging over, dangling as if we were little kids atop a chair that was too tall for us. Mom asked me to hold her hands and pray with her, and so I did. Her hands felt cold, as if she'd iced them down, even though it was a mild summer day, and I could tell just by holding her hands that she was shaking.

Mom clenched her eyes until they were wrinkled in the corners, and we sat there, hoping some higher being could hear us. She was saying things like "Save me. Please, save me." When I heard her pray those words, I prayed, too. "I'll do anything, anything," I prayed. At the time, I really meant it.

We prayed like that for a while on the bridge, till after dusk fell and everything looked gray and grainy. A few cars stopped to see if we were okay, and Mom just said, "Yes—we're fine! Just praying." The drivers looked at us sideways before driving on, trying to determine if they should believe us, two people dressed in rags, hands clasped in prayer.

Once night fell, we prayed silently. I could feel the midnight hour approaching us, even without a watch. Mom was wearing one—it was the only belonging she still had of her mother's—and so when it was eleven o'clock she said, "It's almost time." She took off the watch and handed it to me. "Wear this, baby, and think of me," she said. "It's got powers. Special powers. Powers from beyond. Nothing bad can happen to you when you're wearing it. They told me so."

"Who told you so?" I asked. Remember, I loved my mom.

"The angels. But sometimes you've got to let go, pass it on." I took the watch from her and clasped it onto my wrist.

"Oh, Mom. Don't go," I said. My throat felt like it was closing, and I could barely breathe. I grasped Mom's hand, dug my fingers into it as if I were holding on to the edge of a cliff for dear life. I was half expecting her to rise right off her seat on the edge of that bridge and into the inky sky. I'd never seen anyone die right in front of me before—or levitate, for that matter—so I didn't know how it would happen. Maybe the air would be sucked from her by the invisible mouth of an angel. Maybe God would appear.

At ten till midnight we began to sing "Amazing Grace." Our voices rose high into the night air. The river's lapping waves beneath us sounded like applause. The moon was as bright as a flashlight beam, shining down on us and casting large shadows behind us, twice the size of our bodies. I could see a million stars in the sky. I was struck with the beauty of that moment, right before midnight, and I thought about how the impermanence of things only makes them seem more beautiful. I had to have faith. I tried to hold on to that picture of the sky—burn it into my mind so I'd remember it forever.

With twenty seconds to go, we started the countdown. Nineteen . . . eighteen . . . seventeen. "I love you," she said. Sixteen . . . fifteen . . . fourteen. "I love you, too," I said. My eyes began to water, but I didn't feel like I was crying. It might have been the wind, turning chilly in the night. Thirteen . . . twelve . . . eleven . . . "Now, remember to live your life," she said. "Don't go around feeling sorry for yourself." Ten . . . nine . . . eight . . . "Oh, Mom, don't go," I said. Seven . . . six . . . five . . . "God has his own plan, baby," she said. Four. Three. Two. "Everything happens for a reason."

One.

Nothing.

We both sat there, as if we were frozen through. Nothing. I could feel Mom's heartbeat, but I listened for her breathing, too, and when I heard it, relief washed over me. We sat still, our feet hanging over the bridge, half numb, the night straining our eyes, even beneath such a bright moon. Then out of the darkness grew my mother's laughter, so loud I could almost see it taking shape like a big funnel cloud picking up steam as it rolled. She knew it and I knew it: She'd outrun the curse. She'd been saved.

But what did it mean to be saved? I thought it meant we'd stop moving from place to place. Maybe we'd find a home of our own and live there and grow a little vegetable garden in the backyard. Some of the churches where we'd stayed kept gardens in the warmer months. To me, a garden meant you were rooted, like the plants, and you had to wait at least until their bulbs flowered and fruited before you could move again. That's how gardens worked: through stillness.

But being saved meant something else for my mom. Something in her had shifted. That night on the bridge, as the big hand on my grandmother's watch swept over the little hand, as they both pointed to the twelve, upward, Mom was born again, but born again a different person.

"I had a vision last night," she said the next day. Her voice was scratchy. She'd caught a cold. We were in a motel; the room was square, and the carpet was blue. It smelled like cigarettes, even though the sign said no smoking. Mom's eyes sagged heavily, as if she'd been overtaken by a drug. She'd been awake when I'd gone to sleep and awake when I woke up. I didn't like it when she got this way. She hadn't moved from her spot on the end of the bed.

"Who spoke to you?" I asked.

"Him," she said, then gave me a look like I was sassing her. "We must get you a proper education," she said.

I sat up in bed thinking of the possibilities contained within this phrase. No more moving. School. Friends. I hugged Mom, squealed with delight, then lay my head back on my pillow and closed my eyes to imagine where we might go, who I might meet, where we might stay. I wanted to grow lilies in my garden, because those were the prettiest flowers of all.

Mom took me shopping the next day. I didn't ask where she'd gotten the money. New coat—even though it was still summer—new shoes, new dress. "You'll need these for school," she said. Mom was never the type to look ahead into the future, preferring instead to live in the moment. However, I'd never seen such pretty things before, still stiff in their newness. When we got back to the motel, Mom asked me if I wanted to try my new clothes on again. I said no, because I didn't want to ruin them for school. I wanted my new friends to know me as the girl who dressed neatly. As the girl with the navy blue pea coat, as the girl who wore the dress with pearls for buttons. I wanted my new friends to like me. That night I slept, and I dreamed and I dreamed and I dreamed—all pleasant dreams that lasted through the night—and I woke in the morning feeling rested. Mom told me to put on my new dress, and she called for a taxicab.

It was raining that day, just a light mist, but still I couldn't make out the sky. Mom told me that the sun and the sky were always there; it's the clouds that come and go, and so I thought of that. I stared out the window, tracing my finger against glass, trying to find the point on the horizon where the ground rose up to meet the sky, the place where heaven meets earth. "You can chase it forever, but you can't ever catch it," Mom said. She knew what I was doing. "But that doesn't mean you shouldn't try."

"Where you going?" the taxi driver said, and Mom told him the address. I wondered how she found a new home so quickly, but I didn't care. I watched the trees tick by on the highway, tried to hold my eyes on each one individually so they didn't all blur together.

And then I saw it: this castle in the distance. As we drew closer I could see it was made of stone, and it had spires, and too many windows to count all at once. I could see a cross attached to a steeple. The steeple reached up into the sky, and I thought it might poke a hole in the clouds and reveal the sun. The taxi slowed as we drove down the gravel drive, then stopped right in front of the door.

"Another church?" I said, turning to Mom, but she leaned toward the front to get a better look through the windshield.

"This it?" he asked.

"Will you wait?" Mom asked, but I was too busy craning my neck to look at the gray building that towered above us. Moss mottled the base of the structure, so it looked dirty. I wondered what kind of people lived inside, if they were like us, if they wore the same kind of clothes I was wearing.

The taxi driver opened my door, and in that instant the castle door swung open, too, as though synchronized. I saw a nun dressed in black, her habit covering her hair. She looked like a penguin I'd once seen at the zoo, but she didn't waddle. Rather, she glided toward us as though wheels were hidden beneath her dress.

"I am Sister Frances, but you may call me Sister Fran," she said. She enunciated every word, primness straining her voice. Her cheeks sank into her face, and her arched eyebrows made her appear on the verge of indignation. "Welcome to the Sisters of the Supreme Adoration," she said. She stepped forward, and I stepped back.

Mom didn't move far from the taxi. She held out her arms to embrace me, then kissed each of my cheeks. I realized only then what was happening.

"Don't go," I said, and it was as if we were praying again atop that bridge, me clinging to my mother's arms, hoping someone could hear me. "Don't leave me here alone," I said.

"You're never alone," she said. "I'm right here." She tapped her index finger on my chest. Her eyes were vacant, deep set. I barely recognized them.

"But I want to be with you," I said.

"If you love someone you have two choices: hold on to them or let them go," she said. "But clinging doesn't mean you love them more, and letting go doesn't mean you love them less." Her skin looked waxy. She put her hand over her head to protect herself from the rain, then reached into the car and handed me my belongings. At that moment I saw what the people who watched Mom preaching barefooted in a fountain must have seen: a frizzy-haired woman with wild, flitting eyes.

I felt Sister Fran's hand bear down on my shoulder like a weight that could drop me to the ground, but then it eased up. I wanted to float away, into the sky, and up to the clouds that were covering up the sun. I'd never been without my mother before, not for a single day that I could remember. "Shall we get out of this rain?" Sister Fran asked. She put her arm around my shoulder and helped me walk inside. "There, there, my girl," she said. "The joy of God is the innocent."

The front door swung closed behind us with a click, and we stood in the large foyer. "Let's get you out of these wet clothes," she said. Sister Tabitha appeared with a box, and she handed me my uniform.

"We'll need to st-st-store your belongings," Sister Tabitha said.

"For safekeeping," Sister Fran added. "Dress, shoes, everything you're wearing. Fashion must not be a distraction. And the things girls wear these days!"

"But not my watch," I said defensively, wrapping my fingers around the only relic of my mother's.

"That, too," Sister Fran said. "We're on God's Time here at the convent," she said, then pulled back her robe to reveal her own bare wrists. "See?"

My skin went hot, even though I still shivered from my clothes clinging wet to my body. "But my mom said to wear it. That if I did, nothing bad would ever happen to me. Our family is cursed," I protested. I crossed my arms in front of me and scrunched my shoulders forward, and when I did, I could hear the low ticking of the watch.

"Superstitious nonsense, my dear," Sister Fran said, and I began to cry, quietly at first, but then rising in volume.

"Oh, none of that," she said. Sister Fran looked like a woman who hadn't cried in years, all brittle and dry, white skin hugging bone. "You'll learn, girl. God sent you here for a purpose," she said.

Standing there in the foyer, wet from the rain, I couldn't even begin to imagine what that purpose might be—that there was a grand design larger than myself, larger than the convent, larger, even, than my mother's curse. It didn't occur to me then that there was meaning in my loneliness. Or that there wasn't. I was just a young girl, after all. Hadn't yet met The Guineveres. Hadn't yet met Our Boys. Hadn't yet been taught about all those saints who understood suffering, who embraced it.

Absolution

I helped Gwen sew an elastic band and some extra material into her uniform skirt. Even then, it fit snugly around her stomach, which grew high and round like a small globe beneath her clothing. She swelled with motherhood. Her hair thickened, became shinier and sleeker than it had ever been, and she wore it down, past her shoulders, past the midback length that the Sisters usually made us cut. I don't know if she still rubbed butter into her skin or brushed her hair exactly one hundred strokes every night; we avoided each other in the Wash Room.

I still sat with her in the cafeteria, though. What choice did I have? Between slurps of cabbage soup, the other girls shot us awkward glances that indicated I could never belong with them. Even Reggie ignored us, stared straight into her bowl as if divining her own future there. Lottie and Shirley and Nan and Dorrie Sue made efforts to walk the long way to the tray bin after mealtime so as to avoid our table completely. Maybe they thought pregnancy was contagious, that baby germs could somehow manage to crawl up their skirts as well. Sister Fran never called an assembly to talk about Gwen's "condition." She didn't warn the other girls of the Flesh or lecture about dignity and virtue or make us watch film-strips upon similar topics. I suppose she thought Gwen's changing appearance could speak for itself. And it did. The other girls kept their distance from both of us.

Gwen and I didn't talk much, either. I guess we didn't know what to say. When I'd sit next to her in the cafeteria, our clinking forks filled the silence between us. On occasion, we'd talk about Win and Ginny and wonder what they were doing now, out in the world. But we didn't talk about Our Boys. We didn't talk about whether the baby would be a boy or a girl or what Gwen would do once the baby was born.

Father James asked me to serve as an altar girl just one more time after that. It was during the Mass of the Healing. This time, Sister Tabitha escorted me—walked me up the hill and back down again when mass was over. She didn't let me out of her sight. She sat on the couch in the vestry while I dressed, pulled the rough robe over my head, then finger-combed my hair when static made it stand on end. I saw The Guineveres' robes hanging in the closet, but I tried not to think about them, tried to think only of service and piety. Sister Fran told us that piety was not just being faithful, but being dutiful. She told us that faith and duty are one and the same. I wondered what happened when someone performed her duty but didn't believe in the reasons behind it. Did that still count as faith? I worried so much about those sorts of things then. I didn't yet realize how useless worry is, how we cling to it in hopes of controlling the outcome, but we can never control the outcome.

One server on the altar is difficult, but not impossible. Before mass, Father James had already set up the processional cross and candle in their rightful places, and he carried his gold-edged Bible during the opening hymn. As I walked behind him, the smoke from the incense urn rose up my nose and burned my eyes. Since the Mass of the Healing wasn't a service day of obligation, the church was only half full. A row of soldiers sat in the pew behind the Drexels; I'd never seen them before. These soldiers, unlike the ones in the Sick Ward, were fully awake and wore uniforms so crisp their shoulders had edges. I wondered if they were home for good or if they had to go back to the War again. I could only guess that these were the sons of the parishioners, or the fathers of the fatherless families that I'd seen. I imagined how happy they must have been to come home, how happy their families must have been, too, despite the fact that nobody looked happy. Everyone stared forward with heavy lids, with blank church faces.

During the homily, Father James preached again of the virtue of miracles. He said if we have faith even as small as a tiny mustard seed, we will have the power to move mountains. He said God has the power to heal the sick, cleanse the lepers, feed the hungry, and raise the dead—but only if we hold faith in our hearts. When Father James spoke, he held his vowels just a beat too long. He stumbled as he walked to the pulpit, and then, after his homily, he misplaced his vial of holy oil. I found it next to the tabernacle, then held the jar for him as he dabbed the foreheads of the congregants with a greasy, sloppy thumbprint.

The soldiers strode slowly toward the altar to receive their blessings. Some walked with the help of crutches or canes. One was missing an arm, and his uniform sleeve was folded into a triangle and pinned, like a funeral flag. Others had scars on their faces or burn marks on their hands. Some didn't seem like anything was wrong with them, which probably meant that they had the worst scars of them all, the kind on the inside that take a long time to heal, like My Boy.

When Father James blotted the last person, I whispered to him, "Will you bless me, too, Father?" Father James's face was rosy, and I could see the outline of dye on his hairline from where he recently colored his hair again. He nodded slowly, then dipped his thumb into the jar of oil I was holding and clumsily skimmed my forehead. The oil smelled earthy, like dirt mixed with musk. It tickled my skin as it dribbled toward my eyebrows, then stopped there to rest. After mass, when I returned to the convent, I found Gwen, and I smudged the oil off my forehead and rubbed some onto hers.

"What are you doing?" she complained, and she tried to wipe it away with the back of her palm.

"You can't wipe it off! It's holy oil," I protested. "From the Mass of the Healing."

"What do you think I need healing from? This?" she sneered, rubbing her extended stomach, the weight of which made her appear to lean forward. "You can't cure pregnancy," she said. "At least not around here, you can't."

"I know."

She must have noticed the hurt in my voice, so she softened a bit. "Thank you," she said, and in her breathy voice added, "I now feel Supremely Adored." She twisted her face, pressed her palms into prayer, and offered her best Holy Constipation look.

When she was about eight months along, Sister Fran moved her to the Penance Room on the third floor. Gwen said she was just fine in the Bunk Room, but Sister Fran insisted, claiming it wasn't good for the other girls to see her in this condition. "Let not one lamb lead the others astray," Sister Fran told her. "Sometimes we must sacrifice one for the good of many."

"You'd think I was a leper," Gwen said as she stripped the sheets from her bed. I helped her gather the contents of her basket, her brush and her notebooks, her pajamas and socks. She handed me Her Boy's ring to return to him, then peeled her glossy magazine cutouts from the wall above her bunk.

"Or a prostitute," I said.

I didn't see her much after that.

When it was time, they took her to the Sick Ward and sequestered her from the rest of the patients by hanging a bedsheet divider. I wasn't there when Gwen gave birth, but I heard that Sisters Magda and Connie let her hold the baby for a full hour afterward. I'm told she didn't cry when they took the baby away, didn't raise one word in protest. She simply handed the baby girl to Sister Connie, then rolled over and fell asleep. Gwen stayed in the Sick Ward a few more days, until one morning she woke up to find her packed bags at her bedside. She dressed in silence, tied her shoes, combed her long hair, then sat at the edge of the bed, her knees pressed together, her legs crossed only at the bone of the ankle, as we'd been taught to do. When the time came to leave, she didn't ask to say good-bye, didn't ask for anything except for a glass of water, which she drank in small sips, as if she were drinking from the communion chalice. And then, after more than two years, she disappeared from my life. They sent her off into the world of lost Guineveres.

Years later, before Sister Fran died, she told me that she could never locate Gwen's family, not since the day her father had dropped her off at the convent. She tried calling, she tried writing, but nobody responded—the phone rang and rang, and the postman marked her letters undelivered. "It sometimes happens this way," Sister Fran had said. By then she was a very old woman. Her skin had shriveled to bone, patterned with wrinkles. Her hair thinned to wisps. She wore a headscarf in place of her veil because it was more comfortable as she reclined in bed.

With no other options, Gwen was sent across state to a school for troubled girls. "What else could I do?" Sister Fran asked; age and illness had softened her some. I do believe she acted according to what she thought was right at the time. It was a different world when she ran the convent. Not like it is now.

"I felt badly," Sister Fran told me, "not that we sent her to the home for troubled girls—she *was* troubled—but that her family never knew where she was." Sister Fran licked her lips, white from dryness, and she rested her wizened hands on my own; she'd be dead within the year, suffering a stroke before she slipped away in the very Sick Ward where she oversaw the tending of the sick. I felt sorry for Sister Fran. I don't know why. Maybe I shouldn't have, but she'd known pain, too. "My hope for all of my girls is that they return home," she had told me. "That is the best possible outcome."

I visited the Sick Ward the day after Gwen's departure. The ward was crowded then, brimming with patients and with noise, despite the fact that nobody was actually speaking. It was the sound of starched blankets against dry skin, of shifting discomfort, of mouths smacking with thirst. Another group of comatose soldiers had arrived, and small cots had been set flat against the walls to accommodate them. Sisters Magda and Connie had to scoot sideways through small spaces to deliver their trays of medicine or to empty bedpans. I instinctively walked toward My Boy's bed, and that's when I saw it: In the corner, near the supply closet, the makeshift birthing room. Sheets shrouded the bed like a tent, or like a tomb.

I heard the baby before I saw it. I moved toward the room where Gwen had given birth, and I tugged back the sheets that hung from two coat stands. There sat a bassinet, white wicker fraying at the edges. Inside it, the baby cried, squirmed like a beetle on its back. At first I could do nothing but stare, stare at her wide gummy mouth, opened to reveal a quivering uvula, stare at her downy skin and her complexion turned red from wailing. Her knees were drawn up to her chest. Her fingers tapered to points. She was half My Boy, but not half me.

Sister Connie brushed past me, and she picked up the baby, slung her over her shoulder like a dishrag, and gently patted her bottom. As she did this, she stared out at the crowded Sick Ward, directing Sister Magda. "No, not that one," she said. "Yes, yes. *That* one. No, no. Not like that." Her hair had come untucked from her cap. Droplets of blood were splattered across her apron. "I'll be there in just a moment," she snapped, frazzled. She bounced up and down with the baby, who would not cease her screaming.

"Here, let me," I said. I took the baby from Sister Connie, cradling the tiny girl in my arms like the Pietà. "Shh, shh, shh," I whispered, and her pink-rimmed eyes flicked up at me but could not focus. "I'm here. Don't worry." She smelled like newness, like nothing bad had ever happened to her. I swayed back and forth, moved by an imaginary breeze. Her breathing calmed, her eyes drooped, and then she fell asleep, a bundle of warmth and weight in my arms. That's when I took her to meet My Boy.

I perched on the edge of his bed, pressed up against his legs, angled my body so he could see us, should he awake. I swear I saw his lids pulse, his lashes flutter; I'm certain he struggled to open his eyes. But he couldn't. Sleep overruled his desires, and so we sat, the three of us, a pocket of silence in the clamoring of the Sick Ward. How long I sat like that, I could not say. I sat until dinner trays were delivered and removed. I sat until the setting sun beamed long orange rectangles onto the linoleum. I sat until Sister Connie came back with a warm bottle.

"Do you want to feed her?" she asked.

I nodded.

A few days later, Sister Fran called me to her office. She closed the door and motioned for me to take a seat on the bench. Instead of retreating to the chair behind her desk, she sat down beside me, hip-to-hip, the way The Guineveres used to sit. She smelled like incense and the cafeteria, and like lavender soap. She removed her veil to reveal her slipshod hair, white and wiry, pinned back by an assortment of bobby pins. She looked so small without her veil, like a regular old lady I might see in church. She picked up my hand from my lap and squeezed it. Her hands were papery and warm, and I liked the feel of it, so I let her rest her palm in my own.

"The joy of God is the innocent, Guinevere," she said. She squeezed my hand once more. I didn't respond, because no question had been asked of me. Instead, I leaned against the wall, head bowed, as though I were praying.

In a way, I suppose you could say I was praying. Or I was thinking, anyway, about how this wasn't the ending I had expected when my mother left me here. That sometimes we can't predict the ending, that the cost of loving someone too much is the pain we feel when we lose them.

"I am responsible for you. This is my earnest duty. I was trusted with your care." Sister Fran released my hand and turned her spindly body to face me. "Now listen to me," she said. Her voice was gentle, low, had lost some of its edge and authority. She cleared her throat. "There's a family, from the parish. They have a daughter just a few years older than you, a son who's away in the War. They've agreed to take you in, so you can have a proper home life. You'll go to school. And you'll live with them, of course. You'll still attend mass on Sundays. They've promised to maintain your proper spiritual education, and I have no doubt they'll do just that. They're a good family, and this is an unusual circumstance. Do you understand what I'm saying, Guinevere?"

It's amazing how many thoughts can run through one's mind in only a fraction of a moment, how time can extend. I sat there, numbed through my body, as if someone had swapped the air for chloroform. I tried to think about what life would be like on the outside, with a family, in a house. I wondered if I'd have my own bedroom, and if so, what it would look like. I wondered how many students went to the school, and if they'd like me, and if the teacher would collect homework, and if they'd hold me back on account of the fact that it'd been so long since I'd been in a real school. I didn't even know what I didn't know anymore. I wondered what I'd wear to school, or if the family had hand-me-down clothes from their daughter that I could fit into. I wondered if they'd seen me before in church, serving on the altar, and I wondered if I'd seen them, one of the familiar faces in the rows of pews. I wanted so badly to be part of something. A family.

"Guinevere?" Sister Fran said softly, waking me to alertness again.

"Yes, Sister?"

"What do you have to say?"

I had nothing to say, because I had shifted my thinking to My Boy, to his warm body, a living statue in repose. As I sat against him in the Sick Ward, his daughter nestled in the crook of my arms, I could feel the rising and falling of his chest, each breath washing through me like water. I tried to hold on to the moment. I squeezed the girl tightly, and I kissed her downy head, and I leaned into My Boy so he'd know we were there. When I looked down at the sleeping baby, at her translucent lids fluttering just like her father's, I was overcome with gratitude, waterlogged with it. *They* were my family now, and I couldn't abandon them, even if I wanted to. They needed my protection, and besides, that's not what you do to the people you love.

"I can't," I told Sister Fran.

"You can't? What do you mean you can't? Of course you can. This is your way out, dear," Sister Fran said. Here she paused to place her veil on her head again, and when she did, her voice lost some of its tenderness, and primness returned to the corners of her vowels. "It's a chance for a good girl like yourself."

"I mean I won't," I said firmly. I hardly recognized the words coming out of my mouth. If I could have stopped myself, I would have, because part of me wanted to be as far away from the convent as possible, far away from the reminders of the people who had hurt me the most. But that's not the meaning of sacrifice. That's not how the saints would have acted. "I was sent here for a purpose. You told me yourself the day I arrived," I said.

"And what purpose is that?" Sister Fran asked. "This is an extraordinary offer, Guinevere. These are extraordinary times." She stood and straightened out her skirt. The tips of her black leather shoes peeked out from the hem, and I noticed they were worn at the seams. It wouldn't be long before they wound up in the courtyard, planted with geraniums so as to serve one last purpose of functionality.

I stood and I faced Sister Fran. We were nearly

the same height. I'd grown taller in the years since I'd lived in the convent. I'd grown wiser, too. "My purpose is to serve."

"In the convalescent wing?"

I shook my head.

"The War Effort?"

"With the baby," I said. "She needs someone. She needs me."

"With the baby," Sister Fran repeated, flummoxed. She suctioned her cheeks and puckered her lips as if she were sucking poison from the air, and then she stepped backward, away from me. She turned and walked to her desk and, readjusting her habit, sat down behind it. "I don't know if you realize what that entails. It's a difficult job raising children, especially girls."

I moved toward Sister Fran, placed my palms firmly on her desk, and, listing forward, mustered up the courage the saints must have needed in moments when their convictions wavered. "I know exactly what girls need, Sister." I may have sounded angry—I didn't intend for my words to come out this way—and at that moment Sister Magda rapped hard-knuckled at the door, and she entered in haste.

"Excuse me, Sister," she said, interrupting. Her nurse's hat was off-kilter, and long streaks on her apron resembled tea stains. "Another group of soldiers," she said, catching her breath. Her hand clutched her chest as though monitoring her own heartbeat. "They've just arrived. About a dozen of them."

Silence for a moment, and then Sister Fran spoke. "Do what we must. Phone the church to see if they have cots. If not, we'll bring some bunks down from the girls' room."

"But where will I fit them? There's no space."

"We can't very well turn them away, now can we?"

"No, Sister."

"Well, then, make space."

Sister Magda quickly scooted out of the room, and I turned toward Sister Fran again. Her head was tilted back and her mouth slightly parted, as though she were taking communion on her tongue.

"I can do it, Sister," I said. "I can raise the baby. I want to do it. Please."

Sister Fran leaned back in her chair, pressed her bony hands to her cheeks, and sighed. She gazed upward, toward the heavens, as if for an answer, then looked me square in the face. For the first time I noticed her eyes were blue, not like Gwen's but darker, like the deepest part of the ocean. She nodded slowly, perhaps a nod of resignation, but a nod all the same.

I named the baby Guinevere, after her mother. The Sick Ward was no place for her, so we moved into a room on the third floor, but not the

Penance Room. I remember the way she felt in my arms when she was just a tiny thing, her fingers grasping at air like a wind-up toy, her eyes gleaming with innocence, and round, her skin so soft like her father's. What a miracle life is, an accumulation of history. Her eyes are green; her lips red, red, the way her mother would have liked. She has Win's untamable hair, and freckles, though not as many as Ginny. I prefer to think she looks a little bit like all of us.

It's been just the two of us up here on the third floor all these years. We've made a life of our own. Caring for Guinevere has changed me—for the better, I'd say. I'm no longer the fragile, skinny-legged girl I was when my mother left me. I've gained heft, of spirit and of body. I no longer wear my hair long or rub butter into it before bed for shine. I'm beyond all that. And Guinevere, she's grown into a thoughtful young girl. She's serious and imaginative, sensitive but quick to laugh. She's tall, all arms and legs, yet to fully grow into her body. Just recently, she rummaged through some old boxes in the storage room, and she found one marked with my name.

"Can I open it?" she asked me. I know she tires of convent life, but I've tried my best to see she's been afforded some freedom. I once bought her some makeup, but she wasn't interested in wearing it. Instead, she asks to take long walks in the woods that surround the convent. We've blazed paths through our favorite spots just by traipsing them again and again.

"Of course," I said. When we hike through the woods, I like to observe her from up the path to see if I can detect some traces of her father. I imagine he is as curious as Guinevere. She can stand for hours just observing a tree, its five-fingered leaves that resemble hands, or the way its limbs knot, or the mushrooms that grow off the trunk like little shelves. When she crouches to observe a flower or a toad, I notice the curve of her spine, like a question mark, and I'm certain I'm seeing her father in silhouette. She looks up at me and laughs when she catches me staring at her like that, and it's My Boy's laugh I hear.

Inside the box she found my old clothing and shoes, the coat I never wore, moth-eaten in only a few spots. "It's like what they wore in the olden days," she exclaimed, amused, then slipped the dusty coat on her small frame, but it was short in the sleeves.

Then she reached into the box and pulled out a packet of envelopes bundled with twine. I recognized the handwriting on the outside immediately. It was my own. They were the letters I'd written to my mother as a girl, the letters in which I'd begged her to come back for me, pleaded with her to, at the very least, write and let me know she was okay. Guinevere handed them to me, and I took them, flipped them over to see they'd been unopened. A red hand was stamped on the front, like the hand of Michelangelo's *David* himself. UNCLAIMED, it read. RETURN TO SENDER.

I shouldn't have been surprised. And really, I wasn't. But I can't say it didn't hurt a little, even years later. All those times I'd dropped an envelope into Sister Fran's burlap sack on Mail Distribution Day, I was sending letters to nowhere.

"Who are they from?" Guinevere asked. When she looked up at me, I swear I saw myself in the girl. She cocked her head to the side just slightly, then reached out for my hand as though she instinctively knew I could use the comfort. I wondered why Sister Fran had kept the letters, or why she hadn't told me that my efforts to reach my mother were in vain, that each time I poured out my soul on paper, it was like giving con-fession to a deaf priest. Perhaps she had nurtured my hope; in some way, I could rationalize the act as a gesture of kindness, though I guess I'll never know.

"Look at this," I said, changing the subject, and I released her hand. I reached into the box and held up my mother's watch, my grandmother's before that. The band had oxidized; it was specked with black spots that resembled cigarette marks. I hadn't seen that watch since Sister Fran confiscated it on the day I arrived, all those years ago. As I laid it across my palm, I recalled my mother's promise that nothing bad would ever come to me if I wore it. I wound the dial and brought the watch to my ear: It still ticked. They don't make them like that anymore.

"It's pretty," Guinevere said.

"It's yours now," I told her.

"Really?" she asked. She hugged me, and she smelled of mothballs. My eyes began to water, and her thick hair that she insists on wearing down—no braids for her—clung to my cheeks.

"Now go ask Sister Vickie for some polish," I said.

My mother, she never came back for me. Never called, never wrote. I can't say my heart aches for her—how can you limit it to just your heart? I would say I *am* her when I care for Guinevere, when I mend her clothes, or pray with her, or tell her the stories of the saints, those defiant young women who have gone before. I want a different life for her, one where she's not afraid, where she has choices, not like me. I tell her stories of my own youth, of The Guineveres and the times we walked these same chilly halls. They send postcards from time to time, or gifts around her birthday and Christmas. In this way, they stillplay a part in her life, so I don't think she views them as strangers. She's never asked about her mother, and so I've not told her. Not yet.

But I will soon.

For this is Guinevere's Revival Story. I've written it down for her, all of it, so that when she turns eighteen and leaves the convent she'll know she was loved, by me, by all of us. She'll know she was never alone, not for a single day. She'll know the answers to how she came to be a ward of the Sisters of the Supreme Adoration, and why. Because that's what we all go on seeking in life—the whys. It's the one question for which we may never have the answer, and we turn to faith, so we can keep on asking without seeming redundant. This is my gift to Guinevere: the truth of our stories, the truth of her life. Because if she knows it, the good and the ugly, perhaps she'll be spared the seeking. After all, there's a lot of living to do out in the world, and I'm counting on her to do it.

As for me, I've stayed on at the convent as a layperson, working in the kitchen mostly. I'd like to think that the food these days tastes far superior than when I lived in the Bunk Room as a girl. No more colorless vegetables; no more canned fruit. I've grown a garden out back in the courtyard, replacing the old shoe planters with raised vegetable beds. Sometimes the garden yields so many zucchinis that we can't eat them all before they spoil. I make breads and cakes for the girls, and still have plenty of vegetables to give away. It's an embarrassment of riches, a problem of abundance, and those are the best problems to have.

Once a week I cook for Father James, too, up in the rectory's kitchen. He's a changed man now—stopped drinking years ago, shortly after the War ended, not too long after Gwen left. He experienced his own Revival, and he redoubled his devotion to the priesthood, despite the path that brought him there. He's grown patient and wise, and he treats the young girls well. He realizes he made mistakes, and he's tried hard to correct them. I can't say he feels like a father to me, but he does feel like a friend.

"Do you know why Gwen did it?" he asked me one day, out of the blue. We'd just returned from mass. Now the altar girls and altar boys serve side by side, as if these things happened all along. As though The Guineveres weren't special.

I hadn't considered the question in years, not since Gwen's Boy died and his remains were shipped away to be buried properly with other unknowns. I wrote Gwen to tell her; it seemed like the right thing to do, despite everything. She wrote me back a short note and thanked me. *P.S. Tell Guinevere I say hello,* the letter read. She didn't ask about her daughter, or what kind of young girl she's become. I'm not sure if she doesn't care or if it's too painful or if she's too ashamed. I don't want her to be sorry for any of it.

I don't. Guinevere is a beautiful girl. She's a strong girl, too.

"I guess it doesn't matter, Father," I said.

"But don't you want to know?" he asked.

I remembered how Gwen could hardly bear to look at the scars on Her Boy's face. I was imagining those scars now, the way they oozed, how they were deep and cavernous, as if he hid his secrets in there. "Maybe we'll never know," I said.

"She confessed it to me," he said. I could tell by the way he was looking at me that he was willing to break confessional confidentiality for our friendship. But I also knew that if he told me, I could never trust the sacrament of confession again, my one solace over the years. When I feel things, I confess them—and, like that, the weight lifts away from me. That's the beautiful power of absolution. It's not so much about the ritual as it is about the need to unburden our stories onto someone who will carry the weight for us.

"It doesn't matter now," I said. "And besides, I forgive her."

"You do?"

"I thought forgiveness was our duty, Father," I said.

"It is. Don't be mistaken," he added. His hair is gray now, no longer dyed, and I think it looks better this way, even if he looks older than his age. "It's just . . . forgiveness isn't a natural human propensity."

"Then perhaps you should make me a saint, Father," I said, my face warming.

"Perhaps I will. The Patron Saint of Chicken Pot Pie," he said and took a heaping mouthful of the meal I had prepared him.

When Guinevere turns eighteen soon, I'll be sure she's sent to college. I tell her to go on, go on, and never look back. Don't be like Lot's wife, who turned into a pillar of salt. Look forward; look ahead. She's got her whole life still, and I'll tell her to find someone to love, then love like it's her duty. Love like her heart will explode if she doesn't, like the world will catch on fire. It won't always be easy, I'll tell her. All humans have flaws, and we must love these flaws, too. Such dedication love requires. Such surrender. Love is its own kind of religion, but it's the most rewarding one.

My Boy still sleeps soundly. I used to count the days. But Saint Thérèse of Lisieux says when one loves, one does not calculate, and so I've stopped. Instead, I measure the days with affections: I wash him with a cloth, I shave him carefully, I speak to him while he dreams. When nobody else is around, I speckle his cheeks with kisses. His skin has grown taut and his jaw angular; he no longer resembles a boy. I knead his hands and feet to keep his circulation moving. He's so warm. Sometimes my body grows stiff from sitting beside him for long stretches, and in this way I believe I'm closer to him—I can feel what he feels, the stillness of it. In those moments, I close my eyes and imagine the way his eyes looked when they were open, the way his smile spread slowly across his face like the sun cresting on the horizon. I can still hear his voice as he asked me my name. It's a form of meditation, this remembering.

He hasn't awoken yet, but he will; I know he will. I'll wait. And when he wakes, I'll say: Look, look! I'm the only Guinevere here. I loved you most of all.

Acknowledgments

I've been extraordinarily fortunate for the support of so many individuals, and this book wouldn't exist without them. My sincerest gratitude to the following:

My fantastic agent, Michelle Brower, for seeing the promise in this book and for being my champion every step of the way;

Everyone at Flatiron Books, especially my editor, Amy Einhorn. Working with you has been a dream. Also special thanks to Caroline Bleeke for your thoughtful guidance and to Lauren Harms and Amelia Possanza;

Early readers of bare-boned drafts, in particular Nicola Mason and Annie Hwang;

The Sewanee Writers' Conference, and all those there who workshopped the first chapters of the book, especially Margot Livesey;

My early teachers: Valerie Combs and Katharine Gillespie. You'll never know how much your encouragement meant to me;

The Ph.D. program in Creative Writing at the University of Cincinnati for providing a supportive and challenging environment where writers can flourish. Thanks in particular to Brock Clarke for his mentorship and generosity and to Michael Griffith and Jana Braziel;

517

Lauren Bailey, for your sisterly camaraderie and wisdom. And to Julie Gerk Hernandez and Kelcey Parker Ervick, for your humor, intellect, and spark. I cherish our friendships;

Other friends who have inspired me in both writing and life, including: Jody Bates, Natalie Lamberjack, Kathy Bradley, Kirk Boyle, Liz Tilton, Susan Steinkamp, Darrin Doyle, Laura Van Prooyan, and Annie Jablonski, who once gifted me with a (now dog-eared) copy of Lives of the Saints;

My parents, Luke and Sally, for your unconditional love and your staggering kindness. I'll always be grateful. And to Kevin, Molly, Shelby, Mary Ann, Luke, and, in particular, Laura, who shared with me her own (hilarious) experiences as an altar girl while I was writing this book. I'm glad you're all my family;

Saskia, my daughter, who has been my lucky charm from the start. I wrote this book for you, even before we met;

And last, but always: my husband and first reader, Rob, the most compelling person I know. You believed in me from the earliest days. Thank you for dusting off your English degree and hunkering down for the long haul. You're a partner in the truest sense. I can't believe my luck in love.

Center Point Large Print
600 Brooks Road / PO Box 1
Thorndike, ME 04986-0001 USA

(207) 568-3717

US & Canada:
1 800 929-9108
www.centerpointlargeprint.com